THE NO... ...ATTACHED TO MY

"PLEASE ... ...OU."

I leapt out of my chair, ...ealing off into the bedroom and spilling my iced tea all over the hardwood floor. I edged my way to the kitchen, picked up my butcher knife, and forced myself to look in every room, peeked into the closets and under the beds. How whoever it was had gotten in wasn't hard to figure out—we're not much into security, and every window on the ground floor was wide open. Nothing could make me go down to the basement, so I locked the door at the top of the stairs. Whoever left the note had his goddamn hands on my dog, for Christ's sake, and could be in my house . . .

———◆———

"Alex Bernier is a smart, engaging heroine in this fresh, fast-paced, funny, and suspenseful series debut."
—Judith Kelman, author of *After the Fall* and *Fly Away Home*

"A complex and engaging mystery with a not-exactly-fearless young reporter who has our sympathy even as we enjoy watching her troubles get worse."
—Thomas Perry, author of *The Butcher's Boy, Shadow Woman,* and *The Face-Changers*

RELIABLE SOURCES

BETH SAULNIER

WARNER BOOKS

A Time Warner Company

WARNER BOOKS EDITION

Cover design by Robert Santori

Warner Books, Inc.
1271 Avenue of the Americas
New York, NY 10020

Visit our Web site at
www.twbookmark.com

Ⓦ A Time Warner Company

Printed in the United States of America

First Mysterious Press Paperback Printing: November 1999

10 9 8 7 6 5 4 3 2 1

Dedicated to my mother,
Betty Saulnier
and to the memory of my father,
Wilfred "Bud" Saulnier,
a teacher, handicapper, Yankee fan and lover of books

With deepest thanks to:

Paul Cody
for his constant support and encouragement

Jimmy Vines
for being the best agent a girl could ever want

Bill Malloy
for his deft editing and eternal good humor

John Yaukey and Dr. Boyce McDaniel
for all that science

Micah Fink
for lessons in madness

and

Alexandra Wald, Melissa Levis, Seth Adelson,
Bryan VanCampen and Paul Smith
for their limitless friendship

PROLOGUE

〜

THE CAMERA CREWS CAMPED OUT ON MY LAWN AGAIN LAST night. I peek through the curtains and count the news vans parked along my street. CNN. The networks. The tabloids, who must have driven all the way up from New York. Two unmarked ones, freelancers probably. Sometimes I fantasize they've got my house confused with a crime scene, or some congressman's lovenest. They'll realize their mistake and leave, so I can go outside with my dog again.

But they're really here for me. As proof, I offer the thirty-seven messages on my answering machine. They want me to come on talk shows, give interviews. Some producer even wants to make a TV movie of my life, which with my luck would star somebody from the cast of *Beverly Hills 90210*.

It's been like this since the story broke. The Story. I'm starting to think of it like its own proper name. Journalists wait their whole lives for this—a story that could turn you into the next Woodward or Bernstein. A scoop big enough to make the competition squirm and the readers, well, *read*. You'll do commentary on CNN, Columbia Journalism School will ask you to lecture, and flights of angels will speed you to the *New York Times*.

I was barely twenty-five when the story of a lifetime fell into my lap, and I wish to hell I'd never heard of it.

My name is Alex Bernier. Alex is short for Alexandra, which I have not answered to since first grade. Bernier is French, and I pronounce it that way—rhymes with "day." I'm a reporter at the *Gabriel Monitor,* a newspaper in a small upstate New York city that we kindly describe as "centrally isolated." Gabriel is a college town, the kind of place where the guy slicing your bagel at the deli has a PhD in philosophy. It's five hours to New York City from here, but that's okay. There are enough bookstores and coffee shops to keep you busy forever, or at least until you drop dead from all the clove cigarettes.

Death. That's been on my mind a lot these days. This summer I lost someone very close to me. I also wrote a series of stories on what I thought were unrelated topics. It all turned out to add up to something fantastic, and I choose the word carefully; this all seems like a fantasy, too strange to be real.

I figured the TV people would leave after a day or two, but I should've known better. They're hooked on the story like heroin, and I can't blame them. The whole country is talking about it. Some PBS commentator said it had all the elements of a Shakespearean tragedy: romance, murder, secrets. I hope that doesn't make me Ophelia, or Juliet, or Cordelia.

I tell the reporters that I'm not ready to talk, and still they trample the roses in my front yard. Maybe this is karmic retribution for years of harassing other people, but

I like to think I was never quite this obnoxious. It's strange to be the reported rather than the reporter.

Did the people I've written about feel this out of control? My name is on the news and there's nothing I can do about it. Journalists—my nosy brethren—are sifting through my past, quoting people I haven't seen since junior high. My phone would be ringing off the hook if I hadn't turned it off two days ago.

I can only think of one way to handle this, and that's to do what I was trained for. I'm going to write. Not the sanitized version that ran in the *Monitor*—and on the AP wire, and every news show from here to Maui. When I'm done, I'm going to print it out and leave it on the front steps, with a batch of my ever-popular butterscotch brownies.

Then I'll tell them all to go to hell.

1

I KNOW THE WHOLE THING STARTED A HELL OF A LOT earlier, but I always think of the beginning as the second I stuck my key in the back door of the *Monitor* building. Maybe I just like the symbolism, since unlocking that one door led to the figurative opening of so many others. Anyway, if I were going to make a movie of this crazy story, I would start with a close-up of the key turning in the lock, and the door opening, and me walking up the back stairs to the newsroom. I had the place to myself, no big surprise at nine on a Sunday morning. The sports-writers wouldn't be in until later, to take high school scores over the phone and leave Pepsi cans and candy bar wrappers on everybody else's desks.

Let me interject one thing here. It's intensely weird to me what I remember and what I don't. Like I know just what kind of bagel I had that morning, and I remember a lot of the books I found up in Canada. But ask me what happened right after I first saw the body? No idea.

I remember the scanner was squawking as usual as I walked in the back door of the newsroom. I dumped my backpack by my swivel chair, right across from where the police reporter sits. My desk offers a lovely view of the cobwebby cables sticking out of the back of the scanner, and thanks to the design I can hear the ambulance calls and fire alarms louder than the cop reporter can. The damn thing goes off at the most inconvenient times, like when I'm getting great quotes or schmoozing with that cute guy from the city planner's office.

I don't know about you, but I always seem to get the worst news when I'm in a really terrifically good mood. Like when my first cat died, I'd just interviewed this hunky pair of marine biologists at Benson University. So I'm thinking how I'm going to marry one of them and take up scuba diving and live happily ever after, and there's this message on my machine: Come scrape your dead cat off my lawn.

This is not to say that somebody drops dead every time I'm in a halfway decent frame of mind. Just occasionally. And this was one of those days.

As I said, I was working the weekend shift. Every reporter gets stuck with it once a month or so. The upshot is you get the following Friday off and can leave for a three-day weekend. The drag is to come in on Saturday and Sunday to call the cops and make sure all hell hasn't broken loose. Or maybe more accurately, to make sure said hell is properly documented in the Monday morning paper.

So far, Saturday's calls were less than thrilling: a pair of drunk drivers, a two-car fender-bender, and a minor marijuana bust. Not that I'm hot to cover a big fire or fatal crash, although some reporters live for that kind of thing. But I've got to admit that working cops is a lot more fun if something really heinous happens, like the time this guy killed his wife with a Snap-on screwdriver, grabbed a hostage, and drove around six counties before the police caught up with him. A Snap-on screwdriver. Like I said, it's strange the things you remember.

My actual beat is less exciting, unless you get off on signage and sewage. I cover politics and Gabriel city government, which only really floats my boat during election season. City council meets the first and third Wednesdays of each month, and I've never missed a meeting in the two and a half years I've been on the beat.

But to get back to the day it all started: I wasn't covering government. I was on what I lovingly describe as the flasher beat. I've worked for three papers over the past five years, and—for reasons I prefer not to ponder—I'm always the one who gets assigned to cover nudist colonies. For the Monday page three feature, I'd spent the better part of my Saturday at Shady Acres Nudist Park. If you ever want to visit, it's about twenty miles out of town in Slackville. Dress is ultra-casual. But be warned: One thing I've learned is that nobody you want to see naked ever goes to a nudist colony.

That Saturday, I kept my clothes on. I learned my lesson the hard way, when I was working for a weekly back home in Massachusetts. It was my first flasher story, and when the owner told me I was "welcome to disrobe," I figured, what the hell. The photographer who came out with me swore he wouldn't shoot me, and I was green enough to believe him. So there I am in the newsroom the next day, staring at these negatives of myself, stark raving naked, interviewing a shuffleboard player. The film cost me an entire quart of homemade pesto.

Cooking is pretty much my favorite hobby—second only to falling in love with a succession of smart-ass journalists. I just turned twenty-five, which makes me one of the youngest in the crowd of Monitorites I hang out with. There's only one married couple among us, and most of us aren't even dating anybody, so we spend a lot of time together. The *Monitor* goes to bed at eleven every night except Saturday—there's no Sunday paper—and most of the newsroom moves over to our favorite bar, the Citizen Kane, until it closes at one. Heavy drinking is one of those clichés about journalists that just happens to be true.

To give you a little background: I've worked at the *Gabriel Monitor* for a little over three years. I started out as a part-timer, covering the towns that surround the city of Gabriel in a rural doughnut. When a full-time slot opened up, I started covering the schools beat, then moved over to the city when one of the other reporters left to follow his girlfriend to Belize. They're still down there, in case you're wondering, and I hear they're getting married next summer.

With a circulation of about twenty-five thousand, the *Monitor* isn't the smallest paper you've ever heard of, but it's still a fish-wrapper compared to a metro like the *New York Times*. There are some pretty good people here, though, and since Gabriel is a college town, they tend to stick around. Nobody at the *Monitor* does just one job; the features editor runs the computer system, I write the movie reviews, and the city editor is the only one who knows how to unclog the women's john.

The newsroom itself is a study in chaos theory. People are always amazed that you could put out a supermarket circular from the place, much less a daily paper. None of the desks are the same height, and they're all too short since some handyman sawed the legs half off. The carpet is sort of a mustardy yellow, and the walls have faded to kind of a lemon shade; good luck finding two colors that clash more violently. When the newsroom is full and things are hopping, it makes a trading floor look like the ladies' garden club. There's somebody yelling for the plural of "mongoose," and somebody needs change for the soda machine, and somebody else is telling a dirty joke on deadline. Most people don't understand how you can get anything done in a place like this, but I can't imagine working in some cubicle, with the silence ringing in your ears like a fire alarm.

Most *Monitor* reporters live downtown, but I live up on the hill near Benson University. I rent half of a little two-bedroom house that actually has a picket fence around it. I share space with my dog, my two cats, and my housemate, a law student messy enough to be his own species. Dirk is a great guy and I'd probably be madly in love with him if he didn't have a boyfriend named Helmut.

What else can I tell you? I speak pretty good French and pretty bad Spanish. I see five movies a week and run exactly 3.3 miles every other day in my struggle to stay a size six without giving up pizza. As for romance, I'm fond of saying I've been around the block more times than a beat cop. So far, what I have to show for it is a brief stint in psychotherapy and a cavalcade of ex-boyfriends sprinkled throughout the continental United States, which will probably come in handy if I ever want to drive cross-country. Ex-boyfriends are even cheaper than Motel 6.

Recently, I've come up with three basic rules about men, and this seems as good a time as any to share them with you. The first is simple and nonnegotiable: Never date a man who doesn't like your dog. The second is, never date a man who doesn't wear boxer shorts. Thirdly, never date a man who can't speak at least one foreign language, unless he's a journalist. Rule number three gets tossed most of the time.

To get back to The Story. The first thing I did when I got to the office was make the necessary preparations for my first round of cop calls. To wit: I rescued a legal pad from underneath the Matterhorn of paper on my desk, sucked a few drags from my tub of iced tea, ate half a Long Island bagel with chive cream cheese, and flipped through the want ads in the back of *Editor & Publisher.* Then I picked up the phone.

"State Police. Dispatcher Belding."

"Hi, this is the *Monitor* calling," I said. "Is there anything to report this morning?"

"That's negative, *Monitor.*"

I thanked her and hung up, checking out the Cop-to-English Dictionary a long-gone police reporter tacked on the wall. "That's negative" translates into "Leave us the hell alone, you scum-sucking vultures." Underneath it is "No comment," which means "I know, but I won't tell you." That's followed by "You'll have to talk to the chief about that," meaning "I know, but I'll tell the *Herald* first."

I signed on to my computer and called up the state news wire to give me something to read while I made the rest of my cop calls. The fun stories are usually slugged something like "SCHOOLDECAPITATION" or "MR. SOFTEE-SLAIN." By the time I got no news from the police and sheriffs in the six surrounding counties, I was browsing through a story on a New York City man arrested for exposing himself at three Hasidic weddings.

Once I ran out of fun stuff to read, I moved over to my directory and started my Monday story. It wasn't too taxing.

By ALEX BERNIER
Monitor Staff

 Skip and Marge Wilson are wearing
his-and-hers silver chains and matching
smiles as they lounge outside their
camper, festooned with flags and colored lights.

 That's all they're wearing.

 The Gabriel natives are celebrating
their 25th anniversary as nudists at the
Shady Acres Nudist Park in Slackville.
This weekend, the camp welcomes nud-
ism neophytes for an open house. On
the agenda are volleyball, shuffleboard,
a barbecue and a series of seminars on
life in the buff.

I was debating whether "in the buff" was going to get
past my editor when the scanner went off for real.

"Emergency control to Gabriel monitors. Report of a
body in North Creek Gorge. Subject is believed to be a
male Caucasian, spotted by a jogger on North Creek
Bridge."

After three years of sitting on top of the scanner, I've
come to think of it as a funky musical instrument. The
warning sirens sound sort of like saxophones; the police,
fire, and ambulance responses are repetitive enough to
work as lyrics. I call it the "cop opera," and it was going
full blast as I crossed to the two-way radio.

"*Monitor* base to any photographer," I said with no real
hope of raising anybody at that hour. When no one answered, I went into the darkroom and checked the work

schedule. Jason, the summer intern, was supposed to be on call. I picked up the phone and pushed the button labeled "INTERN," hoping I didn't get somebody who worked there two semesters ago. No answer. I tried Wendell, the photo editor and a genuine Gabriel weirdo who's been at the paper for something like twenty years, and got his machine. Knowing him, he was probably welcoming the sun at the local ashram.

That left Melissa, whom I'd last seen stumbling out of the Citizen Kane after last call. Great, I thought. I hope she and her hangover have some film with them. The phone rang for a full minute before Melissa picked up.

"Good morning, starshine," I said.

"Do you have any idea what time it is?"

"Nine-something."

"Thank you. Can I go back to sleep now?"

"Well, there's this man who wants to meet you."

"Great. Send him over."

"He's at the bottom of North Creek Gorge. We've got ourselves a jumper."

"Call the intern."

"No answer."

"Goddamn students. Okay, where is he?"

"The intern?"

"The jumper, sweet cheeks."

"He was spotted from North Creek Bridge, you know, the one in the middle."

"I'm on my way. Want me to pick you up?"

"Nah, I'll cruise up myself."

I hit the supply shelf for a new notebook and hustled outside. During the week, the cars are packed into the paper's lot so tightly, it can take fifteen minutes to wiggle your way out. I crossed the chessboard of faded yellow lines and aimed my Renault hatchback toward the sirens.

At this point, it might help if I describe how Gabriel is laid out. The city is in the flats between two hills, each topped by an institution of higher education. To the south is Bessler College, a women's school that doesn't seem to know what to do with itself since it admitted men twenty years ago. Across town is Benson University, which is where I was headed. Benson is one of those hugely endowed brick-and-ivy schools where parents pay a fortune to have their kids taught by stressed-out grad students. The real action, of course, is at the graduate level. The school gets a ton of research money—from the government, corporations, and God knows who else. My friend Mad, the science reporter, tells me there are actually a few floors in the supercomputing tower that are owned by a Japanese electronics company; Benson professors aren't even allowed in without clearance.

Benson's campus is beautiful, a city-state on a hill. It's trisected by two gorges, the more dramatic of which is on the west side. North Creek runs through it and over Gabriel Falls before spilling into Mohawk Lake. Three bridges connect the west side to central campus: a gunmetal-gray suspension bridge deemed so inviting to the melancholy, it's surrounded by eight-foot suicide guards; a one-lane bridge linking the campus to a residential area favored by professors; and, in the middle, the two-lane North Creek Bridge that's the main drag.

There was no point in trying to park near the crime scene. This was my third jumper, and I knew the bridge would be blocked off so rescue workers could fish out the guest of honor. The sirens were silent by then, but I could see the red-and-blue lights of city cops, university security, and an ambulance. A fire engine straddled both lanes, dangling a stretcher over the three-hundred-foot drop.

I looked around for Melissa, but I didn't see her among

the crowd, which consisted of twice as many gawkers as rescue workers. A city cop had just finished stretching the yellow tape reading "POLICE LINE: DO NOT CROSS" around the perimeter of the bridge. The policewoman was about to shoo me away when she saw my press pass and jerked her head toward two men leaning against the railing.

Police Chief Wilfred Hill treats the press fairly well, though he's been known to tell us all to kiss his Scotch-Irish backside when we hassle him too much. I'd never met the other man in person, but I'd spoken to him on the phone and recognized him from his picture: Stewart Day, the university's vice president for public relations. I guess it's never too soon to put a positive spin on another gorge-flattened undergraduate.

"Hello, Alex," the chief said. "I didn't think you people would be here on a Sunday morning."

I was the only reporter there, and I didn't expect anyone else to show up. The local TV news only broadcasts Monday through Friday and could pick up the details in time for its evening newscast. The *Gabriel Advocate,* the only other paper in town, wouldn't come out for four days, and the Syracuse paper couldn't care less about another Gabriel gorge diver.

"Yeah, I lucked out," I said. "You ID'ed him yet?"

"Climbers haven't gotten down there. And you know we're not releasing anything until we contact the parents."

"So you think it's another student?" The chief had no way of knowing, but Day looked so uptight in his aqua-blue polo shirt, I felt it was a moral imperative to annoy him.

"Isn't it usually?" Hill said, looking at Day out of the corner of his eye.

"Yeah, Chief. Those calculus finals are a bitch."

"They'll be lining up here when exams start, I betcha. Hafta take a number."

"Wilfred," Day broke in, "why don't you introduce me to this lovely young lady?"

Wilfred? Everybody, including Hill's wife and kids, calls him "Chief."

"Oh, sure. This is Alex Bernier from the *Monitor*."

Day extended a well-manicured paw. "I'm Stewart Day, Benson's vice president for public relations. I recognized you from your movie column. I consider myself a film connoisseur, but I must say that my wife and I wouldn't know what to see if it weren't for you."

Okay, the man was a schnauzer, but I was still flattered. I've been the *Monitor*'s film critic for two years, and I usually only hear from my reading public when they tell me I wouldn't know a good movie if it bit me on the butt.

"Thanks," I said, peering over into the gorge for the first time. "I'd rather be at the movies right about now."

Day clucked his tongue against his canines and shook his head. "It's always such a shame to come out here on an occasion like this," he said. When neither of us answered him, he kept talking. "People find stories like this *so* upsetting. And as I'm sure you know, Miss Bernier, Benson's suicide rate is actually lower than that of many other universities. Most people aren't aware of that. It's simply because so many unfortunate people choose to . . . to . . ."

"Jump."

"Yes. To . . . jump in so public a manner that we have earned an undeserved reputation as . . ."

"As Suicide U."

He looked like he might lose his composure, maybe burst a button on his polo shirt, but he got a handle on himself. "Miss Bernier, you're an excellent journalist.

I'm sure you have no interest in perpetuating untoward stereotypes. So we were wondering if, perhaps, your newspaper might consider . . ."

"Consider what?" I said with the most angelic expression I'm capable of summoning up. I knew what he was after, but I was damned if I was going to help him spit it out.

"I'm new to this city, of course. I'm really a freshman myself." He chuckled at his own joke. "Naturally, I wouldn't dream of telling you how to do your job. But perhaps, in this case, in the interest of your readers, you might be willing to . . ."

"To . . . ?"

He wiggled his eyebrows, and I wondered if he was about to slip me a fifty for hush money. Chief Hill looked in danger of combusting from the laugh he was stifling.

"To overlook this unfortunate incident."

"So you're wondering if the paper could, say, not report that some Benson student jumped in the gorge."

"I think it would be for the best."

"Don't you think everyone will wonder what all the sirens were about? And the roadblocks?"

"Perhaps, but in this case, a certain amount of delicacy may be in order."

"Don't you mean damage control?"

"Call it whatever you like." His voice had a nasty edge to it all of a sudden. "You may not be aware of this, Miss Bernier, but I have had the pleasure of playing golf with your publisher."

"Goodness. I had no idea."

"And he has indicated to me that from now on, the relationship between your newspaper and the university will be very much improved."

Yeah, and if our publisher ever stops by the newsroom

one of these years, we'll all be in a heap of trouble.
"What a relief. It's been keeping me up nights."

"So I think it would be very much in your best interest . . ."

"Don't waste your breath, Stew," the chief interjected.
"If it's in the cop blotter, they gotta write about it. Don't
worry, you'll get used to it. Doesn't hurt a bit." The chief
clapped him on the back hard enough to make Day step
forward to get his balance. He also didn't look like he enjoyed being called "Stew."

"Wilfred, that's really rather shortsighted . . ."

Day was still speaking as I jockeyed to see the body
through the treetops. It was lying facedown on a slab of
rock. The man's legs were bowed out at the knees like a
bullfrog's, his arms outstretched. He was wearing jeans,
a gray T-shirt, and white shoes that I figured were sneakers. It almost looked like he was sleeping—except for the
little rivers of blood that stained the water pink.

From that second there was something familiar, and it
wasn't just that I've covered my fair share of suicides.
Three or four people—usually students, sometimes not—
check out in the gorges each year. Every time the paper
covers one, we get letters complaining we shouldn't pub-
licize such things. But I always figured if the victims
wanted to keep their names out of the paper, they could
have offed themselves in the privacy of their own homes.

I watched the climbers reach the body and motion for
the stretcher. The winch started with a whine and the
man-sized metal tray crawled down toward the riverbed.
One rescuer grabbed the stretcher at shoulder height and
guided it to rest on the rock beside the body. Two of them
rolled the corpse onto its back. Even from three hundred
feet up, I could see the face was coated in blood. *Gross.*

The firemen loaded the body onto the stretcher, covered it with black plastic, and gave the thumbs-up.

I stepped back to give the police and rescuers room to maneuver; it's always good form to get the hell out of the way and let them do their jobs. A cop leaned over and grabbed the stretcher. As he guided it over the side, the body's left arm came free, shaking hands with the air. On his wrist, the face of a black-banded Timex caught the sunlight.

I didn't just recognize that watch. I'd bought it.

I'm lying in my bed, underneath him. His shoulder-length hair falls around my eyebrows. My arms snake around him, touch the back of his neck. We don't talk. The silence is broken only by kisses and his watch ticking in my ear.

I dropped my pen and notebook. My bare knees scraped the pavement as I threw myself down next to the body, ripped back the cover, and screamed.

2

WRITING IS THE ONLY WAY I KNOW HOW TO MAKE SENSE out of life. Put things down on paper. Get them under control. Make order out of chaos.

Maybe that's too simplistic. On the other hand, maybe it's too grandiose. All I know is I can't handle everything that's happened this year—having Adam pop back into my life, then losing him again, and the whole story that came out of it. I can't sleep, and I'm eating way too much pizza and Chinese and not running enough. At least I'm not smoking anymore.

I keep hoping that one of these days it will all make sense. I'll roll out of bed with my three alarm clocks and understand why things happened the way they did. But until then, all I can think of to do is write it down, and let whoever reads this try to figure it out.

Writing about the pain in the past tense makes it seem like it's over, which is a big lie. It won't be over until I can think about Adam without feeling like I've been punched in the gut. They sing songs about broken hearts, but I think most people feel it in their stomachs; that adrenaline-rush sickness you get when something reminds you. Like when I broke up with this guy from Ottawa a couple of years ago, I'd get upset at any reference to Canada. Pretty unfortunate, since it's a big country and difficult to ignore, especially during hockey season.

Since Adam died, I get seasick when I think of California, and mountain bikes, and ultimate Frisbee. Also strong coffee and the *Utne Reader.* And Ernest Hemingway, and Coronas with lime, and those LU biscuits shaped like little schoolboys.

His death is the worst thing that's ever happened to me, which my mom says makes me pretty lucky. No muggings, no starvation, no boyfriends who tried to use me as a punching bag.

Just a thirty-one-year-old man, whom I loved, who died a few hours after he left my bed.

His name was Adam. Adam Ellroy, a native of Berkeley, California, and the most beautiful man I've ever seen with his clothes off. His body was so lovely, so perfect and muscular and wiry, I didn't even care that he wore briefs. *Colored* briefs, no less. So much for rule number two.

That body—to compare him to Michelangelo's "David" is a cliché but I don't care because it's absolutely true—is right now rotting in the Ellroy family plot outside San Francisco. This turn of events might have made me a raging atheist, if I weren't one already.

I met Adam the year before I moved to Gabriel, when we were both reporters in western Massachusetts. He was at the Pittsfield paper, I worked for the Berkshire County weekly. We first ran into each other covering a state senate campaign, at a stump speech for a Republican state rep named Ebenezer Holstein. (As Dave Barry would say, I am not making this up.) I remember—who could forget?—watching the candidate parade around inside a life-size cardboard cow with his name plastered on the side when I heard this incredibly sexy voice behind me.

"Is this guy for real?" he said, and I turned around and that was it. From the moment I laid eyes on him, it was the beginning of the end—brown eyes, dark as new-ground coffee. A scar, short but deep, above his right cheekbone. Hair down to his shoulders, long enough to pull into a stubby ponytail.

A few days after we met, we hiked to the top of Mount Greylock, and stood together as the highest points in Massachusetts. I remember it started to rain while we were up there, and by the time we got to the bottom I was sopping wet and more in love than I ever care to be again. That night, and many nights afterward, I spent in his bed. He lived in a great apartment over a six-car garage on one of those old Williamstown estates with two guys he worked with. Almost every night, the four of us would make dinner and argue about politics or complain about television. Then there'd be that delicious moment when Adam would come up behind me and put his hands on the kitchen counter on my right and left, and dig through my hair with his lips until he found my neck and every cell in my body would say *yes*.

What I didn't know at first but found out soon enough was this: Adam was desperately in love with someone else. Not just deeply, or madly. Desperately. He and Olivia had been on and off since journalism school, and when I met him I thought they were off for good. I should have known better. Adam and I were lovers for eight months, thirty-three weeks of good coffee and great sex. But I guess I always knew it was going to end eventually. I was an illegal alien in his life, with no real hope of getting a green card.

So it was no surprise when Adam leaned against the counter one morning, stared down at the electric bean grinder in his hands, and told me he was moving back to California. I'd half expected him to leave in the middle of the night, a good-bye letter scrawled on a piece of notebook paper, stuck under the windshield wiper of my Renault.

After he left, something truly strange happened. We got to be friends. I'd figured the letters and phone calls would dribble to a halt after a couple of months, but we stayed in touch. Ironically enough, I became his closest confidante on the ever-fascinating subject of Olivia. When they broke up for what turned out to be the last time, he decided he wanted to get away from San Francisco, and I told him about the opening on the *Monitor* cop beat. He started after New Year's, and slid into our social circle as if he'd always been there. He also slid right back between my sheets, which I swore would never happen but made no effort whatsoever to resist.

Throughout the second act of our affair, I kept wanting to talk about it, figure out if there was any future in it this time. But I was afraid confronting him would be like turning on the lights in a movie theater: The screen disappears, the fiction ends. I didn't have the guts to risk scaring him off, although I've since found out that he might have been in love with me after all.

Maybe that should make me feel better. It doesn't. Neither does the passage of time. The intervening weeks have just robbed me of the emotional Novocain that helped me get through it in the first place. Now I feel his absence absolutely; I see it in Technicolor. Nothing's in the past but the verbs.

But back to the story. Where was I? Oh yes—screaming my guts out on North Creek Bridge. I'll jump ahead to later that night, when I was zonked out of my skull. I still remember it pretty well, though; unfortunately, I've never been drunk enough to forget anything.

The thing I recall most vividly is how the streetlights outside the Citizen Kane's plate-glass window turned the line of green bottles on the sill into little Christmas ornaments. This struck me as funny, since it was the middle of July. I leaned back with my feet on an empty chair and counted the six-ounce empties through a red-wine haze. I got to five when I lost track and had to start again.

The voices seemed to be coming from far away, though half the *Monitor* newsroom was clustered around the crescent-shaped table. It's the best seat in the bar, with a view of the local cast of characters that parade around the Green, Gabriel's pedestrian mall. There's the guy O'Shaunessey calls Franz Kafka, and a homeless man with the chest-length beard we named Leonardo da Vinci, and a bunch of different hippies we refer to collectively as Abbie Hoffman.

The conversation hadn't shifted for the past four hours, and I knew it wouldn't for days, weeks maybe. I could picture snow falling as we talked about it, melting into spring and boiling off into summer before somebody changed the subject.

Why? That's what we all wanted to know. Why would Adam kill himself? Why would a healthy thirty-one-year-old man jump off a bridge in the middle of the night? Why didn't any of us realize he was that depressed? Why didn't he say something?

"When did you say he talked to her last?"

Xavier O'Shaunessey, the *Monitor*'s sports editor and one of my best friends, asked the question for the third time, from behind glasses as grimy as the windows of a Bangkok cathouse.

"Thursday," I heard myself answer. I dropped my feet to the dirty wood floor, leaned my elbows into a puddle of beer, and watched the table spin. "Thursday night, late. She told him she was marrying the guy from Cupertino and wanted him to fly out and be her maid of honor or something."

"Her *what*?" Melissa shrieked, pale yellow Labatt's sloshing over the top of her mug.

"She wanted him to stand up for her at the wedding. He told me when he got to work Friday afternoon."

"You have *got* to be kidding me," Melissa said. "Whoever heard of having your ex-boyfriend be your bridesmaid? Jesus! What would you call it?"

"California," I said, leaning forward to add another bottle to the platoon on the windowsill. "I would call it California."

"I'd call it sick," Melissa said. "Not that I ever understood that relationship. It went on for what, five years or something?"

"Six. He met her in J-school."

I reached for the pack of Marlboro Lights I'd been working on all night and lit another one. If I tried to go running the next day, they were going to have to cart me away in an ambulance.

"So do you really think that's why he did it?"

Mad had been quiet up until then, which is pretty unusual for him. Jake Madison covers science for the *Monitor,* and he loves to share his beat with the rest of us—physics, biochemistry, plant science, supercomputing—regardless of our collective disinterest. Truly, the man missed his calling. He should have been a college professor, getting paid to lecture to a bunch of people who couldn't care less.

Everyone's tall compared to me, but Mad is something like six feet four. He's got blue-gray eyes with seriously Nordic bone structure, and if he wanted to he could make it on TV. He works out a lot, and in his own way he's as vain as any debutante.

"I don't know," I said. "I keep running it around in my head, over and over and over and over. I can't believe it. I mean, yeah, he was upset she was getting married. I think he still had hopes they'd get back together. But offing himself? That's insane. Nobody's that madly in love, not even him." Not even me.

"Was he sick or something?" Melissa asked. "Did he have, you know, cancer or AIDS or something?"

"No way," O'Shaunessey said. "The guy was mountain biking the day before he died. No way was he sick. He was fucking thirty-one years old." At forty, O'Shaunessey preferred to think Adam had bowed out of his own accord, rather than succumbing to diseases you weren't supposed to get until you were somebody's grandfather.

"If he had some disease, one of us would have known about it," I said. "And condom or no condom, Adam wouldn't have been screwing me if he had AIDS. No way." On that happy note, the conversation waned, and O'Shaunessey raised the plastic pitcher.

"Another round?" he asked, and everyone looked at him like he'd sprouted a third arm. Of course we wanted another round.

"Fine thing," he said, and toddled off to the bar.

"What did the police ask you?" Marshall asked quietly. The business reporter's lilting Georgia drawl made the question all the more gentle. He sat at the opposite end of the table with his wife, a reporter in the Gabriel bureau of one of the upstate metros.

"Well, after I freaked out, Chief Hill threw me in the back of one of the cop cars. I was half scared they were going to search me and find the Mace in my backpack," I said, draining the dregs of my wine. I hadn't paid for a drink all night.

"You mean he brought you to one of those *interrogation* rooms?" asked Marshall's wife, a lanky blond named Charlotte. Her Dixie accent makes her husband sound like Ulysses S. Grant in comparison.

"I kind of wish he had. I always wondered what the hell goes on back there," I said, lighting what must have been my eleventh Marlboro. I'm what you'd call a hysterical smoker. I won't sit in the smoking section of a restaurant, and I sure as hell won't let anybody light up in my house. But when I'm really upset, I'm a chimney. "No, he let me stay in that little room near the front, the one they use for press conferences. He was pretty nice, actually. Told me I didn't have to ID the body, since half the cops knew Adam anyway. They brought that female sergeant in to take my statement. I guess the chief thought it would make me feel better. I told them about last night, how we all left here together and he went home with me."

"Did they ask if you slept with him?" Melissa asked.

"That was right about when I started smoking. They wanted to know if he was depressed, if he talked about killing himself. 'Any recent traumas,' was how they put it."

When I'd told them about Olivia, the woman cop glanced up from her notebook to the chief. She'd gone on to ask about previous suicide attempts and drug use, but it was obvious that a broken heart was good enough for them.

"So they figure you're the last one who saw him alive," Mad said.

"Yeah, unless he decided to screw someone else on his way up to the gorge."

"I can't believe you wrote the story, Bernier," O'Shaunessey said, raising his beer mug and spilling a little in my lap. "You're a trooper. The girl's a trooper."

"That's off the record. Don't be spreading it around," I said, knowing it was hopeless. Telling O'Shaunessey a secret is as good as putting it on the AP wire.

"What did you do after the police were through with you?" Charlotte asked. She pronounced it *po*-lice, emphasis on the first syllable. I have no idea how people take each other seriously down South, considering they all sound like the third runner-up in the Miss America contest.

"I went back to the paper. Couldn't think of anyplace else to go."

The paper is two blocks from the cop shop, less than a five-minute walk. But I swear it was the longest two blocks of my life. I felt like I was stuck on one of the treadmills I use at the Y when there's too much snow to run outside. The cops were finished with me. I was all by myself. No distractions, except the time-and-temperature clock on the Green.

Adam was dead.

In the movies, they always show the most dramatic moments when somebody dies: the fiery car crash, the troopers knocking on the widow's door. But those aren't the worst moments, not by a long shot. No, you hit bottom when all the drama is over, when you go back to your normal life and realize the person isn't there anymore. There's an empty stool at the bar. You cook dinner and have twice as many leftovers. You reach for a movie in the video store and think: He always wanted to rent this. You put it back.

The walk back to the *Monitor* was like that. Horribly normal. Sunny. People shopping, couples walking to brunch, every third person toting the Sunday *New York Times*. The Green covers two blocks of what used to be State Street before it was turned into a pedestrian mall. Besides the Citizen and a few restaurants, it really only has two kinds of stores: boutiques where you can buy scented soaps and pottery, and hippie emporiums that sell cotton-print dresses and hammocks woven by Nicaraguan peasants. As I passed the shop windows, I thought: My kingdom for a drive-by shooting.

When I got to the paper, I could hear Melissa in the darkroom, working her way down the phone list, telling people what had happened or leaving messages on their machines to call the paper. I dropped the notebook full of empty pages on my desk and tossed the other bagel half in the garbage before it made me gag.

I probably would have started crying then anyway. But it didn't help that my desk is right across from Adam's. There was the swivel chair with his name on the back. The Grateful Dead dancing bears sticker on the side of his computer. His notebooks and accident reports and press releases, piled up like an arsonist's dream.

I put my head down on my desk like they taught me in kindergarten, and cried with these awful, racking sobs that made my ribs ache. Mad found me like that. He didn't say anything, just crouched down by my chair and stroked my hair with one of his huge farm-boy mitts.

"He's dead, Mad."

"I know."

"I saw him, Mad. His face . . . It was *gone*."

"Shh . . ."

We stayed like that for a long time, this six-foot-four jock rocking and shushing me like a baby. Most people can be incredibly kind when you need them to be.

Mad offered to write the story for me, but I couldn't stand the thought of explaining everything. He stayed there as I wrote, reading over my shoulder.

It was obvious I couldn't put my byline on the story; I was way too involved. So when the city editor called to see what the hell was going on and figure out who was going to cover it, Mad told him he was working on it himself.

It ran the next day under the headline "*Monitor* reporter found dead in gorge."

By JAKE MADISON
Monitor staff

A *Gabriel Monitor* staff reporter was found dead in North Creek Gorge early Sunday morning. Adam Ellroy, 31, was the victim of an apparent suicide.

The body was discovered by a jogger crossing the bridge at about 8 A.M., police said. Ellroy, of 275 E. Chandler St., had covered the police beat for the *Monitor* since January.

No suicide note has been discovered, police said. Pending an autopsy, the death has been tentatively ruled a suicide.

"We don't have any reason to suspect foul play or an accident at this time," said Police Chief Wilfred Hill, adding the coroner's report is expected to be released Wednesday. According to police, a friend living in Benson Heights last saw Ellroy at about 3 A.M. when he left to go home.

Ellroy is survived by his mother, Marcia Williams, of Berkeley, Calif.; his father, Dale Ellroy, of Chicago, Ill.; and two older sisters. Funeral services, to be held in Berkeley, have not been scheduled.

Ellroy is the third person found dead in North Creek Gorge this year. Benson University sophomore Catherine James, 19, died in an apparent suicide Feb. 4. The body of 83-year-old René Lecuyer of Ste. Marie, Quebec, Canada, was discovered July 9.

After we filed the story, Mad took my hand and led me down the stairs, out the door, and into the bar.

3

EVENTUALLY, I HAD TO GO HOME; I WAS GOING TO HAVE to face it sooner or later. I'd crashed on Mad's couch Sunday night, and walked the few yards to work the next morning in yesterday's clothes. The managing editor offered me the day off—the week if I wanted it—but I was in no hurry to sleep in my own bed.

It was the last place I ever saw Adam alive. The shape of his body was still imprinted on my feather bed, like those chalk outlines you see on the news.

We weren't going to have a funeral for him in Gabriel; he'd be buried back home in Berkeley. And since Adam's interest in God was confined to orgasms and epithets, the only memorial service that seemed fitting was the Irish wake we'd had for him in the bar.

Calling his parents had been a nightmare, but I couldn't let them hear it from the cops. I picked his dad first, figuring he'd take it better—"take it like a man," I guess. Was I ever wrong. His father absolutely flipped out, beyond hysterical. If Adam's stepmother hadn't been there, I would have called an ambulance for him.

His mother hardly said a word. She latched on to the details of her son's death like a woman overboard would grab for a life preserver. Police report. Autopsy. Travel plans. She wanted to come East for his body, but I talked her into letting me make the arrangements to have it—him—shipped back to Berkeley. To be honest, I wasn't trying to do her a favor. I just didn't want to have to look her in the eye.

When I asked what she wanted me to do with his things, his mother suddenly sounded angry. "Do whatever you want with it. Give it all away. That boy never kept anything more than he could throw in the back of his pickup truck."

I got through Monday by never giving myself time to think. I finished the nudist-colony piece, made some calls for a story on the gay-rights movement at Benson, helped one of the interns with a feature on teen pregnancy. The newsroom secretary—God bless her—picked up Adam's phone the second it rang, telling each caller Adam was "unavailable" and rerouting them all to Mad.

It was late afternoon when I realized something I should have thought of much earlier.

Olivia.

Somebody had to tell her, before she found out about Adam's death on the obit page of the Berkeley paper. It probably wasn't going to be his parents, who never approved of their up-and-down relationship. I had to call her. I looked for her number in Adam's Rolodex, but it wasn't there. I dialed San Francisco information; she was unlisted. The only place I could think to look was Adam's desk in his apartment—and I was avoiding *that* even more than my own bedroom.

I looked around the newsroom to see if there was anyone I could draft into going with me, but everybody was busy, so I walked over to Mad's and found him watching a shark documentary on the Discovery Channel and drinking red wine out of a salsa jar. We walked the six blocks to Adam's apartment and I let myself in with the key Adam gave me when he moved in. The place *smelled* like him. It's hard to describe—an odd combination of Ivory soap, Old Spice deodorant, and fresh-baked bread.

Mad perched on the corner of the unmade bed as I shuffled through Adam's desk drawers. I found his address book almost immediately, which was the last thing I expected. "That's weird," I said. "I was here a couple of days ago, and the desk was stuffed with notebooks. You could hardly open the drawers."

"Maybe he threw them out."

"Adam? No way. He hangs on to his notes forever."

"He probably tossed them. Or maybe they're all in a box someplace. What difference does it make?"

"But it isn't like him . . ."

"You're talking like the guy is still alive. Look, nobody knows what he was thinking right before he . . . did it."

Mad paced around the apartment as I pawed through the desk. His upper lip did an Elvis sneer when he sniffed a plastic ashtray on the orange-crate coffee table. Pot was one of Adam's four basic food groups, but Mad prefers to prey on the liver rather than the lungs.

"Mad, get over here."

"What is it?"

"All his clips are gone." Adam was a slob, but he was meticulous about filing his major stories. Like every other reporter, he always had an eye out for his next job. The black, two-drawer filing cabinet housed his best work, going back to his college paper. "Where the hell are all his clips?"

"Maybe he threw them out with the notebooks."

"Would you throw away everything you've ever written?"

"Would I jump in the goddamn gorge? Look, Alex, you're going to drive yourself crazy. He's dead. It's not your fault."

"I can't deal with this. It doesn't make any sense. Mad, I knew this guy for four years. I was his best friend here. And with no warning at all, he goes and jumps in the gorge? I just can't believe it."

"It's totally understandable that you can't handle it right now, sweetheart. Adam did a really selfish thing, when you think about it. He couldn't handle all his shit, so he jumped."

"What if he didn't?"

"What do you mean?"

"Maybe he didn't kill himself."

"You've been reading too much female private eye crap."

"What if it was an accident? People have fallen into the gorge before. I covered one myself. Last year, that guy from Texas . . ."

"He was drunk off his ass."

"I know, but . . ."

"Let me get this straight. Adam leaves your house. He's stone-cold sober. He stops at the gorge on his way home, takes a little late-night walk, and *accidentally* falls over a three-foot railing?"

"I know, it sounds ridiculous. But Adam . . ."

"Alex, listen to me. I'm not trying to be a monster here. But you're driving yourself crazy. You may never understand why Adam did it. Suicide is hardly a rational act."

"But why didn't he say something? Why didn't I . . ."

"He must have been really fucked up, that's all I can say."

"So how am I supposed to explain it to Olivia? I talk him into coming out here and . . ."

"You can't explain it. Just be straight with her. It's all you can do."

I lit a cigarette with the Zippo on Adam's coffee table. He didn't have that much stuff, but it hurt to look at it all, even the plastic Smurfs on his bookshelves. Sometimes, when he was stoned and stupid, he'd arrange them on the coffee table in tiny blue regiments. He'd ask you which Smurf you'd want to be, like some Rorschach test. Vanity Smurf? Smurfette?

Failing to find Heartbroken Smurf, I picked up a picture of Adam in his college newsroom.

"What am I going to do with all this? I told his mom I'd take care of it. How am I supposed to dig through all his clothes?"

"Screw it. Don't worry about it. Everybody'll help."

"You will?"

"You know us. We'll descend like the vultures we are and clean the place out. Now let's get the hell out of here and go find us a drink."

"I have to call Olivia first."

"Which is why you need a drink."

"Do you ever *not* need a drink?"

"And put the Citizen out of business? Oh, the humanity . . ."

"Oh," I said, touching the cold glass over Adam's face. "The humanity."

4

THE PHONE RANG EIGHT, TEN, TWELVE TIMES. I WON'T LIE about it. I kept hoping Olivia wouldn't answer. I'd already made a deal with myself: Twenty rings and I was off the hook. Midway through ring number seventeen, a woman picked up the phone, sounding out of breath. I suddenly realized that after years of hearing about the mythical Olivia—envying her, maybe even hating her—I had no idea what she sounded like.

"Hello?"

"Hi. Is this Olivia?"

"Yes?"

"This is Alex Bernier. Adam's friend."

No response. Jesus, did he not even tell her about me?

"I work with him at the *Gabriel Monitor.* We met when he was living back in Massachusetts. We, um, dated for a while."

"Oh, *Alex.* Oh God, I am *so* sorry. I didn't make the connection. I just grabbed the phone out of the shower.

I'm on my way to do some damn feature on rooftop swimming pools."

Olivia works for the *San Francisco Chronicle,* doing whatever fluff stories filtered to the bottom of the food chain. From what Adam told me, she's good; you have to be to get a staff job at a metro so early. The mind of Bob Woodward in the body of Heather Locklear.

"I need to talk to you about something. About Adam."

"Okay," she said, drawing the word out slowly.

Even breaking it to his parents hadn't prepared me for this. Maybe having her read about it in the Berkeley paper wasn't such a bad idea.

"Uh, when was the last time you talked to him?"

"You know, Alex, if you're worried something's still going on with us, it's all over. Didn't Adam tell you I'm getting married?"

"It's not that. Are you sitting down?"

Christ Almighty, I thought, I sound like a bad movie.

"Is he okay? What's going on?"

"He's . . . Olivia, he's dead."

"What?"

"He's dead. Adam's dead."

Silence. "That goddamn pickup truck."

"It wasn't a car accident. He . . . Olivia, he killed himself."

"No, he did not." I heard her voice crack from the other side of the country.

"He jumped off a bridge late Saturday night. I covered it myself. I watched them pull his body out of the gorge."

"I don't believe it. Why would Adam kill himself? Oh, my God . . ."

"They're saying . . . They think he couldn't deal with the breakup, that you're marrying somebody else."

"What? That is *not* true. Adam and I settled everything. He was over it."

"He was?" I couldn't have been more surprised if Olivia had told me Adam liked to wear ladies' panties under his Levi's.

"When I told him I was getting married, he seemed really happy for me. He said he'd be in the wedding. He even said he might bring you out with him. Oh, God, Adam . . ."

I could feel the lemon yogurt churning around in my stomach. "Me? What are you talking about?"

"We had a long talk about it about a week ago. It was . . . the last time I talked to him. He said he knew he screwed things up with you when he left."

"He did?"

"He asked me what he should do. I told him he should just tell you how he felt."

"Do you have any idea why he might have . . . done it?"

She didn't say anything for a full minute. It was like waiting for your AIDS test at Planned Parenthood. "I'm trying to figure out how to put this. I haven't seen Adam since he went to New York. And things were pretty bad when he left. I met somebody else, and I guess we both knew it was really over this time. But we've talked a lot lately. He seemed pretty happy—well, maybe not happy, but at least okay. You saw him every day. You should know. Did he seem suicidal to you?"

"Oh, God, Olivia, I don't know anything anymore. I just can't believe he did it."

"I don't believe it."

"I know," I said, wondering if I was managing to sound comforting.

"No, I really don't believe it. He could never kill himself. Even if he wanted to, he would never do that to his parents, or his friends. I don't care what the cops say."

"Then why . . ."

"Was he drunk or something? Could it have been an accident? Were there any witnesses?" Olivia was firing questions as though she were at a press conference. She reminded me a lot of Adam's mother in the way she was handling it. Maybe that had been part of the attraction in the first place.

"I've thought about it, but I don't see how. He was totally sober when he left my place."

"Wait—you mean they think he jumped right after he saw you?"

"It was like three in the morning. He just, uh, we just got out of bed."

"Oh, Alex . . ."

"I don't see how it could have been an accident. He didn't have any reason to be out on North Creek Bridge in the middle of the night."

"Nothing anybody says can make me believe he killed himself. So if it wasn't an accident, that only leaves one possibility. Somebody must have pushed him."

"Olivia, this is Gabriel, not New York City. People don't just go killing each other."

"Apparently, they do. Adam did not kill himself. Unless it was an accident, it had to be murder."

It was crazy. But I had to admit it was the first thing I'd heard in two days that made sense.

"I know," I said. "It's insane, but I agree with you."

"Can you think of anybody who would have wanted to kill him?"

"Other than myself? No."

"What are you going to do now?"

"I don't know. I guess I'll try and talk to the cops. I'm

not sure what I can tell them, except that none of this makes sense. Like, listen to this: When I went to find your number in Adam's desk, all his notebooks and clip files were gone."

"What? Adam would never have gotten rid of them. No way."

"That's what I thought. But everybody here is going to think I'm nuts."

We wound up staying on the phone for an hour. I liked her, the last thing I expected. I'd spent so long picturing her as some flaky bimbo—okay, a bimbo who graduated *cum laude* from Yale—that it never occurred to me we might be a lot alike.

Beware, my lord, of jealousy. It is the green-eyed monster which doth mock the meat it feeds on.

I'd half hated Olivia for years, since the day Adam told me about her. He mentioned her casually, in the normal rundown of exes that comes at the beginning of a relationship. How many people have you slept with? More than a baseball team? Less than the House of Representatives?

But Olivia was more than just a name on a sexual laundry list. He was still in love with her, and I think our affair made him realize how much he missed her. When I found out, the envy burned in my gut like Tabasco sauce. I tossed all my Olivia Newton-John records from junior high. (Okay, so I hung on to the *Grease* soundtrack, but *Physical* and *Xanadu* went right out the window.) I took down my *Gone With the Wind* poster because I got sick of looking at Olivia de Havilland's name every time I went to the john.

And now there we were on the phone, pouring our hearts out like a pair of sorority sisters. I couldn't summon up an ounce of ill will toward her. She understood my loss, and I understood hers. Before we hung up, she gave me her newsroom fax number and I promised to send her all the stories about Adam's death.

When I hung up the phone I felt better, and it wasn't just because the deed was done. It was a relief to hear someone say what I'd been thinking for two days: Adam Ellroy would not have killed himself. Adam Ellroy *did not* kill himself.

Adam Ellroy was murdered.

So why was I so calm all of a sudden? Maybe I'd just been so strung out, I didn't have the energy for more hysterics. The truth is, anything was easier than believing that Adam wanted to die.

The phone was still warm when I picked it up again and dialed Chief Hill. "Alex, I'm glad it's you," he said. "I was about to call."

"You were? About Adam?"

"Yes. We . . ."

"Listen, Chief. I know it sounds crazy, but I really don't think he killed himself."

"Alex . . ."

"I talked to his ex-girlfriend in California, and she said he wasn't upset over their breakup. And all his notebooks are gone from his house, and all his clips. He never throws away his notebooks. Ask anybody."

"Alex, please calm down."

"Chief, I really think he was murdered."

"Alex, we found the suicide note."

"You *what*?"

"This is off the record. This is not for publication. I wouldn't have told you if his parents hadn't given permission. We found a handwritten suicide note on the floor of his pickup truck."

"What did it say? Please, Chief, you've got to read it to me."

"Okay. It says, 'Holy Mary, Mother of God. Forgive our Sins. The End of Hope.'"

"That's it?"

"That's it."

"Does that sound like any suicide note you've ever seen?"

"Frankly, Alex, after twenty years of police work, I've seen just about everything."

"Chief, Adam didn't have a religious bone in his entire body."

"I've seen people that didn't leave any kind of note, and others that left fifty typed pages. A last-minute religious revival is pretty common, believe me."

"Can I have a copy of it?"

"I suppose so. Just come down to the station."

Maybe if I hadn't just gotten off the phone with Olivia, the note would have freaked me out more. But at that point, I didn't know what to think. Olivia seemed so sure Adam would never have killed himself, and the note sure as hell didn't sound like him. Was that cryptic, totally ridiculous piece of paper really his fond farewell? I couldn't believe it. But then again, nobody—not me, not Olivia, nobody—wants to admit they can love someone so much without really knowing them at all.

I knew one thing for sure. If I started howling "murder," my friends were going to think I was nuts. My editor would offer me a nice long vacation—he might even try to make it sound like I had a choice. The cops obviously weren't going to listen to me; between the breakup with Olivia and that ridiculous note, they were more than satisfied. I was going to have to keep my mouth shut about this one. Me, who broadcasts the highlights of my personal life like a sportscaster at the Super Bowl.

I left the newspaper's library, a phone-booth-sized room stuffed with filing cabinets that's a choice locale for personal calls. I wasn't sure where to start, but Adam's desk seemed as good a place as any. I dug through all the crap in his top drawer without finding anything. The files in the stumpy cabinet seemed perfectly mundane, and just seeing his handwriting brought me to the edge of tears. He hadn't been at the paper long, and there wasn't much.

I went out the back door and squeezed my Renault out of the lot, missing the managing editor's bronze Audi by about two inches. I drove an extra three miles to avoid North Creek Bridge, and wondered if I'd ever have the guts to go near it.

I could hear Shakespeare barking in the backyard when I pulled into the driveway; Dirk must still be at the law firm where he was interning, or out with Helmut. I retrieved a mother lode of magazines from the mailbox. Between the two of us, we subscribe to *Vanity Fair, Time, Newsweek, Harper's, The New Yorker, Utne Reader, The Atlantic,* the *Washington Post Weekly, Details,* and *GQ.* The answering machine on the kitchen counter advertised four calls. The second and third were hang-ups—probably my mom, who calls every day and refuses to talk to the machine. The fourth was Melissa, seeing if I needed anything and letting me know the newsroom was convening at the Citizen around eleven.

The first was Adam. It was a message from Saturday afternoon I hadn't bothered to erase, asking if I'd be downtown that night. He spoke lazily, in that studiously casual way of his. Did I want to catch some dinner? What time was everybody heading to the Citizen?

He had no way of knowing these were the final hours

of his life. He certainly didn't sound like a man planning his own demise. I was sure of it. Somebody killed him, and it was up to me to find out who. I hadn't read every Nancy Drew and Hardy Boys mystery for nothing.

It was barely seven o'clock, and the late summer sun shone brighter than it would at noon in a Gabriel December. I might have braved the bugs and taken my *Newsweek* out to the backyard, if Shakespeare hadn't made a meal out of my L.L. Bean hammock. Instead, I went to the kitchen and made myself a sandwich on seedless rye: two slices of dayglow orange fat-free cheese, lettuce, spicy brown mustard, and fat-free mayonnaise.

Although I occasionally wish I'd been born in a more romantic time—eighteenth-century France, say, or the antebellum South—I figure modern technology has had a distinctly positive impact on my life. Without contact lenses, fat-free cheese, and birth control pills, I'd be blind, fat, and pregnant.

I took my sandwich, a Diet Pepsi, and a bag of baked-not-fried barbecue potato chips into the den and curled up in my pink La-Z-Boy. I switched on the TV just in time for the local news. Adam was the lead story; no surprise there. Nine News hadn't had a camera there on the scene, so the reporter—my friend Maggie, whom I'd probably run into later at the Citizen—did her stand-up from the empty bridge. The camera swept the gorge as she described Adam, the retrieval of the body, the presumption of suicide. When the story was over, the anchor shook her head gravely, thanked Maggie, and introduced a piece on a local girl who was trying to break the world record for standing on one foot.

I turned off the TV, put on a Suzanne Vega CD, and let Shakespeare in. The dog jumped on my lap the minute I sat back down: half German shepherd, half beagle, four white paws, forty pounds of pure pleasure. She was going to miss Adam and his expert belly rubs. Come to think of it, so would I.

I tried to straighten out the logistics of Saturday night. Everybody thought Adam went to North Creek Bridge to kill himself. But if he didn't, then what was he doing there? What possible reason could he have to drive out there in the middle of the night? He'd parked his truck along the road as if he'd just come from my house. Did he go straight there, or stop someplace else first?

I couldn't imagine why he would have gone up to the bridge at all, much less alone. He must have been meeting someone. But who? Why? Maybe Adam was buying pot from somebody, and the guy ripped him off and killed him. But that hardly seemed likely; Adam had described his campus supplier as sort of a stoned-out Elmer Fudd.

Could he have been meeting someone for a story? Adam had recently covered a fairly high-profile manslaughter trial, a hunter who was acquitted in the accidental killing of another Bambi stalker. But that had been over for a month. And while Hollywood might portray journalists as notebook-toting Rambos, real life is a lot less interesting. The idea of Adam meeting Deep Throat on a bridge in the middle of the night was almost funny.

So what was he doing there?

I asked Shakespeare each question, slowly. But other than offering her belly for a scratch, the dog was no help at all.

5

I WAS WORKING ON ANOTHER STORY ABOUT THE BENSON gay-rights movement when the coroner's press release came over the fax machine. It was official: Adam Ellroy, 31, died of internal injuries sustained in a fall. All of one paragraph. Along with it came a statement from the police department, saying Adam's death had been ruled a suicide.

"As there is no evidence of foul play, the case is now considered closed."

I consulted the Cop-to-English Dictionary. "The case is now considered closed" meant "Donut Time!"

I reread both pages, but they didn't tell me anything new. I made photocopies anyway, and left the originals in Mad's mailbox. Since he'd ostensibly covered the story in the first place, he'd be the one to write a few paragraphs on the coroner's verdict, to run in the local briefs column on page three.

I stuck my head into the city editor's office. As usual,

Bill had the phone sprouting out of his left ear, balanced on his shoulder with reckless disregard for the laws of gravity. He jotted notes on a yellow legal pad with one hand; with the other, he dangled spicy Chinese noodles into his mouth from a pair of wooden chopsticks. He waved a chopstick to tell me to stay, but I would have loitered anyway; only the newest hires think they have any hope of catching Bill between phone calls.

"What's up?"

"Coroner's report just came in on Adam. Suicide. Thought you'd like to know."

"You okay?"

"I guess."

"Give it to Mad."

"Already did."

"Where is he, anyway?"

"Langston Foundation press conference. Nuclear medicine grants, I think he said."

Bill's phone rang again and I went back to my desk. I was about half done with my piece, one of endless follow-ups to a story that started three months before. Adam had originally covered it from the cop angle, and the first stories bore his byline. It had started late one Saturday night, when a couple of Benson freshmen were walking across campus, hand in hand. Crossing a clearing off the arts quad, they'd met four Gamma Sigma Rho fraternity brothers, commuting from one bacchanalian orgy to another.

It would have been just another drunken crawl across campus—except that both the freshmen were male. And the frat boys, presumably in an alcoholic haze of heterosexual indignation, beat the living crap out of them. The two boys, both still teenagers, were found by the student safety patrol three hours later. They had several broken bones apiece, and required stitches in the triple digits. One of them ended up coming out of the closet to his parents from his hospital bed. The university cops were more than happy to turn the case over to the Gabriel police, and the frat boys were expelled.

Adam covered the original assault, and would have covered the upcoming trial. But the campus uproar that followed the attack fell into my beat. Overnight, Benson's nascent gay-rights group came to the front of the campus political scene. Protesters packed the arts quad and candlelight vigils were held at the site of the assault, which became an impromptu shrine of flowers and bad poetry.

The university president, a dour old Brit who bears a striking resemblance to "Q" from the James Bond movies, was probably going to have to meet with the student activists. I could imagine his Oxford-bred horror at having to sit so close to women in crew cuts and men with earrings, when he would normally have been on the back nine of the school golf course. The meetings I'd covered so far usually degenerated into shouting matches between the extreme and moderate wings of the Benson Gay and Lesbian Action Detail. Apparently, the group, like most campus organizations, wasn't immune from the temptation to concoct a cutesy acronym, in this case, "B-GLAD."

My story for the next day was on B-GLAD's final list of demands, which I'd first written about a month before. The group's "co-chairpersons" had called me that morning to schedule an interview, and later came into the newsroom with a press release on neon-yellow paper. Most of it wasn't much of a surprise, just a rehash of what they'd told me a month ago. The students wanted sensitivity training for campus security officers, more courses on gay and lesbian issues added to the American Studies curriculum, university-sponsored seminars for freshmen on gay life at Benson.

But here was the whopper, the lead of my previous story: B-GLAD wanted a building. The press release called it "a CULTURAL and SOCIAL center for GAY, LESBIAN, and BISEXUAL members of the Benson community, where students can LIVE and WORK together to CELEBRATE the UNIQUE heritage that has been ignored FAR TOO LONG."

Apparently, B-GLAD was also not immune to the wanton use of capital letters in its press releases.

The group didn't just want any building. They weren't going to "get shunted off to a hallway in some crumbling old co-op by the straight white male establishment," according to a Benson senior who seemed to qualify for two out of the three slurs himself. B-GLAD wanted a brand-spanking-new building, they said, equal to the facilities on campus for black, Latino, and Native American students.

"Work on this center MUST be started before AN-OTHER gay or lesbian student is ATTACKED," said the press release, now clothes-pinned to a stand next to my computer screen. "It must stand as a SYMBOL that VIO-LENCE will NOT be tolerated." What' s more, the student leaders said, there was only one acceptable place for the center: the site of the attack, smack in the middle of central campus. The gist of B-GLAD's latest press release was that the university was dragging its feet. The group had made its initial demand a month before, and still hadn't gotten any response from the administration.

"Maybe they think that since it's the summer, they can blow us off," said a Benson junior named Karin Coe, who pronounced her first name in one syllable that rhymed with "barn." "But we're not going away. We're going to mobilize. We'll march every day if we have to, until the administration starts to listen up."

It had been a fun story to cover so far, and it looked to get even more interesting. It was anybody's guess how long the university would put the students off, hoping for the problem to graduate away. I doubted the center would ever get off the politically correct drawing board, but you never knew what might happen on a campus as large and diverse as Benson's. I had to admire B-GLAD's *cojones* in demanding the center be built where the attack occurred, practically within spitting distance of the marble statue of university founder Simeon Benson. It would be a hoot if Benson spent eternity gazing at a gay and lesbian co-op. But even if the university went for it, there were bound to be objections to building on the largest piece of undeveloped land on central campus. Environmental groups like Keep Benson Green (the KBG, known by its detractors as the KGB) would probably go ballistic, claiming it was the last refuge of the rare upstate spotted lizard. But then again, even the greenies might not want to face off against the gay-rights contingent. I could definitely get into covering B-GLAD versus the KGB, in a war of the acronyms.

Come to think of it, it was odd that the spot was empty in the first place. Development had sprawled into adjacent fields and neighborhoods, but nothing had been built in the clearing, even during the growth years of the G.I. Bill. I ripped off a page of my reporter's notebook, scrawled "check out clearing" on it, and tossed it onto the pile of paper on my desk.

As I was getting together a list of who else to call for my B-GLAD story, the phone rang.

"Newsroom. Alex here."

"Hi, Alex, it's Chief Hill. Did you get the fax?"

"Yes."

"Adam's mother said you're taking care of his personal effects. Since the case is closed, you can come down to the station and get his things, if you'd like."

"Aren't they at the morgue?"

"I had them sent here. No need for you to go out there."

You chivalrous old fox. "Thanks, Chief."

I finished my story, spicing it up with quotes from both gay and straight students about the merits of the dormitory plan. I tried calling the fraternity the alleged attackers belonged to, and got hung up on after being called something that rhymed with "bunt." Charming.

After filing the story, I walked the few blocks to the police station and was buzzed into the chief's office. He was gone, but a uniformed officer gave me an oversized manila envelope with "Ellroy" written on it in red marker. I didn't feel like driving home, so I wandered into the Citizen Kane just as it was opening. I passed up the window seat for a change, settling into a dark wooden booth in the back, with a good view of the Rosebud sled replica over the bar.

I broke the seal on the manila envelope and let some of its contents fall onto the table. The bulkiest items were the clothes Adam had been wearing when he died: Berkeley T-shirt, faded Levi's, grungy Reeboks, grayish socks, the Mickey Mouse boxer shorts I brought him back from Disney World. The single blue stone he always wore around his neck was in there, and I realized I'd never seen him without it. His Timex was still working, having taken the ultimate licking and kept on ticking. I fingered his brown leather wallet, worn smooth, its edges almost white. It still contained his California driver's license, phone card, credit card, expired and current press passes, insurance ID, a Trojan condom, and twenty-three dollars in cash. So much for a mugging gone awry.

His car keys jangled when they hit the table. The police found them in his jeans pocket; his truck had been parked on the shoulder at the end of the bridge. If I'd driven that way, I would have run into it on my way to cover the jumper. There were no notebooks.

I bummed a cigarette from Mack, a former radio reporter who decided to quit following jobs around the country and open a bar. He's going slowly nuts from the boredom and follows our stories more closely than we do. Whenever he picks up a choice news tip, he passes it on to all of us, since showing favoritism toward one paper or station is bad for business.

I put my feet up on the seat across from me and watched the smoke rise from the unfiltered Chesterfield. If there were clues to be found among Adam's things, I couldn't find them. I packed everything up and decided to take a look in his truck, presumably the last place he was before he died. The battered white Nissan had been driven to the impound lot, but I could get it anytime.

The lot had a chain-link fence around it, but the gate was open. Who was going to steal cars from the police station anyway? I drove the few miles to Lakeside Park, Adam's plastic Bart Simpson on the dashboard nodding with every pothole. A few families were there, kids feeding stale bread to the seagulls. It seemed as good a place as any to riffle through the truck in relative solitude.

I opened the glove compartment first, and slammed it again when I saw all the crap that threatened to explode onto my lap. I'd deal with it later. I poked around under the seats and found empty coffee cups and soda cans, a fuzzy package of Big Red gum, the wrapper from a king-size bag of peanut M&M's, and about a hundred pens. I took six trips to the garbage can to get rid of all the junk, but I never came across a notebook. A pillow and two blankets were wadded up in the space behind the front seat. I checked in the truck bed, even hopped in for the sake of thoroughness. Nothing.

I emptied the contents of the glove compartment into my backpack, ditched the truck behind Adam's house, and walked back to the Citizen. I sat back down at the table I'd left less than an hour before and spread everything out, separating it into piles. There were Rand McNally maps of New England, New York, Canada, California, and the San Francisco Bay Area. A pile of credit card receipts stacked up half an inch thick. Four unpaid parking tickets were folded together. Most of the tapes were homemade and none had cases: Jim Croce, Rolling Stones, Suzanne Vega, Toni Childs, Counting Crows. An ice scraper guarded against a sudden August blizzard. I found three more packs of Big Red, each one missing a few sticks. I did not, however, find a written confession from the killer.

I was about to toss the credit card slips into the garbage behind the bar when I decided to look through them on a lark. I still wonder what would have happened if I'd thrown them out, whether I would have ever found out the truth. Doubtful.

All of them were for gas, most from the same Gabriel station, dating back to when Adam first moved here. But two didn't make any sense. One was dated two weeks ago, from a station in Watertown, New York, just south of the Canadian border. The other, dated the next day, was from Ste. Marie, Quebec.

What was Adam doing in Canada? He'd told me he was going to Boston to visit friends. Why would he lie? I figured Watertown was just a refueling stop, since everybody tries to avoid buying gas in Canada, where it's twice as expensive. What was he up to in Quebec? Did he go by himself? I knew I'd heard of Ste. Marie before, but I couldn't think of where.

I pulled the map of Canada out of the pile. It should have seemed strange that Adam would have a map of the country in the first place, since as far as I knew, he'd never been there. As I unfolded it, a piece of notebook paper fell out onto the table.

"Holy Mary by the Sea of God? Forgive the Fish. The End of Hope."

It was another version of the suicide note, significantly weirder than the first. It seemed odd the police hadn't come across it, but I guess they weren't looking too closely after they found what they were after.

I laid the map out on the table and found a route plotted in pencil. It stretched north from Gabriel, through Watertown and into Canada. Adam must have crossed the St. Lawrence River in Montreal and continued up the northern bank, about two hundred miles past Quebec City. The name "Ste. Marie," in the typeface for the smallest towns, was circled.

I remembered where I'd seen the name before.

"Mack, do you have a Monday paper back there?"

He dug through the pile and handed it across the bar.

There it was, right on page one. It was under Mad's byline, but I'd written it myself.

Ellroy is the third person found dead in North Creek Gorge this year. Benson University sophomore Catherine James, 19, died in an apparent suicide

> Feb. 4. The body of 83-year-old René
> Lecuyer of Ste. Marie, Quebec, Canada,
> was discovered July 9.

Unless it was one hell of a coincidence, Adam's trip to
Canada must have had something to do with Lecuyer's
suicide. He went up to Lecuyer's hometown, and a week
later he wound up dead in the same gorge.

Don't ever let anyone tell you there isn't some virtue
in being a slob. That slip of carbon paper from Ste. Marie
changed everything. Finally, I had something to go on,
something more concrete than my own intuition. I was
more determined than ever to find out what really happened to Adam. I was going to dig up everything the
newspaper's library had on René Lecuyer. I was going to
read through every story Adam wrote for the *Monitor*.

And I had a feeling I was about to pay a visit to the
Great White North.

6

M̲Y̲ K̲I̲T̲C̲H̲E̲N̲ O̲V̲E̲R̲F̲L̲O̲W̲E̲D̲. P̲E̲O̲P̲L̲E̲, P̲A̲S̲T̲A̲, R̲E̲D̲ W̲I̲N̲E̲, and conversation filled the room and spilled into the hallway, through the den and out onto the back patio. Thursday nights at my house have been a regular thing for a couple of years. The menu varies with my energy level and my checking account: pesto, stir fry, black beans and rice, homemade pizza, salad. Someone usually brings dessert, and Mad and O'Shaunessey kick in two magnums of Concha y Toro Cabernet Sauvignon-Merlot: one to split between them, the other for the rest of us. Adam came nearly every week. He always brought two loaves of French bread, since it requires no effort and goes with just about anything.

That night, I cooked my standard: puttanesca sauce over capellini. As my guests have heard more than once, it started out as the favorite recipe of Sicilian whores, since it could be made quickly (as in between customers), from basics lying around the cathouse larder. The official recipe includes anchovies, but I've never made it that way. I've been a vegetarian ever since I made the connection between a steak and Bessie the Cow.

Mine is a cook's kitchen. It gets better every Christmas and birthday, when Mom indulges my taste for gourmet toys. I have a dozen restaurant-quality Calphalon pans, hanging from a rack with my four-foot garlic braid. When I move out of the house, the holes Dirk drilled in the walls to put it up are going to eat up my entire security deposit. The gas stove was one of my absolute requirements when I was looking for a place to live. My Cuisinart nests on the counter next to the Wusthof knives in their oak holder. When I first moved in, Mom bought me these great French porcelain canisters that say *farine, sucre, café,* and *thé.*

Between six and twenty people usually show up to my Thursday parties. Just about everybody in the *Monitor* newsroom has dropped by at one time or another, along with a few of the reporters from the local TV station, the occasional radio journalist, and my friend who writes movie reviews for the weekly *Gabriel Advocate.* No one has to be invited anymore; if I leave town without telling anyone, they're liable to show up on my doorstep, break a window with a brick, and cook up whatever they find in the pantry.

I've never been to a funeral reception, but I imagine it's something like the first Thursday-night dinner since Adam's death. Everyone was quiet, uncomfortable. No one seemed to know whether it was okay to have a good time when one of last week's guests was on his way to California to attend his own funeral. Things hit the pits when Melissa pulled my wooden cutting board off the microwave.

"Somebody hand me the bread knife. Where the hell is

the bread hiding? Who was supposed to bring the bread? Oh, *shit*."

The five conversations that had been going on in the kitchen all stopped at once.

Adam. The subject everyone had been so carefully dancing around was right there on the blue-tiled counter, and everybody stared down at it like a bunch of kids who'd gotten yelled at by their first-grade teacher. "It's okay," I said, and for some reason I think I meant it. "I'm okay. We're all thinking about it anyway. Let's just try and have a good time. He wouldn't want us to sit around crying in our cabernet."

"A toast," O'Shaunessey said. "To Adam, who'd want us all to have a damn good time and eat too much and get really shit-faced in his honor."

When the last guests—as always, Mad and O'Shaunessey—risked the wrath of the DWI gods and walked out with their leftovers, I was way too wired to sleep. It was only about eleven, and I had the next day off, since I'd worked the previous Sunday. Shakespeare followed me as I paced around the house. I sat down to practice scales at the piano before I realized Dirk was trying to sleep.

"Ride in the car?" I said, and the dog bounded over to the closet where I keep her leash. It was a balmy night, and we drove around town for a while. I stopped at Friendly's for a strawberry frozen yogurt cone, which I split with the dog. Sorry if you think that's disgusting, but her mouth is probably cleaner than mine.

I pulled up in front of Adam's house without really realizing where I was going. Despite my big plans to figure out what happened to him, I hadn't had the guts to go back to his apartment. I was scared. Not so much of the boogeyman, but of the memories.

I parked in the lot behind his house and Shakespeare

and I went around to the front door. It was closed, but unlocked. Had Mad and I left it that way? I wasn't sure. We walked in and I unleashed the dog. Nothing seemed to have been touched. A Cap'n Crunch box sat open on the kitchen table, with an inch or two of stale cereal at the bottom. I poured it into a bowl and set it on the floor for Shakespeare.

I did a quick survey of the kitchen, avoiding the dishes festering in the sink. I figured I'd have to wash them sooner or later—or maybe I'd just throw them in the garbage. I opened cabinets and found memories of a hundred dinners on Adam's unmatched dishes.

I moved to the small living room, furnished like a college dorm: orange-crate tables, battered couch covered by an Indian tapestry, bookshelves made from wooden planks and cinder blocks. What did his mother say? He never kept anything more than he could throw in the back of his pickup truck. She was right. He would have given most of it away when he moved out.

His books were a different story. He collected hardcovers, and had three sets of shelves filled to toppling. Adam kept his nonfiction in one set, mostly journalism basics like *All the President's Men* and Joe McGinniss's *The Selling of the President*. Fiction took up the other two, with titles ranging from *Pudd'nhead Wilson* to *A Clockwork Orange*. I recognized some I'd given him over the years: *The Handmaid's Tale, One Hundred Years of Solitude, East of Eden, The Witches of Eastwick*.

Maybe there was something hidden between the pages of Adam's personal library, but it would have to wait. I'd look through them when I packed them up. They were the only things of Adam's I wanted, apart from a few shirts I'd half adopted anyway.

I moved into the bedroom, and Shakespeare plopped

herself in the middle of Adam's futon. I looked halfheartedly through his closet and bureau; the smell of him was everywhere. I moved over to his desk, and struggled with the top right-hand drawer. When I got it unstuck, I realized what had been jamming it shut: a pile of reporter's notebooks that filled the drawer to overflowing.

Jesus Christ. These were not here before. *They were not here before.*

I opened the drawer underneath it and the one below that and found the same thing. I pulled open the filing cabinet, and knew what I'd find before I saw it: Adam's clips were back.

Someone had been here; that much was obvious. That whoever it was probably had something to do with Adam's death was equally obvious.

How long ago had someone put the notebooks back? Could they still be there? I looked frantically around the apartment, as if the murderer were going to leap out like Tony Perkins in *Psycho*.

Shakespeare didn't seem to sense any danger; but then again, she would probably play fetch with a rapist. I called her to follow me and searched around for her leash. No one grabbed me as I walked out the door, but I was still shaking as I jogged along the sidewalk toward lights and people. No way was I going to get my car from the dark lot behind Adam's place.

It was one A.M., and the last-call drinkers were just starting to filter out of the bars. I stopped at the Citizen, but didn't find anyone I knew. Mad, a notorious insomniac, was probably still awake. He answered the door in boxer shorts, drinking wine out of his favorite salsa jar. He took one look at me and handed it over.

"Jesus, Alex, what's wrong?"

"Can I come in for a while?"

"What's going on?"

"I brought the dog."

"I can see that."

"I just came from Adam's."

"What the hell were you doing there in the middle of the night?"

"Listen, Mad, I'm scared to death, or else I'm going crazy. I've got to talk to somebody. Will you please just listen and not tell me I'm nuts until I'm done?"

"Okay, just a minute." I lay down on Mad's olive drab couch and balanced the wine on my stomach. He got another jar and sat down on the other side of the couch, his long legs dangling onto the floor. "Shoot."

"Remember when we went to get Adam's address book? I looked in his desk and all his notebooks were gone?"

"Right . . ."

"They're back. I went over there to look around, and somebody must have put them back. His clip files too. But that's not all. I was cleaning out his truck and I found this gas receipt. Adam went to Canada last weekend, to some little town way up north in Quebec."

"What for?"

"I'm not sure. The only connection I can think of is that it was the hometown of that old guy who jumped in the gorge a couple of months ago. Remember?"

"Yeah. Didn't he have some kind of French name?"

"Lecuyer. René Lecuyer. He was from someplace called Ste. Marie, way up north along the St. Lawrence. Nobody ever figured out what he was doing in Gabriel."

"Wasn't he dying of cancer or something?"

"I looked up the library file. There wasn't much. Just three stories, more like two and a brief, really. The first was from before they released the name. They were still looking for his next of kin to notify, but they never found any. Anyway, the brief just said they found a man in North Creek Gorge and were tentatively calling it a suicide."

"Adam covered it?"

"Yeah. But I worked with him on the follow-up. Once the cops released the ID, I called Ste. Marie looking for information on him. What I got was that Lecuyer was retired, used to own a grocery store in the next town over, a place called *Le Bout de l'Espoir.*"

"What the hell does that mean?"

"Hope Point."

"Why do you Frogs need so many syllables to say something that short?"

"Well, literally, it means 'The Point of Hope,' or 'The End of Hope.' That's cheery. Oh, my God. That's it."

"That's what?"

"The suicide note. 'The End of Hope.' That's what the suicide note said. Only it wasn't any suicide note."

I jumped up and displaced Shakespeare from on top of my backpack. I pulled out a photocopy of the note and gave it to Mad.

"Look at this. It says. 'Holy Mary Mother of God. Forgive our Sins. The End of Hope.'"

"So?"

"So, it's not a suicide note. It's a list of places. 'The End of Hope' is *'Le Bout de l'Espoir,'* where the dead guy worked. 'Holy Mary Mother of God' has got to be 'Ste. Marie.' I wouldn't be surprised if the full name of the place is *'Ste. Marie, Mère de Dieu'* or something."

"That means 'Holy Mary Mother of God'?"

"Yep."

"And what about this other one? Forgive our sins?"

"I don't know. Maybe it's a street name."

"How do you say it in French?"

"*Pardonnez nos péchés*. But that doesn't sound like a name at all."

"I thought '*pêcher*' meant fishing."

"How did you know that?"

"You know, Alex, I went to school too."

"Sorry. You're right. '*Pêcher*' is to fish. Wait a minute. You're brilliant." I went back to my backpack, rolled the dog off again, and showed Mad the stranger version of the note I'd found in his glove compartment.

"'Holy Mary by the Sea of God, Forgive the Fish.' What the hell does that mean?"

"Nothing. Don't you get it? It's just a bad translation. Adam's French was awful. He mistook 'sea' for 'mother' and 'fish' for 'sin.' The words are really close."

"What's the point of all this?"

"I don't know. But I'm going to find out."

"What do you mean?"

"Mad, Adam was murdered. I'm sure of it."

"Alex . . ."

"No, listen. Adam covers some old guy who jumps in the gorge. A couple of weeks later—why, I don't know yet—he takes a trip to the guy's hometown, without telling anybody about it. A week after he goes to Canada, he winds up dead. All his notebooks are missing from his apartment, then they suddenly reappear." I went in for the kill. "Look at all the reasons he supposedly killed himself. Was he sick? None of us thought so; nothing in the coroner's report. Was he heartbroken? Olivia says he was totally over their breakup. Did he leave a suicide note? It turns out he didn't. Was he just having a goddamn bad day? He'd just slept with yours truly."

"It could kill a lesser man."

"Very funny. But what do you think? Am I crazy or what?"

He rose to refill his jar. When he came back, he said, "Alex, you've got to go to the cops."

"Not yet. The chief has been really sweet, but I think he's ready to have me sedated. I need to have some proof before I try to get him to listen to me for real."

"Alex, you could be in danger. If somebody killed Adam . . ."

"I know. I realized that just before I came running over here."

"So what are you going to do?"

"I'm going to Canada. I'm going to follow the same route, try to figure out what Adam was after."

"Did you find out anything else from the story file?"

"Not much. According to the autopsy, the dead guy had pancreatic cancer—didn't have more than six months to live anyway, and not very enjoyable months at that."

"Sounds to me like a good reason to kill yourself."

"Me too. Back when we were working on the story, I called around Ste. Marie and finally found somebody who knew him fairly well—the local librarian. She gave me some quote about how he was nice and quiet, read a lot, good to kids and small fuzzy animals, you know the drill."

"But nobody knew why he chose our fair city for his final exit?"

"No. Nobody could tell me what the connection was, if there even is one. The only way I'm going to find anything more about this guy is to go up there."

"So when are you leaving?"

"Tomorrow. I'm going to tell everybody I'm going home to my parents. You have to promise not to say where I'm really going."

"Cross my heart and hope to die."

"You wouldn't be the first."

7

THE ST. LAWRENCE RIVERBANK FELL OFF TO THE RIGHT AS Shakespeare and I drove north. The dog rode in her favorite position: three-quarters out the window, snout smiling into the wind. I have no idea how she keeps her balance, but she hasn't flown out of the car yet. We'd left Quebec City behind more than two hours before. With the air screaming past Shakespeare, I'd given up hope of hearing the French-language radio station I'd tuned in after crossing into Quebec from Ontario.

Shakespeare and I had hit the road before dawn, in the hopes of reaching Ste. Marie before the library closed. I didn't have much of a plan, beyond wandering around town for a few days trying to talk to people who knew Lecuyer. The librarian I'd interviewed seemed as good a starting point as any. If she was still feeling friendly, maybe she could direct me toward some of Lecuyer's favorite hangouts—if an elderly guy did much hanging out in the first place.

As we cruised along, I thought of Adam covering the same pavement, just weeks before. What could have been worth driving all this way? If he was working on a story, why wouldn't he have told me? *Monitor* reporters aren't secretive about their work; the shop is too small for anybody to try to scoop anyone else. People aren't even particularly protective of their beats, since stories, especially breaking news, are generally assigned to whoever can get down the stairs fastest.

But Adam had always been different, more competitive. He kept to himself more than most. I'd tried to give him space, especially since he moved to Gabriel. But his emotional barriers were invisible, like those electric fences my neighbors use to keep their dogs in without marring the lawn. And I didn't have a collar around my neck to give me a shock when I crossed the line.

We never spent the night together in Gabriel, never once had to deal with the morning after. The last night I ever saw him, we met up at the Citizen for the usual Friday postmortem: Mad boring everybody with the details of Langston Foundation science grants; O'Shaunessey and a couple of his staff writers debating the upcoming Benson football team; me holding forth on B-GLAD. Just before one—as O'Shaunessey was launching into his argument for the fifth time, with as much gusto as the first—I caught Adam looking at me across the table. When we closed the bar half an hour later, his hand brushed the small of my back and he whispered, "*I'll follow you.*" Ten minutes later, my Water Lilies sheets were strewn around us in a pastel sea.

I'd ached for him that night, and I still do. I wonder when I'll stop.

After another half hour of driving, a road sign said that Ste. Marie was five kilometers ahead. A few minutes later, I pulled off the road to read a wrought-iron sign wishing us *bienvenu* to *Ste. Marie Mère de Dieu.* The sign, hanging from a wooden frame above a small box of flowers, told us the town had been founded in 1825, and had a population of 2,382.

Downtown Ste. Marie consisted of all of six buildings, each a two-story wood frame. There was a coffee shop, a combination general store and post office, a gas station with an ancient Coke machine out front. I felt like I'd just landed on Walton's Mountain. The library was on the first floor of a well-kept maroon building; a small brass name-plate indicated a dentist's office above. I left Shakespeare in the car and went in, the heavy screen door slamming behind me. A seventy-something woman behind a dark wooden desk looked up.

"Bonjour, madame," I said, trying to resurrect the Que-becois accent of my childhood. *"Je cherche Madame Lavoie, la bibliothécaire."* I'm looking for Madame Lavoie, the librarian.

"You've found her," the woman said in French. "How may I help you?"

"My name is Alex Bernier. I work for a newspaper in New York. I interviewed you a few weeks ago about Monsieur Lecuyer."

"Yes, I remember you," the librarian said, fingering the tight bun at the nape of her neck. "You look younger than you sounded on the telephone."

"Everybody tells me that."

"So what brings you all the way up to our little town? You aren't still interested in poor Monsieur Lecuyer?"

"Well, yes and no. It's complicated."

"Then do sit down." She looked out the window over my shoulder. "And your dog, she would prefer to come inside?"

Ten minutes later, we sat opposite each other in a pair of lumpy chairs, with Shakespeare curled up on the floor. The older woman had offered tea, and smiled approvingly when I declined both milk and lemon.

"You speak French well for an American."

"It was my first language. I had a Quebecois babysitter from the time I was two weeks old. She used to give me tea in my baby bottle, just like this."

"Your family is French-Canadian?"

"Bernier on my father's side, Rougeau on my mother's. I'm not sure when they came down to the States."

"So what can I tell you?" the librarian said, switching to English so efficiently I didn't notice at first.

"You speak English?"

"Of course. Most of us do, though we don't like to be expected to."

"Touché."

"So what brings you all the way up here?"

"Two weeks ago, a friend of mine came up here. A young man, about thirty years old. I think he was looking for information about Monsieur Lecuyer."

"Another journalist?"

"Yes. His name was Adam Ellroy. About six feet tall, curly brown hair, glasses."

"He spoke horrible French?"

"Horrible would be a compliment."

"Yes, I remember him. He came into the library, asking questions about René—or trying to ask them, in any event."

"What did you tell him?"

"Very little, I'm afraid. He was polite, and quite a handsome young man. But we have very little patience for English around here, you know."

"*Je le sais bien.* You didn't speak English to him?"

"I'm afraid not."

I could picture Adam standing there in linguistic agony, a reporter's notebook in one hand and a Berlitz phrasebook in the other. "Do you know where he went after he left here?"

"I did give him René's home address. He lived on *La Rue du Pardon des Péchés.*"

"'The Forgiveness of Sins.' There seem to be so many religious names here, madame. Why is that?"

"I know it must seem overwhelming to an outsider. Let me explain. Ste. Marie was founded by a group of monks who left their monastery in France because they believed it had become too liberal. They lived here for more than one hundred years, but their numbers eventually dwindled. The last few brothers left to join a group near Montreal when I was just a little girl. The ruins of the old friary remain, on the hill just outside of town."

"Could you tell me how to find Monsieur Lecuyer's house? I'm trying to retrace Adam's steps as best I can."

"Continue down the main street—*La Rue de l'Avènement*—for approximately three kilometers. Turn right onto *La Rue du Sacré Coeur*, and you will find *La Rue du Pardon* on the left. Monsieur Lecuyer lived on the second floor of number thirty-two."

"Can you remember anything else? Did Adam seem to be looking for anything in particular?"

"I don't believe so. But now, I am curious. What was the young man searching for here in Ste. Marie?"

"I don't know. That's what I'm trying to figure out."

"If he is your friend, why do you not ask him?"

"He's dead, madame."

"Dead? How very sad. I am so sorry."

"Everyone thinks he killed himself, but I don't believe

it. His body was found in the same place as Monsieur Lecuyer's, not long after he came up here. I think there's some connection between his death and Monsieur Lecuyer's suicide."

"But what possible connection could there be? René was an old man, a gentle soul, really. He ran the grocery store in *Le Bout de l'Espoir* for fifty years. Everyone liked him, although I can't say that anyone knew him very well. He was a bachelor, with no living relatives that I know of. He was an avid reader, though—something of a scholar, I think. I always wondered why he spent his life as a merchant. Not that it's not an honorable profession, mind you. But René always seemed quite intellectual. I know he read English, Latin, Italian, and German, as well as French. He used to like to talk with me about the books he ordered from Montreal."

"Is anyone still living who grew up with him?"

"Oh, René wasn't born here. I'm not sure where he was from. As far as I know, he arrived when he took over the store—sometime in the 1940s, I would expect."

"Did he have any close friends in Ste. Marie?"

"Not that I know of, not what you'd call intimate. He was on cordial terms with everyone, as far as I know. This is a very small town."

"Did he ever leave on long trips?"

"Again, not that I know of. He certainly left town occasionally, but he also worked long hours at the store in *Le Bout de l'Espoir*—we don't have a real grocery market here in Ste. Marie."

"Did he ever have, uh, a girlfriend?"

Madame Lavoie laughed. "I'm afraid there's no gossip there. René really was your stereotypical old bachelor. He lived alone, and seemed perfectly happy to do so. He didn't invite questions. I flatter myself to say that I was the closest thing he had to an intimate. We spent many hours together in the library, he and I."

"Forgive me, Madame Lavoie, but were you surprised to hear he killed himself?"

"Yes, I suppose I was. But then again, I had no idea poor René was ill. He did seem weaker, more tired. But when one reaches old age, one hardly expects anything else."

"Do you have any idea what he was doing in Gabriel, New York?"

"I believe you asked me that question over the phone all those weeks ago. My answer is unfortunately still the same. René never mentioned visiting the States. I have no idea why he did so, or why he chose to end his life there."

"Is there anyone else in town you think I should talk to? Anyone who might be able to help me figure out what Monsieur Lecuyer was doing in Gabriel?"

"I'm afraid most people will be able to tell you even less than I. But you might speak with his landlady, Madame Beaulieu. I will call her and tell her to expect you."

"Thank you," I said, and stood up to leave.

"It's been a pleasure talking with you, mademoiselle," the older woman said, switching back to French. "You have asked me many questions, and I have just one for you. This Adam, he was more than just a colleague, was he not?"

"Yes," I said, and smiled when I realized the truth of it. "He was my lover."

8

THE HOME OF THE LATE RENÉ LECUYER, GROCERY-STORE owner and scholar, looked much like every other building in town. It was old but lovingly maintained, with flowers lining the walk and a three-story birdhouse on a pole in the front yard. The one thing that distinguished it from its neighbors was the "FOR SALE" sign on the lawn. I knocked lightly on the door and a woman of about sixty emerged from the first-floor apartment.

"Bonjour, mademoiselle," she said, offering a solid handshake and continuing in French. "You must be the young lady from the newspaper. Madame Lavoie has just phoned me."

"You're Madame Beaulieu?"

"Yes," she said, friendly as a hostess in a mid-priced restaurant. "Please come in, and be mindful of the carpet."

I wiped some imaginary dirt off my feet and was instantly reminded of my grandmother's house. There were lace doilies covering the arms of worn easy chairs, and peppermint candies languished in a red glass dish. I almost expected Mémère—God rest her soul—to be sitting in the rocking chair, watching *The Newlywed Game* with the volume turned all the way up.

"Madame Lavoie said you could speak French. I'm afraid my English isn't as good as hers," the woman said, inhaling vowels into a particularly thick Quebecois accent. She gestured for me to have a seat on the tapestry sofa, and I sat down beneath an enormous ceramic triptych of the Holy Family that read *"Bénissez nous—Jésus—Marie—Joseph."* If there was an earthquake, the thing was going to decapitate me.

I must have been staring, because the woman suddenly sounded apologetic. "I'm afraid very little has been done with the house since my mother died."

"Oh, I'm sorry," I said automatically. "Did she die recently?"

"Yes, just a few months ago—shortly before poor Monsieur Lecuyer."

Le pauvre Monsieur Lecuyer. "*Le Pauvre*" was starting to sound like his first name, sort of like Dirty Harry Callahan, though probably without the .357 Magnum.

"I'm not sure how much Madame Lavoie told you," I said. "I'm trying to find out as much as I can about him, and what he was doing in Gabriel when he died."

"I'm afraid I can't help you. I hadn't really spent any time with him in quite a few years."

"So you didn't know him very well?"

"No, not very well, not since I was a young girl. I grew up here, but I've lived in Montreal most of my adult life. I'm a nurse, you see, at a Catholic hospital. I came back home to take care of *maman* at the end. I'm the only child, and I could never have put her in a nursing home."

"Your father is no longer living?"

"He died when I was quite small. At first we thought he just had a bad cold, but it turned out to be lung cancer. It's part of the reason I went into medicine. Of course, if I'd grown up as one of you girls today, I might have been a doctor."

I was itching to get a look at Lecuyer's apartment, and I cast about for a way to steer the conversation away from Madame Beaulieu's life story.

"Was that around the time that Monsieur Lecuyer moved in?"

"Yes. My mother was recently widowed. But she was a practical woman, and she spent part of my father's life insurance turning the upstairs part of the house into an apartment, so we would have some monthly income. In a way, my father kept providing for us, even though he was gone. I think he would have liked that. Of course, my mother never remarried."

Of course. Here we go again.

"I'll bet she never thought she'd have the same tenant for so many years," I said, paddling valiantly against her stream of consciousness. "Madame Lavoie told me he lived here since the forties."

"We were very lucky to find Monsieur Lecuyer. He was a great help, always willing to fix anything."

"He was handy at that sort of thing?" At least now we were talking about the right corpse.

"Oh, yes," she said. "He could do plumbing, and electrical work, and carpentry. He even made a birdhouse for us—you'll notice it's an exact copy of the house."

I hadn't noticed. But I was beginning to get an image of Lecuyer. He seemed to be a small-town Renaissance man—a hard-working good neighbor who could speak five languages and fix a leaky faucet. If he wore boxer shorts, I probably would've wanted to sleep with him.

"What did people around town think of him?"

"Everyone liked him, though no one knew him very well. *Maman* and I lived in the same house with him, but we never really got to know him personally. I must say, a few of the ladies were hoping he'd look their way, but he never seemed interested." She leaned forward and lowered her voice, apparently to keep the candy dish from hearing her. "You know, some people used to wonder if he was . . . well, *feminine*. But I never thought that for a moment myself."

Feminine? Was the woman's tongue going to fall off if she used the word "gay"? An image of B-GLAD protesters marching down Main Street Ste. Marie popped into my head. "Is there anyone new living in Monsieur Lecuyer's apartment now?"

"There's not so much demand, not since the highways took away most of the river traffic. Most of the young people have gone to the city. Some prefer the small-town life, though, and commute to *Le Bout de l'Espoir.* I'm just staying long enough to have the house modernized a bit, so it can be sold."

"Is your husband in Montreal?"

"Oh, I have never married."

I had forgotten that, in French, women of a certain age are often called "madame" whether they've been married or not—the image of an elderly "mademoiselle" is apparently a bit unseemly to the Gallic mind. "Madame Lavoie may have mentioned that a friend of mine came up here a few weeks ago, also looking for information on Monsieur Lecuyer. I was wondering if he visited you?"

"Yes. He came by here. But his French wasn't very good, and I couldn't help him very much. I just let him go through Monsieur Lecuyer's things and then he left."

"You did?" Let me get this straight. Ten years of reading Flaubert and Proust and Marguerite Duras gets me your life story, and Adam's lame high school French gets him an express ticket upstairs? Where's the justice?

"He seemed like such a nice young man, so very handsome. His French was abominable, but he had a lovely smile. As Monsieur Lecuyer didn't have any living relatives, I didn't see the harm."

I rose and smiled my best Catechism smile, the one I use on political candidates just before asking them why they accept PAC money from the NRA. "I'd hate to take up any more of your time. Would it be all right if I took a little look at Monsieur Lecuyer's apartment?"

"Certainly. It's up the stairs. I've only just started boxing up his things. I suppose I'll give most of it to the church charity, but the clothes are terribly outdated. There's certainly nothing valuable. If you see anything you like, I don't see any reason why you can't have it."

"Did Adam take anything?"

"No. I would have let him, but we had such a hard time conversing—his poor French and my poor English."

Madame Beaulieu led me up the brown carpeted stairs and opened the unlocked door. The sensation of walking back in time was even stronger. Each room seemed like the set for a movie from the 1940s. The parlor had no television, and a handsome radio dominated one corner. The kitchen, with its hulking icebox and massive range, reminded me of *The Honeymooners*—although that probably wasn't quite the right time frame.

"It's quite something, isn't it?" Madame Beaulieu said. "Nothing's been changed since the apartment was first built. Even my mother updated her kitchen back in the 1960s, but Monsieur Lecuyer never wanted her to change a thing up here."

"Is it okay if I look around a bit?"

"Go ahead. I'll leave you, if you don't mind. I'll be downstairs if you need anything."

She shut the door behind her, and I wandered slowly around the five rooms: kitchen, parlor, bedroom, bathroom, study. The last seemed the most modern, and it took me a moment to realize why. The room was lined with books, practically floor to ceiling. Some of them were recent, and their colorful dust jackets were just about the only evidence that the room had been touched by the past fifty years. Their subjects were so varied, it was hard to believe they'd been collected by the same person. In just a cursory tour, I noticed Rilke's *Dueno Elegies* in German; the complete works of Honoré de Balzac; three biographies of Albert Einstein; pulp novels by Michael Crichton, Anne Rice, and John le Carré; a beginner's guide to organic gardening; physics textbooks that I couldn't begin to understand; the poetry of William Butler Yeats; a collection of *Doonesbury* comics; an Indonesian cookbook.

A halfhearted attempt had been made to pack a few things into cardboard boxes, but I could understand why Madame Beaulieu was reluctant to tackle the library. I was in no hurry to deal with Adam's books, and Lecuyer easily had ten times as many. Maybe Madame Beaulieu didn't think there was anything valuable up here, but the books had to be worth thousands.

For lack of a better idea, I started with the desk, an ugly walnut affair that took up most of the floor space. I dug through the top drawers without finding anything interesting. The heavy file drawer revealed household bills, meticulously organized, going back through the past fifteen years. I pulled a folder at random, and flipped through Lecuyer's household accounts for September–October 1986. The notes were in neither French nor English, but a mishmash of both—the "Franglais" of the truly bilingual. There was the usual assortment of utility bills, plus drugstore receipts and a whopping order from a Montreal bookseller. Lecuyer had even documented every item he took from his own store, and billed himself for it, down to the last can of peas and roll of toilet paper.

The files in the drawer only went as far back as 1980. I found the rest in a tall wooden cabinet by the study's only window. I poked through them without ambition, unable to see where any of this was getting me. The files began with January–April 1945 and ran, unbroken, up to the month before Lecuyer's death. Apparently, his illness hadn't made him slack off on the anal-retentive house-keeping. What could possibly have interested Adam enough to get him all the way up here? To look at some dead guy's phone bills from thirty years ago?

Phone bills. I went back to the desk and pulled the most recent file. The phone bill was there, but there were no long-distance calls to Gabriel, or anywhere else in the U.S. Ditto the previous six.

What was I looking for? If I was going to hide some deep dark secret, where would I put it? I went into the bedroom.

Lecuyer had slept on a narrow twin bed that was still neatly made; judging from the files in the other room, he probably made perfect hospital corners before driving south to leap into the gorge. Feeling like an intruder for the first time, I poked through Lecuyer's drawers, filled with sleeveless undershirts and black socks. Other than the fact that he was indeed a boxer man, I didn't find anything of interest. I peeked under the bed and found nothing; Lecuyer didn't seem to have been a stash-it-under-the-bed kind of guy.

I moved over to the tiny closet, where neatly arranged

pairs of shoes stood at attention beneath ancient-but-clean shirts and pants. I'd never met Lecuyer, never even seen a photo of him other than his body being hauled out of the gorge. But I was piecing together an image of an old man tossing a red apron over these clothes and stacking apples into a neat pyramid, like a character in a Norman Rockwell painting.

Over my head, three hats rested on the narrow shelf just above the clothes rail. I jumped high enough to pluck one down and found it was an old-fashioned fedora, like something out of *The Maltese Falcon,* or maybe *The Front Page.* I tried it on and looked at myself in the grainy mirror over the bureau; not a bad fit. I was about to put it back when I noticed a box, pushed way back on the upper shelf. I went into the kitchen, took one of the chairs from the table, and carried it into the bedroom. I hopped up on it, pulled down a yellowed cigar box, and carried it into the kitchen, where the light was best. The papers inside seemed to have been tossed in hurriedly; they didn't match the meticulous order of the study.

Had Adam looked through this box? I spread the contents out on the kitchen table and discovered a stack of old black-and-white photographs. In one, three men in lab coats toasted the camera with glasses of champagne. Another showed a man in his late twenties—I thought it was one of the guys from the lab photo—with his arm around a young woman as they stood in front of a waterfall.

The scene was so familiar, it took a moment for it to register. The picture was taken at Gabriel Falls.

Here, finally, was a link between Lecuyer and Gabriel. I had no way of knowing if the young man in the photo was Lecuyer, but the fact that he had a picture taken in Gabriel meant there must be some connection. I turned over more of the pictures and found a half-dozen shots of the woman in hiking clothes. The woman had a natural, fresh-faced kind of beauty, like a young Katharine Hepburn. The photos could have been taken at one of the Walden County state parks, but I couldn't be sure.

By the time I dug down to the bottom of the pile, I was even more confused. Turning on the light over the table, I examined a yellowed Benson University ID card from the academic year 1944–45. The photo was a head-and-shoulders shot of the same man as in the other pictures, but with a name I didn't recognize: André Sebastien, an assistant professor in the department of applied physics. Beside the ID card was Sebastien's New York State driver's license, describing him as 5'10" with black hair and blue eyes.

Who was André Sebastien, and what was his ID doing in René Lecuyer's closet? I looked through the contents of the box again, but didn't find anything more. Opening all the cabinets in the kitchen didn't do any good, nor did a brief look through the parlor and the bathroom. I did discover that the radio still worked, and turned it on for background noise.

I went back into the study and took a long look around, walking slowly past the bookshelves. There were so many different subjects, I hadn't noticed the preponderance of physics books on my first tour. But with the Benson ID in mind, I counted dozens of books on the science in its many, utterly confusing forms—applied, theoretical, high energy, nuclear. I opened a few, but they might as well have been in Sanskrit. There was only one thing in school that I hated more than science, which was gym.

Did Lecuyer really read this stuff? What's more, did he understand it? I thought about what the librarian had said—that Lecuyer always seemed so intellectual. A reading knowledge of German was one thing. But did anybody really pick up a fancy for nuclear physics in their spare time?

I dug through the desk and filing cabinets one more time, visions of a dozen old movies forming into an idea. A thorough search didn't turn up anything to contradict my suspicions. Although Lecuyer had obviously been a meticulous man, his documentation only went as far back as his arrival in Ste. Marie. It was as though René Lecuyer hadn't even existed until then.

I retrieved one of the black-and-white photographs from the box, one with a clear shot of André Sebastien. A quick trip down the stairs to Madame Beaulieu confirmed it. The secret that Adam must have discovered was simple, really.

André Sebastien and René Lecuyer were the same person.

9

THE *GABRIEL MONITOR*'S MORGUE WOULD MAKE A GREAT setting for a horror movie: dark and damp, with God-knows-what hiding in the corners. It's the worst possible environment for storing newspapers, and a serious fire hazard to boot. It's huge—runs all the way through the building, underneath the press room and business offices—and you can't walk two feet without tripping over stacks of papers and gigantic rolls of newsprint. Between the stacks, you can just make out some faded white letters painted on the floor. I'd been working there nigh on two years before I realized what it said: "FIRE LANE! DO NOT BLOCK!"

So much for the power of the written word.

People mostly come down to the morgue to look up the past year's newspapers, which are kept on wooden shelves, stacked by date. To see complete papers before that, you have to use the newsroom microfilm machine, which is never quite in focus and makes everybody seasick. The current subject and biography files are kept up-stairs in the library, but the older ones are stored in a cor-ner of the morgue, in hulking black cabinets that would be right at home in an episode of *Perry Mason*. Until that Saturday night, I'd never had any reason to dig through them.

As Shakespeare sniffed among the stacks, I poked around with my flashlight until I found a series of cabi-nets marked "BIO (deceased) to 1960." The "S" files were in the last one, and it only took me a minute to find what I was looking for. Ironically, the files kept down-stairs are in much better order than the newer ones up-stairs. Back when they were filed, the paper actually paid for a full-time librarian. Now, we have a spaced-out high school kid with a blond buzz cut.

The file labeled "Sebastien, Dr. André" stuck out a bit from the rest, as though it had been carelessly returned to the drawer. Adam? I pulled it out and found it was thicker than I'd expected—a lot of the bio files only have one story in them, usually a single, one-shot profile.

I settled down on the concrete floor and spread the file out, using a stack of 1987 "Holly Jolly Christmas" edi-tions as a desktop. I doubted anyone was going to show up in the newsroom, but I didn't want to chance it. My friends and I are a curious bunch, and I didn't feel like ex-plaining why I was reading fifty-year-old clips on a Sat-urday night.

The Sebastien file was a mess, further proof that Adam had pawed through it. It had been put back haphazardly, some of the yellowed pages creased around each other in the manila folder. I sorted through the neatly clipped ar-ticles and started to put them in order, according to the date stamped in the top right-hand corner. A banner headline caught my eye: two-inch letters screaming, "BEN-SON SCIENTISTS DIE IN CRASH."

The article, cut from the front page, was dated January 28, 1945. Three small photographs were nestled below the headline in the right-hand corner. I recognized one, labeled "Dr. Sebastien," from the ID I'd found in Lecuyer's closet; the other two were Dr. Langston and Dr. Adelson. I thought I recognized them, but to make sure I compared the newspaper photos with the pictures I'd found in Lecuyer's strongbox. I was right. They were the other two men wearing lab coats, toasting the camera along with Sebastien.

The story was printed in the delicate type the *Monitor* had used for its first seventy-five years:

By CHRISTOPHER McCOOK
Monitor staff

Three Benson University scientists died yesterday in an aviation accident in the mountains near Salt Lake City, Utah. According to the U.S. Army, the three physicists—Dr. William J. Langston, Dr. André Sebastien and Dr. Seth Adelson—were killed when the small Army transport plane in which they were traveling went down in a severe thunderstorm. The three, all prominent physics researchers at Benson, were on their way to an undisclosed government facility as part of their scientific work to aid the war effort.

The article went on to discuss the professors' years of service at the university, their educational backgrounds and various scholarly awards. Toward the bottom, it gave some family information: Langston left a wife and young son; Adelson, a wife and two teenage daughters; Sebastien was a bachelor.

I riffled through the rest of the articles and found half a dozen that post-dated the crash. All were follow-up stories, with headlines like "Students Mourn Professors' Deaths" and "Memorial Service Held for Hero Scientists." The latter contained a quote from an army colonel, who the story said had flown in to speak at a ceremony in the university chapel.

> "Although they did not die in battle, there can be no doubt that these men are war heroes. They, like so many other Americans, dedicated themselves to the war effort. Though they did not wear uniforms, nonetheless they gave their lives in the cause of freedom."

The memorial service story included a photograph that reminded me of that famous shot of John Kennedy, Jr., saluting the flag at his father's funeral. Underneath was the caption: "IN MOURNING: Mrs. William J. Langston and her son, William Jr., at the memorial service for her husband and his colleagues."

I don't want to break the mood, but I think I should pause here to share with you my feelings about science.

I don't like it. Never have. I was always the kid in school who couldn't light the Bunsen burner. Like when

I was taking chemistry at boarding school, we were supposed to make candy canes at Christmas. I don't know what I did wrong, but mine refused to harden, and I kept them for two years. What I'm trying to explain is I know zip about science, and I could care less who's looking for quarks or quacks or whatever. So if I've heard of a physicist, he's got to be the scientific equivalent of Steven Spielberg.

Dr. William J. Langston Jr. is a very, very famous guy.

He's Benson's superstar. Whenever the university ends up in the national press, nine out of ten times it's because of Langston. His field is nuclear medicine (and if you want details, go read something else), but he's more charismatic than you might think. How many scientists hang out with the President of the United States *and* David Letterman?

Langston is the head of the Langston Foundation, which gives out grants to people much smarter than yours truly. They hold press conferences every couple of months, and even one of the *New York Times* science guys troops up here to cover them. Mad talks to the foundation's flack so often, he's got the number programmed into his speed dial.

Sure enough, "Langston Foundation" was one of the subjects cross-referenced on the back of the Sebastien file. It also listed Langston, Dr. William J. (BIO); Adelson, Dr. Seth (BIO); Benson University, science departments (SUBJ); and Accidents, fatal, 1945 (SUBJ). It was way too much for me to go through in one night, especially sitting on the floor of the morgue. I put the clips back into the Sebastien file, pulled the Adelson and Langston bio files, and stuffed them all into my backpack. The active files on Dr. Langston *fils* and the Langston Foundation itself would be upstairs. I'd get a look at those later, not that I had any idea where all this was going.

I leashed up Shakespeare and headed for the Citizen, one of the many fine Gabriel watering holes that let you bring your dog in for a drink. As we walked, I tried to sort out what I'd learned in the past two days. Sebastien was supposed to have died in a plane crash back in 1945. But if René Lecuyer and André Sebastien were really one and the same, then Sebastien obviously didn't die in the crash. So was the whole thing a mistake? Was somebody else on the plane instead? If he really wasn't dead, why did he let everybody think he was? And why did he come back fifty years later to kill himself?

And most important of all: What did any of this have to do with Adam? Assuming he figured out Lecuyer was Sebastien, was that what got him killed? How could something that happened so long ago possibly be a motive for murder? Or—and this was something I thought about constantly—was I just totally on the wrong track?

I didn't have any answers by the time I got to the Citizen. I could see O'Shaunessey—a.k.a. The World's Whitest Man—sitting in the window from half a block away. I waited in line behind a gaggle of Bessler students, who tend to take over the place on weekend nights. They packed the bar five-deep, nose rings and dyed-black hair glinting green under the neon Rolling Rock sign. Shakespeare spotted O'Shaunessey and lunged for him, dragging me up the steps to the window table. As far as I can tell, Shakespeare is the closest thing O'Shaunessey has to a girlfriend.

"It's the Shakes factor!" he said, whacking her on the snout. "Shakes! You big poocherooni! Give your Uncle 0 a kiss! What a huge doggie! Alex, what the hell are you doing back already?"

"Glad you're so happy to see me."

"Didn't you go to see mumsy and dadsy?"

"Drove me nuts. Kept wanting me to talk about the Adam thing."

"So you just cut out?" Melissa asked.

"More or less. I told them I had to see movies for my column tomorrow. My mom was sort of pissed because she had this whole Sunday dinner planned, but my dad was just as glad to get the dog off his wall-to-wall carpeting."

Okay, so I always tend to overdo it when I'm lying. Mad—the only one at the table who knew about the trip to Canada—was smirking at me from behind his beer mug. I joined them for one drink and ended up closing the place at one. There was a movement afoot to migrate over to the Acropolis Diner (open twenty-four hours), but Mad and I hung back.

"Want to go over to my place?" he asked.

"People will say we're in love."

"Come on," he whispered, breath smelling heavily of Labatt's. "I'm dying to find out what happened up in Canada. What are you doing back already?"

"Inquiring minds want to know, do they?"

"Cut the crap."

"Okay. Sorry, I'm a little punchy. It was a long drive and I've been down in the morgue for two hours."

"Come on over. I'll buy you a drink."

"By which you mean Gallo burgundy out of a jelly jar?"

"Salsa jar. Much classier."

A few minutes later I was installed on Mad's couch, and it was déjà vu all over again. Same ugly green sofa, same jelly jar—sorry, salsa jar—balanced on my tummy, Cocteau Twins crooning weirdly on the stereo.

He settled down opposite me and I filled him in on my trip to Canada. When I got to the part about my survey of the morgue, I dropped the pilfered clips into his lap. "What do you make of all this?"

Mad rubbed his face and stretched out his long legs, feet encased in scruffy grandpa slippers. "Ah . . . Let's take it piece by piece. You're pretty sure this guy Lecuyer is really Sebastien?"

"Yeah, unless it's his identical twin."

"Maybe he is."

"What?"

"Maybe it *is* his identical twin."

"Jesus, Mad, I hadn't thought of that. Maybe they aren't the same person after all, they just look alike. That would explain a lot of things."

"Like what?"

"Like how a guy can die in 1945 and then kill himself fifty years later."

"That *is* a neat trick."

"Wait a minute. If Lecuyer isn't Sebastien, then how come nobody in Canada ever heard of him before 1945?"

"Heard of who? Which one?"

"Lecuyer. I told you, the man kept meticulous records, archived his bills back to the forties. But nothing before then, no pictures or letters or anything. It was like he never existed."

Mad leafed through the clip files. "Well, whoever Sebastien was, he was one smart son of a bitch."

"What do you mean?"

"He was how old when he died? Twenty-eight? Pretty young to be a tenured physics professor."

"Hard to believe a guy like that would spend fifty years running a grocery store, isn't it?"

"Oh, my poor little Vassar girl . . ."

"Shut up, Mad. I just mean it's another thing that indicates maybe they really weren't the same guy. But Lecuyer *did* have all those physics books up in his library, which your average Joe Grocer wouldn't have."

"True enough."

"And what about the plane crash? Looks like it was one mother of a big story when it hit. Take a look at that headline."

Mad held up the yellowed page, the header as tall as the top line on an eye chart. "Yeah, but remember, papers used to love those screaming heads, hundred-point type and all. When's the last time the *Monitor* ran a headline that big? 'Man Walks on Moon'?"

"Did you ever hear about this plane crash before?"

"Sure. I mean, that's how Langston's father died. He was a pretty hot scientist himself, in his day. The Langston Foundation is named after him."

"I thought it was named after our guy Langston."

"No, it was founded like fifty years ago. Started off pretty small. I did a feech on it for the fiftieth anniversary a while back. It was started in Langston Senior's memory; I guess he was some kind of war hero. He was on his way to Los Alamos to work on the Manhattan Project when he died."

"You mean, as in the atomic bomb?"

"Yeah. They brought scientists from all over the place to do research there. Langston and the other two were supposed to be among them, for the final push. Anyway, the background should all be in the Langston Foundation file."

"I guess I'll look for it on Monday."

"You know, I was just up there last week at one of their press conferences."

"What about?"

"Grants for nuclear medicine research. Langston's pet project."

"Oh, yeah. It was on the story budget. Was he there?"

"No, he was at a conference. San Francisco or Chicago or someplace."

"Is he back yet?"

"I have no idea. Why?"

"I think I'll try to talk to him. Maybe he can give me some information about Lecuyer."

"Good luck getting a hold of him. He's out of the country half the time. But he's a pretty solid guy once you nail him down. Not too much of a prick. Obsessive-compulsive, but it goes with the territory. You back to work on Monday?"

"I guess."

"You up to it?"

"It's better than hanging around at my house. And I was only half lying about my parents. If I went home, they *would* drive me nuts."

"Seeing any flicks tomorrow?"

"The new Van Damme just opened, thank God. I could definitely use some senseless violence, Belgian guys in their undershorts."

"What would they say back at Vassar?"

"I believe they would say, '*J'aime les hommes grands et bêtes.*'"

"Meaning?"

"'I like 'em big and stupid.'"

"Of course you do."

"And look whose couch I'm on."

10

IT WAS MY OWN FAULT, BECAUSE I FORGOT TO TURN THE ringer off. I was eating crepes suzettes off the tummy of a mostly naked Jean-Claude Van Damme when the phone woke me up. I fumbled for the receiver and squinted at the clock: nine-thirty on a goddamn Sunday morning.

"Hi," said this incredibly perky voice. "This is Suzie calling from the *Gabriel Monitor.* How are you today?"

"Not working today. Sleeping."

"What? This is Suzie calling from the *Gabriel Monitor.* How are you today?"

By then I was awake enough to realize what was going on. The *Monitor*'s circulation department is legendary around town—the sort of legend reserved for Cossacks and Mongols and Hitler's SS. They have been known to track people down *in their hospital beds* to try to get them to subscribe. Their telemarketers, armed with an automatic dialing system of dubious value, actually call the *newsroom* and pitch subscriptions on a regular basis. We get complaints about them all the time, mostly from the people they wake up on Sundays.

"Listen, lady," I said. "I work for the *Monitor.* I've worked there for three years, which is a fact I shared with you the last time you called."

"Yes, uh, well," I could hear her riffling through her script. "Well, let me tell you about the advantages of convenient home delivery . . ."

"I already get home delivery. You know how? *I bring it home myself.*"

"Well, with convenient home delivery, we offer one week absolutely free . . ."

"Listen very carefully. There are exactly two tangible benefits to working for the *Gabriel Monitor.* One is a prime parking spot in beautiful downtown Gabriel. The other is a free newspaper each and every day. That's a thirty-five-cent value, fifty cents on Saturday, when all the coupons come out." I hung up on her; I'm not proud of it. I paid for it, though; if I'd just hung up in the first place—without the smart mouth—I might have been able to get back to sleep. Instead, I lay there for a while with the dog on my feet and tried not to admit I was awake. After about twenty minutes, I gave up and got out of bed. Shakespeare followed me downstairs, and I let her out the back to run around while I put in a quick call to Mom and Dad, who'd already been up and arguing a good two hours by then. Mom wanted me to come home the following weekend. I told her I'd think about it, and she went back to her true-crime show. I dug out yesterday's socks and underwear from the laundry basket and found my sports bra, designed by the Army Corps of Engineers. I changed into my black spandex biking shorts and leotard and pulled a tent-sized T-shirt over it, to avoid frightening the children.

Shakespeare, who started bounding around like a maniac as soon as I put on my running shoes, could barely sit still long enough for me to clip the leash to her choke collar. We did a slow trot around the corner and through the neighborhood. After less than half a mile, I felt terrible. Another quarter, and I suspected I was going to die. At the one-mile mark, I was absolutely certain I would keel over any minute, to be eaten by the rabid raccoons who live in the woods around here.

Then I sort of felt better. It's always that way, my love-hate relationship with physical exertion. The first mile is hell, the second mile is pretty much fine, the third mile starts off okay and winds up back in purgatory. I'll usually look for any excuse to quit, and "my lover just croaked" worked quite well, thank you, right in the middle of mile number three.

I walked back to the house, put Shakespeare inside, drove to the Y, and went upstairs to the weight room, where the average age is about forty-five. Very few students use the Y, which is one of the reasons I like it. It's filled with sweaty middle-aged folks and little kids, the farthest you can get from the meat markets near campus. I tried one of them when I first moved here, and it was packed with sorority girls talking and chewing gum on the StairMaster with their little gold earrings bobbing up and down, not even sweating.

Unlike jogging, I actually like Nautilus. There's something medieval about the machines, with their pulleys and metal bars and clunky stacks of weights, that I find really satisfying. I was on inner thigh when the trainer on duty nearly got cut in half by my madly scissoring legs.

"You're Alex Bernier?"

"Yeah," I grunted, plucking the headphone out of my right ear.

"There's a phone call for you."

"For me?"

"You can take it in the office downstairs. I guess it's an emergency or something."

I ran downstairs, convinced Shakespeare was dead by the side of the road. It turned out to be Bill.

"What's up? They said it was an emergency."

"Oh, yeah. I had to say that so they'd go get you. You've got to get your butt over to Benson. The natives are getting restless."

"I'm not on today. Am I? Isn't Mad Sunday reporter?"

"Yeah, but he's out covering some vigil at the Rainbow Camp." The Rainbow Peace Camp, located near an army depot in the next county, can always be counted on for a story on a slow weekend. They've always got a vigil or something going on over there, everybody wearing Birkenstock sandals and braiding daisies and singing "Where Have All the Flowers Gone." Mad, who's a big fan of the military-industrial complex, would like to napalm the lot of them.

"What's going on at Benson?"

"Looks like that gay thing has gone nuts."

"Aren't we politically correct! 'That gay thing'?"

"Whatever. Somebody just called the newsroom—said they're pissed the administration isn't even considering the living center B-GLAD wants. Apparently there was a leak from somewhere."

"So B-GLAD is less than glad."

"Yeah. Funny. There's talk about taking over Yaukey Hall. Check it out. I already sent the intern, but he's gonna get eaten alive."

I jumped in the shower at the Y, got dressed as fast as

I could, and was on campus in twenty minutes. Since it was a Sunday, parking was no problem—during the week, the university stormtroopers write tickets at forty dollars a pop. If you don't pay them—and nobody I know ever does—they'll tow your car on sight. I left my Renault behind one of the engineering buildings, pulled my university press pass and a notebook out of the glove compartment, and hiked in the direction of all the shouting.

There were fewer than two hundred people at the demonstration when I got there—a pretty lousy turnout, considering Benson is a campus of thirty thousand, if you count all the pasty-looking graduate students. But for the crowd's relatively small size, they sure were making a lot of noise. The ruckus I heard when I opened my car door solidified into the usual editorial chanting; by the time I got to the fray, they'd arrived at "Hey, hey! Ho, ho! Homophobes have got to go!"

To expose a little journalistic bias: I totally agree with B-GLAD's basic premise of equal rights for gays and lesbians. But that doesn't mean I don't find them ridiculous a lot of the time, mostly because they're so damn humorless and often their own worst enemy. They alienate people when they don't need to, make outrageous demands when they probably ought to compromise. They run around with their pierced eyebrows and Mapplethorpe T-shirts, scaring the pants off the conservative white guys who run the place, then wonder why there's very little "meaningful dialogue" going on.

There was exactly zero meaningful dialogue happening in the middle of the little grove off the arts quad, as far as I could see. Karin Coe—the girl I'd interviewed for last week's paper—was standing on a folding table that had been dragged onto the grass as a makeshift dais, holding a microphone connected to a couple of guitar amps. Karin led the crowd, which was growing steadily now, in a chorus of "What do we want? (Fill in the blank.) And when do we want it? Now!" Her round face looking awfully flushed, Karin suggested the crowd wanted a whole host of things, including freedom, peace, equality, justice, beauty, love, understanding, and truth.

I wanted a bagel with cream cheese. From the look of things, I wasn't going to get it for a while.

"But what do we really want?" Karin shouted.

I really, really wanted a bagel. The protesters looked confused.

"A gay, lesbian, and bisexual living center!" she answered herself. The crowd, looking a little relieved that she hadn't demanded the head of William Wallace on a pike, went wild with glee. After a few rounds of "We want a home!" Karin passed the microphone to Bryan Kahn, the senior whom I'd interviewed in the *Monitor* newsroom. He calmed everybody down a little and introduced the next speaker.

He was still very young-looking, tall and skinny and easily mistaken for a high school kid. He had a shiny earring in his left ear, and was wearing a black T-shirt with a pink Act-Up triangle on the front. He looked uncomfortable, his hands stuck in the back pockets of his jeans, awkward in his role as gay-rights poster child. Public speaking was new to him—that was obvious from the tentative way he spoke into the microphone. But there was something tough about him. It took guts to come back to the scene of the crime, when all he had to do was transfer to Brown or Columbia.

"Uh, hi. My name is Tony Cerutti. You've probably heard what . . . happened to me here last fall." He stared down at the laces of his sneakers for a while, then looked up again. "Karin and Bryan told me I didn't have to come back here if I didn't want to. I almost didn't, actually." Down to the laces again. "But I don't want it all to be for nothing, I guess. So here goes." He took a deep breath.

"Last October, I was hanging out here with my"—he hesitated just a little on the word—"my boyfriend. Franklin. We were just hanging out here, right here, together on the grass, when these guys came by. They called us names." He relaxed enough to try to make a joke out of it. "Quite a colorful array of names, actually. Fag. Homo. Queer. Rump ranger. Rump ranger. That was my favorite." The crowd laughed, tentatively, totally with him. I liked this kid already. "They poured beer on us. I told them to fuck off—Franklin tried to stop me, but I did it anyway. One of them, not even the biggest guy, punched me in the face. That got them all going. It didn't last very long, but they did a job on us. Broken ribs and shit." He paused, and Karin patted his ankle from where she was standing on the grass.

"I'm pretty much okay. I decided to come back to school in the fall." The crowd started to clap lightly, but he waved them off. "Franklin won't, or can't. He went back to his parents in New Jersey. They didn't even know he was gay, before this. He's still not sure where he's going to go for college, but he's not ready to go back yet. That'll be two years of his life he's lost over what they did to us. That's why I'm here now. They got expelled, but it's not enough. I want them to go to jail for what they did, and I don't want anyone to forget that this kind of thing can happen at Benson." He was warming to his role as orator, and it showed. "I believe the living center is a good idea, and it has to be built right here, right on this spot." There was no stopping the applause now. He waited until it died down.

"We shouldn't let the administration dump us off with a bunch of excuses. I want something good to come out of what happened to us. I don't think we should leave them alone until we get it." More applause, and Tony leaped down ungracefully from the folding table. I waited until the rally started to break up, and walked over to where he stood with a handful of B-GLAD leaders. Before this, Tony had consistently refused to speak to the press; even Adam had been unable to talk him into an interview after the attack. But before I got two words out, he offered to go somewhere and talk. We sat together for nearly two hours in one of the smoky coffee houses in Collegetown, and I finally got my bagel. He obviously believed in his cause—believed in it enough to give up his privacy, even to talk about coming out of the closet and facing all the publicity back home in rural Maine.

Fifteen minutes into the interview, I realized I was sitting across from a large chunk of tomorrow's paper. I called Bill from a pay phone, and he whooped into my eardrum when I promised an interview with one of the gay-bashing victims; so much for Mad's Rainbow Camp feature. Tony consented to have his portrait taken, and I set up a time for Melissa to meet him. Bill wanted it to be shot in the clearing where the attack happened. Tony agreed, even to that.

He was not yet nineteen years old. He sat in the battered wooden chair drinking plain black house blend and smoking a Camel. He offered me the pack, and I inhaled down to my toenails. *Adam.* Adam used to smoke Camels. Adam used to drink his coffee black, but not anymore.

What's that expression? Is it Nietzsche?

"That which does not kill me, makes me stronger."

I hadn't realized I'd said it out loud.

"I know," he said. "I know."

11

MY PROFILE OF TONY CERUTTI RAN ON PAGE ONE THE next day, and jumped to take up most of page 4A. Melissa's portrait of Tony turned out to be one of her best. He stood in the middle of the clearing, hands in his back pockets, face half in shadow from his Boston Red Sox cap. The sun looked eerie, bouncing off the trees and buildings in the distance, and the overall tone was of a kid utterly alone. That's probably not accurate, since Tony has both B-GLAD and his family behind him. But it sure was dramatic, and drama means more coins in the vending machines.

The paper hits the streets around six in the morning. When I got to work at nine, my phone was already ringing.

Karin was furious because she thought the article didn't focus enough on B-GLAD's struggle for a gay and lesbian living center.

Stewart Day was irked—off-the-record irked, that is—

because he thought my piece "sensationalized an unfortunate incident that is best forgotten."

Tony's mother (how she saw the story so fast, I don't know) screamed at me for "forcing" her son to talk to the press.

There's a saying in journalism: If everybody's pissed at you, you're probably doing your job. As it turned out, though, not quite everybody was pissed. Tony himself called around one, to thank me for my sensitivity.

Now *that* was a first.

Right after I hung up from talking to Tony, my phone rang again. It was Dr. William J. Langston's secretary up at Benson, returning my call to say he'd be available to talk to me tomorrow. Could I come at nine? Bill called me into his office then, and closed the door behind me. The room reeked of Thai peanut sauce.

"Alex, this newspaper can't keep running without a cop reporter."

This turned out to be Bill's attempt at tact and sensitivity. "I realize that."

"We hired somebody."

"Already?"

"Buyer's market."

"Who is it?"

"A guy who's been freelancing up here for a while." He dug around on his desk for a résumé and passed it over. It was sticky with duck sauce. "Name's Gordon Band."

"Gordon Band? From the *Times*? Are you being serious?"

"Yeah. I guess he really needs a job."

"What do you mean? The guy works for the *New York Times*. The *New York* Fucking *Times!*"

"Used to, actually."

"I don't get it."

"He had some major falling out with his editor. Something about the story he broke on that state trooper scandal up in the Adirondacks, from what I hear. Anyway, I guess there was some major-league scene in the *Times* newsroom. Band went ballistic, and now nobody wants to touch him. Apparently, he does not play nicely with the other children."

"So if he's so hard to work with, what did we hire him for?"

"Look around, Alex. Who do you know in this newsroom who's *not* hard to work with? Band is smarter than all you jokers put together. Who cares if he's a nut? He'll fit right in."

"But I still don't get why he wants the job."

"I guess he needs the health insurance, 'cause he committed to a year. Basically, I think he has to prove he can work in a newsroom without being some raving maniac prima donna. He'll probably slink back to the *Times* with his tail between his legs at the end of the year. Besides, who else do you know that's hiring, especially white guys? Where's he gonna go, *New York Newsday*?"

Since *New York Newsday* shut down in the summer of '95, Bill has taken to holding its fate over our heads when we whine about stupid assignments. It's a reminder that even folks who win bloody Pulitzer Prizes can get fired, roughly the equivalent of threatening to sell us all down the river. "So when does he start?"

"Tomorrow. That's what I wanted to talk to you about. Somebody needs to clean out Adam's desk. If you don't feel up to it, I can get the intern to do it. Up to you."

I told him I'd rather do it myself and went down to the morgue for some cardboard boxes. Adam's top drawer was, as always, stuffed with crap from the Mesozoic Era.

There were dozens of scraps of paper jammed in there, and I was wary of throwing out anything that might be important, so I designated one box for miscellaneous notes. The desk was full of old pink message memos and random slips of paper with phone numbers scrawled on them. Some of them had names attached, but most were just numbers, jotted down to be used once for a callback. I've always had this theory that messy people make the best lovers, and Adam sure didn't prove me wrong.

I moved on to his filing cabinet, in the bottom drawer of the right side of the desk. Reporters keep their active files in their desks; the older files, the ones you're not likely to need for current stories, go into filing cabinets sprinkled around the newsroom, two drawers to a customer. I'd already looked through Adam's two, and found nothing.

I decided to leave the active files where they were, since Gordon Band would need them, just as Adam had, when he took over the beat. Adam's personal clip files were in the back of the drawer, and I pulled those out. Reporters are supposed to clip out all the stories they write, to make them easy to find for future reference. Most of us keep them in bunches of a month or two per file, depending on how busy we've been.

Since Adam had only been at the *Monitor* for half a year, all his clips fit into three file folders. I flipped through them, mostly stories about car accidents and fires, and was reminded of why I never want to be a cop reporter as long as I live. "Gabriel High Seniors Die in 'Joy Ride'" "Infant Dies in Slackville Trailer Fire." "Boy, 9, Still in Coma After Kemp Ave. Crash." I can handle that stuff once in a while, but every day? I'd turn into a clocktower sniper.

I put Adam's clips in one of the boxes, then changed

my mind; they might as well stay here, in case the temperamental Mr. Band wanted to see what his predecessor had been working on for the past few months. I was about to close the file drawer when I noticed how sloppy everything was. Newsprint corners peeked out of the manila folders, organized by a system more esoteric than alphabetical. I'm not sure why it was important to me, but I didn't want Mr. *New York Times* to think of Adam as some incompetent slob. Band would probably reorganize it all, like everybody does when they take over a beat. But I felt like I owed it to Adam to clean up his act for him.

I started by pulling all the folders out and classifying them in stacks on the floor: fires, car accidents, petty crimes, felonies. That was how Adam had organized them when he first got here, though everything had gotten shuffled around in the rush of daily newspapering. Given Gabriel's topography and glorious tradition of public self-destruction, there was even a folder labeled "jumpers." That one, I knew, was missing at least one name. I'd referred to the file myself, when I wrote the first story about Adam's death. I cut my story out, dated it, and stuck it at the front of the "jumpers" file, which is kept in reverse chronological order. I am aware that it was totally unnecessary, not to mention more than a little psychotic. I did it anyway.

Once I had all the files separated into piles, I opened up each folder and neatened it. The felony stack was just a bump on the floor, since Gabriel is hardly a high-crime area. Still, there's usually one good murder every year, and once in a while someone goes on a burglary spree. Since we're in a college town, the petty crimes stack was a veritable Leaning Tower of Pisa of vandalism, graffiti, public nakedness, and general drunken misbehavior. Adam kept separate files on those and many other youthful pursuits, and I waded through them, returning them to the proper section in alphabetical order.

I flipped open another file, and thought for a second I was holding something that belonged in my desk, not Adam's. What was labeled "lost pets" turned out to be filled with photocopies of my stories on B-GLAD and the living center movement. Every article I wrote on the subject was in there, from the time I took over the story from Adam until a few days before he died. And here's the thing that really shook me up: He hadn't just clipped the stories himself. He'd taken the file out of my desk and copied everything without telling me. I could tell, because notes and dates were written in the margins in my own handwriting.

Why would Adam have been so interested in my stories—and yet never even mentioned it to me? He'd filed the whole thing under "lost pets"—I couldn't believe it was an accident—so he must have wanted to make sure no one ran across it. Was there some connection between this and the Lecuyer-cum-Sebastien story he'd been working on? And did either thing have anything to do with his death?

The more I found out, the less I understood. This was not what I would call progress.

Hoping to find something else, I pawed through the petty-crimes file, looking for the most mundane things I could find, and ran across a large file marked "jaywalking." When I opened it, a reporter's notebook fell into my lap. The first dozen or so pages in the file were photocopies of the stories I'd stolen from the morgue, about the plane crash that killed Sebastien and the others. So it *was* Adam who'd been through them before me.

I realized what an idiot I'd been the first time I'd looked through the drawer, when I was too upset to think clearly. Normally, I like to think I would have noticed it was ridiculous to keep a quarter-inch-thick "jaywalking" file in a town where nobody's ever been ticketed for crossing against the light.

I must have been staring like a zombie, because the next thing I knew O'Shaunessey was whacking me on the shoulders. "Earth to Bernier," he said, loud enough for them to hear him down in the pressroom. "Earrrrrth toooo Bernier!"

"What's up?" I said, absurdly worried he was going to rip the file out of my hand and start reading it out loud.

"Stop spacing and come to lunch." He worked his way around the newsroom, repeating "You lunching? Lunch action!" to everybody, pointing with his thumb cocked up like a gun.

I put the file back in the drawer where I found it and went out for a falafel on the Gabriel Green, which is paved. After lunch, I finished rearranging Adam's files and cleaning out his desk without finding any other hidden explosives. Then I went up to campus to talk to students for a reaction story to Tony Cerutti's speech: Did people think it would be hard for him to come back to campus? Was Benson a hostile place for gays and lesbians?

After I filed the story, I declined O'Shaunessey's usual after-work invitation to the Citizen, and got Mad to help me carry the boxes to my car. "We've got to talk," I told him as he dropped the box into my hatchback. "I found some files in Adam's desk that seem pretty important."

"But I thought you already searched through his files."

"Don't ask. One of them seems to be all about Lecuyer and Sebastien. I haven't had a chance to read it yet. But the other one is even weirder. For some reason, Adam was really interested in what's been going on with B-

GLAD. He copied all my stories on it, right out of my desk."

"You mean that gay thing?"

We agreed to meet later that night, after Mad had finished his stories, run seven miles, and spent the requisite two hours at the gym. At home, I settled into my pink chair and tried to make sense of Adam's self-styled shorthand. It seemed like notes from an interview; the date was at the top, about two weeks before his death.

> Anon. wom.—'70s? 80s?
> LECUYER, RENE (jumper)
> sez no sside; <u>murder</u>!!!
> no name, no #
> see GM 7/8
> "he wd nvr have klled hself. He
> wantd 2 make thngs rt."

Adam had done some doodling at the edges of the page, little squiggles and faces—and, more tellingly, the word "NUTS" ringed by filigreed question marks.

The rest of the pages in the notebook were easier for me to figure out, since I recognized the names of some of the same people I'd talked to up in Ste. Marie. Adam had taken meticulous notes on what he'd found in Lecuyer's apartment. He'd copied down all the information on Sebastien's Benson ID and driver's license, taken notes on the photographs of Sebastien and his girlfriend cavorting at Gabriel Falls. Strange to think that the things Adam had studied so carefully were presently tucked away in the back of my underwear drawer.

The top sheets in the file folder were copies of the morgue stories on Sebastien's death. Underneath those were pages torn from several news magazines, all fiftieth anniversary features on the Manhattan Project. I wanted to talk to Mad about it, but he never called. I tried his apartment, but there was no answer. That was nothing new; outside of work, he rarely does anything when he's supposed to. It boils down to booze, or some girl, usually both.

Shakespeare and I went to bed around midnight, but I couldn't get to sleep 'til two. My appointment with Langston was for nine the next morning, and Mad had only given me some basic bio information about him. It was a lousy time for him to blow me off, and I was more than a little pissed.

I read the new Anne Tyler novel for a while, and was about to turn out the light when I saw the file on my nightstand. I stared at the word on the manila tab, printed neatly in Adam's handwriting, and pressed my lips against it. Jaywalking. Crossing the street when you're not supposed to. Was it just Adam's little random in-joke? Or did it signify something else, whether he realized it or not? Had Adam stumbled onto something he wasn't supposed to, gotten himself killed as surely as if he'd wandered into the street without looking both ways?

I wonder, I thought. I wonder if he ever saw it coming.

12

DR. WILLIAM J. LANGSTON JR. DOESN'T HAVE AN OFFICE. He doesn't have a suite. The man has a *wing*. His research facility, and the headquarters of the Langston Foundation, take up a third of the new supercomputing facility, perched on the edge of Benson Gorge. Though Benson is considered to be the less dramatic of the two gorges that cut through campus—North Creek Gorge, where Adam died, is the big one—the view is still spectacular. You may wonder why a guy who does nuclear medicine research works out of the supercomputing building. I wondered the same thing. According to Mad, it's because the National Supercomputing Facility is the fanciest building on campus. And the Langston Foundation is *always* in the fanciest building on campus. Period.

The building, made of what looks like pink granite, curves to follow the contour of the gorge; the Langston wing's facade comes out in a semicircle, with a fountain in front. It's a very impressive building, but if you look at it just the right way . . . Well, you get the idea. Nobody can believe the architects didn't realize they were building an eight-story penis, but there it is. When it was being, uh, *erected,* two years ago, lots of people protested it; not just the die-hard environmentalists, but folks who liked to hike there and resented having the view ruined by a pink granite schlong. Graffiti—"Kick the dick," "Circumcise it!"—was spray-painted all over campus, but the thing went up anyway.

The lobby, with its vaulted ceiling and enormous windows, looks more like a hotel than your typical university science building. The receptionist, a guy about my age wearing a coat and tie, sat in the middle of a circular desk as wide as a jacuzzi. He asked to see my press pass, called up to Langston's office, and noted me in the log. I was wearing my usual summer uniform: white T-shirt under a floral-print hippie dress and sandals. After looking me up and down and sniffing like a rabbit, he decided I wasn't there to steal the silverware, and buzzed me through the glass doors behind him.

"Dr. Langston's private office is on the top floor," he said.

"Of course it is."

Through the doors, I found an alcove with a framed botanical print and an elevator waiting open. That was it—no way out, nowhere to wander unobserved. I got in and pushed the button for the eighth floor. Just for a lark, I tried to see if it would let me ring for any other floor; it wouldn't. I thought about every James Bond movie I'd ever seen, and wondered if the floor was about to open up and drop me into a pool of bulimic sharks.

I made it up to the eighth floor, and the doors opened with nary a whisper. Langston's secretary was a suicide blond dressed like a refugee from Condé Nast; I doubted she bought one stitch of her clothing within the Gabriel city limits. She wore her hair up, didn't seem to chew her nails, and was probably even wearing panty hose. Mad, who is usually discreet about such matters, tells me she's quite a tiger in the sack. She ushered me past the cluster of forest-green chairs in the waiting room. I was right about the panty hose. Langston got up from behind his desk and crossed to greet me. It took a while, since the office was large enough to be carpeted in Astroturf. A door in the corner probably led to a bathroom, maybe even a bedroom. Instead of the usual diplomas and awards, the walls were lined with art. I couldn't identify most of it, but I could have sworn there was a genuine Edward Hopper over the right side of the desk.

Up close, Langston turned out to be no more than five feet nine, with one of those nuclear-powered handshakes that makes you want to run to the bathroom and soak your fingers under the cold water. He had on a kelly-green polo shirt with the requisite horse and rider over the left nipple, tropic-weight slacks, and Docksides with no socks. Either it was ultra-casual day at the office, or Langston had an appointment with his sailboat.

As I describe him, you might assume Langston's your average white-bread asshole. He's not. Mad had described him to me, and of course I'd seen his picture in the paper, but nothing prepared me for the sheer charisma of the guy. It's not exactly that he's good-looking, although I'd definitely put him in the "attractive older man" category, along with Sean Connery and Harrison Ford and the sexy Italian who runs the Gabriel Department of Public Works. He has that quality that separates movie stars from journeyman actors, trial lawyers from tax attorneys. Adam had it too.

His hair was graying nicely, and he wore it surprisingly

long, brushed back over the top of his head. He had a respectable tan and deep lines at the corners of his eyes, either from laughing or squinting into the sun a lot. He wore a wedding ring, and he was fit enough so the flesh didn't bulge around it. I knew, again from Mad, that Langston's wife had died in a car accident a little over five years ago. I couldn't help but be touched by the fact he was still wearing a ring; it's a lousy way to pick up coeds.

"It's an honor to meet you, Miss Bernier," he said, pronouncing my name perfectly. If he was trying to throw me off balance, it worked. Mr. Nobel Peace Prize for Medicine was honored to meet *me*?

"Uh, thank you . . ." I stammered, wondering if he could see the C-minus in chemistry tattooed across my forehead.

"I've always thought your movie reviews are exceedingly well written. Very intelligent commentary," he said, as if he actually meant it. "Not that I always agree with you." He smiled, and his teeth were as white and straight as my dog's.

"Are you, um, a big movie fan?"

"You sound surprised."

"I guess it seems rather mundane for someone who . . ." I wasn't sure how to put it. "For someone who's so . . ."

"So goddamn *smart*?"

"I guess so."

"Well, I do like movies. I try to see at least one a week, if I'm not traveling. I do a lot of renting."

"Mostly arthouse films?"

"Oh, God, *no*. Too pretentious. Gives me a headache. Lately, I've gotten very much into action movies from Hong Kong. Have you heard of John Woo? Of course you have. Do you like him?"

I do like John Woo, and I was starting to like William J. Langston. For a while, we debated the shoot-outs in *The Killer, Bullet in the Head,* and *A Better Tomorrow.* Turned out we both liked that part at the beginning of *Hard-Boiled,* when Chow Yun-Fat is covered in flour and the bad guy's brains explode all over his face. Wild. I'm not quite sure how I'd expected the conversation to go, but exploding brains definitely hadn't figured in. "Is that a Hopper?" I hoped my tongue wasn't lolling all the way down to my waist.

Eerie light played across a nude woman reclining in a spartan apartment. It was the same mood Melissa had captured in her portrait of Tony Cerutti. Loneliness personified. "I bought it for my wife for our tenth anniversary. It's my favorite painting, and since I spend the better part of my life in this building, I decided to keep it here."

"It's wonderful."

He stared at it for a moment, then leaned back in his leather office chair. "But I don't suppose you came here to talk about movies and art with me all morning."

"No, not really, Dr. Langston."

"Please call me Will."

"All right."

"So what can I do for you?" He leaned way back, hands clasped behind his head, and propped his Docksides on the corner of the desk. His pose was casual, but the mood in the room had shifted from chatty to what-the-hell-do-you-want.

"I was wondering if you could help me with a story I'm working on."

"What's it about?"

I had no intention of pouring my heart out to him about my dead lover, though I had a suspicion Langston, a widower with a wedding ring, might actually understand. But

I'd come prepared with a pretext. "It's a feature package I'm working on about French-Canadians in Walden County. You probably know there was a big immigration wave at the beginning and middle of the century, mostly menial laborers. I want to do some side profiles on individual people who emigrated here, and I was looking for some standouts." As lies go, it was pretty mediocre, but it was the best I could come up with. And now that I'd told it, I was going to have to sell the idea to Bill, so I wouldn't get caught. "There was a tenured physics professor here back in the forties, one of the few Quebecois in the area who was extremely well educated. His name was Dr. André Sebastien. I thought he might be an interesting man to profile."

He put his feet down on the oriental rug and leaned toward me, forearms on the desktop. "Ah . . . Dr. Sebastien. You know, he died with my father. In a plane crash."

"I looked up the newspaper stories when I started working on this piece. I don't mean to upset you . . ."

"Oh, not at all. Not at all," he said, one time too many for me to really buy it. "I was just a little boy when he died. I don't even remember him, or Dr. Sebastien either, I'm afraid. I do know he and my father worked together, quite closely, in fact. They were both physicists, doing research for the government."

"What kind of research?"

"You've heard of the Manhattan Project?" I didn't answer, thinking of Adam's hidden file. "The Manhattan Project? You've heard of it?"

"Yes, of course. The atomic bomb."

"The most massive, intensive research effort this country had ever undertaken, led by Robert Oppenheimer. I'm not sure how much you know about physics . . ."

"Try nothing."

"Then I won't bore you with details. My father and Sebastien and a few others here at Benson, along with scientists all over the country, were doing pieces of preliminary work that eventually led to the creation of the atom bomb, dropped on Hiroshima and Nagasaki." He pushed his bangs over his head, a gesture that made him look like a sophomore. "That is, the work in general led to the bomb; my father died before he had a chance to contribute much. He and his colleagues did some research here, but there were no facilities at Benson back then for anything very advanced. When they died, they were flying to Los Alamos. You're familiar with the work that was done there?"

"Vaguely. That's where the bomb was invented."

"Yes. My father was quite well known in his field when he died, and I know he hoped to contribute to the war effort. In those days, no one wondered whether nuclear weapons were a good idea. *Someone* was going to have the bomb—either the Allies, or the enemy. The race was on, and my father planned to win it. When he died, it was . . . Suffice it to say it was a great loss to the scientific community. That's when the Langston Foundation was started, in his memory. It's his foundation, really, not mine. His and my wife's." He paused for a long moment, staring out the window. The view stretched across the gorge and beyond, to Mohawk Lake and the horizon. "But I'm afraid I haven't told you much about Dr. Sebastien, have I? All I really know is that Sebastien was a promising young professor. He was in his twenties when he died, I think, and he already had tenure. I couldn't tell you where he got his doctorate, but I assume it was somewhere in the States. I'm sure you can look that up with the university."

"Do you happen to know anything about his personal life?"

"Almost nothing. All I know is what I read when I was older, and what my mother told me. Sebastien wasn't married. The other man in the plane, Dr. Adelson, left behind a wife and family. As, of course, did my father. Odd to think I'm nearly fifteen years older than he was when he died."

"Do you happen to know if there are any documents still around from those days, anything like personnel files?"

"That may be difficult, given how much time has passed. Have you tried the head of the physics department? He might be able to help more than I can."

"Do you think there's anyone around who might remember him?"

"I doubt it, but there may be a few professors emeriti still around. Let me make a few calls, have my secretary do some checking."

"I'd really appreciate it."

"Anything for a fellow John Woo fan. If there's anything else I can do for you, please don't hesitate to call," he said, pulling a business card from a brass holder. He stood up, and I gathered the interview was over. I hadn't even pulled out my notebook. "I don't want you to get the wrong idea, but I'd enjoy having dinner with you some time." I opened my mouth to babble something. "Don't worry. I'm not hitting on you. But even I have to get out of this building once a week."

"I'm the only Bernier in the Walden County phone book."

At home, there was a message from Mad, who wanted to hear how the meeting went. I dialed his direct line and he picked up on the first ring. "Where the hell were you last night?"

"Sorry," he said, but didn't elaborate. "So how did the thing on campus go?"

"That place is a fucking fortress."

"No kidding. You check out the view?"

"Fabulous."

"Did you find out anything? He remember the other guy?" I had to give Mad credit for not naming names in the middle of the newsroom.

"Not personally, but he said he'd ask around, see if anybody's on campus who remembers him."

"How much did you tell him?"

"Not much. I could hardly say I think Sebastien was still alive until a few months ago. How do I know who he's gonna tell?"

"Smart." I could hear Mad typing away, working on his story with one half of his brain and talking to me with the other. "So what did you think of him?"

"He's definitely not what I expected. Less uptight. Totally charming. Very . . ."

"Intense?"

"How did you know?"

"That's what they all say. Didn't I warn you?"

"And get this: Here's something my mom always wanted to hear."

"What?"

"I think I've got a date with a doctor."

13

WHEN I GOT TO WORK WEDNESDAY MORNING, GORDON
Band was already at the desk across from mine, talking
into a phone headset. He had on a long-sleeved white oxford, khakis, and a Liberty of London tie with pink and
blue flowers on it. His glasses were little round John
Lennon lenses with wire rims. As he did the interview, he
finger-combed his sandy hair so it stood up an inch and a
half on one side.

"What was the victim's name, Captain? Could you
spell that? Her age, please? Address?"

It was mundane stuff, probably some car accident. But
there was something incredibly intense about the way he
asked the questions, as if this fender-bender concealed
the secrets of the Kennedy assassination. Who did you
say was on the grassy knoll, Captain? He banged notes
into his computer, never once peeking at the keyboard.
Disgusting.

The idea had started to form when I walked out of

Bill's office, after he told me Gordon Band was joining the staff. Mad didn't think it was the brightest idea I'd ever had—"How can you trust this asshole from the *Times*?", I believe, was his graceful way of putting it. But a real investigative reporter, a digger, had fallen into my lap—or at least four feet from my swivel chair. "Hi. I'm Alex Bernier, your friendly neighborhood politics reporter."

"Gordon Band. Cops." He shook hands across our desks and went back to his computer.

"How was your first day?"

"Fine," he said to the screen.

"Where'd you get the headset thing?"

"I asked for it." Type, type, type.

"When?"

"Yesterday." More typing.

"You asked for it *yesterday* and you got it *today*?" The *Monitor* has been known to be without reporter's notebooks for weeks at a time, and this guy gets a headset within twenty-four hours?

"Of course."

"Wow. I want one."

Band didn't seem inclined to chat, so I got to work on my story for the next day's paper. Thanks to one of the publisher's bright ideas, I've been profiling members of the Gabriel city council. I saved my favorite for last: a Benson law professor who does pro bono work for death row inmates and spends his summers selling potato pancakes at folk festivals. The story pretty much wrote itself. When I was done, I cornered Gordon at the coffee machine and asked him to lunch. He was about to turn me down when, perhaps, it occurred to him that it might be nice to be cordial to someone you're going to work with for a year, and we walked down the stairs into the sun.

The Green was crowded with the usual bunch of fair-weather lunchers, dogs, kamikaze roller-bladers. Nobody in their right mind stays inside this time of year; the clouds come in November, and they stay put until April. One of the shops on the Green has a T-shirt in the window that says "Gabriel Rain Festival: Jan. 1–Dec. 31." Nobody thinks it's funny.

We went to King David's, where an Israeli family makes fabulous pitas. In the summer, they have a cart on the Green, and I might as well have my paycheck direct-deposited into their account. Gordon ordered chicken kabob, I went for baba ghanoush, and we brought our food and a couple of Snapples over to one of the cement benches in the center of the mall.

"So what do you think?"

"The chicken? It's not bad. Tahini's good. And I thought I was going to be the only Jew in six counties."

"Not the food. The *Monitor.* What do you think of the new job?"

"Fine."

"So you said. I'd expect something a little more eloquent from a journalist of your stature."

He looked as if he were going to say something ungentlemanly, then changed his mind. "You've been here awhile. What do you think?"

"Oh, no you don't. Nice try. I doubt you're in the habit of letting people weasel out of questions."

"What is this, an interview? I thought it was lunch."

"How else am I going to get to know you?"

"Are you always this incredibly nosy?"

"Of course I am. So are you. Or else you don't get hired by the *New York Times.*"

"Yeah, I got hired by the *New York Times.*" I thought

he might bean me with his sandwich, but tossed it onto the paper plate instead. "And look where I wound up."

I decided to try a different tack. "How did you hear about this job, anyway? It wasn't even advertised in *E&P* yet."

"My girlfriend heard about it. She used to cover this part of the state for the AP."

"Have you spent much time around here?"

From the look on his face, I might have asked him if he voted for Reagan. "Not much."

"It's not so bad, you know. It's really beautiful." He didn't look convinced. "There are great places to hike, and the people are friendly. There's weirdos from all over the world who end up here, one way or another. And did you know there are more bars per capita in Gabriel than anywhere else in the world? No? Well, they don't exactly put it in the tourist brochures. Do you like movies? There are seventeen screens. Also tons of concerts— all the college circuit bands come here." He looked as though he wanted to throttle two teenagers whose game of barefoot hackeysack threatened to land in our laps. "You're going into Manhattan withdrawal, aren't you? Poor baby. Don't worry. There's tons of renegade New Yorkers up here for you to play with."

"I don't wanna talk about it."

"Homesick for the Upper East Side?"

He looked even more insulted. "Upper *West* Side."

"And now you're stuck up here in the wilderness, and you're terrified you won't be able to find anyplace that delivers Ethiopian food at four in the morning?"

"Something like that," he said, almost smiling.

"But nobody gets mugged around here, either."

"You upstaters don't understand the value of muggings as performance art."

"Yes, but we do understand the value of sheep as sexual surrogates."

"Then maybe I might like it here after all."

I stared at him for a minute, assessing. "You know, you're not nearly as much of a prick as you pretend to be."

"Don't let it get out. It'll ruin my reputation. I've worked very hard to become an asshole."

"So now that I've discovered your secret, are you going to tell me how you like your job?"

"If you'd been in line to do investigative pieces for the *New York Times,* and screwed up so badly you ended up doing morning cop calls for a twenty-five-thousand-circulation paper in West Bumblefuck, how do *you* think you would like your new job?"

"My grandmother would tell you to take your lemons and make some lemonade."

"My grandmother would tell you when the noodles go bad, it's time to throw out the kugel."

"But you didn't go flack for somebody. You're not writing press releases for nuclear power plants. It takes chutzpah to try and work your way back to the *Times,* if that's where you want to be."

"Chutzpah? What kind of a shiksa are you?"

"The kind with lots of Jewish friends from boarding school."

"So, what are you still doing here? You've been here, what? Two years?"

"Three."

"Isn't it about time for you to go somewhere bigger?"

"Have you met Mad yet?"

"The science guy? Yeah. He's good."

"He's been here eight years. And O'Shaunessey, the sports editor? Try eleven."

"What are they, nuts?"

"It's not lunacy, exactly. It's Gabriel. People just come here, and they never leave. Everybody I know in this town is some kind of misfit or other; Gabriel is like a witness relocation program. People belong here who don't belong anywhere else."

"But in the city, you're in the center of everything. Up here, you're just . . ."

"Five hours from everywhere?"

"Thanks for reminding me. I'll just go kill myself now. Thank you very much." He feigned getting up, and sat back down again. "But from what I hear, it goes with the job."

"What?"

"The previous cop reporter, Adam Somebody. He committed suicide, right?" The look on my face shut him up. "Oh, Jesus, I'm such an asshole. He was a friend of yours. That was really lousy. I forget sometimes other people have actual feelings. In New York, we don't have feelings. We have them delivered by little Chinese men on bikes, and when we're done, we throw them out with the paper cartons. We don't even recycle."

In the short time I've known Gordon, I've never been able to stay mad at him for long, and that first day was no different.

"They found his body at the bottom of North Creek Gorge," I said simply. "But he did not kill himself."

I told him. Not everything, not at first. Just that I knew Adam better than anyone, and I didn't believe he would have killed himself.

"Have you told the cops?"

"I tried, but they found this cockeyed suicide note. I know, I know, it sounds crazy. But sometimes you just have this gut instinct about something."

"Well, then, you should trust it. Every good story I ever

wrote came down to instinct—who to believe, who not to, what questions to ask. Instinct is the name of the game, baby."

I believe in love at first sight, and I believe in friendship at first sight as well. I'm not sure why I decided to trust Gordon right from the beginning, before I really knew him, but I did.

"Can you keep a secret?" I asked. "I mean, are you the kind of guy who'd go to jail to protect a source?"

"Don't you think I'd kill to have that on my résumé?"

"Well then, think of me as your source. I'd like you to help me with a story, sort of a personal, freelance kind of thing. It's either the investigative adventure of a lifetime, or I'm just some lovesick twit who can't believe her boyfriend did himself in an hour after boffing her. Take your pick."

"Alex, I am stuck in Gabriel, New York, for an entire year. I have derailed my career, which is the most important thing in my life, because I am not humanly capable of keeping my goddamn mouth shut. My girlfriend is in Manhattan, probably being snatched out from under me as we speak by some jerk from ABC News. I will do anything, repeat, anything, to take my mind off my own misery."

I told him everything then. The story, beginning with the day I met Adam and ending with my meeting with Langston the day before, took up the rest of our lunch hour. Gordon was a good interviewer. He knew when to ask questions, when to nod and make encouraging noises, and when to shut up and listen.

"So, what's the verdict?" I asked. "Am I nuts, or what?"

By that time he'd fiddled with his hair so much he looked like some kind of Jewish intellectual punk rocker.

He gave his scalp a final, climactic scratch. "Man, oh man, oh Manischewitz. It sounds like your guy Adam really got himself in deep."

"Do you really think so? You're not just—I don't know, being sympathetic?"

"You may not have realized yet, my little shiksa friend, but I am not that nice."

"Okay. That I believe. So what do we do now?"

"I know what we don't do. We do *not* tell anybody else about this. Agreed?"

"I wasn't planning on it."

"Who else knows this?"

"Just Mad. And Olivia. She's Adam's ex-girlfriend who lives in San Francisco. But she doesn't know all that much, just that I'm looking into it. What are you so worried about?"

"You idiot, don't you realize you're sitting on one hell of a news story?"

"News story?"

"Alex, a journalist was *murdered* because of a story he was writing. That sort of thing happens in Medellín, not upstate New York. Apparently, this has something to do with the Manhattan Project, though I have no idea what. And plus, you said Adam was interested in that gay thing?"

"Oh, no, Gordon, not you too."

"What?"

"Forget it. Go on."

"There's a hell of a lot of hot buttons being pushed here. The *Times* would be more than interested in breaking this thing."

"Don't you *dare*. Gordon, if you leak this to the *Times*, I'll arrange to have your foreskin painfully reattached. And I mean *staples*."

"I didn't mean . . . Jesus, Alex, I'm not *that* much of an asshole. I promised I'd keep my mouth shut. Besides, the *Times* is the last place I'd give it to. The bastards fired my ass. It'd serve them right if I broke a story like this." He looked positively gleeful. And on a face like Gordon's, that's not easy. "Jesus. It would absolutely *kill* my son of a bitch of an editor. This could be my ticket back to civilization . . ."

"Wait a minute. I'm not doing this for any story. Adam was one of the best human beings I've ever met. He made people laugh. He sure got them high often enough. He took care of you, in his own weird way. He was one of those guys you could always count on to help you move, even if he'd been partying late the night before. He was the most amazing Frisbee player you ever saw. When he got on a mountain bike, he was absolutely fearless." I stood up and stretched. "I'm babbling, and we've got to get back to work. All I'm trying to say is, I owe it to him to find out the truth about how he died. I don't want everyone to think the last thing he ever did in his life was drive to North Creek Gorge and jump in, like some miserable coward. If your big news story comes out of all this, fine. But don't go thinking that's the point of it, because it's not."

"All right, all right. I gotcha. I solemnly promise I will not even think about breaking this without your permission. So what do you want me to do to help?"

"I'm not sure. Asking you to help was one of those instincts—and you said to follow your instincts. All I know is, you seem like one of those people who likes asking questions no one wants to answer. I bet you get a hard-on just thinking about exposing a scandal at the traffic board."

"Hubba hubba."

"You're a digger. I'm not. I'm much more of a writer than a reporter. I don't really know much about doing research. I'd like the three of us—you and me and Mad—to get together tonight and go over everything we know so far. Maybe you'll notice something I've missed. At the very least, you'll get to see the inside of Mad's apartment. Not many men in this town are so honored."

"Most of the women are, though?"

"Another triumph for investigative journalism," I said. "Give the man a matzo."

14

~

IN THE SUMMER, THE GABRIEL FARMER'S MARKET DOWN by Mohawk Inlet has lush bouquets of organic basil for sale, yet another seasonal wonder that makes winter seem so dismal by comparison. Once September comes, you can only get a few measly leaves, in little plastic coffins in the supermarket. Fresh basil, like garlic sautéing in olive oil, is one of the culinary world's great aphrodisiacs. And as Shakespeare and I walked down the packed-dirt aisles of the farmer's market, I found myself thinking not of linguine al pesto, but of Adam. The first time I went to the market after he died it was the epicenter of basil season, and the scent of the deep green leaves surfed on the humidity. It smelled like life.

I made a quadruple batch of pesto for dinner that night; if you go to all that trouble, you might as well have some to give away. You're never supposed to wash basil leaves under the faucet, because it weakens the flavor. But you also don't want to grind up bugs and dirt into your dinner, so you have to wipe each leaf carefully with a soft towel before you toss it in the Cuisinart with the cloves of garlic. Then come the walnuts, which I prefer to pine nuts, and are also much cheaper. After that, you alternate the freshly grated parmesan and pecorino-romano cheeses with enough extra-virgin olive oil to make the mixture circulate through the food processor. Salt and pepper to taste. Some people's pesto is distinctly liquid, but mine is a thick paste. You can freeze it, serve it on French bread, and it makes a great filling for omelets.

In her book *Heartburn,* which is one of my favorites, Nora Ephron writes that mashed potatoes are one of those labor-intensive foods you serve at the beginning and end of a relationship—first to show your devotion, then to give yourself something to do while you're trying to get over the guy. Every woman I know who's read the book nods her head, and goes on to tell which food is her personal mashed potato. It could be something elaborately French, like coq au vin, or maybe lasagna, which takes a lot of steps to make. For me, it's pesto.

Mad has always been a big fan of my pesto, though he complains he has to run an extra two miles the next day to work it off. I made it that night partly to make sure he'd show up. As further insurance, I arranged to bring the food over to his apartment, though even that couldn't guarantee he'd be there. But when Gordon and I came over at eight, he was there, wearing shorts and a holey T-shirt from some bar in D.C. He'd dispatched a good half foot of the first magnum of Concha y Toro, but didn't seem a bit drunk. "I thought it would be a good idea if we got together and talked about where to go next with this," I said once we were all settled in the living room. I pulled the various exhibits from my backpack, spreading everything out on the floor. I handed the two file folders to

Mad, who was sprawled on the couch. Gordon, who seemed just as happy to vacate Mad's dilapidated wicker chair, sat on the floor next to me. I gave him the box I'd found in Ste. Marie, and left them with their reading to go into the kitchen. I came back with a loaf of French bread and some smoked Gouda.

"Do you know how much fat there is in that?" Mad asked, and sliced off a chunk.

Gordon held up one of the snapshots. "Who's the woman?"

"I have no idea. Those photos were taken at Gabriel Falls. You haven't been down there yet?" Gordon poured a world of sarcasm into one raised eyebrow. "It's a prime spot on parents' weekend. Great swimming hole too. We should go sometime, before it gets too cold."

"Swimming hole? How quaint. What a pity I left my fishing pole back at the old homestead."

I took the photo from Gordon and studied it. "They look happy, don't they? Young and in love. They found Lecuyer's body right near there, you know. The water was high enough to carry it down to the falls and right over. Adam told me by the time they pulled him out of the water, his clothes had been completely ripped off by the current. Just this naked, scrawny old corpse."

Gordon made a queasy noise. "So much for this happy little upstate oasis of yours."

"What the hell does this gay thing have to do with this?" Mad asked from the couch. "I mean, why would Adam have copied all your stories about B-GLAD? *B-GLAD!* I hate those obnoxious acronyms. Why do people think they're so goddamn cute? What was I saying? Oh, yeah. There's got to be a reason Adam was following your story. It's got to be connected to whatever it was that got him killed. Agreed?"

"So what's the connection?" Gordon asked. "Wait. Let's write this down. Give me the notes you've put together so far, and I'll start to formulate a list of questions."

"Notes?" we asked in a lame duet.

"You've been documenting this whole thing, right? Writing down all the research you've done, everyone you've talked to so far?"

"It's sort of all up here," I said, sticking a finger to my temple.

Gordon fell back onto the carpet with more melodrama than the moment probably warranted. "Jeeezus! What kind of goddamn reporters are you? It's all *up here*? You've got to be kidding me!"

"Come on, Gordon, spare us the outraged journalist act for five minutes, would you please? We'll write everything down from now on. You can be in charge of all the notes. You probably couldn't read my handwriting anyway."

"Ever heard of a typewriter? Or don't they have them this far north?" He sighed, sat up, and pulled out a notebook. "All right. Let's start from scratch. At the very least, we need to make a list of all the questions we need to have answered. Number one . . ."

"Number one," I said, standing up. "Who killed Adam?"

"Right. That's the big one. But maybe we should stick to the smaller questions first, and they'll help us figure out the answers to the big ones."

"Fine. Organize it however you want. I've got to go see if the water's ready." I went into the kitchen, and listened to Mad and Gordon kibitz in the other room.

"Number one, who killed Adam Ellroy?" Gordon went on. "Number two, who's the woman in the photograph?

Number three, what does the B-GLAD situation have to do with Adam's death? What else?"

"Number four . . . Let me see . . . Number four, are Lecuyer and Sebastien really the same person? And assuming that's true, that obviously means he didn't die in the plane crash. So, question number five, what was the deal with the plane crash?"

"Or was there ever a plane crash in the first place?" Gordon added.

I came back into the living room. "And if there wasn't any plane crash," I said, "what happened to the other two guys? Langston and . . . what's his name?"

Mad consulted the morgue clips. "Adelson. Dr. Seth Adelson."

"Do we think there's any chance they could still be alive?" Gordon asked.

"Doubtful," Mad said.

"But Sebastien was probably still alive until last month," I said.

Mad held up the clips. "But you're forgetting he was younger than the other two. Langston was in his forties. And Adelson . . . Let me see . . . He was fifty-three. Fifteen years makes a lot of difference when you're talking about eighty versus ninety-five. And with Adelson, we're talking about somebody who'd be over a hundred."

"Well, we'll just leave the question, acknowledging that it's unlikely," Gordon said.

"Fair enough," Mad said. "Now where's my pesto?"

"The linguine needs five more minutes."

"Bernier, I'm *hungry*."

"Calm down. I put a whole batch of it in your freezer. You can bathe in the stuff."

"Ooh, baby . . ."

"Can we concentrate here?" Gordon said. "What about

the Manhattan Project? What does that have to do with the rest of it? Why did Adam clip magazine stories about it?"

"The three scientists were on their way to work on it," I said. "They were supposed to help invent the bomb. But if they never got there, what difference does it make?"

The pasta was done, so I drained it and put some linguine in three mismatched bowls. Mad scooped out a tennis-ball-sized lump of pesto and mixed it meticulously into his pasta. Gordon tried a little, gave a satisfied grunt, and dolloped on some more. If the way to a man's heart were really and truly through his stomach, I'd have no problem. Gordon was the first to come up for air.

"What about the interview?" he asked.

"What interview?"

"The one in the notebook you found in Adam's file. Apparently, somebody called Adam and said Lecuyer's death was no suicide. Now, if we're right, that caller was telling the truth."

"We've been wondering all along what set Adam off to begin with," I said. "What if this is it? An anonymous tip?"

"A Deep Throat?" Mad said through a mouthful of pesto. "Jesus, that's just *too* Woodward and Bernstein."

"Yeah, it's melodramatic, I'll admit," I said. "But who hasn't gotten that sort of call?"

"Try once a week," Gordon said. "Once you get a reputation as a whistle-blower, every nut in town comes out of the woodwork. And look"—he held up the notebook—"this Adam of yours apparently thought she might be a crackpot."

"She?" Mad asked.

"Yeah, she," Gordon said, passing the notebook to him. "According to his notes, it was a woman."

"'Seventies or eighties,'" Mad read. "I wonder whether he was talking about age or years."

"What do you mean?" I asked, flopping down on the other side of the couch and using his legs as a footrest.

"Was this an old lady who called him, somebody in her seventies or eighties, or was he talking about something that happened in the 1970s or 1980s?"

"God, how many questions is this?"

"A lot," Gordon said. "I stopped counting."

"And what about this?" Mad asked. "'GM 7/8'? Was that some appointment he had or something? Who's GM? General Motors? Do we know anybody with those initials?"

"Sure we do," I said. "*Gabriel Monitor.* Maybe he was talking about the paper from July eighth. You think?"

"It's possible," Gordon said. "We have to get our hands on a copy of that day's paper. Want me to run over to the morgue?"

"Hold it," Mad said. He ducked into the bathroom and returned with a stack of newspapers, pale and wavy from weeks of shower steam. "Got it." He plucked a paper from the pile and tossed it to Gordon. "Aren't you glad I don't recycle?"

"Here we go again," Gordon said. "Take a look at what's on page one." He held up the newspaper. The lead story was my piece on B-GLAD's initial demand for a gay and lesbian living center.

By ALEX BERNIER
Monitor Staff

A gay and lesbian living center is at the top of a list of demands issued Wednesday by Benson University stu-

dent activists. Leaders of the Benson
Gay and Lesbian Action Detail (B-GLAD)
called for a dormitory and social center
to be built on the site of an April attack
on two gay freshmen.

"We don't want apologies. We want
action," said B-GLAD co-chairwoman
Karin Coe, a Benson junior. "A living
center will be a symbol that hate crimes
will not be tolerated."

University Vice President for Community Relations Stewart Day said Benson officials plan to schedule a meeting
with student leaders to discuss B-
GLAD's demands, which include sensitivity training for campus police and
more courses on gay and lesbian issues.

"The attack on the freshmen was
reprehensible," Day said. "The university is committed to ensuring such a
tragedy does not occur again. But a
major project such as the building of
a new campus center cannot be undertaken in haste."

Day said the student proposal will
be studied over the next few weeks. He
would not comment on whether the subject would be on the agenda of the next
trustee meeting.

"So that's what set him off," I said. "Whoever called him must have told him that B-GLAD had something to do with it—or else maybe just to look at that day's paper, and he figured it out for himself."

"And here's something else," Mad said, tossing the notebook to Gordon. "One thing that's obvious from these notes is that the caller told Adam that Lecuyer's death was no suicide, it was murder. So the question is . . ."

"The question is," Gordon interrupted, "was she right? Are we really looking at not *one* murder, but *two*? And if we are—if Adam and the old guy were both killed—is the same person responsible for both of them? Or is it two different people?"

Mad gave a strangled sigh. "Two jumpers, two murders, two murderers. We're gonna need a flow chart to follow this thing. Bernier, where the hell's dessert?"

"Frozen yogurt's in the freezer." Mad vaulted up from the couch toward the kitchen.

"We've got to find out who made that phone call," I said. "But where the hell do we start? If this were one of your *New York Times* stories, what would you do?"

"Jesus, Bernier, there's four grams in this stuff. What are you trying to do to me?" Mad said. "Peanut butter fudge ripple. Yum . . ." He wandered back into the kitchen.

"Is he always this obsessed with fat?"

"It's a hobby of his. Go on."

"Okay. We're basically dealing with two separate issues here. Well, separate, but maybe—probably—connected. What happened fifty years ago, and what happened this summer. So what I would do is think of them as two separate stories we have to cover."

"But how do you cover a story that happened fifty years ago?"

"I suppose the same way you'd cover anything: interviews, and documentation. In this case, we can safely assume most of the people we would have used as sources are no longer around. So that means we're just going to have to concentrate on the paperwork."

"What paperwork?"

"Anything we can get our hands on," Gordon said, starting to lick his chops. "University records. Payrolls. If these three scientists were doing any government-sponsored research, there's got to be a record of it somewhere. I'm sure it was all classified back then, but with a little digging . . . Maybe I'll have to go down to D.C., or at least New York . . . If I have to, I could always do a FOIA request, but that takes time . . ."

"Wait a minute, Gordon. Don't go off half-cocked on me. Remember what happened to Adam. He tried to investigate this, and it got him killed. We've got to be careful. I told you about the notebooks and files that were stolen from his house, then brought back. It scared the shit out of me. The only reason why anybody would do that is to make sure nobody found out what Adam was working on. What I'm trying to say is, there's somebody out there who has a serious interest in keeping this quiet, whatever it is. If he killed Adam to shut him up, what makes you think he wouldn't do the same thing to us? So I think we need to be a little more subtle than filing under the Freedom of Information Act. Anything we do, we have to have a decent excuse for."

Mad came in with bowls and spoons for the three of us. "Christ, Band, you look like hell."

"Alex was just reminding me of my own mortality."

"She's good at that."

"I don't know how you can drink wine and eat ice cream at the same time," I said. "That is so disgusting.

And you ate all the fudge out of this. *Mad!* Watch where you're walking. You're stepping on the pictures." I squatted on the floor to pick them up, and froze. "How old do we think this lady in the pictures is? Twenties maybe? Mid-twenties? So what would she be now?"

Gordon answered. "If she's still alive, obviously, she'd be in her seventies or eighties, depending on when those were taken. So what's your . . . Holy *shit.*"

"You think she's our mystery woman," Mad said. "The one who called Adam."

"It's just a guess. But she obviously knew Lecuyer—I mean Sebastien. And the age is right."

"So where does that leave us?" Mad asked.

"Are you going to pout if I speak French?"

"Probably."

"I don't exactly know how," I said. "But I think it's time to *chercher la femme.*"

15

In case you've been wondering why I've barely mentioned my beloved roommate Dirk, it's because I hardly see him these days. He's a law student, so he's holed up in the library a lot, even in the summer. But he's also madly in love, and his boyfriend is not only a serious German hunk—I call him *der Ubermensch,* which I think Dirk secretly likes—he's house-sitting for a professor who's on sabbatical. Dirk, damn him to hell, not only has access to regular sexual gratification with a hairy Bavarian, but a hot tub as well.

I mention this because when Dr. Langston came to pick me up at seven on Friday, he asked if I lived alone. I gave him an abbreviated version of my housemate situation, opting to omit my intense admiration for Helmut's buttocks. He didn't seem fazed, either by the fact that I live with a gay man, or by the dog hair Shakespeare left on his khakis. Clearly, this guy was a lot less uptight than my dad, who gets apoplectic at the mention of homosexuality, and vacuums the carpet five times a day whenever I bring Shakespeare home to visit her grandparents.

"I thought we'd eat at Thai Palace," Will said, opening the car door for me. I got into one of the leather seats of his new-smelling BMW, noting that his idiosyncrasies apparently didn't extend to driving around in a battered Volvo. NPR was playing something classical as we drove down the hill toward the restaurant, located downtown on one of the side streets off the Green. We talked about the new Spike Lee movie, which he'd liked and I hadn't. Thai Palace has a reputation for great food but lousy service, so I was surprised that the hostess smiled like the Cheshire cat when we walked in, and seated us at a table big enough for four in the restaurant's new glassed-in terrace. I always got a table for two with a view of the coat rack.

A reedy blond waiter with a close-cropped beard came over and lit the mirrored oil lamp on the table.

"How are you this evening, Dr. Langston?"

"Fine, thank you, Stephen. How's your dissertation going?"

"Another couple of months at least. I'm stuck between the Scylla and Charybdis."

"Stephen is getting his doctorate in classics."

"I gathered that."

"I'm only in it for the money," the waiter said with a laugh. "Actually, I tried to think of something more useless, but I came up empty."

"What's your thesis called again?"

"Hera, Phaedra, Medea: Olympus Hath No Fury Like a Woman Really Pissed Off."

"You're kidding," I said.

"Nope. At first, I called it something horrible, like *An Ontologically Hermeneutic Deconstruction of the Female Strategic Role in Ancient Greek Myth,* and I wondered why I never wanted to work on it. Now, I just can't wait to get to the library."

Will tossed off a remark in Latin. Apparently, it was quite a knee-slapper, because our waiter nearly keeled over with mirth. If Will's French was better than mine, I was going to kill him before I got my free Pad Thai.

"I'm sorry, I didn't introduce you. Stephen, this is Alex Bernier, from the *Monitor*."

"Hey, aren't you 'Alex on the Aisle'? I didn't recognize you from your picture. It makes you look a lot . . . A lot . . ."

"Better. It's been remarked."

"You were *totally* wrong about that Jodie Foster movie. My girlfriend and I really liked it."

"I'm glad somebody did. You know, I would just *love* a Thai iced tea."

"Oh, certainly," he said. "Anything for you, Dr. Langston?"

"I'll have a Singha."

"Excellent." Why do waiters always say that, no matter what you order? I mean, it can't *all* be excellent, can it?

"Sorry about that," Will said after he'd gone. "When you come here as often as I do, you get to know the waiters. If I'm in town, I eat here two or three times a week."

"For the food, or to quiz the waiters on their grad school plans?"

"I'm interested. And it's someone to talk to."

"Do you usually come here alone?"

"Usually. I like to. It gives me a break from my work. Maybe it's a strange habit. Most people don't like to go to restaurants by themselves."

"I feel a little strange about it. Back at boarding school, you'd stay in your room and starve before you'd go to the dining hall by yourself. It would have been a badge of shame."

"So it's still like that, is it?"

"Did you go away to school yourself?"

"Exeter."

"Exeter, then Harvard?"

"Exeter, then Yale. Then Harvard. No, wait. Then Oxford, *then* Harvard."

"You got a Rhodes?"

"I'm afraid so."

"Then you got your medical degree?"

"MD-PhD. Harvard offers a combined program."

"That's disgusting. What are you doing having dinner with me?"

"You hardly strike me as the product of a community college, if you'll forgive a bit of elitism from an old man."

"*You* hardly strike me as an old man. And to answer your question: Middlesex, then Vassar. Then I did my postgraduate work at the *Gabriel Monitor,* otherwise known as the school of hard knocks. Actually, it's true—journalism is one of the last fields where you really do learn better by apprenticeship."

"You never got a master's in journalism?"

"I got a job at a weekly right out of college. You don't leave a reporting job to go to J-school. It would be like quitting a Broadway play to take acting lessons."

"See, you've already taught me something I didn't know."

"I'm willing to bet it will be the first and last time this evening."

I stirred the cream floating on top of my drink into the bloody tea underneath, and the resulting mixture was Creamsicle orange. Heaven. The waiter took our orders. I asked for Pad Thai, hold the shrimp. Will ordered a vegetable curry, medium hot, so we could share.

"So how is your story going?"

"What story?"

"The illustrious French-Canadians of Walden County."

"Oh, that." To tell the truth, I'd totally spaced on the cover story I'd given him for all my questions about Sebastien. "It's still in the early stages yet. I've got lots of interviews to set up."

"When do you expect it to run?"

"I'm not sure. There's no fixed date. Just whenever it gets done."

Awkward silence time. I whisked the straw around my drink and watched an orange nimbus swirl around the glass. When I looked up, Will was staring at me so intently, I thought he was about to tell me to stick out my tongue and say "ah."

"So," I said. "What's your major?"

"I suppose that's a lot of what passes for conversation in this town."

"At least during Freshman Week."

"So are you saying you're not much for small talk?"

"I tend to want to cut to the chase."

"What would you like to talk about?"

"Anything but physics."

"You mentioned before that you weren't much for science."

"That's an awfully polite way of putting it. I practically flunked chemistry. Thank God, Vassar had no science requirement, or it would have been the end of my college career."

"Maybe you just didn't have good teachers. I believe that anyone—any intelligent person—can learn science, if it's taught the right way."

"What's the right way?"

"Passionately. You have to look at the sciences as living things, constantly changing things, not just numbers and theories and formulas. Considering the excruciatingly dull way science is usually taught, it's a miracle more students aren't turned off the way you were. The foundation has just started a new grant program, giving small sums of money to creative teaching projects at public high schools. Hopefully, it will do some good."

"Do you give out all the awards yourself? Are you the one who decides who gets what?"

"Oh, Lord, no. There's a committee for that. I'm the president of the foundation, but it's really just an honorary title. The board of trustees runs everything. I'm their spokesman, more than anything else. I go to parties and shake hands with the money men, flout the Langston name so they feel like they've gotten something for their cash. Does that sound terribly crass?"

"Not if it does some good in the long run."

"It does. Last year, the foundation gave away more than twenty million dollars in grants for education, AIDS research, nuclear medicine research. Since that's my field, I actually do oversee the dispersal of those grants."

"What is nuclear medicine, anyway? I'm sorry to be so ignorant . . ."

"Not at all. I don't know much about German expressionist cinema."

"Neither do I."

"Do you want the complex technical explanation, or would you rather I keep it simple?"

"Very, very simple."

"I always start off by describing nuclear medicine as the ultimate use of nuclear technology for humanitarian purposes. In terms of actual medicinal applications, a very common example is positron emission topography."

"I thought you were going to keep this in English."

"I'm sorry. It's more commonly known as a PET scan.

You've heard of it? In a PET scan, the patient is injected with a low-level radioactive tracer, called a radionuclide, most often carbon-11, fluorine-18, or oxygen-15. The patient is placed in a chamber, rather like a man-sized tube, that's made up of many tiny radiation detectors. Now, I don't want to get too technical here. Suffice it to say that the instrument monitors the reactions of the photons and electrons in the radioactive agent, and from that we can paint a very accurate picture of the biochemical processes going on in the body. Do you follow?"

Was he kidding? "Did you decide to specialize in this because of your father?"

"You *don't* go for small talk, do you? But you're certainly not the first person to ask." He paused for a long drink of Thai beer. "I suppose the short answer would be yes. I always grew up knowing what a great man my father was. At least"—he smiled—"my mother always made sure I didn't forget. She was very faithful to his memory, never remarried. But when I got to college, I started to question it, to question everything. It was the sixties, after all. Perhaps you've heard of them?"

"I've seen pictures."

"My junior year at Yale, I started hanging out with the anti-war crowd. This was before the Vietnam War movement was at its height, but there were protests. I grew my hair long, got my ear pierced. I believe I even had some love beads."

"Are you for real?"

"My mother nearly died of shame. Luckily, it didn't last long. The trappings of that sort of lifestyle always seemed ridiculous to me. I'm a cotton-and-khaki man at heart. But what *was* important was the underlying philosophy. I realized that I didn't believe in what my father had been trying to do—or would have, if he'd lived. I didn't believe in the arms race, or even that dropping the bombs on Hiroshima and Nagasaki were morally defensible acts. For a while, I think I even hated my father—at least, I hated what he stood for. It took me a long time to come to terms with the fact that he lived in another time, and I might never understand what drove him."

The food came then, and I was afraid Will might not keep talking. But as soon as the waiter left, he picked up where he'd left off. "I always knew I wanted to go into medical research. After I got my degrees, I was offered a position at Benson. I had some qualms about coming back to where I'd grown up, especially since my father was such a legendary figure. I didn't want anyone to think I was trying to ride his coattails—masculine pride, and all that. But I knew I'd have more freedom here than anywhere else, and my wife always loved Gabriel. So we came. And when research into nuclear medicine began in earnest, I was one of the first to specialize in the field. It was like coming full circle—what my father and his colleagues created in anger and hatred, I could use to do some good for mankind." He drained his beer. "Good Lord, but that sounds pretentious. I didn't mean to give you the Sermon on the Mount."

"I'm interested."

"But I've been monopolizing the conversation. Why don't you tell me something about yourself?"

"If you don't mind, I like listening while I scarf my Pad Thai."

"I'm flattered. But you've essentially heard my life story."

"Do you have any children?"

"My wife and I wanted them, but we never quite got around to having any. We both worked so much, and all the traveling . . . She died a few years ago."

"I'm sorry."

"So am I. She was an amazing woman. A Vassar girl, actually, just like you. Class of '64. We met at Harvard Med."

"What was her name?"

"Laura. Laura Langston. She used to joke that it made her sound like one of Superman's girlfriends, but she took my name anyway. You might call it the dark days of patriarchy."

"I call it romantic."

"She was a pediatrician, and she had her own practice. But her real passion was the foundation. That's how she died. She was in Kenya visiting a clinic that wanted a grant. Her Jeep overturned." The silence lingered, and neither one of us felt like eating anymore. "So much for casual dinner conversation. I'm sorry."

"You already know I'm not much for talking about the weather."

"Perhaps we should change the subject. May I turn the tables and ask the story of your life?"

"If I can dish it out, I'd better be able to take it."

"Why aren't you married?"

"Ouch!"

"Fair is fair."

"Okay. I'm too young. And I haven't met the right chap. At least not the right man at the right time." I realized I was playing with my noodles, and put my fork down. "Oh, I don't know. Maybe I've just had bad luck. Dating men in their twenties is no picnic."

"How so?"

"They're obsessed with their careers; they're determined to be as successful as their fathers were even though it's a lousy economy; and they think they're going to live forever. They think they want strong women, but when they get one, they run like rabbits. How's that for a tirade?"

"You sound bitter."

"I am, a little. It seems like everything used to be simpler. Of *course* you got married. Everybody got married. Don't get me wrong; I'm glad I have choices. We've had it drilled into us all along that we can do everything as well as men, make as much money. But men don't have to worry about their biological clocks ticking all to hell."

"Are you involved with anyone? Or is that too personal?"

"Not anymore. I was. He . . . died recently."

"Ah . . . so you know what it's like. I'm sorry. That was probably an utterly inappropriate thing to say."

"No it's not. It's been hard. It was only a few weeks ago, actually. We weren't really a couple anymore, but we were still close."

"You don't have to talk about this. Would you like to get going?"

He called the waiter over and asked him to pack up our leftovers. He suggested coffee, and we walked to one of the outdoor cafés and had cappuccino and hazelnut biscotti dipped in chocolate. We chatted about movies and Gabriel politics, debating whether the city's raving socialist mayor was going to be unseated by a Republican restaurateur. He offered his jacket for my shoulders on the walk back to the car, and the conversation followed us up the hill until he pulled up in front of my house.

"Do you want me to walk you to the door?"

"This is hardly a high-crime neighborhood. But thank you for a great dinner. I really had a good time."

"I can't tell you how much I enjoyed myself. To be honest, I wasn't sure how much we'd have to talk about. But you're very easy to talk to."

"Are you back to the lab now?"

"I'm afraid so."

A slightly uncomfortable silence settled over the car.

My hand lingered on the car door and it took me a second
to realize I was waiting for him to kiss me good night.
And it took me quite a few more seconds to realize that I
actually wanted him to.

He turned toward me in his seat, constrained by the
seat belt.

"I'm old enough to be your father."

"I'm aware of that."

He leaned forward across the gearshift and pressed his
lips against mine, softly. I could have pulled back from it,
but I didn't. Without even knowing I'd done it, I touched
the side of his face lightly with my right hand, the hand I
could have sworn was still on the door handle. It was an
excellent first kiss, gentle and not too sloppy, and our
tongues only connected for a second. We said good night
with a surprising lack of discomfort and I got out of the car.

When I walked in the front door, Shakespeare ran down
the stairs to greet me. I wasn't tired, so I filled the tub with
hot water and peach bubbles and lay down against my in-
flatable bath pillow. The dog sat by the side of the tub and
licked the bubbles off my skin as I petted her, leaving
streaks of damp fur on her head and snout. I tried to read
The New Yorker but couldn't concentrate, and tossed the
damp magazine onto the closed cover of the john.

I lay back and closed my eyes. It was about twenty
minutes later when, pruning in the tepid water, it struck
me that Adam was no longer the last man I'd kissed, and
he never would be again. I'm not sure why the thought
made me cry, but it did, and the tears ran down my face
and between my breasts and into the water, where the
bubbles had all gone flat.

16

Before work Monday, I called the head of the Benson physics department. His secretary gave me the usual brush-off, until I dropped Will's name. It worked like magic—or maybe like physics, which as far as I can tell is the same thing. She transferred me to her boss, and I gave him my song and dance about wanting to exalt the glory of Walden County's French-Canadians, yadda, yadda. I was starting to think it wouldn't make that bad a feature package after all.

"Oh, yes, Miss Bernier," he said. "Will Langston sent me an E-mail about you over the weekend. He asked me to see what I could dig up on Professor Sebastien's tenure with the department. I'm not sure if I can be of much help. I had my secretary look through the old personnel files, but we couldn't find anything going back that far."

"There aren't any old payroll files or anything? I was hoping to find someone who might have worked with him."

"Payroll? I'd have no idea about that. Back then, that would have been handled out of the Arts and Sciences business office in Lloyd Hall."

"Lloyd Hall? Where's that? I've never heard of it."

"That's because it doesn't exist anymore. It was torn down years ago, to make room for a new law building, I think."

"So where would the files have gone?"

"I couldn't tell you. You might try the university archivist." He gave me the phone number.

"So there isn't anyone on the faculty who was around back then? Dr. Langston said there might be a professor emeritus or something."

"Emeritus . . . Emeritus . . . Let me think. There is one, but I'm not sure if he'd be much help. He retired quite some time ago, and I don't think his memory's very good."

"I'll give it a try."

"His name's Singer. Dr. Henry Singer. I believe he lives in Liberty Towers now. Do you know where that is?"

Liberty Towers is an old-age development, four twenty-story buildings on the outskirts of the city. It's the kind of place where you have your own little apartment, but there's also a staff to look after you in case you need some help getting dressed, or think Truman is still in the White House. I've done various feature stories there over the years, the most recent one on a "sister-senior" partnership, which pairs up sorority girls with old ladies for some wild nights of quilting and chugging kegs of prune juice.

I left a message on the university archivist's voice mail and decided to drop by Liberty Towers on my lunch hour. According to the directory, Singer lived in Building Four,

distinguished from the others by a man-sized green nu-
meral painted on the cinder blocks over the entrance. I
walked in through the glass double doors and heard the
dish-clatter of the lunch crowd off to my left. Through
another set of doors, and I was in the main dining room.
The walls were decorated with works of art—I use the
term generously—that looked to be made out of colored
yarn wrapped around a wooden frame in diamond patterns, like you used to make in arts and crafts at camp. Elderly folks were clustered in tables of eight, eating and
talking. As retirement homes go, I guess it's pretty nice.
But ending up there is still horrifying to me; there's
something so desperate about this last gasp of privacy before you vegetate your way to the nursing home, where
they stack you three to a room like cordwood.

Two women about my age, wearing white uniforms
with cobalt-blue aprons, strolled around the dining room,
chatting with the residents and, I thought, making sure
they got enough to eat. I stopped one of them to ask
where I could find Dr. Singer, and she told me he was eating in his room.

"He's not doing so well today," she said, pushing her
permed hair behind her ears. "He has his days, and he has
his days. Sometimes he's pretty good, but he's been
pretty out of it lately."

"Out of it?"

"You know, senile." She rolled her eyes. "Sometimes
he thinks I'm his daughter. He thinks we're *all* his daughter. He's a nice old guy, though."

"Would it be all right if I went up and knocked on his
door?"

"Sure. Good luck getting out of there, though. Once he
gets going on about something, he really gets going." Her
index finger orbited her ear in the universal sign for "nut-

case." "He's on sixteen—1609, I think. All the names are on the doors."

I took the elevator up to the sixteenth floor, found the right apartment, and knocked. A voice called me to come in, and I opened the door on an elderly man sitting in a BarcaLounger with a TV tray in front of him. Despite the heat, he had on a brown cardigan over a tan shirt with faint blue pinstripes, faded gray corduroys, and slippers: the official old-man uniform. He was eating macaroni and cheese and a fruit cup topped with maraschino cherries that probably glowed in the dark.

"How are you today, Dr. Singer? Is it okay if I come in?"

He waved me in, smiling broadly. "Come in, come in. Have a seat." He indicated a plaid sofa next to his chair.

"Thank you." I sat down and upped the wattage on my smile. "Dr. Singer, I'm a reporter with the *Gabriel Monitor*. I was hoping to ask you some questions about . . ."

"Oh, by all means, by all means. Now tell me, dear, how was school today?"

"School?"

"Is that Johnny Kellerman still bothering you? Now, Margaret, you know little boys only pick on the girls they really like. I gave your mother a devil of a time . . ." He chuckled softly to himself. The girl downstairs was right; Singer was a nice old guy. He was also crackers.

"Uh, Dr. Singer . . ." I decided to go for the gusto. "I mean, uh, Dad . . ."

"Are you hungry? Would you like some fruit cup? Here, have some fruit cup."

"Er, uh, no thank you."

"But it's your favorite. You love fruit cup." He was holding the bowl across to me and his hand was shaking, and I was afraid the beloved fruit cup was going to land on the linoleum floor. I took the fruit cup and the spoon that followed it, and gagged down a couple of maraschino cherries and a piece of what I guessed was a pear. They both tasted exactly the same, like a tin can.

"Um," I said, trying to make a convincing yummy sound.

"There's a good girl," he said, smiling beatifically and tucking into his macaroni and cheese. Well, if nothing else, at least I was making the old guy happy. I hope some nice young reporter stumbles into my place when I'm eighty-five and senile and eating canned fruit cup all by myself.

"Uh, Dad, I was hoping you might want to talk about teaching at Benson." I made a shameless stab in the dark. "Remember when you used to tell us all about teaching at Benson?"

"I was a full professor." He seemed to sit a bit taller in his chair. "I was the Paul T. VanCampen Professor of Physics," he said, as if every syllable still gave him pleasure.

"That must have been a very important job," I said. "You must have worked with lots of very important people."

"Oh, yes. Yes, of course. People from all over the world came to study with us."

"Do you remember a man who worked with you, named André Sebastien? He taught physics?"

He seemed to search his memory for the name. Either the memory itself, or his inability to access it, upset him. He leaned an elbow on the arm of the easy chair and buried his face in his hand.

"Sebastien, Sebastien, Sebastien . . ." He looked stricken now. "Can't say as I do. Sebastien, Sebastien . . ."

"What about a Dr. Seth Adelson?" He shook his head apologetically, and the fissures in his skin deepened even farther as he knit his brows. "Or Dr. William Langston?"

"Dr. Langston. Oh, of course. But you mustn't bother him, dear. He's a very busy man." I wasn't sure if he was talking about Langston Junior—Will—or if he was living so far in the past, Langston Senior was still alive.

"Oh, don't worry. I won't bother him."

His face lit up suddenly. "But I could show you a picture! Would you like to see a picture, dear?"

He started to get up, and I moved the TV tray out of his way. He was bent over, but still seemed in fairly good shape as he shuffled across the room to a hutch covered with china cups and saucers. He pulled open a long drawer and drew out a box. He shuffled back, laid it on the laminated coffee table, and lifted the lid, covered in faded Santas. I tried to curb my impatience as he shuffled through a lifetime of keepsakes. After about five minutes, he pulled out an eight-by-ten photograph, black and white, and held it out to me.

There were a few dozen people in the picture, gathered for a group photo. Some of them wore shorts, while a number of middle-aged white guys had on shirts, dark ties, and long pants. Some had beer bottles in their hands, and everyone seemed to be having a good time. Underneath was written, "Benson Physics Department Picnic, Summer, 1944." I turned the picture over. Jackpot. Someone— presumably, Singer—had been anal enough to record the names of everyone in the photo, just like my dad used to do when I brought my class picture home from school.

"If I promise to bring it back, can I take this with me?"

"Of course, dear, of course. I wonder what's keeping your mother . . ."

I stayed for another hour, out of guilt or kindness or blind gratitude. I brewed us some tea, and Singer made me eat three Pecan Sandies, and he complained about how badly the Brooklyn Dodgers had been playing lately.

Finally, the permed girl from downstairs showed up to bring him to his chair-caning class (does anyone under the age of eighty cane chairs?) and I walked out into the sunshine with the photo in my hand.

Idling in neutral, I laid the photo against the sheepskin-covered steering wheel and read through the names on the back, recorded with blue pen in meticulous Catholic-school handwriting. Langston was there, with his wife, and there was Will, just a toddler on the grass in front of them. I stared at the tousle-haired little boy and thought, I've kissed this kid on the lips. *Weird.* I found Adelson and his wife, who looked very forties with a kerchief in her styled hair. In the same row, a few people off to the left, was André Sebastien. He had his arm around the girl next to him, and since he was looking at her instead of the camera, he was shot in profile. If the picture hadn't been labeled, I wouldn't have recognized him. But his companion was looking straight ahead; it was the same woman from the waterfall, the one who looked like Katharine Hepburn. I turned the picture over: Miss Betty Barrows.

I studied the rest of the faces and read through all the names on the back, but I didn't recognize anyone else, except for Singer and his family. I drove back to the newspaper and parked in the circulation row, which you're not supposed to do, because all the reporter's spots were taken. I found Gordon eating at his desk yet again. He left his burrito and followed me into the library, where I showed him the photograph.

"How the hell did you get your hands on this?" I was tempted to make up some valiant tale of journalistic agility, but wound up admitting that it had basically tumbled down from the heavens. He whistled. "Sometimes, you get lucky." He copied all the names from the back of the picture, and we agreed to split them three ways and see what we could dig up. Mad and I each got eight names, with nine for Gordon. We left off the children, the three scientists, and Singer; I doubted he was going to be any more help, unless we wanted Mickey Mantle's batting stats. I gave Mad his list when he got back from his midday run, and the three of us agreed to rendezvous at the Citizen Kane at nine.

I sat down at my desk and studied my list: Mrs. Rosalyn Adelson, Dr. Seth Adelson's widow. Mr. and Mrs. Yitzhak Dershowitz. Miss Marion Hazel. Prof. James Catalano. Michael Gibson. Prof. Stephen Landesman. And last, but definitely not least, Miss Betty Barrows. I'd held on to her for myself, hoping more and more that I was right about her being Adam's mystery caller. I decided to start in the most obvious place, and opened my trusty Walden County phone book. None of the names popped out at me, though there were three Dershowitzes, plenty of Gibsons, and one Adelson. I found a Barrow, but no Barrows with an "s." No Hazels, and no Landesmans.

I decided to call all the similar names I'd found in the phone book, just as a long shot. Since I could hardly do it from the *Monitor* newsroom, I figured I'd wait until after work that night, when people were more likely to be home anyway. I flipped through the Benson faculty directory and found nothing. What were the odds of looking up people who'd been on campus fifty years ago? I don't even know what my own parents were up to back then. I got up and wandered around the newsroom, between the closely packed desks that would give the fire marshal night sweats, if we didn't rearrange the furniture before the safety inspection every year.

My phone rang, and I went rushing back to my desk. It was Will Langston. "I was wondering if you might be free Wednesday night," he said. "I know it's short notice . . ."

Watch it, Bernier. You're on the rebound, big time. Say no. Say you're busy. Say you have to go watch Sylvester Stallone kill people, or wash your hair, *anything*. "What's happening Wednesday?"

"The foundation is hosting a reception for some major donors, followed by dinner at the faculty club. I was hoping you might like to go as my guest."

"I'd like that." Who said that?

"After dinner, I have to host a presentation on our latest projects. Essentially, that means two hours of speeches during which we hope our benefactors will get drunk enough to write some checks. But you're welcome to skip that; I could run you home."

"Two hours of physics? To avoid that, I'd be willing to walk home. But let me see how I feel."

"May I pick you up at five? Is that too early? What with the cocktail hour . . ."

"No, five is fine. I can get out of here early if I need to."

"Then I'll look forward to Wednesday."

"Me too."

We hung up and I whacked myself on the head with the receiver. What was I doing? Was I just trying to do anything, anything at all to fill up the hole Adam left? Or was there something about Will that really attracted me, despite the age difference, despite the lousy timing, despite the fact that his family history might have something to do with Adam's death? I barely knew him. He seemed hunky and trustworthy and slightly creepy all at the same time. The only thing I knew for a fact was that he was an above-average kisser. Should I give up all this investigative stuff and go find myself a good shrink?

17

Every Monday afternoon, the *Monitor* reporting staff gets together for a budget meeting, which has nothing to do with finance. A "budget" is the list of stories the reporters are working on, organized by the day they're slated to run in the paper. The weekly meetings are held in Bill's office, and since there's no way to squeeze eight chairs in there, a couple of us get stuck sitting on the radiator, having warm air blown up our backsides in the summer, freezing cold air in the winter. The budget meetings are supposed to be when Bill assigns the stories for the following week, but we generally spend the hour trying to talk him into letting us do stuff we're actually interested in.

Either budget meetings are the same in newsrooms around the globe, or Gordon just comes by his talent naturally, because at his very first one at the *Monitor* he managed to side-step a week's worth of ride-alongs with the new "community policing" officers.

"That sounds really interesting," he said, ignoring the

fist Mad was grinding into his snout in the universal symbol for "brown noser." "But I thought I might jump into this gay-bashing story Alex has been working on. If you don't mind, Alex?"

"Well, I . . ."

"From the cop angle, of course. Wasn't that Adam's story anyway? I was thinking of trying to talk to the two fraternity brothers, the ones who were charged in the initial attack." He glanced down at his notebook. "Trevor Hoffman and James Caruso."

"Good luck," I snorted. "They're not what you'd call eager to talk to the press."

"I'd still like to give it a whirl. Maybe they'll respond to a fresh face, someone who wasn't around when it all hit the fan. They might want to tell their sides of the story."

I expected Bill to retaliate by sticking Gordon with covering the Mohawk Strawberry Festival, but no; he went for it.

"See what you can dig up," Bill said. "Alex, make sure he's got all the clips."

I walked into the Citizen Kane at five after nine that night and found Mad and Gordon sharing a pitcher of Labatt's at a back table.

"Jesus, you guys drink that much already?" I said, indicating the two inches of beer at the bottom of the pitcher.

"Sweetness, you don't really think this is the *first* pitcher of the evening, do you?" Mad countered. I slid onto the bench next to Gordon, who's a good six inches shorter than Mad and not half as broad.

"Goodness, Gordon," I said, "you've decided to take time out from kissing Bill's butt to meet with us? How nice of you."

"You know, if you'd dig out some tough assignments for yourself, you might actually get out of this shithole one of these days. Besides, I'd rather get a million doors slammed in my face than ride around with some fucking dogcatcher all week."

"Did you take some time out from your search for truth, justice, and the American way to make some calls about this thing we're supposed to be working on?"

"I wasn't just kissing ass. I'm really interested in the story. And besides which, we know the B-GLAD case may have something to do with what happened to Adam. What the hell is wrong with you?"

"Okay, I'm sorry. Maybe I'm just being defensive. It was Adam's story, and if he couldn't get an interview with the frat guys, I guess I'd like to think nobody can. Let's just forget about it. Deal?"

"Deal."

"So, what did you guys come up with? I've got a great big zero."

"You didn't find anything either?" Mad asked.

"Nothing useful. I found out everybody's dead—at least, everybody I could dig up."

"That's better than nothing," Gordon said. "Look at it this way: There's some truth to be found out about all these people. Either they're dead, and useless to us, or they're alive out there somewhere, and we need to find them. So if you found out for sure they're dead, that's progress."

"I guess you're right," I said. "What if we each go through our lists, and go over what we found? Okay. Here we go. Mrs. Rosalyn Adelson, who was married to Dr. Seth Adelson, who died in the plane crash."

"Allegedly died in the plane crash," Gordon corrected.

"Right. I found a separate bio file on her. She died in Florida in the mid-seventies. The *Monitor* did a news obit on her, widow of hero scientist and all that. So she's been out of the picture for a while. Mr. and Mrs. Yitzhak Dershowitz and family. From what he's wearing in the picture it looks like he was a janitor or grounds worker. I called every Dershowitz in the phone book, but none of them were related, so I need to keep looking. I found Marion Hazel in the cross-reference file down in the basement. Whoever did the filing back then was incredibly efficient, not like that space cadet we've got now. Anyway, she died in a house fire back in 1945. I found the story in the morgue.

"Professors James Catalano and Stephen Landesman I got by calling a friend at the alumni mag. They both retired over twenty years ago, and they're both dead now. According to the Benson alumni directory, Michael Gibson got his PhD in 1947. He must have gotten a teaching job somewhere else, because my friend couldn't find him in the directory of past faculty. And as for Miss Betty Barrows . . . Nothing. Zip. I even called somebody named 'Barrow' in the phone book, in case it was a typo or something, but no cigar."

Mad and Gordon had similar results. It seemed that just about everyone in the picnic photo was either dead or incommunicado. Mad was in the middle of reading through his list when Gordon interrupted him. "Wait. Go back to the last one."

"Peter Murphy, janitor, died in a car accident, 1945."

"When in 1945?"

"January 28. The story said early in the morning, just after midnight."

"Unbelievable!" Gordon looked like he was about to spontaneously combust.

"What is it?" I prompted.

"Alex, when did what's-her-name die in the house fire?"

"Who? Marion Hazel?" I looked through my own notes. "January 27, 1945."

"And when was the plane crash?"

"The *alleged* plane crash," Mad interjected, starting to look fairly delirious himself. "The alleged plane crash was January 27. Holy *shit*."

"Do you realize what this means?" Gordon asked. "This means five people in that picture, five people from the Benson physics department, died within a day of each other. *One day*. What are the odds of that?"

"You think these are connected? All five of them?" I asked. "I need a drink." I took two steps over to the bar and asked Mack for a gin and tonic, which he made just the way I like it: really weak, with two limes. He caught me eyeing his pack of Chesterfields behind the bar and offered me one, but I managed to turn it down. Self-control is very unsatisfying sometimes. I carried my drink back to the table.

"I'm trying to make some sense out of this," said Gordon, who'd been crafting some kind of diagram in his notebook while I was up at the bar. "Look at it logically. Either these people died back in 1945, or they didn't. Now, we're fairly sure Sebastien, or Lecuyer, was alive until very recently. So I've got to wonder whether any of the others are still around, despite the evidence to the contrary."

"You mean, reports of their deaths were highly exaggerated?" Mad offered.

"Something like that. How old was this Murphy guy?"

"Forty-six," Mad answered.

"Hmm. Not likely, then. He'd be nearly a hundred. What about Marion Hazel?"

I handled that one. "Thirty-one."

Gordon raised an eyebrow. "Could still be around. What did she do in the physics department?"

"The obit said 'research assistant,' whatever that meant back then."

"Something else just occurred to me," Gordon said. "What if *she's* the one who called Adam, rather than the other one—Betty Barrows?"

"You may be right," I said, feeling exhausted and resting my head in my hands. "I just don't know. So you think we should be looking for her, too?"

"Listen," Mad said. "This may be premature. But does anybody else think we should be talking about who we think did this?"

I turned toward Mad with my chin still stapled to my palms. "You mean, like, a list of suspects?"

"Yeah, for lack of a less melodramatic way of putting it, a list of suspects."

Gordon took off his glasses and wiped them with his shirttail. "Usually, I like to do as much research as possible before forming any theories. But I see your point—this is overwhelming, from a research point of view. We could go off in any one of a half-dozen directions."

I perked up a little. "So we go back to question number one: Who killed Adam? I mean, that's the point of all this, isn't it? Somebody's out there—somebody who pushed Adam off that bridge, somebody who did the same thing to René Lecuyer."

"But who says it's necessarily the same person?" Mad interjected.

"You're right," I said. "We may be talking about more than one person, either working together or separately."

"Okay," Gordon said, scrolling to an empty page in his notebook. "Whodunit? Fire away." The three of us sat there staring at each other. "Come on," Gordon prodded. "Don't get caught up in trying to prove anything. Who do we know that's connected to this, who might possibly have had a reason to commit murder?"

"Who had both motive and opportunity?" I said. "It's like something out of an Agatha Christie book. Only this time, I think truth is stranger than fiction. Do you know the difference between a classic drawing-room mystery and a police procedural?"

"Come on, Bernier, you know I don't read that crap," Mad said. Gordon, slightly more polite, just shook his head.

"Listen up for a minute. This is just an analogy. In a drawing-room mystery, you have a finite number of suspects. The classic examples are by Agatha Christie, Ngaio Marsh, Ellery Queen. At the end the great detective gets all the suspects together and says, 'J'accuse!'"

"What's your point?" Mad interrupted.

"Listen. In a police procedural, on the other hand, the cops are looking for a killer. He's somewhere out there. But when you finally find out who it is, at the end of the book, it's usually not someone you've ever met before. It's some guy out there in the shadows, who they hunt down bit by bit."

"Once again, I ask you, why the fiction lesson?"

"Hold on," Gordon said. "I think I see her point. You're wondering which we're dealing with."

"Right," I said. "Look at it this way, Mad. Either whoever did this is someone we've heard of, in which case we can make a list of suspects and he'll be on it somewhere, or it's someone we don't know about yet. It's just two separate ways of looking at things. My point is, if we're dealing with someone unknown, we can make all the lists we want and it won't do us any good."

"You're right," Gordon said. "And I agree with you that whoever did this is probably someone we haven't even heard of. But it can't hurt to talk about it."

"That's my favorite block of the news pyramid," Mad said. "'Speculate wildly.'"

We laid our notes out on the table and shuffled through them.

"There's those two women, the ones we think might still be alive," I said. "Betty Barrows and Marion Hazel."

"You seriously think Adam was pushed off a bridge by a seventy-year-old woman?" Mad said.

"Don't be such a goddamn sexist. If he was taken by surprise, knocked off balance, it could happen. I thought we weren't supposed to rule anything out."

"Fine. But I'd rather concentrate on people who aren't collecting social security," Mad said.

"You know who I can't stand?" I said. "Stewart Day. I'd love to pin this whole thing on that little weasel."

"Do we have any reason to think he's involved?" Gordon asked.

"Well, no, nothing concrete," I admitted. "But there's something about him I just don't trust."

"You just can't stand his type," Mad said. "He's a preppy prick, buttoned down to his butt."

"That's not it. I don't know. I always thought there was something totally fake about him."

"You mean, besides the fact that he's an Ivy League flack who lies for a living?" Gordon asked.

"He's connected to the university," I said. "And he's definitely got a nasty side under all those smarmy manners." The whole argument was starting to sound lame, even to me.

"Yeah," Mad said. "So's two-thirds of this town. Should we put the whole phone book on the list?"

"Forget it. Let me see . . . Who else have I talked to? What about the head of the Benson physics department? What's his name?"

"John Sydenstricker."

"What do you know about him?"

"He's Benson's resident string theorist. Smart son of a bitch too."

"String theory? What the hell is that?"

"It's a new concept about the fundamental nature of matter. It theorizes that the smallest element of matter, even smaller than the proton and the neutron, is something they call a string. It's. . ."

"Can we cut to the chase?"

"You have no idea how fascinating this stuff is. It's really on the cutting edge of physics. There are only a handful of people out there working on it, and Sydenstricker is one of them. Essentially, the theory states that . . ."

"Mad . . ."

"Suffice it to say that it's so new, a lot of the physics establishment thinks it's a loopy bunch of crap."

"And the man himself?"

"Oh, yeah. Sydenstricker grew up in New York, went to Bronx Science, won a Westinghouse and I think a Fulbright, or maybe it was some kind of genius grant, I can't remember. Undergrad at MIT, got his PhD from Stanford in about five minutes."

"So, what do you think? Is this a guy we should be looking at?"

"You mean, does he strike me as a psychopathic homicidal maniac? How the hell do I know? The man's got tenure, he can do whatever he wants."

"Do we know where he was the night Adam died?"

"Interesting you should ask. I looked this up. The weekend Adam died, practically the entire Benson physics department was at a big conference in Chicago. I know because I did a local sidebar to go with the wire stories and threw some of it in my Benson tech column."

"So he was out of town?"

"Nope. He was the only Benson physicist of any note that *didn't* go to the conference."

"Why not?"

"I have no idea."

"Find out."

"You're really good at all this bossing around, Bernier. Ever thought about being an editor?"

"You don't have to get nasty."

"What about your friend Langston?" Gordon interjected. "I mean, after all, it was his father who supposedly died with Sebastien."

"I don't know. I like him. He's way more interesting than he has any right to be."

"He was at the same conference in Chicago," Mad said, "so I guess he's off the hook."

"Nobody's off the hook, Mad. Nobody."

"Are you seriously telling me you suspect Langston? Man, what a story that'd be. 'Nobel Nominee Whacks Reporter.' I'd live to cover that one."

"It's not funny. And no, I don't seriously suspect him. But there's something about him I just don't get. And I thought we weren't supposed to be in the business of believing everything everybody says."

"What do you know?" Gordon said. "Our little girl is growing up to be a real reporter."

"Alex, where did you find this asshole?"

"Same place I found you. He just sort of crawled up on the rocks."

"Okay, sorry," Gordon said. "Back to business. Did Adam have any enemies that you know of?"

"What are you talking about?" I said.

"I don't know. Isn't that something you're supposed to ask? What about other reporters, somebody who might have been working on the same story?"

"Come on, Gordon, would you kill to break a story? Wait. Don't answer that."

"You probably don't want to hear this," Gordon said, "but we're leaving out a whole other group of people. The *Gabriel Monitor* newsroom."

We stared at him until Mad finally broke the silence. "Fuck you, Gordon."

"Don't get so goddamn defensive. Can you possibly say that you know everyone you work with so well, you'd bet your life that they didn't do this? Your friend Adam bet his life, and he lost."

"I can't deal with this," I said. "We can't start suspecting all our friends, start wondering who's got some dark side we don't even know about. Can't we just call that Plan B?"

"Alex, if you're going to call yourself a journalist, you're going to have to pull your head out of the sand and investigate all the possibilities. And aren't you the one who just said nobody's off the hook?"

"Gordon, man, leave her alone."

"It's okay, Mad," I said, half-afraid he was going to cold-cock Gordon in an excess of chivalry. "He's got a point. We can't rule anybody out. But before we go suspecting all our friends, maybe we should have this picture blown up, so we can get a better look at everybody."

"Why?" Gordon asked. "Does somebody look familiar to you?"

"Maybe. I don't know. Everyone's so small, they all sort of look the same. But for a second I thought . . ." I caught sight of Charlotte and Marshall coming toward us.

"Hey, *what* are y'all doin' back here?" Charlotte asked. "Why are y'all hidin' in the corner?"

"There was somebody in the window when we got here," Mad lied.

"Well, there's no one there now," Marshall said. "Y'all care to move?"

We packed up our notes and moved to the window seat. Charlotte sent her husband to the bar—"Fetch me a Tom Collins, sugah"—and sat next to me. "You poor thing." She patted my cheek. "Oh, Alex, you poor darlin', you look like something the cat dragged in."

"Gee, thanks, Charlotte. Thanks a lot."

"Now, don't take offense, sweetie pie. I'm just sayin' you look like you've got the weight of the world. Don't you think you should take a vacation or somethin'? I mean, it's hardly been two weeks since . . ."

"I know. I think I'll feel better if I keep working. It's nice of you to worry about me, though."

"We girls have got to stick together, honey. That's what my momma always told me." Charlotte is a riot. I'm willing to bet she's a lot less Southern when she's actually down South. Up here, playing the belle is what sets her apart.

Before long, O'Shaunessey walked by the window, spotted us, and detoured inside. The bunch of us stayed at the Citizen Kane until after midnight, and I most unwisely imbibed another pair of gin and tonics. Marshall and Charlotte ended up having to drive me home, and I rolled into bed without even taking out my contact lenses. I woke up at two A.M. with my eyes glued shut, excavated my contacts, and tried to go back to sleep, but I couldn't. I just lay there with the ceiling fan whipping around over my head, imagining Shakespeare's fleas crawling around inside my sheets.

Goddamn Gordon. What he'd said that night wouldn't get out of my head. Could someone from the *Monitor* be involved? I went through the cast of characters, one by one. O'Shaunessey, the very picture of the jolly Irishman. Bill, who worked too much to possibly have time to do anything sinister. Melissa—well, that was just plain ridiculous. Marshall, whom I'd always thought of as the quintessential Southern gentleman. Wendell, the photo editor, who'd be too busy chanting his Buddhist mantras to kill anybody. Marilyn, the managing editor—granted, the woman has a black belt in tae kwon do, but Adam was always one of her favorite newsroom weirdos. Jimmy, the obese wire editor, who's been at the paper since before the Korean War. Benjamin, the features editor, who wears red suspenders and walks around with a pipe clenched in his teeth quoting *A Shropshire Lad*. The sportswriters, both recent Benson grads whom I barely know, but who seem like nice guys and couldn't give a rat's ass about what happens over on the cityside of the paper. Mad . . .

I tried to picture any of them luring Adam to his death, pushing him off the bridge when his back was turned. I'm not sure when I fell asleep, but the next thing I knew I was dreaming we were all marching out of the newsroom and down the stairs, across the Green and up the hill to the bridge. We jumped off one by one, and when it was my turn I sprang off the cold rail and felt myself falling. Unlike Adam, I never hit the ground.

18

I WOKE UP WITH A NASTY HANGOVER TUESDAY MORNING, having gotten all of four hours of sleep. I had to drag myself out of bed and into the shower, where I nearly threw up from the smell of my Body Shop tangerine-and-beer shampoo. I slimed into work forty-five minutes late, but Bill was still cutting me a certain amount of slack. I felt guilty enough to make a halfhearted effort at cleaning off my desk, which as usual was frosted with notebooks and press releases. It was then that I came across a note I'd written to myself right after Adam died. "Check out clearing." I'd been so preoccupied with everything else, pretty much just treading water at work, I'd forgotten about it.

But it *was* curious. After the war, when Benson had been besieged by veterans studying on the G.I. Bill, the university boomed. Dorms and classrooms went up overnight, and the number of campus buildings more than doubled. Benson's land mass stretched out to both gorges and beyond—but the grassy spot where Tony Cerutti and his boyfriend were attacked stayed fallow. The university didn't seem in any hurry to give in to B-GLAD and build a living center on the land—not that that was much of a surprise. But I still wondered why nothing had ever been built there before. Maybe it had been endowed as a park by some alum. But if that were the case, the university would have just slapped a plaque on the ground and gotten B-GLAD off its back.

I gave up on the cleaning project and went down to the morgue, where I looked up the Benson University files. Benson has always been big news around here, and the stories took up three whole filing cabinets. I hunted until I found a series of folders labeled "construction" and "buildings" and waded through dozens of lame stories about new dormitories and classrooms—endless shots of white guys in front of halls whose ivy hadn't had a chance to sprout.

Then I found something. It was a story labeled "New All-Women's Dorm Planned," and what struck me was the small clipping stapled to it: "Planned Dorm to Be Relocated." I flipped back to the first story and read more carefully. Elizabeth P. Gillman House, which is on north campus, was apparently originally planned for central campus. "To the west of the chemistry building," said the story, from the mid-fifties. Unless I had my directions turned around, that's where the clearing was.

I looked through the rest of the files, and found one other, similar story. It was from the early seventies, and talked about plans for a student activity center. As far as I could tell, it was supposed to go on the same spot. The story ran with a picture of a girl in a cropped T-shirt and cut off shorts, carrying a sign that said, "Our lives, our center, ourselves." *The more things change* . . . There was another story following it, showing jubilant students at the building's dedication. But the photo showed the center not where it was first planned, but where it was eventually built and still stands, at the edge of North Creek Gorge.

"Alex? Are you down here?" Gordon said. "Christ, I hate this place."

"Wait until you see what I found."

"Wait until *you* see what *I* found. That's what I came down here to the fifth circle of hell to tell you."

"What's going on?"

"I think—I'm pretty sure—that I found that dead janitor's grandson."

"Peter Murphy's grandson? Gordon, you are incredible. How did you do it?"

"Elementary, my dear Alex. His obit said he left a wife and son. The son's name was Sean. Now, I figured that since Murphy was forty-six when he died, the son was probably in his teens or mid-twenties. Anyway, I went down to the County Clerk's office to look through the birth and death records . . ."

"They just let you riffle through their stuff? Those chicks *hate* reporters."

"You have no idea how far a friendly smile and a box of Pecan Delights will get you. So like I was saying, I found a birth certificate for a Peter Murphy, who was born in 1961, and the father was listed as Sean Murphy. I guess Sean named his son after his own father, which makes sense. Now, here I thought we were screwed, because how many Peter Murphys are there going to be in the State of New York? And that's assuming he's still going to be in the state. But then I noticed his middle name: Kozlowski, which was his mother's maiden name, and quite unusual, thank God. Then it was just a matter of calling a guy at the DMV who owes me a favor. Peter

K. Murphy"—he waved a piece of paper triumphantly—
"lives at 593 East 86th St. in that goddess of all cities,
New York, New York."

"Gordon, this isn't just some big lie you're telling me
so you have an excuse to go to Manhattan, is it?"

"I'll admit, I'm glad the guy doesn't live in Buffalo. So
let's go. There's this great bar I want to show you in the
Village."

"What village would that be?"

"Greenwich Village, you little hayseed. Only the
hippest place on the planet."

"I know. I was just being difficult."

"Cute. So what did you find out yourself?"

I showed him the files I'd been sifting through. "Now,
I'm not sure what this has to do with anything. But doesn't
it strike you as a little weird? Three times, there have
been plans or proposals to build on that clearing, the
largest undeveloped piece of land on central campus.
Twice, those plans have been canceled, for no good reason that I can find. And now that B-GLAD has its knick-
ers in a twist about building there, the administration
seems totally unwilling to even consider it."

"What if it's—I don't know—the groundwater or
something?"

"Then why don't they just say that and get it over
with?"

He scratched his head for a bit. "I still don't understand
how this ties in to the rest of it."

"Neither do I. But there had to be some reason Adam
was copying all my stories about B-GLAD and the living
center. It has to be connected somehow."

"Curiouser and curiouser. So when are we going to
New York?"

"Couldn't we just call the guy?"

"Perish the thought. We can't risk something this important to a mere phone interview. I think it definitely calls for the personal touch."

"You are just salivating to go down there and get mugged, aren't you?"

"Alex, at this point, getting mugged would be the closest thing I've had to getting laid in I don't know how long."

"Oh, that's right—you've got a girlfriend down there, don't you?"

"Andrea. She lives in Chelsea. We could both crash there for the weekend."

"In her one-bedroom apartment?"

"Studio."

"Thanks just the same. I'll call my friend at Columbia and see if I can stay with her."

"Do you realize that's almost in Harlem?"

"That's still safer than listening to you screw all weekend. But what about your magnum opus with the frat boys? I thought you were going to scoop us all and get them to pour their homophobic hearts out."

"Not to worry, princess. I've got it covered."

"Is this for real, or are you just mouthing off?"

"Me? Mouth off? No, ma'am. After you dragged your semi-inebriated little butt home last night, I went down to the frat house to commune with the brothers."

"Gordon, do *not* tell me you were in a fraternity in college. You're hardly the type. And besides, I refuse to believe any of them would have you."

"Hell no. But my worthless younger brother belonged to one at Dartmouth which, according to legend, inspired the movie *Animal House*. I visited him there once, and from what I can remember, it was the worst weekend of my life. However, it did allow me to observe the beasts in their native habitat."

"You mean you . . ."

"Passed myself off as one of their own. I talked the talk, I walked the walk, and without having to exactly *lie*, convinced them I was some long-lost brother from the St. Lawrence chapter."

"Gordon, do you even know where St. Lawrence University *is*?"

"Somewhere north of Westchester, I assume."

"Farther north than you ever want to be, believe me."

"Alex, *this* is farther north than I ever want to be."

"So what did you find out?"

"Not as much as I would have liked. I had a hard time steering the conversation around to Hoffman and Caruso without tipping them off. But after I did enough Jaegermeister shots to prove my manhood, I did manage to find out that Caruso is working in some pizza joint in Poughkeepsie."

"Poughkeepsie?"

"Yeah. I guess his parents were angry enough about his little escapade to ship him off to an uncle and make him work for a living—at least until sonny boy gets convicted for assault and sent to Ossining."

"Gordon, this kid is about to go on trial for a felony. There's no way he's going to talk to you."

"Just leave it to the master."

"And his ego."

"So here's the plan. On our way down to the city, we stop off in Poughkeepsie for a snack, and have a little talk with our friend the gay-basher."

"Stop off? Do you realize Poughkeepsie is, like, three hours out of our way?"

"Upstate New York is way bigger than I ever imagined,

I'll grant you. But Poughkeepsie's where my boy Caruso is stashed, and Poughkeepsie's where we're going."

"Oh, Christ, no. Anywhere but there. I went to *college* in Poughkeepsie. Gordon, *please*. Can't you just go by yourself next week or something?"

"Come on, it'll be fun. Think of it as an early reunion. Where's your school spirit, Vassar girl?"

"Gordon, listen very carefully. I did not like college. I did not like *myself* when I was in college. I was fat and clueless and obnoxious and generally a complete and total fool. I wouldn't go to a reunion if Brad Pitt delivered the keynote speech in his boxer shorts. And I have spent enough time in the hellhole of Poughkeepsie to last me the rest of my life."

"Perfect. Then you know your way around."

"I was afraid you were going to say that."

Will took me to the awards dinner on Wednesday night, and I was having such a good time I didn't even leave before the god-awful science speeches. I regretted it an hour later, though, when I'd heard plenty about experimental models and lit reviews and who knows what else. I stopped paying attention, and started thinking about Adam and about how my whole entire life was spinning out of control—or maybe that was the screwdrivers talking. I guess I was quiet on the walk to the car, or maybe he just sensed something, because he asked what was wrong.

"Remember I told you there was someone I knew who died?"

"You used to be involved."

"We sort of still were. And the last . . . He died just a few hours after we, um, after we spent the night together."

"Alex, my God . . . Was it someone from Gabriel?"

"His name was Adam Ellroy."

"The reporter?"

"Did you know him?"

"Only vaguely. Didn't he . . ."

"Didn't he kill himself, you mean."

"I must have read it in the paper. Alex, I . . ."

"I know, you're sorry. Everyone's sorry."

"It doesn't mean much, does it? It's what people always say, but it doesn't mean anything."

"Not a whole hell of a lot, no."

"Is there anything I can . . ." He stopped short. "Listen to me. That's the other thing people always say, isn't it? 'Is there anything I can do?' But they never really mean it, do they? It's nothing but an empty platitude. But, Alex, please believe me. *I* mean it. I mean it more than I can tell you. If you need to . . ."

"Look, Will, I really don't want to talk about it. I only brought it up because I don't think I can—I don't know—I can't keep this up."

"What are you trying to say?"

"I feel like I'm losing it, Will. I can't deal."

"You mean you don't want to see each other anymore?"

"Is that what we're doing?"

"I suppose it is."

"We can't be. I mean, *I* can't be. This is crazy."

"It doesn't seem crazy from where I'm standing."

"What are you getting mad at me for?"

"I'm not."

"You sure sound like you are."

"You just took me by surprise, Alex, that's all. I'm not angry with you. Go ahead and say whatever you've got to say."

"Will, I can barely think straight. I told you, he just . . . It all just happened a couple of weeks ago."

"It's too soon. Is that what you mean?"

"Of course that's what I mean."

"Don't you enjoy my company?"

"You know I do. But that's hardly the point."

"I think it's precisely the point."

"Are you listening to a word I'm saying? Jesus, Will, I'm in *mourning,* for lack of a better word. Maybe that sounds Victorian to you, although I don't see why it should. I may not be traipsing around in a black veil, but I'm telling you, he's all I think about."

His arm snaked around my back. "Alex, it's okay, just calm down. Come on, let's keep walking. You must be freezing in that little dress. All I'm trying to say is I think you need to be around other people right now. You shouldn't be alone."

"I don't get you." I shrugged his arm off. "You've spent the past five years holed up in that gold-plated lab of yours, and you're telling *me* I shouldn't be alone?"

"Call it words of wisdom from the grieving front. Believe me, Alex. I learned something when my wife died. You go through something like this, and you realize the world is separated into two kinds of people: the ones who understand, and the ones who don't. It's as though you join a club, Widowers Anonymous or what have you, and all of a sudden you know the password. You find that you gravitate toward people who understand what you're going through. I apologize if I'm coming on too strong. Perhaps I'm overstepping the bounds. But, Alex, from the moment I met you, I felt a certain connection. I didn't know what it was at the time. But there it is. You understand what it is to lose someone. We have that in common."

His arm went around me again, and this time I didn't resist. "Is that all there is?"

"I don't suspect so. I certainly hope not. All I'm saying is, please don't close me off."

"It's not that I want to. It's just that . . . Listen, Will. I've never been much on self-control. I tend to leap first and ask questions later, and it's gotten me into more trouble than I care to think about. But right now, I need to get a grip. So please, *please* cut me some slack and be the grown-up here. I need a friend. What I don't need is a lover."

An actual smirk appeared on his face then. "So you're saying I should keep my lips to myself."

"I'm glad it amuses you."

"Alex, you sweet girl, I'm not laughing at you. Forgive me. I'm just savoring the thought that a ravishing twenty-five-year-old can't trust herself to keep her hands off an old man like me. It's rather flattering, really."

"Ego."

"There you go. I like it when you smile."

"Something I haven't done a lot of lately."

He opened the car door for me. "Let's get you home. You need to go to bed. And don't worry. I won't even try to tuck you in."

19

We took off for Poughkeepsie Friday afternoon, with Gordon at the wheel of the '85 Honda he'd been forced to buy when he moved to Gabriel. We headed toward Binghamton on back roads, planning on picking up Route 17 and winging it from there. There's no direct way to get from Gabriel to Poughkeepsie—or from Gabriel to anywhere, for that matter—and we had no idea how long it was going to take us. After my furtive trip up to Canada, it was a relief not to have to lie about where we were going. We just said we were going to hang out in New York for the weekend after Gordon bagged—or failed to bag—the Caruso interview, and only Mad knew that the real point of the trip was to track down Peter Murphy.

On our way across the state, Gordon outlined his strategy for getting Caruso to open up to him. I wasn't particularly optimistic. I doubted even Gordon could sweet-talk someone who probably thought of date rape as a spectator sport.

We pulled into town just after six o'clock, and the pizza place where Caruso worked turned out to be one of my occasional undergrad haunts. The Isle of Capri is too far out on Route 44 to be popular with the college crowd, but I pride myself on my ability to sniff out a decent Greek salad.

I told Gordon I knew what James Caruso looked like, since his face had been all over the news following the attack. But he brought a photo of him along anyway, to make sure he'd be able to spot him. Gordon had worked out plans to cover every contingency—if we didn't see him in the restaurant, I was supposed to rave about the pizza and ask to talk to the guy who made it, in the hopes of finding him in the kitchen. If he wouldn't talk to us, we were going to wait around until closing and follow him home. It wasn't exactly Watergate, but I'd never seen Gordon so psyched. The little pit bull was having an absolutely splendid time.

"Keep your eyes open," Gordon said as we walked in. "It's been a few months since that picture was taken. He might have longer hair, or a beard or mustache. Maybe after what he did, he's tried to change his appearance."

"Are you being serious? Gordon, we are in a pizza place in Poughkeepsie. Will you spare me the *Mission: Impossible* routine?"

"You never let me have any fun."

"You just live to get people to spill their guts to you, don't you?"

"Who doesn't?"

The restaurant was a casual, family-style place, with big plastic cheeses and salamis hanging from the ceiling, mesh-wrapped red lanterns on the tables, and a gigantic ivy plant covering most of one wall. The tables were wide and solid, with paper place mats of Italian tourist spots. Gordon and I followed the hostess to a booth, where a teenage girl filled our water glasses, making a show of lighting the lantern on the table with a blue plastic Bic.

When our waiter came, I had to stifle a laugh. Carrying an ordering pad, wearing a red-checked apron over an Isle of Capri T-shirt, was James Caruso.

Though Caruso hadn't affected an eye patch or had plastic surgery, he did look different. He'd lost weight, maybe thirty pounds off the huge grizzly bear frame that had appeared in the paper—first in the *Monitor* sports section in his varsity football uniform, and later in handcuffs on page one. But even without the extra poundage, Caruso was still a very big guy, and the hands that held the notepad were as thick as catcher's mitts.

"Hi. I mean, um, '*Benvenuto* to the Isle of Capri.' The special tonight is eggplant parmesan, and it comes with a small Greek salad and garlic bread. Can I get you guys some drinks?"

I stared across the table at Gordon. This was his show. I'm not sure what I expected him to do—maybe whip out his tape recorder and ask Caruso if he'd broken into the Democratic National Committee—but what he did was order himself a beer. I asked for a Diet Pepsi with lemon, and Caruso lumbered off to the kitchen.

"So, Mr. Bernstein, what's the plan? I grab the drinks, you wrestle him to the ground and get some good quotes?"

"Okay, so I didn't expect him to land in our laps. Took me by surprise. But I've got it covered."

I never did find out what Gordon's plan was, because what happened when Caruso came back to our table totally derailed it. He brought our drinks, laid them in front of us, and just stood there. He didn't pull out his notepad, didn't ask what we wanted for dinner. He stared at us, the noise of the diners filling the room like a barn full of poultry.

"You guys are here for me, aren't you?" he said finally.

I guess Gordon isn't used to being on the defensive, because for once he seemed at a loss for words.

"For you?" I echoed lamely.

"That's why you're here, isn't it? You're from that newspaper. The *Gabriel Monitor.* I was wondering when somebody would show up."

"How did you know?"

"You're Alex Bernier. 'Alex on the Aisle.' I didn't recognize you for a minute."

It seems pretty stupid in retrospect, but it had never occurred to me that Caruso would know who I was. Benson students *never* read the *Monitor,* which is one of the reasons we've been through four circulation directors in three years. And I'd never met Caruso; by the time I started writing about him and his pals, they were banned from campus.

"So what do you guys want?" he asked.

"We were hoping you'd be willing to talk to us about what happened at Benson," Gordon said. "I don't know if you've heard, but there's been a lot of publicity about the case lately. There was a big rally a few days ago, and . . ."

"And they want to chop off my head in the middle of the arts quad. I know."

"We thought you might want to tell your side of the story."

"There's not much to tell."

"People want to know why you did what you did, Mr. Caruso."

Caruso stared down at the floor, chewing absently on the nail of a sausage-sized pinkie. He looked like he was about to bawl, which was the last thing I expected. In

fact, nothing about James Caruso fit my image of a frat
boy run amok.

"Listen, I have to put in some orders and then I get to
take my break. If you want, I'll come back and talk to
you, but I only have, like, fifteen minutes."

"Okay," Gordon said warily. "You understand, we'd
want to be able to publish what you say. It wouldn't be
off the record."

"Oh. I guess that's all right. I'll be right back."

Caruso walked off toward the kitchen, and as soon as
he passed through one of the swinging doors, Gordon
leaped up from the table.

"Where are you going?"

"Around back, where do you think? The guy's obviously trying to give us the slip."

"You think so? He didn't really seem like . . ."

Gordon didn't stick around to let me finish, elbowing
his way through a family of five to get out the door. I was
debating whether to run after him when Caruso appeared,
minus the apron.

"Sorry that took so long. Things are kind of screwed up
in the kitchen. Where did the other guy go?"

"He's out back, trying to cut you off at the pass. Don't
worry, he'll be back."

A weak smile crossed Caruso's face, and for the first
time I noticed the freckles jogging across the bridge of
his nose.

"How come you're still here?"

"I didn't think you took off."

"Why not?"

"I guess I figured if you didn't want to talk to us, you
could have just told us to go to hell."

"I, um, I don't have a whole lot of time," he said, rocking back and forth in his seat. "Do you think we could, like, get it over with?"

"James . . ."

"Jimbo. That's what everybody calls me. Jimbo."

"Jimbo, I'm wondering . . . I don't want to put you off. But how come you're willing to talk now? The paper's been trying to get an interview with you for months, and you wouldn't have anything to do with it." He seemed fascinated with the place mat in front of him, with its red and green drawings of the Coliseum and the Duomo. He ripped the Leaning Tower of Pisa into tiny bits, and I started to worry I'd put my foot in it. If he clammed up now, Gordon was going to kill me.

"It's one of the steps I'm supposed to do," he said, still talking to the place mat.

"Steps?"

"Yeah, there's a bunch of them I'm supposed to do for the program."

"You mean, like . . . twelve?"

"How did you know?"

"It's fairly common."

"Yeah, well, one of the steps is to try and make up for all the shit I did. Uh, sorry," he mumbled. "I mean all the bad stuff I did. I'm supposed to accept responsibility and ask for forgiveness. Or maybe it's the other way around, like, ask for forgiveness and *then* accept responsibility. I'm not real sure about the order."

"I don't think the order matters that much."

"Oh. Yeah."

"So what's this program like?"

"It's not bad. There's a lot of meetings, but I feel pretty good. A hell of a lot better than when I was in school, anyway."

"You didn't like Benson?"

"No way. I totally loved it. Problem was, I was too fucked, uh, screwed up most of the time to know what I was doing."

"And you regret that now?"

"Hell, yeah. I had a scholarship to one of the best colleges in the country, and a starting spot on the football team, and I totally fucked it up." He glanced up at the plastic provolone hovering over the table and shook his head. "You know, I was supposed to be the first kid in my family to graduate college. And now I'm stuck here, waiting tables and tossing pies."

"You could still go back to college, couldn't you?"

"Who'd take me?"

Since I didn't have an answer for him, it was a good thing Gordon picked that moment to come back to the table.

"Hi. Sorry about that," he said, pushing me aside with his body as he sat down. "Thanks for talking to us, Mr. Caruso. I know you don't have a lot of time, so I was wondering if we . . ."

"Listen," Jimbo interrupted. "I don't mean to be rude or anything, but do I need to talk to the both of you? I mean, this is pretty hard for me, you know."

"Sure," I said, motioning for Gordon to let me out of the booth. "That's okay. I can go get myself a salad."

"No, don't," Jimbo said, looking like a boy whose mother was about to leave him at day care. "I meant, would it be all right if I just talked to you?"

"This is really Gordon's . . ."

"No problem," Gordon said. I was about to protest again, but Gordon's look shut me up. I gave him a look that said, "This is not my fault," and he palmed me his tape recorder under the table. "I'll just find myself a table over there until you're done."

I felt like a heel as Gordon stalked across the dining room. I didn't believe his conciliatory act for a second, and I had a feeling he was going to chop me into my constituent parts as soon as he got me alone. I took a deep breath, turned back to Jimbo, and laid the tape recorder on the table between us. "This okay with you?"

He nodded. "So what do you want me to say?"

"Why don't you just tell me your feelings about what happened?"

"How do I feel about it? It's funny, nobody's ever asked me that before." He leaned against the table with his chin in his hand and spoke through his fist. "I don't know. I feel awful, I guess."

"You regret what you did?"

"Course I do. Why wouldn't I?"

"Well, Jimbo, if you think what you did was so bad, why did you do it in the first place?"

"You gotta understand how messed up I was. I know I'm not supposed to blame what I did on the drinking or all the weed, but I gotta tell you, I was totally out of control. Man, my coach wanted to beat the crap out of me when he found out. I mean, I never pulled that kind of shit when I was practicing, but after the season ended I just kind of went wild. I always drank, like, at parties and stuff, but I got so I was partying every day. If I hadn't gotten booted out, I probably would have flunked spring semester anyway."

"So you're saying you were drunk when you attacked the freshmen?"

"Shit, yeah. I barely remember it. We were going across campus from a party at another house, and we ran into these two guys, and Trev said, like, 'We got ourselves a couple of faggots,' and he said, 'let's fuck them up.' Wait. You probably shouldn't say that in the newspaper. The f-word, I mean. Anyway, it was really easy. They didn't put up much of a fight. When I think about it, it seems like we beat on them, like, forever. There were other guys there, but Trev did most of the damage. Him and me, I mean. That's why the rest of them only got hit with misdemeanors and we got the felonies. We all got expelled, though. I guess we deserved it. Anyway, that's why I decided to make a deal."

"A deal? What deal?"

"My sponsor said I had to own up to what I did and take the punishment, so I'm pleading guilty. I've got to go to court next week. It's a lower charge, but it's still a felony. Did you know convicted felons can't even vote? Boy, did I screw my life up but good."

"You mean you're not going on trial?"

"Nope. But they're giving me house arrest for a whole year. You know, where they strap this thing to your ankle and you can only leave to go to work? And I've got like ten thousand hours of community service. And I have to do a . . . What's the word? Where I say what I did and why I shouldn't have done it?"

"Allocution?"

"Yeah, that's it. Allocution. Kind of sounds like electrocution, huh? And besides that, I'm going to write letters to the two kids we . . . to the two victims."

"That's part of your deal, too?"

"No. I just sort of want to. Do you think they'd, like, read it?" Jimbo's beagle eyes were anxious, and I thought of Tony Cerutti's nerve at the B-GLAD rally. The guy who'd been assaulted had recovered a hell of a lot better than the one who did it to him.

"I think one of them would. The other may not be able to deal with it yet."

He scratched what was left of his thumbnail along the

graffiti etched into the tabletop. "Plus, I have to testify at Trev's trial. That's part of the deal too."

"That must be hard. Having to testify against your friend, I mean."

He pushed away Gordon's abandoned beer with a nauseated look. "If you told me a year ago I'd be squealing on one of the brothers, I'd have said you were nuts. But now . . . You probably think I'm a rat, don't you?"

"No, I don't. But how come you decided to do it?"

"After what happened . . . I don't know. Trev seemed so proud of it. Like he wasn't sorry for what he did, but he was real sorry he got caught. He even said . . . After we got busted, he said we should've killed them, so there wouldn't be any witnesses. I mean, I figured he was probably just blowing smoke. He always talked real big, like about how all the homos should have their . . . um, you know, cut off so they couldn't hit on the rest of us. And after we got arrested, he was a hundred times worse. He seemed so pissed off, like it was the gay kids' fault we got in trouble. He was way out of control. Everybody was pretty freaked out. The brothers were going to have him kicked out of the house, but once we got banned from campus, they didn't have to. Not that he even cares."

"How do you mean?"

"I probably shouldn't . . . Oh, fuck it. Listen, can this be—what do you call it—off the record?" I clicked off the tape recorder. "I still talk to a few of the brothers sometimes, and they told me he's been hanging around the house. Not a lot, but he's still pretty tight with some of the guys, and he showed up at a couple of parties. I said I didn't want to hear about it. Staying out of the county was one of the conditions of our bail. You didn't look him up too, did you?"

"Not yet. So far, he's refused to give any interviews."

"Good," he said, relaxing back into his seat. "Promise me you won't try and talk to him."

"Why?"

"You seem like a nice lady. I don't know what . . . Trev's really lost it. He blames those two kids for getting us in trouble, and he's pretty pissed at your paper for writing about it. He nearly took a swing at that reporter that kept coming around the frat house after it first happened, told him he'd rip his head off if he didn't leave us alone."

"You mean he threatened Adam?" I tried to keep my voice steady.

"Who?"

"Adam Ellroy, the reporter who was covering the story. What did Trevor say to him?"

"I don't know," he shrugged. "He was all freaked out. Something like, 'If you don't leave us alone, I'll knock your ass from here to the bottom of the fucking gorge.' I can't remember exactly. Are you okay?"

I tried to stay calm, but my voice was ragged and weak. "Jimbo, is there any way . . . Do you think Trevor Hoffman could really kill someone?"

"No, I . . . Oh, Jesus, I don't know. I can't believe he really could. But he was awful angry at that reporter guy. I guess some of the stories he wrote ended up in Trev's hometown paper, and he was pretty pissed. And when he's drunk, he can be a total maniac . . ." Jimbo stopped short and stared at me. "I don't get it. What's the point? I mean, it's not like Trev killed anybody."

"The reporter, the one who covered the assault for the *Monitor.* He's dead. They found his body in the gorge a couple of weeks ago."

Jimbo looked like a deer caught in headlights. "You don't think . . . No. No way. Forget it. I shouldn't have said anything. Please believe me, Miss Bernier. Trev's an asshole and all, and he likes to talk big. But there's no way he would have . . . Look, what he did before—what we both did—was, like, in the heat of the moment. I shouldn't have said anything."

"Jimbo . . ."

"Listen, I've got to get back to work. Write whatever you want about me. But you can't use anything I said about Trev. You promised, right?"

"Yes, but . . ."

"I really gotta go." He slid out of his seat and ran for the kitchen before I could think of a way to stop him. Gordon was in the booth a heartbeat later, smiling blandly.

"So how did the interview go?" he said, leaning back with his arms crossed. "You get anything good? You obviously charmed the savage beast."

"You know damn well I didn't want to. You're the one who dragged me here."

"What's wrong?"

"First off, we have to call Bill and get him to hold some space on page one. Caruso is cutting a deal, and if we bust our butts we can get it into the Saturday paper."

"Way to go, Alex," Gordon said, glee replacing petulance behind his wire-rimmed glasses.

"Wait a minute. That's not the half of it. Remember Trevor Hoffman?"

"The other frat boy."

"This was off the record, but apparently he's been violating his bail. And Caruso told me that back when the assault story broke, he made some threats."

"Against who? The gay kids?"

"The *Gabriel Monitor* reporter who was covering the story."

"Are you serious?"

"Dead serious."

20

~

WE FOLLOWED THE HUDSON RIVER SOUTH, REHASHING
the Caruso case through the miles of farmland. We'd
banged out the story together on Gordon's laptop and
modemed it into the paper for Saturday's *Monitor.* Gordon had managed to corral Jimbo for a few more questions, and Mad, working the Friday night shift, would fill
in the holes—he said he'd at least try to track down
Caruso's lawyer, Stewart Day, and Tony Cerutti. When
we got back to Gabriel Sunday afternoon, Gordon and I
were going to co-write a follow-up story for Monday.

Once we'd sent our Saturday story off into electronic
oblivion, we spent most of the car ride talking about
Trevor Hoffman. As far as we knew, he was living with
his parents in Manchester, New Hampshire; the whole
family had refused to talk to the press from day one.
Adam had called them several times after Hoffman's ex-
pulsion, and had gotten nowhere—except to have his sexual preference called into question by Hoffman's father.

Adam had laughed about the phone call in bed one night, on one of those occasions when his heterosexuality was particularly evident. If Adam ever thought he was in any danger from Trevor Hoffman, he never let on.

"We have to find out if Hoffman was in town the day Adam died. Do you think any of these frat brothers will talk?" I asked, waving the list of names Jimbo had given us.

"If they do, it'll save us a lot of effort," Gordon said. "Listen, I've been thinking. We were trying to figure out why Adam wouldn't have told you, or anybody else, that he was meeting someone that night. Right?"

"Yeah, well, I guess I've figured all along that the source, whoever it was, must have asked him not to. If that was the case, Adam wouldn't have told his own grandmother. Nobody."

"Well, if it really was Hoffman, maybe there could be another reason. Maybe he didn't want you to think he was horning in on your story about B-GLAD."

"Gordon, at that point, he *would* have been horning in on my B-GLAD story."

"And he never would have done that?"

I tried to think about it objectively, which was sort of ridiculous. I'd never had any sort of perspective about Adam, so why should this be any different? "Okay," I said, sighing. "Maybe not *never*. But probably not without a good reason, like he could get something that I couldn't. But he wouldn't just go scoop me for the hell of it." At least, I hoped he wouldn't.

"Did you ever try to get an interview with Hoffman or his family?"

"Not seriously. I left a couple of messages on their machine, but that's it."

"You left your name?"

"Of course."

"Alex, I don't want to freak you out," he said, checking the traffic in his rearview mirror. "But if Hoffman was the kind of guy who made threats about nosy reporters, then what if he was making them about you too?"

"You mean, what if he was making threats about me, and Adam found out about it? Jesus, Gordon . . ."

"Look, I'm just putting it out there. But if we're serious about Hoffman as a suspect, we have to think of why Adam would climb out of bed and meet with him. Assuming that Adam wasn't trying to scoop you, then he had to want to talk to him about *something*. If Hoffman was telling his frat brothers he was going to get that little bitch from the *Monitor*—sorry, Alex—then it might explain why Adam wanted to talk to him. Maybe some source told him Hoffman was going to be in town that night. Where's the frat in relation to the gorge?"

"It's practically *in* the gorge. It perches right on the edge of it. Oh, my God."

"What?"

"This whole time they've been assuming Adam fell off the bridge. But what if it was from the frat house—one of the balconies or windows or something?"

"Is that possible? Logistically?"

"I have no idea. And hold on a minute. Aren't we forgetting something? What does Trevor Hoffman have to do with Adam's trip to Canada? And the missing files?"

Gordon was at a loss for the second time in one day, which cheered me up. "I couldn't tell you. But maybe his death and Sebastien's aren't connected after all."

"So what are we doing driving down to New York City?"

"Because maybe they are."

The farmland segued into Catskill resorts, then suburban sprawl. When we got to the outskirts of the city, he turned off the Bob Dylan tape we'd been listening to and switched on the radio. "We should be able to pick up Andrea's station by now."

"Who does she work for?"

"Steinberg Information Radio."

"You're dating someone in *broadcast*? Gordon, you of all people. I'm shocked." There are a lot of hard feelings between print journalists and people who work for radio and TV; don't let anyone tell you different. We think they're shallow and couldn't string a decent paragraph together if their mother's life depended on it. They think we're a bunch of throwback losers who don't know how to do their hair. For the most part, we're both right.

"She wasn't always in broadcast. She used to work for the AP."

"Where'd she go to school?" He pretended to concentrate on the road. "Come on, Gordon, where did your Jewish American Princess go to school?"

"I do not recall, Senator."

"Oh, *please*."

"She's not . . . exactly . . . Jewish."

"You're dating a shiksa who works for a radio station? Does your mother know this?"

"Are you insane?"

"So you're really not going to tell me where this girl went to school? Come on, Gordon, how bad can it be?"

"The University . . . the University . . . All right, the fucking University of Hawaii. Are you happy? Would you please shut up and stop laughing?"

Gordon dropped me off on West 110th Street, and I went to a little Mexican place with my friend Sarah, who was my senior-year roommate at boarding school. We went out to dinner, and the inevitable conversation about

Adam was lubricated with liberal amounts of guacamole and sour cream. The next morning, I met Gordon for breakfast at this great pancake house on Broadway, where they'll feed you an omelet served on top of a waffle, with basil and tomato and mozzarella cheese stuffed in between. Sometimes, I think I can almost see why people live in New York.

After we ate, we hauled our stuffed carcasses across Central Park to the East Side. It was a beautiful day for walking, and we strolled past the runners and rollerbladers and homeless guys stretched out on benches with everything they own in plastic bags.

"What are the odds this guy is even going to let us in the door?" I asked Gordon as we left the park and crossed Fifth Avenue. "Maybe we should have called first. What if he isn't home?"

"If he isn't home, we'll come back later. And I never call first if I can possibly show up in person. It's much easier to get rid of somebody on the phone than standing on your doorstep. That's nosy reporter rule number one."

Less than ten minutes later, we were standing out in front of 593 East 86th St., a modern-looking building with bricks arranged in geometric patterns to form an entryway. According to the directory, Murphy lived in apartment 1-B. Luckily, somebody was on his way out the door, so we didn't have to talk Murphy into buzzing us in. I rang the bell and heard a faint ding-dong from inside. Nothing. I tried again, waited. Footsteps came toward us, and someone stopped on the other side of the door.

"Yes?" The voice was muffled by the door; not hostile, but not exactly welcoming, either.

"Hi," I said, trying to sound as little like a criminal as possible. "We're looking for Mr. Peter Murphy."

"Yes? What is it?"

"Um, it's kind of complicated. We're from Gabriel. My name is Alex Bernier, and this is Gordon Band. We work for the *Gabriel Monitor*."

Umpteen Medico security locks retracted, and a nose poked out through the safety-chain crack.

"Do you have some sort of ID or something?" We dug out our press passes and handed them through. After a minute, the door opened. Murphy was very slim, looking older than thirty-something. His hairline had receded to the North Pole, and the fluorescent light from the hallway reflected off his skull. He wore a white cotton sweater and blue jeans, and I thought I wouldn't be scared of him in the subway.

"The *Gabriel Monitor*?" he was confused, but not unfriendly. The smell of bacon wafted through the apartment; even after a decade of vegetarianism, it still makes me want to kill a pig with my bare hands. "What's the *Monitor* want with me?"

"Is it okay if we come in?" Gordon asked.

"Sure, I guess," he said, and I thought there was no way he could have grown up in the city, or he would have called the cops by now. He offered us coffee and we settled in the cramped living room. I found it hard to think with all the bacon in the air. "So what can I do for you?"

"It's kind of complicated," I said. "It's related to a story we're working on."

"Are you sure you've got the right guy? I mean, I haven't lived in Gabriel since college. This is so strange, having you show up like this. How come you didn't just call?"

I shot Gordon an I-told-you-so look. "Oh, we were coming down to the city anyway, so we thought we'd just stop by." It sounded lame even to me, and I was the one saying it.

"We were hoping to ask you a few questions about your grandfather," Gordon said, and I was shocked at how sensitive he sounded all of a sudden. Silky smooth, like your best friend. He reminded me of those vampires from the movies, that speak to you and you have to obey their every command.

"My grandfather? What possible interest could you have in him?" A little defensive now, like anybody would be when perfect strangers ask personal questions.

"We're working on a story about the Benson physics department in the forties," Gordon said. This much at least was true. "Your grandfather worked there, didn't he?"

"Yeah, I guess, after he got out of the army. But I don't know much about it. We're talking fifty years ago."

"Oh, sure, I understand. We weren't going to quote you or anything. We were just hoping for some background information. You know, fifty years later, and all that. You can imagine how hard it is to find *anybody* who's still around from back then. We were just hoping for some anecdotal stuff, what it was like to work there, and not just the big-deal scientists, but the janitors and secretaries and everybody too." Listening to Gordon weasel information out of someone was like hearing Pavarotti sing. Assure him nothing will go into print, make him feel a little silly for not wanting to answer, appeal to his vanity. What a pro.

"Well, like I said, I don't know very much. You know, my grandfather died before I was born. He was in a car accident."

I was about to tell him we knew that, but Gordon got there first. "How awful. Was he very young?"

"Just in his forties, which is starting to seem awfully young to me." He ran a hand over his bald head.

"What happened?"

"It wasn't something my folks talked about very much. My dad was only a teenager when it happened, and I think it really screwed him up." It's always amazed me how some people treat reporters like shrinks. Get them talking, and it all comes gushing out. "I guess my grandfather had been drinking and crashed into a tree. There was a fire. They found a couple of liquor bottles in the car." I made some sympathetic noises, and hoped Gordon approved.

"We had no idea," Gordon told him. "We never would have come in and upset you like this if we'd known." Yeah, and there's this lovely bridge in Brooklyn . . .

"It all happened a long time ago. It was just one of those things in the family you didn't talk about, you know?"

"I totally understand. My uncle had a terrible problem with drinking and driving. It was amazing he didn't kill someone." I wondered if this was true. I doubted it. Gordon, you shameless slug. Not that it was any worse than me pretending to be old Dr. Singer's daughter.

"That's the thing," Murphy said. "My dad always swore his father didn't drink and drive. I guess one time is all it takes."

"And your family stayed in Gabriel?"

"I guess they could have left, what with the insurance money and all, but they didn't. I went to Gabriel High and I got through Benson. Took me a while," he chuckled.

"A while?"

"Yeah, I was on the six-year plan."

"Did you like Benson?" I asked, wanting to have something to do with the conversation.

"Oh, I loved it. The university was great to me. It was

my dad's alma mater, but I was still amazed I even got in, and then they gave me a scholarship for all six years, and paid for my tuition and all my books and room and board. I never could have gotten my Wall Street job if it weren't for Benson."

That was pretty much the end of the interview, such that it was. Murphy apologized profusely for not being able to help us more and wanted to know when our story was going to run. We told him we weren't sure yet, and walked out with our fingers crossed behind our backs.

"Nice shootin', Tex," I said when we were safely a block away.

"'T weren't nothin', ma'am. Besides, I had to prove my manhood after that mess in Poughkeepsie."

"So what do you make of that?"

"Several things. The most salient of which is, you generally don't get insurance money if you get all liquored up and do a header into a tree."

"Also, people who struggle through college in six years don't generally get full-boat scholarships."

"That also occurred to me."

"So what do you think happened?"

"I don't know. The guy said his grandfather wasn't a habitual drunk driver, which may mean that the DWI was as fictional as the plane crash."

"So you think somebody killed Murphy too, then tried to make it look like an accident?"

"Could be. Who knows? At this point, the bodies are piling up like dirty laundry."

"That was eloquent."

"How much does a Benson education go for these days?"

"With tuition and everything else, maybe a hundred thousand dollars."

"Between that and the so-called insurance money, it adds up to a nice payoff, doesn't it?"

"You see payola under every rock, don't you?"

"You bet your ass."

We found a one-hour photo place and dropped off the Benson physics department picture to be enlarged. Gordon went off to see his girlfriend, and Sarah and I split a prix fixe dinner for two at a hole-in-the-wall Indian restaurant on Seventh Avenue. We wound up at Gordon's favorite bar, a close, smoky place on Hudson Street in the Village where you can sit on little couches, listen to jazz, and read books from the shelves that line three walls. He showed up around one carrying his duffel bag, a nasty look, and no desire to talk about it. What he did want was a Gibson, which a woman with a blond chignon brought over, spraying the cocktail onions with vermouth from a tiny blue dispenser. He downed about a third of it in one gulp, leaned back against the blue velvet cushions, and brooded as I pulled a Shakespeare volume off the shelf behind me.

"Cheer up, Gordon. Take it from the Immortal Bard. *As You Like It,* Act Four, Scene One: 'Men have died from time to time, and worms have eaten them. But not for love.'"

On our way out of the city, we picked up the blowup of the physics department photo; the grainy, poster-sized enlargement cost me twenty bucks. I studied it as we crossed the George Washington Bridge into New Jersey, and when I took a good look at one of the faces I swore so loudly, Gordon nearly sideswiped a taxicab.

"Jesus, Alex, what is it?"

"I thought I recognized somebody before, but I wasn't sure. It still seems impossible . . ."

"You're killing me. What the hell is it?"

"Pull over."

"Where? Into the Hudson?"

"I mean, pull over whenever you can. You've got to take a look at this."

"What?"

"I may be wrong. But there's a guy in this photograph who looks exactly like Stewart Day."

21

His name was Yitzhak Dershowitz. At least that's what it said in the photo. But the face in the grainy black-and-white looked amazingly like Stewart Day, especially the eyes and mouth. "Wild," Mad said when we brought it over to his apartment. "How the hell do you explain this one, Nancy Drew?"

"Damned if I know."

"You realize it couldn't be the same guy."

"Yes, thank you, Mad. Unless he's a bloodsucking creature of the night, the guy in the picture is dead, or he's a hundred."

"Alex and I talked about it all the way up from the city," Gordon interjected. "We're thinking it's got to be one of the kids."

"Kids?"

"Look at the caption," I said. "It says it's Mr. and Mrs. Yitzhak Dershowitz *and family*. There's, what, six kids? Unless it's a major-league coincidence, Stewart Day has got to be one of them. The family resemblance is incredible, isn't it?"

"Yeah," Mad said. "Except for the nose."

"Rhinoplasty," Gordon offered.

"Excuse me?" Mad said.

"Nose job. Believe it or not, there are some who feel the Semitic schnozz doesn't conform to some goyish standard of beauty. I prefer to hang on to the original, thank you very much."

"You're telling me Stewart Day is *Jewish*?" Mad said, his eyebrows nearly colliding with his hairline.

"Hard to believe, I know," I said. "Never have I seen a Waspier dude in my life. But I always said there was something off about him. So, voilà! Day is really Dershowitz. Go figure. And the real pisser is that not only is Day a big phony, he's in the thick of this whole thing. This whole time, we've been looking for somebody connected to André Lecuyer. I don't know how, but it looks like Stewart Day may be our man."

"Then let's nail the son of a bitch," Gordon said.

"Wait a sec," Mad said. "I can't believe I'm about to be the voice of reason, but don't you think you two are going just a little nuts? How do you know you're right about Day being one of these kids? What if it's just a coincidence? Or what if it's a distant relative or something?"

"But, Mad, what are the odds?" I said. "Like I told you, there was always something about Day that just wasn't right. Everything he says sounds like a lie."

"But how do we know he had anything to do with Adam's death? I mean, so let's assume the guy's a fake. That doesn't exactly make him a killer. We still have a long way to go before we can prove anything."

"All right. Point taken," Gordon said. "But this is the

first time we've actually had something to go on—a link between the past and the present."

"But what about a motive?" Mad asked. "What possible reason could Day have for killing Adam—not to mention André Sebastien?"

"Maybe Adam figured out the same thing we did," Gordon said. "If we're right about this, Day has gone to a lot of trouble to pretend he's something he's not. What if somehow or another, Adam figured out that Mr. Ivy League School Tie is really the son of a Jewish janitor? If the man's whole life is a fiction, don't you think he might kill to cover that up?"

"And Sebastien?"

"I don't know yet," Gordon admitted. "We've got to do some serious digging."

"You were there the morning after, on the bridge," Mad said. "Think back. Was there anything suspicious about the way Day was acting?"

I tried to remember everything Day had said to me on the bridge, how he'd reacted when they'd pulled Adam's body up on the stretcher. I had to admit he hadn't acted particularly guilty. Would a murderer have blithely chatted about my movie column? "All right, so he didn't confess right then and there and tell the chief to slap the cuffs on him. That hardly means he didn't do it."

"Well, at least we've got a suspect. It's sort of a relief to have something to go on for a change," Mad said.

"Oh, we've got a suspect all right," Gordon said. "In fact, we've got two. You're going to love this. Tell him, Alex."

"Remember that frat boy Gordon was going to try to interview? You are not going to *believe* what he told us."

Gordon and I spent the afternoon writing the Caruso profile. After we filed it, I dragged Melissa to a truly

awful movie called *Love at First Sigh*. I mention it because it turned out to have some redeeming value; seeing
it must have made the right neurons fire in my brain, and
the hunch that formed after I wrote my column eventually
led to finding Betty Barrows. Up 'til then, we'd combed
through birth certificates, marriage records, property
deeds, and Benson alumni directories, tapped Gordon's
friend at the DMV. It had all gotten us no closer to finding Betty Barrows, or Marion Hazel either. Then I saw
that stupid movie. Strange how so much can turn on
something so irrelevant.

In case you were lucky enough to miss it, the movie is
about a neurosurgeon who falls madly in love with a
waitress in a diner. He spends most of the film trying to
convince his family to accept her, which they finally do
when our heroine saves his mother from choking on her
shrimp cocktail at the country club.

"It never convinced me that they belonged together,
not for one single minute," I was saying to no one in particular. "Why are they together? Because the damn script
says they are."

"I thought it was kind of romantic," Melissa said.

"Oh, give me a break," I said. "Like some guy who
spends fifteen years in college is going to have anything
to talk about with some girl who dropped out of high
school."

"But she had to take care of her ailing mother."
Melissa clasped her hands over her heart for dramatic effect. "Didn't you think it was nice that she liked to go to
the airport and watch the planes take off and wonder
where they were going?"

"Oh, gag me."

Later, Mad, Gordon, and I repaired to the Green to talk
about our so-far fruitless search for Betty and Marion.

"We know who Marion Hazel was," Mad was saying. "At least, we know she was some kind of lab assistant. But we're still totally in the dark about this Betty Barrows, other than the fact that she was Sebastien's girlfriend."

And that's when that wretched movie, still taking up valuable space in my cranium, did me some good. "Wait, Mad, say that again."

"I just said, we don't know anything about Betty Barrows, except that she was going out with Sebastien, right?"

"But maybe that in itself should tell us something," I said. "We know Sebastien was some kind of *wunderkind*. He was a full professor at, what, twenty-eight? So doesn't it follow that he'd be going out with somebody pretty smart herself?"

"I hate to disillusion you," Mad said, "but we fellas have been known to go for a nice pair of bazongas, which our Miss Barrows had in spades. Did you see those pictures? Hubba, hubba."

"But something tells me he wasn't the kind of man who'd go for some bimbo. You should have seen all his books up in Canada, Mad. I think he prized knowledge above everything. Even, believe it or not, a nice pair of bazongas."

"So, fine," Mad countered. "What good does that do us?"

"Let's just take the leap of logic that like mated like, and Betty Barrows was well educated. Now, back then, where did a woman go to college?"

"Seven Sisters," Gordon said. "Smith, Vassar, Radcliffe, et cetera."

"Don't let's forget Wellesley girls," Mad said. "They're my favorite. Stuck up, but once you get them in the sack . . ."

"Here's my idea," I cut in. "I think we should call the alumni offices at the seven schools, give them some excuse, and find out if a Betty Barrows graduated in the late thirties or early forties. If we flop, we'll start on other schools that admitted women."

"Don't you think this is kind of a long shot?" Mad asked.

"What have we got left?"

I went back to the office, locked the door to the library, and struck gold on the third call. Betty Barrows graduated from Barnard College in 1943.

"Barnard!" Gordon said, tossing his pen in the air in a rare moment of euphoria. "Ha! Back to New York!"

"Calm down. We may not need to go down there ourselves this time. I'm going to ask my friend Sarah to check out the Barnard-Columbia alumni rag."

"But isn't she too busy? I mean with law school and all . . ."

"Oh, Gordon, don't be so goddamn transparent. She's got the summer off. And yes, if she can't do it, we'll have to go back down to the city."

Unfortunately for Gordon, Sarah—who's going to make one kick-ass lawyer, by the way—was willing to help. She left me a message Thursday night to tell me to watch out for a FedEx package the next day. From the pages she'd photocopied out of the 1943 Barnard yearbook, we learned that Elizabeth Beaton Barrows had majored in art history and played varsity tennis. In her senior photo, she wore a form-fitting cardigan with tiny pearl buttons, her hair swimming to her shoulders in sleek waves. She looked like something out of an old movie, and I was struck again by the resemblance to a young Katharine Hepburn.

Under the photo I found a Post-it note from Sarah, attached to another set of papers.

"Thought I'd go one further and check the B.C. alum mag for you. Didn't take long; just ran through class notes. Come back down soon! Hope all goes OK up north.—S. P.S.: Also looked through the necrology, and didn't find B.B., so it looks like the old gal's still around!"

It was all there: Betty Barrows's life, reduced to a collection of squibs covering five decades in the Class of '43 notes column. There weren't more than a dozen entries. (Her peers, by contrast, wrote about such joys as buying a house on Martha's Vineyard and adopting a cocker spaniel named "Muffin.") I learned about her marriage in 1945 to a banker named Alan L. Spencer; apparently, she didn't write in about it, because the note didn't appear until the following year.

> Heard through the grapevine that Betty Barrows tied the knot way back in July. The lucky fellow: Mr. Alan Spencer, an exec with Empire Federal Trust. Naughty, naughty Betty B. for not informing her classmates of her nuptials! Heartfelt congrats to the (not-so) newlyweds, who are residing in NYC.

If Betty Barrows—now Spencer—hadn't been eager to keep her alma mater informed about her personal life, she hadn't been as reticent about things professional. The class notes said she'd earned a PhD in art history from Columbia in 1951. In the next issue was an item congratulating her on her first teaching position, an assistant professorship. I read about her rise to full professor; the awarding of an endowed chair; sabbaticals in Paris and Florence.

Professor Elizabeth Barrows Spencer had had a distinguished career. And she'd spent nearly all of it at Benson University.

I'd read the whole package on the stair landing, sitting on the navy-blue carpet covered with dog hair. Now, I went over to my desk in the corner of the living room and pulled out my Benson faculty directory. The elusive Betty Barrows had been there all along, sandwiched between an economist and an astronomer. Elizabeth B. Spencer, professor emeritus of art history. I was beginning to think we could solve the whole mystery just by calling up every emeritus professor on the Benson campus and asking them what the hell was going on.

According to the directory, she lived at 401 Sherman Ave., which is on the opposite side of campus from my house. I could walk there inside of forty minutes. I stared at her phone number, went so far as to pick up the phone, but hung it up. Now that I knew where to find Betty Barrows, I had no idea what I was going to say to her. And I couldn't shake the suspicion that she was the key to the whole thing.

As Gordon said, never do by phone what you can accomplish in person. So instead of calling Professor Spencer, I showed up on her doorstep at noon on Saturday. The retired art history professor lived in a forest-green clapboard house with white shutters and a door painted bright red. The yard was a brilliant jungle of flowers, surrounding the house in a giddy sea—sunflowers, snapdragons, peonies, lots more I couldn't name. Geraniums and salvias in the window boxes matched the door, as did the wooden mailbox at the curb.

I wasn't much clearer on what I was going to say to Professor Spencer than I'd been the day before, but I decided to plow ahead and knock. Nothing. For a second I thought I heard music coming from inside, but with the cars going by the house, I couldn't be sure. I waited a minute, knocked again. No answer. As I closed the white picket gate, I thought I saw one of the lace curtains on the second floor shift a little. But the window was open, and it might have been the breeze.

After psyching myself up to have all mysteries revealed, it was quite the anticlimax to get back into my car inside of ten minutes. Suddenly at loose ends, I drove down the hill to the supermarket. After I got home and unloaded, impatience got the better of me, and I tossed Gordon's rule out the window and picked up the phone. I figured I'd at least leave a message for Betty Barrows, but that didn't work either. No one picked up the phone, and she didn't seem to have a machine.

I couldn't think of any good reason not to go running, so I did. Shakespeare dragged me over sideways chasing a squirrel, and I barely finished the second mile, near death and in a foul mood. I drove to the Y and did my nautilus circuit, sat in the sauna until I couldn't stand it anymore. The endorphins were kicking in by then and I felt a little better, so I decided to give Professor Betty another shot. I went back to her house, but again no one answered the door. This time, I left a note in the crack where the front door met the jamb.

> I'm looking for information about André Sebastien, a physicist who worked at Benson in the 1940s. I'd like to talk to you about him. It's important. Please give me a call as soon as you can.

I'm not sure why I decided to dispense with the pretense that I was working on some generic news story. I guess I had a feeling that with Betty Barrows it wouldn't do any good to lie. I peeked at the second-floor window as I left, and again the curtain ruffled a little. This time, there was no wind.

I felt like I was going a little nuts from the suspense, so in fine journalistic tradition I went out for a few drinks with the boys. I stumbled home to my answering machine shortly after midnight, but there was no message from Betty Barrows. I called her again the next morning. Still no answer. I went back to her house and found my note was gone, so I assumed—at least I hoped—Betty had read it. But she still hadn't called. I hadn't thought far enough ahead to know what I was going to do if I never found her, or if she refused to talk. Pleading with her was starting to sound like a fine idea.

I wrote out another note, a facsimile of the first, only more pathetic. I tucked it where I'd left the other, and as I walked out of the gate this time, I stared straight up at the second-floor window and tried vainly to see beyond the curtains. I bet you're in there, I thought. But if you are, why won't you come out?

What are you hiding from?

22

"TELL ME ABOUT HIM."

Will's voice was gravelly with sleep, muffled by the pillow resting against his cheek. We lay together in his king-size bed, wide as an ocean, sheets warm and damp from the past two hours. Will's arm was around me, the flesh tanned but loose around the muscles. I'd never seen a fifty-year-old man with his clothes off before, and I can't say I found his age unattractive. What his body lacked in firmness it made up for in mileage, and there's nothing sexier than experience. Maybe most importantly, his body couldn't have been more different from Adam's. There was nothing to remind me, only comfort, and an arm around me that said I didn't have to be alone.

I'd come to Will's house around ten the night before, and I'll tell you why just as soon as I figure it out myself. I'd been at the Citizen with Mad and Gordon and everybody, drinking the same drinks we always have and saying the same things we always say, and all of a sudden I had to get out. It wasn't exactly like the walls were closing in. I wasn't even drunk. I just told everybody I was tired, got in my car, and drove to Will Langston's house with total malice aforethought. He might not have even been there, in which case I would have probably gone back to my house and drunk myself into a crying jag. But he was, and when I knocked on his door he didn't even seem that surprised.

How could I be doing this? you may be wondering. How could I fall into bed with another man just a matter of weeks—days, really—after Adam's death? Even as I sit here writing this now, I couldn't tell you. Will said there was a certain connection, and he was right. I guess you don't have a choice about when you meet a person. It can be the worst time in the world, it can be right before you go off to war or a week before you're supposed to marry someone else, and it won't make a difference. I still loved Adam. I love him now, love him as I sit here on the couch with my computer and my dog and write all this down. My feelings for Adam and my feelings for Will have never precluded each other. That's the only way I can describe it.

Adam Ellroy and Will Langston are the two most attractive, complicated, utterly maddening men I've ever come across. One is dead, the other is alive, and maybe it's only human to want a new lover, even when your memories of the old one haven't even begun to fade. Or maybe I'm just like Captain Benwick in *Persuasion*. "He has an affectionate heart," the heroine says. "He must love somebody."

There was always something frenetic about sleeping with Adam, probably because I wanted him so badly. I can't even think of it as making love, it was so fast and violent and amazing. God, when I was in bed with him, I couldn't have told you my own name. Will was different that first time, gentle and funny, and we talked a lot. I can't say it was fabulous, because it wasn't. Part of me was in bed with him, and the other part of me was sitting over by the nightstand wondering what the hell I was doing. But he was very sweet, told me I had the most beautiful shoulders he'd ever seen, and I wondered how many women he'd been with since his wife died.

"You don't have to talk about him, you know. It's just that . . . I don't want there to be anything between us."

"There isn't," I said, rolling over to face him, brushing the hair back from his forehead.

"Alex, honey, don't kid a kidder. I just want you to know it's all right to talk about it if you need to."

"I really don't . . ." My voice trailed off as Will kissed the side of my neck. "Adam was . . . Adam was the love of my life. Not much of a life, I know, but he was it. I loved him from the moment I saw him, maybe obsessively. He never felt the same way about me. Now that he's gone, I'm really tempted to rewrite history, tell myself things were different than they were, but what's the point? Do you know what it's like to love someone you can never really have? Christ, it's the worst thing in the world—at least I thought it was, until he died. I remember one time, after he'd gone back to California, I was watching a movie and some actor—I think it was Daniel Day-Lewis—looked just like Adam. Just for a second, he had the same smile and the same jawline, and I started crying, right there in the dark. And there didn't even have to be a reason. I'd be unloading the dishwasher, and the idea of him would hit me like a tidal wave, wash over me and knock me down. Jesus, Will, do you really want to hear this?"

"I'm a big boy. I can take it."

"But, Will, there's more. There's something I haven't told you."

"Someone else?"

"No, not the way you mean. Adam didn't kill himself. He was murdered."

I poured out the whole story to him then as we lay together with nothing but the light from his bedside clock. I told him about the day I'd watched Adam's body pulled out of the gorge, my trip to Canada, the search for Betty Barrows and Marion Hazel. When I finished, he was quiet for a long time.

"It's . . . it's unbelievable," he said finally. "Alex, sweetheart, are you sure about this?" I nodded against his chest. "You really believe the old man who died in the gorge was the same person who was on the plane with my father when he died?"

"That's how it looks."

"I don't know what to say. My whole life, I thought . . . I don't know," he said again. "I wish I could shed some light on this. I know my mother always believed my father died in the plane crash, with Sebastien and Adelson. I'm sure of it. She never would have kept something like that from me."

"I'm sorry I lied to you, when we first met. But I didn't know if I could trust you."

"You can trust me."

"I know."

"Do you have any . . . Good Lord, I suppose the correct word would be 'suspects.' "

"Yes, but we can't prove anything yet. It's a long story, but there's another whole part of this thing I didn't tell you about. There's a former Benson student involved, somebody who was expelled for assault last year. He isn't even supposed to be anywhere near Walden County, but it turns out he was on campus the night Adam died. And there's someone else, someone high up in the Benson administration, who I'm almost positive is involved in this."

"Who?"

"I'm sorry, Will. I just can't name names until I'm sure."

"But, Alex, this concerns me too. It might have something to do with my father. Isn't there anything I can do? I'm not without resources, you know."

"I don't know . . ."

"And I don't like the idea of you poking around in this. If your friend Adam was really murdered, don't you think you might be in danger?"

"I don't have any reason to believe whoever did this has any idea I'm on to him. Can't we just . . . forget about this for a little while?"

"And how would you like to accomplish that?"

"You can't imagine."

I went straight from Will's house to work the next morning, and Mad lost no time in commenting on the fact that I was wearing the same clothes from the day before.

"Alex, are you nuts? Isn't this guy old enough to be your father?"

"And what about that Bessler freshman you were shtupping last summer? And the intern from Wells? The one whose baby tooth . . ."

"So . . . what are you up to today?"

"Subtle change of subject."

"What can I say? I've got style."

"Stewart Day. I'm going to try to bump into him, accidentally on purpose."

"What are you going to tell him?"

"I guess I'll just have to wing it."

"You're going to wing it with a suspected murderer? Jesus, Alex, you *are* in a flaky mood. Dr. Langston must still have some protons in the old particle accelerator, eh?"

"Would you please shut up?"

"Not unless you want to miss the scoop on Sydenstricker."

"What'd you find out?"

"A conversation with one of the secretaries in the physics department has yielded the sinister reason behind his absence from the conference in Chicago."

"Spill it."

"Our favorite string theorist was doing the chicken dance at his cousin's wedding in South Carolina."

"Bummer."

"Did you get anything out of Day's bio file?"

"Just what we ran when he got the job."

"You do it?"

"You kidding? That's why God created interns. Bill tried to strong-arm me into doing a profile, but I managed to weasel out of it."

"So write it *now.*"

"Write what?"

"Alex, concentrate. What's the best way to get somebody to spill their guts inside of an hour?"

"Do a profile of Day. Mad, you are brilliant."

"If you wish, you may touch the hem of my khakis. And hey, have you heard the latest? About the redecorating?"

"What redecorating?"

"Our beloved publisher has decided to turn this place into an insurance agency. We're talking gray plastic dividers all over the place."

"No way."

"Way. Marilyn's worse than pissed. I guess Chester had some efficiency expert up here, and we're not 'making optimal use of our work space,' or some goddamn thing."

Chester Davenport, the *Gabriel Monitor*'s esteemed publisher, has logged something like two weeks in a newsroom his entire life. He spent way too much time in the military in his youth, and would love to make the reporting staff drop and give him twenty whenever he deigns to walk upstairs. The newsroom basketball team, though officially called the Monitor Press, has nicknamed itself the Chester Detesters.

"Take a look," Mad said, pulling a sheet of paper from the garbage can next to his desk. "They're screwing everything around."

"They're moving the features desk into *sports*? And what the hell is this? The arts and leisure clerk is halfway across the newsroom from the arts and leisure editor? What's the point of that?"

The man himself walked up the stairs, and I beat a hasty retreat to my desk. When Bill seemed calm enough, I pitched him a Day profile. Ever desperate for quick-hit copy, he nodded like a dashboard Jesus and told me to fill out a photo assignment. I called Day's office to request an interview, and the self-promoting little schnauzer agreed to do it that very day, even offering lunch at the faculty club.

Parking on the Benson campus is like playing musical chairs with the Marquis de Sade: There's always fifty cars roving around pathetically, competing for the handful of empty spaces left after nine A.M. It was a good thing I'd left myself half an hour before my interview, because I wound up in an overflow lot on the hinterland side of the football stadium. It took me so long to hike back to central campus that I was five minutes late by the time I got to the faculty club. Through the etched-glass windows, I could see Day schmoozing his way from table to table, shaking hands with an astounding variety of middle-aged white men. I went inside and was heading over to him when a short, balding man with enormous Woodsy Owl glasses blocked my path.

"I'm sorry, miss, but this is the faculty club," he said, his British accent clipping at my toenails.

"You mean it's not the janitors' dining hall? What a disappointment."

"Students are not allowed here, unless they are accompanied by a member of the faculty or the senior administration. I'm afraid you'll have to leave," he said, trying manfully to look down on me. I may be five-three, but I had at least two inches on the guy, and I thought I could have bench-pressed him. But since Stewart Day appeared forthwith, I never got the chance to prove it.

"He seems to take his duties seriously."

"Simon? Oh, he's quite protective of us. The faculty club is supposed to be a haven from the rest of the campus. He simply tries to make sure it stays that way."

"Teaching would be a great job if it weren't for all the damn students, right?"

"The Benson faculty is deeply committed to its undergraduates."

"I was just kidding."

"Of course."

For lunch, I asked for a big salad with blue cheese dressing and an iced tea. Day ordered a joint of rare roast beef, which a liveried waiter sliced to order at the table.

Actually, no, he didn't. I wish I could report that he ordered some sickeningly rich country club lunch and washed it down with three martinis, because it would have fit so well with his overblown aura of noblesse oblige. But there he did not cooperate, ordering a tuna club, a double order of cole slaw, and an orange juice. He was, however, wearing a tie with large green whales on it.

We'd agreed to eat first and do the interview over coffee, and I spent the better part of an hour making small talk about the glory of all things Benson. Day was trying to convince me to do a feature story on a new kind of carrot the ag school was developing—Benson red rather than Princeton orange—when the waiter finally cleared our plates. Before he could sing the praises of the university dairy herd, I pulled out my notepad and, mercifully, he got the hint.

He was born, he said, in Darien, Connecticut. His father had worked on Wall Street, his mother had stayed home with him, their only child. He'd attended private day school in Darien, then Andover, then Dartmouth, where he majored in history and was president of the Beta Chapter of Gamma Sigma Rho. He'd gotten a job in the Dartmouth admissions office after graduation, he said, planning to go to law school after a year, but found he liked the work. In five years, he was assistant director of admissions at Dartmouth; by his early thirties, he was Boston University's admissions director, then vice president for student services. He'd served as V.P. for university relations at Swarthmore before coming to Benson. He was married, with two daughters; his wife had already enlisted in the Gabriel Junior League. They had a country house in the Berkshires, and an English springer spaniel named Eloise.

In short, Day had mail-ordered his life from L.L. Bean.

It was an odd, slightly distasteful experience—sitting there scribbling down the facts of a life that, I suspected, probably belonged in the fiction section. I'd interviewed my share of squirrelly politicians before, but when they tried to dodge, I could call them on it. With Day, I couldn't let on that I didn't believe him. But I had to admit the man was a pretty good liar. Either that, or he'd told the story so many times, he'd begun to believe it himself.

Had he ever been to Gabriel before he took the job? I asked. Just for a few Benson-Dartmouth football games. Was his family particularly religious? His wife was a staunch Methodist, and they were raising the girls in the church. I was getting nowhere, but I was afraid to go too far out on a limb. All I could do was nod and take notes in my horrible handwriting, and I hated every minute of it.

Through it all, Day was on his best behavior. There was no hint of the creepy authoritarian side I'd seen that day on the bridge. He'd let his control slip in front of me once, and I got the feeling that he wasn't going to let it happen again. But at the very least, I'd expected him to try to talk me into sending an advance copy of the story for his approval—something no self-respecting reporter would ever do—but he didn't even ask.

I was driving down the hill when I realized what a lousy situation I was in. I suspected that Day had just told me a passel of lies, at least about his origins. But in four hours, the night editor was going to expect a pithy profile of no more than twelve inches, newsprint being at a premium these days. So what was I supposed to do? File a story that probably contained a slew of factual errors? Goddamnit, why didn't I think of this before I pitched the story to Bill? Why didn't Mad, or Gordon the wonder boy?

I dragged Mad into the library as soon as I got back. "What am I supposed to do? File the thing? Or try to get out of it somehow? Christ, Mad, Bill will kill me. Melissa's up there right now, shooting his goddamn portrait. It's the page three feature for tomorrow."

"Pretty slow news day, huh?"

"Believe me, I've been praying for a trailer fire all afternoon."

"Don't worry. Just write the story the way you've got it down. Something'll come up, don't worry."

"But, Mad, you know this guy is full of shit. Christ, what did I think I was doing, barreling up there for an interview? It wasn't like I was going to get him to confess or anything. I am *such* an idiot. And now I've got to go file a story that I know is probably all wrong. Do you realize I could get fired for this?"

"Shh . . . Calm down. Just write it. You don't really have any other choice, do you? Think about it as the lesser of two evils, or the ends justify the means, whatever you want."

"Jesus, Mad, don't go all Republican on me."

"Cheer up. You always told me you wanted to write fiction. Now, here's your chance."

Mad left me stewing in the library, and as I was gathering the courage to face my computer, Gordon came in. "Mad said you were in here. I wanted to let you know I'm going up to ye olde frat house to hang with the brothers tonight."

"Great. Have fun."

"What's wrong? You look awful. How did the interview go?"

"Don't ask."

"That bad?"

"Worse." I explained the whole ugly situation to him. "Damn it, Gordon, you're supposed to be this bastion of journalistic ethics. Why didn't you tell me what I was getting myself into?"

Gordon sighed and pulled the tail of his shirt from his waistband to clean his glasses. "I guess I didn't think about it. But you're absolutely right. You can't file the story."

"But, Mad said . . ."

"Alex, what's the point of doing this job for shitty money, if you're not going to take it seriously? Listen, I'm hardly what you'd call a nice guy in my personal life, but when it comes to my work, I don't fuck around. I have never printed a fact that I didn't check at least twice, and I certainly have never written anything I knew to be false, and I never will."

"Not under any circumstances?"

"None at all."

"But what if . . ." I tried to think of something really juicy. "What if somebody—say the FBI—asked you to plant a false story to help catch a criminal, and by doing it you could save hundreds of millions of lives and protect the free world? What about that? Huh?"

"Must you be so melodramatic?"

"But you said you wouldn't do it under *any* circumstances. What about it? What about what I just said?"

He sighed again, this time with exasperation. "In that case, I would tell them to find themselves another reporter."

"Even if it costs millions of lives?"

"A minute ago it was *hundreds* of millions."

"Whatever, fine, hundreds. You still wouldn't compromise your ethics as a reporter to save people?"

"It would never come to that. My life is hardly that interesting."

"Gordon, stop wriggling around. We're talking theoretically now."

"Boy, you will do anything to avoid writing this story, won't you? What is it that Day told you that's got you so upset?" I gave him the Cliffs Notes to Day's life. "Wait a minute, Alex. Do you really think he's lying about all this?"

"I told you, I just don't trust the guy. And if we're right about that picture, his name is *not* Stewart Day, it's something-or-other Dershowitz."

"But it's not a crime to change your name. And as for the rest of it, Alex, think about it. Day has a top position at one of the best universities in the world. There's no way he could fake his way into that, so let's assume his job history is for real. And if he's spent his entire working life in higher education, I cannot possibly believe that he faked his academic credentials. Either he went to Dartmouth and Andover, or he didn't. And in his line of work, he's going to run into graduates of those schools. Someone would be sure to catch on."

"You know, you're right. But that still doesn't mean we're wrong about him. He could have gone to those schools, and still be lying about where he grew up, what his parents did. I could still write the story, and sort of fudge over that part. Would that pass your ethics test?"

"Forget about my ethics, Alex. What about your own?"

Gordon's dressing down had the desired effect, and I went back to my desk to make some phone calls. Working backward, I called every school Day had claimed to have worked for; they all checked out. When I mentioned his name to the woman who answered the phone at the Boston University admissions office, there was something loaded in her voice when she said that yes, she remembered him. I asked her for a comment on him just to see what she'd say, and all I got was dead air. "Oh, I don't think it's my place to say anything on the record," she said finally.

"How about off the record?"

"Off the record?" Another long silence.

"Off the record, as in, just between you and me and the wall."

"My mother taught me that if I have nothing nice to say, I shouldn't say anything at all. And in that spirit, I have nothing to say about Mr. Day."

"Look, I promise not to print anything, or even tell anybody I talked to you."

"Oh, all right. I know I shouldn't say anything, and maybe you'll think it's just sour grapes. But I've been in this office for ten years, and in that time we've had three different directors. Let's just say that Mr. Day was the least popular, by a mile."

"You mean, he wasn't a very good boss?"

"Oh, he was quite good at being bossy."

"You don't say?"

"The girls—myself and the other secretaries—we used to call him Mr. Puff Pastry. As in, 'Fat Little Napoleon.'"

"So you weren't exactly sorry to see him go?"

"We never had a party for him when he got the Benson job. But we sure as heck had one for ourselves after he left."

"Did you have any idea why he was so . . ."

"Arrogant? Overbearing? Yes, I'm talking about Mr. Day," she said to someone in the background. "Some reporter from Benson. No, she's not going to *print* this!" She laughed merrily. "One of my coworkers here says to add 'autocratic.' Also, 'badly dressed.' What was the question?"

"I asked, why do you think he was so difficult?"

"Oh, I can't imagine. I guess, because he could get

away with it. Let me tell you, he has a mean streak a *mile* wide. Once, when one of the interns got some applications mixed up, we printed out hundreds of rejections by mistake. We nearly rejected the entire freshman class— the ones we'd intended to accept, that is. Luckily, some-one caught the mistake. When Mr. Day found out, he not only fired the intern in front of the entire office, he threw a can of coffee at him. He apologized later, said he'd been aiming for the trash can, but nobody believed him."

My new confidante would have kept me on the phone for another hour, but I managed to escape after ascertaining that the coffee can incident was Day's single most violent act. I could hardly call that a harbinger of murder; after all, Mad has been known to throw pens across the newsroom so they stick in the wall like darts. Still, if Day had a temper . . .

I confirmed that he had, indeed, graduated from Dartmouth and Andover, and at that point I felt free to write the story. I'd already done ten times as much background work than I'd done for any other profile. I mean, I *never* check stuff like that. If somebody says they were at Woodstock, I print that they were at Woodstock; I don't call around to every ex-hippie I know to see if they can vouch for them, for Christ's sake.

I finished the story about seven and was on my way out of the newsroom, planning on going home to change before meeting Will for dinner. "Hey, Alex, you finish that Day profile yet?" Bill asked.

"Just filed it."

"I was just going to tell you not to bother. We can't run it tomorrow."

At that point, after half a day of jumping through Gordon's little ethical hoops, I wasn't sure if I was relieved or just pissed off. "Why not?"

"Melissa's portrait didn't come out. Bad batch of film, or else it was loaded wrong. Whatever it was, the negative was all black. She's going to have to reshoot it."

"But what about page three tomorrow? Wasn't that supposed to be main art?"

"Yeah, we're going to have to use some enterprise. The intern's out looking for something. If he brings me back another kid eating a goddamn ice cream cone, I swear I'll wring his neck."

"Remember, it takes a whole village to raise a photographer."

The film accident was just too convenient to be true. And since I don't believe in fairy godmothers, I hiked over to Mad's place. "Jacob Ebenezer Madison, you *didn't*," I said when he opened the door. "Please tell me you didn't."

"And, hello to you too. Come on in. Want a drink?"

"What I'd like is an explanation."

"Take it easy, Alex. Didn't I tell you something might come up? Besides, I was the one who suggested doing the profile. I should have known you'd work yourself into a moral quandary, and I felt sort of responsible. So, Jake Madison to the rescue," he said, humming the theme song to *F-Troop* on his way into the kitchen.

"Mad, if they find out you tampered with film like that, you could get fired," I said to his back. "What the hell did you do?"

"It's like it says in the Bible. God said, let there be light," Mad said. "And there was light."

23

WILL TOOK ME BACK TO THAI PALACE THAT NIGHT, AND as I was stealing marinated tofu off his plate, he told me he was leaving town the next day to give some guest lectures at Stanford. I was more than a little appalled at how much I didn't want him to leave. "I'm supposed to stay through Sunday, then I go to Houston, but most of the weekend is devoted to cocktail parties. I was thinking you could come out and meet me."

"Will, I can't possibly get a plane ticket on this short notice, at least not one I could afford."

"You don't think I'd invite you to go to San Francisco with me and expect you to pay for the plane ticket, do you?"

"Well, I'd hardly expect . . ."

"Why not?"

"But, Will, I don't know if I can accept . . ."

"Nonsense. You'd be doing me a favor. This way, I don't have to be in a lonely hotel room all by myself, and

I get to show off my beautiful young mistress." He laughed, and his eyes sparkled like streetlights on snow. "Truly, I'll be the envy of every physicist on the Stanford campus. Say you'll go."

It was obvious that I shouldn't. I mean, not only was it wrong to accept what would probably be a thousand-dollar plane ticket from a guy I'd known less than a month, but I had to stay in Gabriel and keep working with Mad and Gordon on the story. Plus, my roommate hates it when I stick him with Shakespeare. Clearly, I should have just thanked Will very sweetly, told him I had a ton of work to do, and begged off. But the temptation to get out of town for a couple of days was just too strong, and the part of me that slices off a second piece of cheesecake took over and told him I'd go. When I got to work, I asked Bill to take me off the on-call list for the weekend.

"Where are you off to, Bernier?" Mad asked.

"Uh . . . San Francisco."

My answer actually surprised Mad enough to make him stop typing and look up at me. "San Francisco? Since when?"

"Since . . . this morning."

"This wouldn't happen to have anything to do with a certain member of the medical profession?"

"Shut up. Okay, it might."

"Alex, as one who is older, wiser, and considerably more self-destructive than yourself, allow me to warn you that you are out of your mind."

"Mad, it's just a weekend, for Christ's sake. I'm not marrying the guy."

"No, that will be next weekend."

"It will *not*."

"Are you going to keep Bernier, or will you go by Langston professionally?"

"Are you aware that you're a real asshole? Because if you're not, I feel it's my duty to point it out."

"I'm sorry, Alex. I just don't want . . . Who am I to be doling out romantic advice? The longest relationship I ever had lasted"—he counted on his fingers—"eight days. I just hate to see you jump into something."

"I know. I wish I could tell you what I'm doing, but I don't have a clue. It just . . . Oh, Christ, I don't know. You probably know Will a hell of a lot better than I do. What do you think?"

He leaned back in his chair and put his feet up on his desk.

"You want honesty? Or a whitewash?"

"Pretend I'm your sister. The one you like. Not the one who keeps sending you pamphlets from A.A."

"That would call for honesty. Okay. Here goes. He's smart as hell."

"Of that, there can be no doubt. Go on."

"You in the mood to hear about his wife?"

"I guess," I said, actually guessing that I'd rather not.

"Quite the couple. Went to all the big social wingdings. Gave money left and right. She was on some board for children's welfare, made a couple of trips to Africa, and wound up on *Nightline*. Oh, and she volunteered for that bunch of French doctors—the one that goes into war zones."

"*Médecins Sans Frontières*. Doctors Without Borders."

"That's the one. You know, you could look her up in the croaked bio files. I'm sure there's a ton on her."

"You ever interview her?"

"A couple times, sure."

"What was she like?"

"Total babe."

"That's very enlightening."

"Okay, all right. She ran the Langston Foundation, built it up from some pretty small spuds to this big international whatever. I guess she was good at bringing the money in—crusading lady doctor and all that. And I'm telling you, the chick had *legs*. Short, but legs."

"I think I get the picture."

"You hear how she bought it?"

"Will said Kenya."

"Yeah. She was out there checking out some clinic, and wham, her Jeep runs off the road. Deader than dead. Local reax went on forever. I got stuck covering it for like a week. Tragic story. Won me an AP award."

"Don't get all choked up on me."

"Listen, I gotta know. Christ, I can't believe I'm asking you this. It is *so* unmanly. But I gotta know. What's he . . . like? You know what I mean."

"Mad, do I understand correctly that you're asking me what Dr. William J. Langston Jr. is like in the sack?"

"Inquiring minds want to know."

"Have you ever known me to kiss and tell?"

"All the time, and to anyone who'll listen."

"He's . . . sweet."

"Sweet? That's it? That's all you're giving me? Sweet?"

"What's wrong with 'sweet'?"

"Please, please, don't say that word again. It's every man's nightmare. You give a woman your all, and the next day she's comparing you to an eclair."

"Somebody go to the bakery?" Gordon said, stowing his canvas briefcase under his desk. "Man, I am *starved* for some good Italian pastry."

"Morning," I said.

"I tried to call you last night."

"What's up?"

"I thought you might be interested to hear what I found out at the frat house."

"Anything good?"

"Better than good."

"Spill it."

"Too complicated. Let's go someplace out of the way for lunch."

"I'll die. C'mon, let's go for coffee. Or down to the morgue. Gordon, you're killing me."

"You're just going to have to hold your breath for a couple of hours. I just got here, and I've got a ton of work. *Somebody's* got to write something that actually runs in the paper."

I spent the morning working on three stories: an update on the city's notorious pothole problem, a petition to make yet another street one-way, and the Red Cross's annual summertime plea for blood.

Why is it, I wonder, that you never see reporters in the movies working on stories about potholes?

Lunchtime finally rolled around, and Gordon and Mad piled into my Renault to drive out to a Chinese buffet place out on Route 13, where you can eat all you want for five bucks. Gordon refused to say anything until we were settled in the restaurant, savoring his moment of investigative triumph.

"So spill it," I said to Gordon, who'd just stuffed half an egg roll in his mouth. "All right, chew first, then spill it. But chew quickly."

Gordon washed his egg roll down with a cup of weak tea, then wiped a splotch of duck sauce from the corner of his mouth. "Okay. Get this. I went to the frat house last night to see those guys that James Caruso said might talk, and they did. Not at first. I had to admit I was a reporter, and they seemed to think I'd deceived them a little the first time I was there."

"Imagine that," I said.

"It took some fast talking to convince them I wasn't trying to drag the frat through the mud, or Caruso either. They're incredibly loyal, I'll give them that."

"But what about Hoffman?"

"He's no longer in the fraternity. Deactivated, is what they called it. Anyway, they kicked him the hell out. I gather it caused quite a schism. Most of the brothers wanted him gone, but a few of his buddies stuck by him, said if he went, they were going too. Never mind that he's already expelled; I guess kicking him out of the frat is a whole separate issue. I guess his pals backed down, because they never did move out. Now, we all know that Trevor Hoffman isn't supposed to be anywhere near that frat house. He's supposed to stay out of the county, or he's in violation of his bail. And that in and of itself is unusual; normally, the cops tell you *not* to leave town. But after all the hue and cry about the gay-bashing, I guess these guys were considered a real threat. Is that right, Alex?"

"They're basically the frat-boy equivalent of the Ebola virus. Go on."

"Okay. So these two guys I talked to—their names are Marks and Vargas, but everything is off the record anyway, so what difference does it make? They told me Caruso hasn't been near the place. Hoffman, on the other hand, has crashed there a couple of times, usually drunk off his ass. Seems he holds some sort of fraternity record for never missing a keg party in three years, and doesn't want to let a little thing like the threat of incarceration stop him. Now, most of the house is not exactly in favor of this. If Hoffman's caught there, the whole frat could get kicked off campus, maybe for good. Their reputation wasn't exactly spotless, was it? I looked it up, some story about a girl who said she was raped."

"Yeah, I covered it when I was on cops," Mad said. "It was maybe six years ago. Halloween party. Some freshman came dressed as Minnie Mouse and passed out in one of the bedrooms. Woke up without her costume. Didn't remember a thing, but there was a certain amount of, uh, physical evidence."

"And no charges were filed?" Gordon asked.

"Only internally," Mad said. "The university put the house on two years of probation for underage drinking, but that was it. The girl had no idea who'd done what to her, and if anybody in the house knew anything, they never talked. Rumor was you'd need a paddy wagon to round 'em all up."

"She was gang-raped?" I gasped.

"Alex, you go to a frat party and get so drunk you pass out, what the hell do you think is going to happen to you?"

"Are you saying she asked for it?"

"Doesn't she have some responsibility for her putting herself in that situation?"

"Thank you, Camille Paglia."

"Who?"

"Hold it," Gordon interjected. "I'm sorry I brought it up. All I was trying to do is show that the administration wouldn't thank the frat for more bad press. The school would probably love an excuse to kick them off campus, and the brothers know it. But one of Hoffman's good buddies is president of the fraternity, and the way the place is structured, it takes an act of God to veto him. These guys have a code of honor that would scare the Sicilians."

"I still don't see what's so earth-shattering," I said.

"I'm getting there. As I said, Hoffman has never missed a Sigma Rho keg party. And guess when the last one was?"

"You don't mean . . ."

"You got it. The night Adam died. And that's not all. It gets better—or maybe I should say it gets worse. Those frat parties go until, what, four or five in the morning? According to my sources, at some point in the early morning, Hoffman left the party to, quote, 'take a piss,' unquote. Eloquent little bastard, isn't he? My guys have no idea what time it was—they're not exactly choir boys themselves. Anyway, he eventually wandered back in, and he'd upchucked all over his clothes. Now, that in and of itself is nothing to write home about. But get a load of what he said."

I realized I was holding my breath and forced myself to exhale. "What did he say?"

"He said he ran into the motherfucker from the *Monitor* trying to crash their party and, quote, 'kicked his ass.'"

"And these guys will testify to this?" Mad asked.

"I guess they'll have to. They don't know it yet, of course. I told them everything was off the record, which it is—in regard to the gay-bashing incident. If they're called as witnesses in a murder case, that's another thing. If I get the same information in court, I can use it without breaking my word. God, I *love* this job."

"When you're done gloating, we need to figure out what to do next," Mad said. "Like maybe call an ambulance for Alex. Are you okay? You look like you're about to lose it."

"Gordon, couldn't you have told me all this *before* I scarfed down an entire plate of Chinese food? If I throw up on anybody, it's going to be you."

"Sorry."

"God, I would trade my dog for a cigarette. Okay, let's deal with this. How are we going to nail this guy?"

"What do you mean, nail him?" Mad asked. "Isn't this when we go to the cops?"

"With what? The testimony of a couple of drunken frat boys? How much good is that going to do? The case on Adam's death is *closed*, Mad. Do you really think this is enough to get the police to open it up again?"

"Sure. There's Caruso's testimony about Hoffman's threats against Adam, and the fact that his body was found in the gorge right next to the frat house. There's the two guys who can say that Hoffman was gone from the party, then came back claiming he kicked Adam's butt. What more do you want?"

"I want the son of a bitch to admit to it to my face."

"You're dreaming," Mad said. "The guy probably doesn't even remember doing it. Hell, half the time I don't even remember how I get home from the Citizen, and it sounds like Hoffman could drink *me* under the table."

"Hold on," Gordon said. "We have to look at how this fits in with the rest of the evidence. I mean, I think Hoffman is probably our man. But if he is, does that mean that he was the person Adam was going to meet that night?"

"He must be," I said. "Hoffman must have contacted him, said he'd finally agree to an interview, but it had to be in the middle of the night because he wasn't supposed to be on campus, and made Adam promise that he wouldn't tell anyone. Later on, he starts to freak out that maybe Adam had something in writing about the meeting, so he busts into his apartment to look, but there's so much paperwork, he panics and takes it all. Maybe he found something, maybe not. Either way, he tries to return it before it's missed."

"Hold on," Gordon said. "Are you suggesting Hoffman

planned to kill Adam, then went and bragged about it? Even he couldn't be that stupid."

"Maybe he only meant to rough him up, and things got out of hand. Maybe he was so drunk, he didn't know what he was saying. I don't know."

"But what does all of this have to do with the Sebastien case?" Mad asked. "Aren't we forgetting that?"

"Maybe nothing," I said, starting to feel tears pricking the backs of my eyeballs. "Wouldn't that be the mother of all ironies? Maybe after all this, it really was just a coincidence. I'm sure there's still a story to be dug up about Sebastien, and the plane crash and everything. It could very well be that Adam was on to that story; considering his trip to Canada, he obviously must have been. But maybe it had nothing to do with his death after all."

"And what about our friend Stewart Day?"

"Jesus, Gordon, I don't know," I said, sniffling. "What am I supposed to do, tie everything up right here in the goddamn Chinese buffet? Right now, all I can think about is that I'm fucking glad New York has the death penalty now. And to think I voted Democratic . . ."

Gordon and Mad looked abashed when I started to cry for real. "Shh, Alex, try not to get all upset," Mad said. "Let's just call the chief and get this thing over with."

"No. Please, Mad, I need to finish this. For Adam. I've got to."

"Precisely what more do you think you can do better than the cops can?" Gordon asked.

"Look, so far this kid thinks he's gotten away with it. He thinks his worst problem is this assault charge. He's already shown us what a careless slob he is by waltzing in and announcing he beat the crap out of Adam. But once we go to the police and he gets charged, it's all over.

He'll totally batten down the hatches. He'll clam up. He won't talk to anybody."

"Alex, he's not talking to anybody *now*," Gordon said.

"So who says I have to tell him I'm a reporter? This isn't business anymore, Gordon. This is way personal. I'm not going to his house with a notebook. I'd be more likely to show up with a gun and put him out of my misery."

"I'm going to assume that's the hysteria talking," Gordon said.

"Don't worry, I'm not going to go vigilante on you. I'll let the state take care of Trevor Hoffman. And bless my liberal little heart, I want to be there when they stick the needle in."

24

WHEN I GOT HOME FROM WORK THAT NIGHT, I FOUND THE first note in the mailbox.

"Leave it alone. Let the dead rest in peace." That's all it said. My name and address were typed on a plain white envelope, postmarked Gabriel, one sheet of paper inside. At least whoever sent it didn't have enough of a flair for melodrama to cut the letters out of a magazine and paste them together, like in TV cop shows.

I won't pretend I'm any braver than I am. The note really shook me up. I read it standing at the mailbox, and looked around as though whoever wrote it was going to hop out from behind my neighbor's rhododendron with a hockey mask and a machete. The only person in sight was the Widow Winsecker, who was working on her rosebushes next door, and I didn't feel too threatened by her pruning shears. I headed straight for the phone and called Gordon. He came up the hill as soon as he'd filed his story, telling me he'd hunted for

Mad in the usual haunts but hadn't been able to find him.

"'Leave it alone. Let the dead rest in peace.' What the hell does that mean?" Gordon asked.

"I'd say it's fairly straightforward. Whoever wrote it wants us to keep our snouts out of Adam's death."

"Doesn't strike me as the work of a drunken frat boy."

"Me neither."

"I thought you quit smoking."

"Yeah, until about fifteen minutes ago."

"Are you really upset?"

"Of course I am, you idiot. Why wouldn't I be?"

"You can't tell me this is the first anonymous note you've ever gotten."

"Other than some hysterical movie fans who didn't like me panning *Babe, the Gallant Pig,* it is. What, is this something normal where you come from?"

"Alex, I have a whole psycho file full of threats I've gotten over the years. Somebody wanted to bash my skull in with a lead pipe over a story once. Even included a picture of what my head was going to look like. In red crayon, no less."

"Jesus, Gordon, what story was that?"

"Hmm . . . let me see. That one was an investigative piece for *Newsday*—a couple of Girl Scout leaders were embezzling a ton of money. We called it 'Cooking the Books.'"

"The *Brownies* threatened to brain you? You seem to have taken it remarkably well."

"Part of the job. You can't let it get to you."

"But doesn't this strike you as a little different? Or are you just trying to make me feel better?"

"I just don't want you to get all freaked out over nothing."

"Nothing? Gordon, are you nuts?"

"Hoffman must have found out you talked to Caruso about him."

"But a second ago, you said it didn't sound like anything a drunken frat boy would write."

"Maybe he didn't write it. It's postmarked Gabriel, after all. He must have gotten somebody to send it for him. He'd have to. A New Hampshire postmark would be pretty obvious, don't you think? He must be trying to scare us off."

"Us? Don't you mean me? And come to think of it, how come I'm the only one who got this thing in the mail? You're as deep as I am in the fraternity end of this thing, aren't you?"

"Yeah, I am. Alex, if you're this upset, maybe Mad is right. You've done enough. Maybe it's time you went to Chief Hill."

"I don't know . . . I don't want to. Not yet." I breathed in the smoke as far as I could, and was rewarded with a coughing fit. "I mean, look at this thing. Not much of a threat, is it? 'Let the dead rest in peace'? It's not exactly, 'I'm gonna bash your head in with a lead pipe.'"

"You don't want to go to the cops?"

"Do you want to?"

"Well . . ."

"Be straight with me."

"Okay, no, I don't. My instinct is to hold on to the story as long as I can before handing it over to the cops. But that's just because I'm an anal-retentive control freak."

"And those are your best qualities."

"But it's not up to me, Alex. As you've so cleverly pointed out, I'm not the one who got an anonymous note. It's not my butt that's on the line. Mad wants you to be safe, because he's your friend and he's not the self-serving son of a bitch that I am. Maybe he's right. It's got to be your call.

If you want to go to the cops, that's okay with me. I'll get my hands on a piece of this story one way or another. But if you want to hold out awhile longer, I'm with you."

"Then let's stick with it."

"Maybe it wouldn't be a bad idea if you get the hell out of here for a while. Aren't you going to California?"

"I was supposed to. But after what we just found out about Hoffman, I was going to cancel. It hardly seems like a good time for me to blow town."

"Maybe it's the best time."

"Huh?"

"When Mad finds out about this, he's going to try to talk you into going to the police. Maybe this is a compromise he'll find acceptable."

"You mean, instead of calling the cops, I retreat to San Francisco?"

"Something like that. Whoever sent you this note is trying to scare you off. Maybe the best thing to do is let him think he succeeded."

Then the second note came, a couple of days later.

"Leave it alone. The past is past. What's done is done."

By the time the third one came on Thursday—*"Some things are better left as they are"*—I had my hand on the phone to call Chief Hill. I'm not sure what stopped me, other than the most basic, knee-jerk refusal to be scared off by some homicidal nimrod. Gordon hadn't had any luck figuring out who was sending the notes; his sources in the frat house didn't seem to know anything. The tone of the threats was so strange, so weirdly esoteric. It was hard to imagine Trevor Hoffman cleaning the vomit off his Benson football jersey and repairing to a typewriter to warn me that "some things are better left as they are."

It was a relief to get on the plane to San Francisco, though it was just my luck to be seated next to a couple of newlyweds. If their halogen wedding rings hadn't given them away, I would have been clued in by the smooching and groping they kept up for the better part of three thousand miles. I scrunched into the wall as far as I could without stepping out onto the wing, turned Beethoven up really loud on my Walkman, and prayed for a little turbulence.

Will wasn't waiting for me when I emerged from the gate, rumpled and cranky. Instead, there was a chauffeur holding a sign with my name on it.

"Hi, I guess you're looking for me," I said, not sure whether to shake hands with him or what. It was my first chauffeur. "Um, I wasn't expecting a car."

He handed me an envelope containing a sheet of paper and a room key. "Got caught in meetings. Had the hotel send a car. Hope you don't mind. See you at 8. Will."

The San Francisco airport is south of the city, and it took about half an hour to get to the Fairmont. The hotel looks like an embassy, very fancy and official, and way too grown-up for yours truly to be spending the night. The front door was held open by a guy who looked like he should've been carrying a trumpet in a road company of *Henry V.* Will opened the door to room 316 wearing a business suit and looking tired. He kissed me briefly, which was a considerably less enthusiastic greeting than I'd expected, and I could taste the memory of a martini on his lips.

"Are you okay?" I asked.

"I'm fine. No, I suppose I'm a little drunk. I wanted to meet you at the airport, but I couldn't seem to bow out gracefully after my talk. I hope you didn't mind that I sent the car."

"No, of course not. Don't be silly. It's fine. Are you sure you're okay? You seem pretty tired."

"It's been a long day on top of a long week. I'm just . . .

exhausted. I'm sorry, Alex. I shouldn't have dragged you all the way out here. Now I'm not even sure I can get away tomorrow to spend the day with you."

"Is that what you're so riled up about?" He didn't answer, just collapsed into a blue velvet easy chair and plucked his drink off the end table. "What's the matter?"

"You don't ask a woman to fly across the country, then leave her alone in a hotel room for two days."

"Don't worry about it. It's no big deal. It's just good to see you."

"Oh, Alex, you have no idea how sorry I am. I wanted to . . ."

"Would you cut it out?" I said, kneeling by his chair. "I told you, I don't mind. Now stop apologizing, or I really am going to get peevish."

"Peevish?" he said, cracking a hint of a smile. "That's a rather elderly word for one so young."

"You've caught me. I confess. I'm a closet Jane Austen freak."

"I don't deserve you," he said, a comment so weird and out of the blue, I had no idea how to respond.

"Oh, yeah, sure," I said finally. "You've got seventeen advanced degrees and you cure cancer for a living. You're right. I'm way out of your league."

"No," he said, "don't joke. I'm very serious. I really don't deserve you," and slipped out of the chair so we were facing each other on our knees. He kissed me then, and there was more behind it than there had ever been before, something deliciously intense and out of control as he pulled me down to the floor with him. Eventually we wound up in what proved to be a very wide and comfortable bed, and the last coherent thought I remember having was that although there was nothing even remotely sweet about it, it felt pretty goddamn good.

25

~

The House of Nanking is one of those little hole-in-the-wall restaurants that has so much atmosphere simply because it has no atmosphere at all. The customers sit at what amounts to one long table—actually, lots of little tables shoved together. Once you cram into your seat, the owner basically tells you what to order, and although the food is fantastic, you eat it at the risk of having your eye poked out by some stranger's chopstick.

In short, when I used to fantasize about meeting the mythical Olivia, the House of Nanking wasn't the sort of place I imagined. Frankly, I don't know what I expected; maybe her calling me up, begging for career advice, once I'm chief film critic for *The Boston Globe*. But as it was, my first vision of her was walking down Kearny Street in a bright yellow slicker with the hood thrown back and a blond ponytail bobbing in the rain, looking for all the world like a five-year-old kid. Okay, make that a five-year-old supermodel. She had these impossibly long legs connecting the bottom of her raincoat to a pair of ankle-high Timberlands, and eyes as big and blue as the YMCA pool. I've always wondered why it is that pouring rain makes some women look so damned alluring, and others—like, say, myself—look like drowning groundhogs. I guess the secret is probably a pair of really good cheek-bones, which I lack, and which Olivia has by the yard.

As she walked toward me, I wasn't entirely sure it was her. I mean, Adam had described her to me, but for a few seconds I held out the hope that maybe I was really supposed to be meeting the obese lady in the flower-print muumuu who was crossing the street. For about the tenth time, I questioned the wisdom of calling Olivia that morning; even though she'd been extraordinarily nice in the half-dozen times we'd talked since Adam's death, I still wasn't sure if I was in the mood for a face-to-face meeting with the woman he'd dumped me for. What's the proper etiquette for two women who've been crazy in love with the same man? How's a civilized person supposed to act? I mean, like Mad says, female tigers just skip the formalities and *eat* each other, for God's sake.

"Alex?" she said, and when I nodded, she took me by surprise by wrapping her arms around me and holding on tight; she was a lot stronger than she looked. The top of my head barely came to the collar of her raincoat, and my face got wet from being pushed against the yellow plastic. "It's so wonderful to finally meet you. After hearing about you all this time, I feel as though I already have."

"You look, um, just like I thought you would." So much for impressing her with my rapier intellect.

"You look just like your picture."

"Picture? What picture?"

"You know, the one Adam used to keep in his apartment."

"He kept a picture of me?"

"You didn't know?"

I shook my head. She brushed away some of the damp hair that was sticking to my cheeks, and there was something motherly and totally genuine in the gesture. "Isn't that just like him? Lord, sometimes I forget all the things about Adam that drove me out of my mind. He always did have a talent for hiding his feelings from everyone, including himself. Let's get out of this rain. We're both getting soaked. Are you hungry?"

"A little."

"I'm starving. Do you still feel like Chinese? This place is cheap, and it's the best in town."

"It looks like a pretty long wait, but I don't mind waiting on line if you don't."

"Screw the line." She laughed and cut ahead of the dozen or so people standing on the sidewalk waiting to get in for lunch. A man in a stained apron smiled broadly when he saw her, and the two of them launched into a torrent of Chinese—don't ask me if was Cantonese or Mandarin. I wouldn't have thought anyone else could fit at the table, but the owner made everyone else slide down a bit and jammed us into two seats he squeezed in at the far end. He brought us water, tea, and chopsticks and said something to Olivia, which must have had something to do with lunch.

"Where'd you learn to speak Chinese?"

"I spent my junior year of high school in Taipei," she said. "It didn't exactly hurt when I was applying for jobs around here."

The owner—who seemed to be the waiter and occasional cook as well—returned with a plate of vegetable dumplings and a dipping sauce that was sweet and slightly peppery. I managed to snag one with my chopsticks without dropping it in my lap. As Olivia ate, I noticed she was left-handed, and glinting off that hand was a diamond the size of a peanut M&M.

"Do you like my rock? I think it's sort of much, but what are you going to do?"

"When's the wedding?"

"Next spring. The Ides of March, actually, isn't that a laugh? At least Michael won't forget our anniversary. He was a classics major."

"Oh, I get it. So does he teach?"

"Hardly. He sold out. He's in advertising. He and a friend from Stanford started their own firm. They've done some political campaigns, and some pro bono, AIDS awareness, and that sort of thing. They swear they'd never do a Marlboro ad, but if the money were good enough, who knows? Do you have any idea what a house costs around here? It's out-of-this-world expensive."

"How did you two meet?"

"Oh, it's a great story. Very romantic, if I do say so myself. You really want to hear? All right. I was flying back from Philadelphia—I'd been visiting a friend from J-school who works for the *Inky*—and I had my pillow with me . . . Wait, I suppose I should back up. Whenever I go on an airplane, I always bring a pillow with me, a real feather pillow, or I can't sleep. So I had my pillow, and I'd taken over the middle seat too, but there was this man sitting on the aisle. I was hungover and bitchy, and I remember being really annoyed—like how dare the airline sell that seat when I needed to stretch out? The last thing I wanted to do was talk. But he said something cute like, 'I hope you've got an extra ticket for that pillow,' and we started chatting, and he told me he'd been visiting his family in New Hampshire. And then when they turned the lights out for the movie, he gave up his seat so I could stretch out."

"He switched seats? I guess chivalry isn't dead after all."

"Oh, no. He slept on the floor."

"You've got to be kidding me." Just for five minutes, I'd like to know what it's like to be six feet tall and blond. "Okay, keep going. Now I'm dying to hear how he went from sleeping at your feet to proposing marriage."

"Okay," she said with a grin, and her smile was really endearing. She was obviously crazy about the guy. "So I woke up just as we were landing, and he had to sit back down and put his seat belt on, right? I don't know why I didn't notice before, maybe because I was so tired, but I realized this man was absolutely gorgeous, not my type exactly, but just incredibly attractive. And I thought, I've got to find out who he is."

"So you asked him for his phone number, and the rest is history."

"No." As she shook her head, her ponytail flopped from side to side like a happy blond squirrel. "I wanted to, but I didn't have the nerve. The plane landed, and I just let him get up and walk out of my life."

"So how did you ever get together?"

"Guess."

"Oh, God, I don't know. He sent up smoke signals. No, wait. I've got it. He hired one of those planes to fly over San Francisco with a sign that said, 'Marry me, O blond goddess.'"

"Nothing that good."

"I give up."

"It was the pillow. That night, I found his business card inside my pillowcase. I guess he must have put it in there while I was asleep, because when I went to wash it, there it was. And he'd written on the back of it . . . Oh, no, I can't tell you. It's too much."

"Go ahead. It can't be any worse than sleeping on the floor of a 747."

"Here." She reached into her brown leather backpack, pulled out her wallet, and extracted a card. On the front it said "Michael Hoffman, Denali Advertising," with the usual contact information. On the back was written: "You are the most beautiful creature I have ever seen, and unless you call, I will spend the rest of my life in loneliness and misery."

"Is that all? He could at least have written it in his own blood."

She laughed, and a piece of tofu fell off her chopsticks onto her plate. "You're funny. Adam always said your sense of humor was the thing he liked most about you."

I stared down at the card, wrinkled from being shown off to untold gaggles of girlfriends. How come this Michael could pour his guts out to Olivia within five minutes? And why couldn't Adam and I ever talk about whatever it was we really felt for each other? And what the hell was I doing with Will?

"Why's it called Denali Advertising?" I asked, grasping for something else to think about.

"He and his friend decided to start the business one summer when they climbed Mount McKinley up in Denali National Park in Alaska."

"And I take it you called him?"

"How could I not? Believe me, I was prepared for him to turn out to be a total jerk with a wife and three kids. But he wasn't."

"And you lived happily ever after."

"Not hardly. We broke up twice, and once he had a fling with one of his ex-girlfriends from Palo Alto, and Adam and I . . . Well, you already know that part."

"It *is* a good story."

"Thanks. But what about you? What are you doing out here, anyway?"

"I came out to stay with a friend who's at a conference in the city. He's a professor at Benson."

"Is this a romantic thing?" I didn't answer. "That's all right, it's none of my business anyway."

"I don't know how to explain it. I don't want you to think I just . . . That I just forgot about Adam. Or maybe it's just my own guilt talking. I guess I'm not particularly proud of myself."

"Let me tell you a secret. I left something out of my story about Michael. When we met, when he left me that note, he was engaged to somebody else. He didn't even tell me until he'd broken it off. Now technically, when he started pursuing me, he was cheating on her. My best friend said that meant he couldn't be trusted—that any man who would dump his fiancée for you meant he would eventually dump you for someone else. But you know my theory? I think the heart wants what it wants. I think life is messy and it's complicated. And I think that if this man is right for you, in the long run the rest won't matter."

I told her about Will as we finished lunch, and by the time we walked out onto Kearny Street, the rain had let up and the sun was peeking out. She asked if I felt like coffee, and we walked over to North Beach, San Francisco's version of Little Italy, and found a café where we got giant cups of cappuccino and split a hunk of tiramisù.

"I really miss him, you know," she said, licking the froth off her spoon. "I get the feeling you don't want to talk about him, but it feels strange not to, like we're dancing around the one subject that really matters."

"I'm afraid if I start, I'll never stop."

"Never stop what?"

"I don't know. Crying. Thinking about him. You name it."

"I'm sorry, Alex. I know it's much harder for you than

it is for me. He and I didn't leave anything unresolved. We'd made our peace, and I think in the end, we really were friends. Maybe we understood each other better apart than together."

"I'm not sure I understood him at all."

"Sure you did. Better than me, I think. From what Adam told me, I think you really did understand his mania for independence, for the freedom to pick up and go anywhere, anytime. I used to call it his pathological need not to be needed. It was one of the things we used to fight about most—I wanted to get married, he didn't want to settle down; I wanted to move in together, he wanted to keep his own place. It took me a long time to realize that it was just the way he was, and I was never going to change him, and it was a mistake to try."

"I know the feeling."

"Alex, I don't want to upset you, but I need to know what's going on back in Gabriel. Have you learned anything new?"

"I'm sorry. I should have said something right away, but I guess I've been trying to escape from it."

"I don't blame you. But I feel so . . . isolated out here. There's nothing I can do to help you find out what happened to Adam. I hate to think of you trying to do this all by yourself."

"I'm not exactly alone. Two friends of mine have been helping me—Mad, who's the science guy, and Gordon from the *Times*. But there's something I should have told you from the beginning, I mean ever since we met today. We think we know who killed Adam."

"Why didn't you . . ."

"Like I said, Olivia, I'm sorry. I guess I've been waiting for the right time. It's a pretty long story." I started from the beginning, telling her about the assault on the two gay students, and how Adam had covered the story. I was so caught up in what I was saying, it took me a few minutes to notice that her expression had morphed into something like real fear.

"Oh, my God, Alex," she said, sloshing coffee into her saucer as she put it down hard. "Please tell me you don't think this has anything to do with Trevor."

I stared back at her. "Are you telling me you know Trevor Hoffman?" The man at the next table looked up from his Italian newspaper. I tried to lower my voice and leaned closer to Olivia, who looked on the verge of tears. "You know him, don't you?"

"Trevor is . . . He's Michael's younger brother. Once we get married, he'll be my brother-in-law."

"Oh, Christ."

"It's like they say," she said after a glacial minute. "You can choose your friends, but you can't choose your family. Trevor is a problem kid, to say the least."

"Olivia, we have some pretty solid evidence that he's the one who killed Adam."

"No, he couldn't have." She shook her head violently. "I can't believe it."

"He was back in Gabriel the night Adam died. He was at a party just a few hundred yards from the bridge where Adam fell off. He disappeared for a while, and came back saying he'd beaten up the *Monitor* reporter who'd been bothering him. What do I have to do, draw you a picture?"

"But why would he have wanted to kill him?"

"I don't know. I'm not saying he was really in control of himself when he did it. Apparently he was pissed off that Adam had been writing stories about his attack on the two freshmen."

"But he wasn't."

"What do you mean?"

"Adam wasn't writing about Trevor, at least not any more than he had to."

"How do you know?"

"Because he did it for me."

"What?"

"Wait. Hold on. I know this is going to sound terrible. Let me go back to the beginning and explain everything."

"I really wish you would."

"Michael is ten years older than Trevor. There's just the two of them, and Trevor was the baby, and I suppose he was spoiled, not that it's any excuse. But it probably wasn't easy to follow Michael. He was a big soccer star, magna at Stanford, the perfect kid. Trevor was trouble from junior high—lying, stealing from his mother's purse, sneaking drinks. In the ninth grade, he went away to school, just like Michael did. I think their father went to the same place. It's called Holderness, somewhere in New Hampshire."

"It's in Plymouth."

"So he went away to school, and he didn't do very well. Scraped along academically, but socially he fell into a bad crowd—if you ask me, he's the kind of person who'll find the wrong crowd wherever he goes. He only lasted a year before he was expelled for drinking and his parents sent him to another school, and he got expelled again, and then went to military school. He finally graduated from there. I'm not sure how he got a scholarship to Benson, except that he's apparently a very good football player, and he probably tested well on his SATs. Trevor isn't stupid."

"What happened once he got to college?"

"His parents stopped worrying about him. Michael says the military really suited his brother, and he hoped he'd do ROTC. Their grandfather was a Marine in World War II, and their father was career army—a drill-sergeant, no less. Trevor was supposed to be the first one in his family to become an officer."

"But it didn't work out that way."

"I think his first semester went well, but then he got into that horrible fraternity and started backsliding. Only from what Michael says, there was something really ugly about him that wasn't there before. And then one day Michael's parents called and said Trevor had been arrested. Their father is a real law-and-order type, and he just about put Trevor through a wall. His mother still can't believe he did anything wrong. Either way, he's just about ruined his life."

"But if you know what this guy is like, why are you so unwilling to believe he killed . . ."

"Because he had no reason to. Let me finish. After Trevor was arrested, Michael flew home and when he came back, he was really worried about his mother. He said all the publicity was killing her. I know that sounds melodramatic, but his mom is diabetic and she can't take stress. It was an incredible coincidence that Adam was covering the story, but then again I suppose it isn't that odd; we work in a pretty small world. I'm not saying I did the right thing. But I was worried about Michael and his family, and I asked Adam to lay off. I know it wasn't fair. Maybe you could say I called in a favor."

"And he agreed?"

"Kind of. Adam was happy at the *Monitor.* He said he wouldn't do anything that might jeopardize his job. But he did promise he wouldn't try too hard to track Trevor down, that he wouldn't go out of his way to keep Trevor's name in the news. But obviously, when it came to the cops or the trial, he'd have to cover it. He just wouldn't be as . . . enterprising as he might have been otherwise."

"Adam told our city editor that he couldn't get him to

talk. He said he called and got hung up on. Are you telling me he was lying?"

"I honestly don't know. Maybe. Probably. But believe me, Alex, the family wouldn't have talked anyway. Think about how much time we spend harassing people who we know aren't going to talk to us. We just keep after them, so we can say we did."

"Forgive me, but that's a load of crap. We keep after them because it's our job." As soon as I'd said it, I felt guilty. She was obviously desperate to rationalize the whole thing. Still, the idea of Adam soft-pedaling his job, lying to Bill for Olivia's sake, really pissed me off. "But wait a minute. A source in the frat house told us that when Trevor came back to the party that night, he said he'd just beaten Adam up. If Trevor didn't have anything against him, why would he say that?"

"I don't have any idea. But one thing I do know is that Trevor always has to make people think he's a big man. Maybe he was just bragging. Maybe he ran into Adam, and later he boasted that he'd roughed him up."

"He knew who Adam was?"

"Sure. He couldn't stand him, or any of the other reporters who covered the story. You can't really blame him for that."

"But did he know you'd asked Adam to leave him alone?"

"I didn't want anyone to know about it. But I told Michael, and he told his mother, and naturally she went and told Trevor. So you see, Trevor had no reason to kill him. He knew Adam was a friend of mine, and presumably he knew that as long as Adam was the one covering the story for the *Monitor*, he didn't have to worry about being hassled."

"Do you really think he would have thought about it so logically?"

"Alex, I know we hardly know each other. But I'm going to ask you a favor. Have you gone to the police with your suspicions about Trevor?"

"Not yet."

"I'm glad. He's a creep, but I don't want him punished for more than he's done."

"That's what you want me to do? Keep quiet about Trevor?"

"I want you to find out what really happened to Adam. If Trevor turns out to be guilty, we'll all have to live with it. But I still can't believe he's a murderer. I think that when he attacked those freshmen, he hit bottom. And if he didn't kill Adam, there must be some other explanation. I'm asking you to put Trevor aside for now, give him the benefit of the doubt. Would you do that for me? Please, Alex?" She looked at me pleadingly, her big blue swimming pools starting to overflow, and I could imagine all the times Adam must have gazed into them. "Don't you have any other suspects? Anyone at all who could be involved?"

"There's someone in the Benson administration. But . . ."

"Then please, Alex, just consider the possibility that Trevor didn't do it."

"There were some loose ends . . . Things that don't really make sense, that we haven't tied up yet."

"See? So it could be that Trevor really isn't responsible." She seemed so relieved, she was positively giddy. "Thank you so much, Alex. You're great. It's easy to see what Adam saw in you."

Cheap shot, I thought. But I just said, "Do you think they let you smoke in here?"

26

I WAS LOUNGING IN THE HOTEL ROOM IN MY LITTLE BLACK
dress, waiting for Will to take me to dinner at Greens,
when the phone rang. I figured it would be Will saying he
was late, but it turned out to be Gordon—which was
funny, because nobody knew where I was staying. "How
did you track me down here?"

"Lucky guess."

"No really, how?"

"No joke, lucky guess. I just called the best hotel in
town and asked for Will Langston's room. Got it on the
first try."

"As always, I stand in awe."

"Listen, Alex, are you alone?"

"What's up? You sound all weird."

"Is Langston there?"

"You mean right this minute? No. What's up?"

"I was doing some research, and there's something

odd." Odd. That was the word he used, but the tone in his voice said *very, very bad.*

"What is it?"

"I went through all the bio files for the Benson faculty—just the sciences, not arts or vet or anything."

"You've got to be kidding me. There must be, what, hundreds of them in there."

"Three hundred sixty-three."

"Must've taken you forever. What the hell for?"

"I skimmed them. It only took me last night."

"But what for?"

"It's just the way I do things."

"Leave no lead unfollowed?"

"Something like that."

"So what did you find?"

"I'm not exactly sure. But there was something in the file on your friend Langston."

I sat down on the shiny walnut coffee table. "What?"

"It's . . . Okay, let me start from the beginning. Most of the files were a complete mess. Who's the librarian, anyway? I've never even seen him. Forget it, it's not important. Anyhow, some of the library files look like they got mixed up with circulation. Neat trick, since they're on different floors."

"Its happened before. The guy works in both departments, and he's an idiot. Come on, Gordon, what did you find?"

"You know how circulation has these cold-callers that phone people up and ask them to subscribe?"

"Yeah, sure. So what?"

"Jesus, those guys are a pain in the ass. They've already called me twice and I've only been here a couple of weeks. Don't they even know who works for them?"

"What's your point?"

"Okay, I gather they do everything by computer, and they keep a log of who they call and when and what happened. You'd think with all that they'd figure out when enough is enough, but apparently not. Anyway, in Langston's file I found the calling list under his phone number. They called him eight times in three months."

"So what?"

"Alex, one of those calls was on July 24. The same day Adam died."

"And so? I don't understand."

"I talked to one of the troglodytes down in circulation. Those logs only list calls where they actually *spoke* to the person."

"I still don't . . ."

"Alex, he was supposed to be out of town at a conference. Isn't that everybody's alibi? But according to the circulation log, he was there to answer his phone."

"But Mad said . . . It doesn't make any sense. Mad showed me the clips from the conference. I saw his picture in the paper. There must be some other explanation."

"There very well may be. But after I ran across that and I knew you were out there with the guy, I thought I should . . . I don't know, warn you."

"Warn me?"

"Alex, minus the fact that he was out of town, don't you realize that Langston is as connected to this as anybody? More even."

"But he was out of town . . ."

"*Allegedly* out of town."

"I don't . . ."

"How well can you possibly know this guy, anyway?" I flashed back to the night before, all the heat and intensity and Will saying *I don't deserve you.*

"I . . . No, Gordon, I can't believe it. You don't know him."

"Do you?"

I heard a key turn in the lock. "I've got to go."

"Be careful. Alex, promise me you'll call me back as soon as you . . ." I hung up just as Will was walking in the door. Except that I'm not blond, it was positively Hitchcockian.

"Good Lord, Alex," Will said, freezing in the doorway. "I feel as though I should call the police."

"Police?" I squeaked.

"That dress. It should be illegal. My God, it looks as though it were painted on with a fire hose. You know, a man could get used to coming home to this." He came over and kissed me hard and quick, then crossed over to the bar. "I'm going to fix myself a drink. Want one?" I just gaped at him. "Well, do you want one or not?"

"Oh. Absolutely."

"How was your lunch date?" he asked over his shoulder.

"Fine."

"Who did you meet?"

"My friend Olivia."

"Where did you go?"

"Chinatown."

"Are you ready for dinner?"

"Sure."

"Would you still like to try Greens?"

"Okay."

He turned from the low table where he'd been mixing a couple of gin and tonics. "You're awfully monosyllabic this evening."

"I'm just a little tired."

"We don't have to go out if you don't want to. But it would be a shame to waste that dress . . ."

"I don't think I'm that hungry."

"Is everything all right? You don't seem like yourself."

"I'm fine." Okay, so I wasn't trying very hard to convince him that nothing was wrong. But I was only half paying attention to what Will was saying; all I could think about was what Gordon had told me. Should I just ask him straight out if he'd really been home that weekend? I tried to summon up six years of acting classes. *Smile. Think about something that makes you happy. Adam. No, not that. Something else.* "I'm perfectly fine. It's just the time change. It always freaks me out."

I must have looked more convincing than I felt, because he seemed to buy it. He crossed the oriental rug, put his arms around me, and rested his chin on top of my head. I could hear his heart beating through his cotton shirt, so pale blue it was almost white.

"Would you just like to go to bed?"

"Oh, no," I said, maybe a little too fast. "Let's go out to dinner."

"I thought you weren't hungry."

"I'm not." I pulled away from him and retreated to the other side of the sofa. I don't think I sprinted, but I can't swear to it. "But, I mean, I've always wanted to try Greens. For a vegetarian, it's like Mecca."

"Are you sure you're all right? You look rather shaken."

Say you're fine. Go out to dinner. Have a lovely plate of arugula. Then get on a plane and get the hell away from him until you can figure out what's going on. "What was with you last night?"

He'd been on his way toward me, but he stopped. "I'm not sure what you mean."

Actually, I didn't mean anything. I was only trying to stall, give myself a chance to figure out what to do. But as I stared at him across the four-star hotel room, I realized I'd whacked the nail on the head, and I couldn't think of a way to back out of it. "Last night. You seemed like a different person all of a sudden. Like somebody I didn't know."

He shrugged. "We all have our moods."

"It seemed like more than a mood."

"What was it then?" He took a step toward me, and I backed up. Another step. I backed up again. It was a weird little waltz, with half a room between us, and it seems funny in retrospect. At the time I can't say I appreciated the humor. "Alex, what's going on?"

I forced myself to stand still. "That's what I'm asking you."

"My God, Alex, you're scared of me. Aren't you? I can see it in your eyes."

"Why would I be scared of you?"

"It was last night, wasn't it? I came on too strong." He looked genuinely stricken, and it threw me off balance. But he was right; last night was part of it. I just didn't have the guts to open my mouth and ask him about the rest. "I'm sorry, Alex. I get like that sometimes. Brooding, I suppose. Please don't take it personally."

"How am I supposed to not take it personally?"

"I know I'm not a particularly easy person to be around at times."

"But why did you say you didn't deserve me?" He didn't answer. "Will, what was that supposed to mean?"

"Just that. Alex, I'm more than twice your age. You're young, and beautiful, and smarter than you give yourself credit for. Here I am barging in at what is very probably the worst moment of your life. I feel as though I'm taking advantage of your grief."

I didn't know what to say. Maybe he was right. But he sure wasn't talking like a killer.

"You're not taking advantage of anything."

"Yes I am. You asked me to behave like a grown-up, don't you remember? You looked me straight in the eye and told me that you tended to rush into things, begged me to be the one with the self-control. But I've let you down, haven't I?"

"Will, I showed up on your doorstep and practically threw myself at you."

"And I should have been man enough to tell you to go home."

"I wouldn't have listened."

"I should have made you." There was a thin lick of anger in his voice, and I wasn't sure if it was at himself or at me. "I told myself that if there was any hope for us, I had to take things slowly. But there you were, offering yourself up to me like some gift I didn't have any right to unwrap, and I wanted you so badly, I couldn't stop."

"Will . . ."

"Alex, tell me what to do."

There was this voice in my head saying, *Ask him.* Ask him about the weekend Adam died. Find out if the man you're sleeping with could possibly have had anything to do with killing the man you love. But I couldn't come up with the words. "Will, what the hell is going on here?"

"Do you really want to know?"

"Of course I do."

"I'm falling in love with you."

I stood there staring at him, and he all but leaped across the room at me. He grabbed me by both arms, and I had one second of pure fear before I realized he was kissing me, and going at it with more force and intensity than anyone ever had. He pressed his lips against me so hard it cut my tongue against my teeth, and when I bit his neck a little smile of blood came through the skin. *Vampire,* was the only coherent thought I remember having, and at some point we must have rolled off the couch and onto the floor. Afterward, as I lay panting with my skirt hiked up to my waist and my head jammed against the leg of the coffee table, I realized two things. For the first and only time in my life, I'd had sex without any birth control. And when he came, and dug his fingers into my shoulders so hard it left a three-day welt, he called me Laura.

27

~

I FLEW BACK TO GABRIEL ALONE ON SUNDAY AFTERNOON, and this time I had the whole row to myself. Three thousand miles is a long way to go, even in the jet age, and I finished the new Robert B. Parker mystery somewhere over Denver. With nothing to distract me but the complimentary peanuts, I couldn't stop thinking about Will. I wasn't frightened of him exactly. There had to be some simple explanation for what Gordon had found, a mistake in the newspaper's notoriously flaky circulation department. But sitting there in coach hoping the pilot hadn't drunk his lunch, I was starting to seriously doubt my own sanity. Did the *Monitor* health plan cover Prozac?

I got home after midnight Sunday, and as soon as I could drag Gordon and Mad into the newsroom library on Monday morning, I told them Olivia's story. "Don't tell me you bought it," Gordon said. He'd forgotten to take the headset off, and he looked like he belonged in Mission Control. "You really think that just because some chick says Hoffman didn't do it, he didn't do it?"

"I don't know. She seemed so sure . . ."

"She just sounds desperate to me," Gordon said. "She's trying to protect her boyfriend. Who the hell is this woman anyway? Where does she get off being so sure about people she hardly knows?"

"She works for a metro."

"Oh. Why didn't you say that before?"

"So what do we do now?" Mad asked.

"For better or for worse, I promised Olivia we'd lay off Hoffman for a couple of days, look into possibilities before we went to the cops about him."

Mad brushed some bits of the drop ceiling off the librarian's desk and sat down. "What other possibilities? We've got witnesses who heard him saying he knocked Adam's block off. What else do you want?"

"Olivia swears it was just bragging. You know, drunken frat boy stuff."

"Alex," Gordon said. "It's my understanding that 'drunken frat boy stuff' means panty raids and swallowing goldfish. This is what we call manslaughter."

"I know. I'm not trying to make light of this, believe me. It's just that . . . Look. You may not understand, but Olivia gets to have a say in all this. She loved Adam as much as I did, and she knew him way longer. For her sake, I hope it isn't Hoffman. Olivia's engaged to his brother. How's she going to deal if it turns out Hoffman killed him?"

"So what are we supposed to do now?" Gordon said. "Wait for a confession to move over the AP wire?"

"Let's try and find out what Stewart Day was up to the night Adam died, whether or not he went home after the fund-raising dinner."

"How are we supposed to do that?" Mad asked.

"Gordon's the wonder boy. Let him figure it out."

When I got home from work, I forced myself to check the mail—which might sound brave if it hadn't taken me ten minutes to get up the nerve. But there were no new threats, nothing in there at all but a Victoria's Secret catalogue, which is depressing in itself since none of the really pretty bras ever come in a 34DD.

The anticlimax set the tone for the rest of the week. Gordon hadn't had any luck figuring out where Stewart Day had been when Adam died. Olivia's conscience must have been getting to her, because she called three times to see how things were going. I didn't have the heart to tell her that both Gordon and Mad still had Trevor Hoffman all but strapped to the gurney.

And what the hell was going on with Will? I'd taken his bio file home, sat in my backyard looking at pictures of him shaking hands with Bill Clinton. Could he possibly be mixed up in a murder? It was hard to even think of him parking in a handicapped space.

The week dragged by, fruitless and frustrating. I went to Professor Spencer's house twice a day, knocked on the door, called out pathetically for a while, and left another note. But after the first one disappeared, the rest just started to pile up between her front door and the screen. Could she possibly be holed up in there?

By the time I got home Thursday night, I'd quit looking at the mailbox like a kid eyes a measles shot. There'd been no more threats, not that I could really have described them that way in the first place, more like Zen riddles. It wasn't until I was sitting in my pink easy chair with the dog on my lap that I noticed something attached to her collar. Something small, and white, and folded. Typed.

Please don't make me hurt you.

I leaped out of my chair, sending the dog squealing off into the bedroom and spilling my iced tea all over the hardwood floor. Whoever left the note had been in my house, had his goddamn hands *on my dog,* for Christ's sake. I edged my way to the kitchen, picked up my Wusthof butcher knife, and forced myself to look in every room, peeked into the closets and under the beds. Nothing could make me go down to the basement, so I locked the door at the top of the stairs. If anyone was down there, they could damn well stay put. How whoever it was had gotten in wasn't hard to figure out. We're not much into security, and every window on the ground floor was wide open.

I tried to call Mad and Gordon; neither was home. I must have some good karma with the universe, because just as I stood there shaking in the middle of the kitchen, Dirk came home. I threw myself into his arms the second he walked in and cried all over his favorite red cotton shirt.

"Lexie, my sweetheart, what's wrong?" I gave him the butcher knife and sent him downstairs to make sure no one was lurking in the basement. Then, for what felt like the thousandth time, I told the whole story. I had to; Dirk had a right to know if some psycho was planning on killing us in our beds. The story had grown so much by now it took half an hour to get through it. When I was done, he looked a little dazed.

"Lexie, darling heart, I don't know whether you're very brave or very, very stupid. This is just about the craziest story I've ever heard. But if there's even a little bit of truth in it, don't you think you'd better go to the police before something bad happens? If you're right, then whoever sent you this has already killed at least one person, maybe more. It's not someone you want to futz with."

"I know." I laid my head on the cool blue tile of the kitchen counter. "Dirkie, I don't know what to do. We must be close to the truth. We must be close to *something,* because whoever sent this is trying to warn me off." He picked up the phone. "Dirk, please. You can't call the police. Not yet."

"*Guten abend, liebling,*" he said into the phone. The rest of the conversation proceeded in German, which I have no knowledge of beyond *Hogan's Heroes.* "Okay. It's settled."

"What's settled?"

"Helmut is coming over, and we're going to guard your life from all evildoers."

"What did you tell him?"

"Don't worry, Lexie"—Dirk is absolutely the only person I allow to call me that—"I just said somebody was sending you threatening letters because of a story you were working on, and you were scared, and we needed to keep you company. It'll be fun. The *Ubermensch* is making schnitzel."

"Vegetarian schnitzel?"

"What other kind is there?"

Helmut came over an hour later, with a case of wheat beer and a copy of *Der Blau Angel* on videotape. We watched the movie, which is so depressing it makes your life look like a picnic, even if you're being threatened by an anonymous sociopath. I drank a few beers, which I never do, and when Helmut brought out a couple of joints I didn't turn those down, either. We sat there laughing and eating garlic bread and singing German beer-drinking songs, and I think I actually managed to forget about the whole mess for fifteen minutes.

I lay in bed and tried to look at things rationally, which was difficult considering the room was spinning in both directions at once. Who the hell had broken into my house? And why? Or rather, why now, when we'd learned practically nothing all week? I'd done nothing for the past five days but stake out Professor Spencer's like some extra on *NYPD Blue*. Could whoever had sent the notes have seen me there?

I woke up the next morning at ten, with my tongue stuck to the roof of my mouth and cotton balls where my brain used to be. Thank God, I was working the swing shift that night, and didn't have to be at work until three. Shakespeare was asleep at the foot of my bed, and it drove me insane to think that some bastard had gotten his hands on her. He could have killed her, if he'd wanted to. What would I have done if I'd found her head in my bed, like the horse in *The Godfather*?

I had to have some answers, and all my instincts were telling me there was only one place to find them. I took a shower to get the beer smell out of my hair and drove over to Betty Barrows Spencer's house. I'd had just about enough of playing Jehovah's Witness, and my rap on the door was less than polite. No answer. I walked around to the back door, knocked on that one. The one-car garage was attached to the house, and I peered in the small window. The burgundy Volvo station wagon was still parked inside. I circled the house again, too riled up to realize I was trespassing. All the first-floor windows were closed.

I stopped in the middle of the backyard and looked up to the second floor. There were five windows, small ones like you find in older houses. Two were open, and I flirted briefly with the idea of climbing the rose trellis before I came to my senses. "Hello," I yelled up to the open windows. "Professor Spencer? Are you home? I know you're in there. I'm not leaving. Go ahead and call the police, but I'm not moving until you talk to me."

I might have been talking to the sunflowers, for all the response I got.

"Professor Spencer, *please*. Adam Ellroy was my best friend. Please, you have to let me in." The back door opened a crack then. Just a crack. I thought I was imagining it for a second, then got a definite glimpse of a face topped by a helmet of white hair. I walked toward the door slowly, terrified she was going to slam it again. She opened it a little wider.

My first thought, ridiculously, was that she still looked just like Katharine Hepburn. Her figure was good, and she wasn't hunched over at all. She had on a simple, rose-colored dress, and it suited her. Stockings and heels, even though she'd apparently been holed up in her house by herself. A heavy gold chain circled her neck and disappeared into the top of her dress.

"Professor Spencer?" I asked. She nodded, and the mass of hair piled on top of her head swam gracefully with the motion. "Can I come in?" She nodded again, and stepped back to let me pass. The room was breathtaking. Four deep burgundy velvet chairs, their backs covered with delicate pieces of ivory lace, surrounded a circular table of intricately carved wood. Paintings hung three-high on the walls; statuary, china, and crystal figurines covered every surface, and nestled in mahogany hutches that stood against three walls. A Steinway grand dominated one corner, its cover open.

"Do you play Beethoven?" She nodded. "Were you playing on Saturday?" Another nod. "Why wouldn't you let me in?"

"Please sit down," she said in a low voice, and I was

startled to hear her speak for the first time. We stared at each other; I wasn't sure whether to act the interviewer or just wait.

"You're probably wondering why I'm here . . ."

"I know why you're here, Miss Bernier," she said, and I realized all at once that this woman was very, very frightened.

"What are you scared of?" I blurted out. She pulled a handkerchief from her sleeve to dab at the corners of her mouth. Her hands were shaking.

"Miss Bernier, please, I have to ask you to leave this alone. Please trust me. You seem like a very intelligent young lady. You're certainly a persistent one. But nothing good can come of this. Some things are better left as they are."

Some things are better left as they are.

"Oh, my God," I said. "You sent the notes." No answer. "Someone has been sending me threatening notes. One of them said exactly what you just told me: 'Some things are better left as they are.' I'm asking you, *did you send them?*"

"You've gotten them too?"

She rose from her seat opposite me, back straight as a rifle, and went to a rolltop desk crafted of the same rich wood. She reached inside her neckline, drew out a key, and unlocked the desk. Rolling back the cover, she drew a stack of white envelopes out of one of the pigeon holes. I only had to read a few lines to realize that whoever had sent the notes had done it in duplicate. I wondered who else might be on the mailing list.

"Professor Spencer, I don't mean to be too forward, but would you like me to make you some tea or something? You don't look very well."

"Would you like some?" I said I would, as much to

have an excuse to stay in her house as for the caffeine I craved like crack. She made the Earl Grey with loose leaves, served in an antique teapot covered with a cozy. On one small cut-glass plate, she arranged lemon wedges studded with whole cloves; on another, English short-bread biscuits half-dipped in chocolate. Our cups were delicately painted with roses and vines, so thin you could hold them up to the light and see the outline of your hand through the bone china.

The absurdity of the whole scene struck me as I watched her balance a small silver strainer over each cup to catch any wayward leaves; the ritual seemed to soothe her somehow. We were strangers who might be in danger because of something that had been set in motion more than half a century before. And there we were, nibbling butter cookies and sipping tea like we were at the Junior League. It was all too crazy for words.

She tried to balance her cup and saucer on one knee, then seemed to think better of it and placed it on the three-legged table at her side.

"Miss Bernier, I really wish you weren't involved in this," she said finally.

"So do I. But I am involved. I have been since someone pushed Adam Ellroy off North Creek Bridge. And I'm going to stay involved until I find out what happened to him."

"You were close to Mr. Ellroy, I believe you said?"

I gave her the *Reader's Digest* version of my relationship with Adam, but even though I glossed over most of the details, I couldn't keep the tears out of my eyes. I'd been close to crying in her backyard just a while before, and now the grief melded with the anger and the fear. The cookies, which had tasted pretty good a minute ago, threatened to come back up on me. Her patrician eyebrows drew together into a deep furrow, and she pulled the lace handkerchief from her sleeve.

"My dear, I'm truly sorry for you. Please, try not to cry. Take this. I'm afraid I don't know a great deal, not nearly as much as someone seems to think I know."

"Please . . ." I barely got the word out. She made soothing sounds and patted my knee.

"Try to calm yourself, my dear. Here, drink your tea. Drink your nice hot tea, and I'll tell you everything I know about André Sebastien."

28

THE WORD EVERYONE USED WHEN THEY TALKED ABOUT André was 'brilliant.' That's how they always described him, even in passing—'that brilliant young man.' And he was. He was the youngest professor ever to be tenured in the Benson physics department, and as far as I know that's still true. He had an incredibly facile mind, could grasp any concept almost instantly. But he wasn't like so many of the other scientists he worked with, men for whom science was the whole wide world. André loved art, and literature. He spoke several languages. French, of course, and he was fairly fluent in German, which was the lingua franca of the scientific world in those days. He also spoke Italian, which I studied in college, and we often spoke it together.

"We met in the fall of 1943. It was in the university art museum, and I must confess that in all the hundreds of times I've been in that building over the years, I always think of the day I met André. I'd just graduated from

Barnard, and come to Benson to pursue a PhD in art history. I had it in mind to be a professor, though my parents hoped I'd meet a suitable man here, fall in love, and get married. I did fall in love, and I did get married. But not to the same man. But now I'm getting ahead of myself." She leaned forward to take a sip of tea and settled back into her chair. "If we had a matchmaker, you might say it was Sir Lawrence Alma-Tadema."

"The painter?"

"One of my favorites, quite popular during the Victorian era for his rather racy Greek and Roman scenes. But, of course, even in a repressed age, you could show a little leg in the name of classical art. Benson owns a number of his works, two of which, I'm proud to say, I helped the museum acquire. But you didn't come here for an art history lecture."

"I want to hear the whole story."

"I met André just a few days after I started my first year at Benson. As I said, it was at the museum. It was a Saturday, I remember. A very sunny Saturday morning, which as you know is rare here in Gabriel, and I remember wondering what a young man was doing in a museum on a day like that. As for myself, I was just wandering through the galleries hoping for inspiration. You see, you were supposed to come to school with at least a vague idea of what you'd write on for your dissertation. But I've always been quite a generalist—I still am—and I was having a terribly difficult time trying to decide.

"André was pacing around the main gallery, stopping at various points to stare at one particular painting, an Alma-Tadema. *Women of Amphissa*, it's called, depicting the morning after some bacchanalian festival. He was quite absorbed in it. We were the only two people in the room, and although I tried to concentrate on the art, I found myself glancing at this young man, who was behaving so eccentrically. He was quite striking-looking, with black hair and blue eyes, very bright blue, like the sky in a Magritte painting. I wouldn't have called him untidy exactly, more rumpled, as though he never gave a thought to his dress, just tied his tie around his neck and threw on his jacket and had done with it.

"'No matter where you go, she looks at you.' That was the first thing he ever said to me. 'Pardon me?' I said, or some such, and he explained that the woman at the center of the painting, the one in the plain brown dress, was looking straight at him, regardless of where he stood in the room. I told him that the model for her was the artist's wife, and I'd always thought of her as the conscience of the painting.

"He introduced himself then, and it seemed perfectly natural that we should walk around the gallery together, then continue through the rest of the museum. I showed him my favorite John Singer Sargent painting, the one of the woman all dressed in white over a pot of incense, and we had a little debate over what mood the Goose Girl was in when Bougereau painted her.

"When our tour was over, he asked if I'd like to go for a walk. We went all over campus, hiked the trails in the wildflower preserve near the reservoir, and he bought us lunch from one of the carts by the duck pond. It was all terribly romantic. I think I fell in love with him that day, not so much at first sight but over the course of a few hours. There was an ease to being with him, a sense of not having to talk all the time. I've often thought the definition of a perfect mate is someone with whom you can just be *quiet*.

"We spent most of our free time together after that. There wasn't much, of course. I was starting my PhD, and he was immersed in his research, and his teaching. After that first day, we made a habit of going on long walks together, and we'd sit in front of the sundial on the engineering quad and read each other poetry. He was very fond of Victor Hugo, and also Alexander Pope, although the latter remains beyond me. We both loved Yeats, and one of the first poems he ever read to me was 'When You Are Old.' I think about that poem a great deal now, now that I really am old. Do you know it? No? Well, perhaps you'll recognize the second verse.

"How many loved your moments of glad grace,
And loved your beauty with false love or true,
But one man loved the pilgrim soul in you,
And loved the sorrows of your changing face."

"Those were heady days, and as I look back, I'd call them the happiest days of my life. I had everything. I was young, and in love, and spent my days studying art. Of course, I did my dissertation on Alma-Tadema—or, rather, I started to. But I'll get to that in good time.

"I don't mean to romanticize the past. I loved André, and he loved me, but he wasn't an easy man to know. Brilliant men never are, nor truly talented men, for that matter. There's always a part of them you can never truly know. You just have to accept it, understand it's an integral part of the man you fell in love with. In any event, that's how I tried to think about it. It wasn't always easy. André never told me much about his work, but I never asked questions. There was a war on, and loose lips, as they say, sank ships.

"He never actually told me he was doing research for the government, but I always suspected that was the case.

There was just too much pressure, too great a sense of urgency, for his work to be purely academic. And on a practical level, I knew that if André wasn't doing something to help the war effort in his research, he would have joined up. You can't imagine what it was like for an able-bodied young man to walk down Main Street, U.S.A., in civilian clothes in those days. You could see the disapproval in people's eyes. As I say, he never told me any of this outright. But when you spend a great deal of time with a man, his moods can become your own.

"We were engaged a year after we met." She pulled the gold chain out of her blouse a second time, drawing it over her head. Next to the desk key was a platinum ring, a diamond mounted on an intricately filigreed band. "We never set a date for the wedding. Everything was too uncertain. André knew he might be called away suddenly to do research elsewhere, perhaps for a long time, and it wasn't clear if I'd be able to go with him. We saw each other less and less, as his work put greater demands on him. Again, he never said anything specific, but I gathered there was considerable tension in the department, or perhaps within his research team."

"Did he get along with the people he worked with?"

"Well, yes and no. It was a close-knit department. Physicists aren't like other scientists; I think their research into the fundamental nature of matter makes them more creative, perhaps more eccentric, than people in other fields. I've often wondered if anyone can understand a physicist, except another physicist. André and his coworkers socialized together, barbecues and picnics in the summer. In the winter, there were cross-country skiing parties. I got to be quite close to Rosie Adelson, and also Joan Langston. I used to baby-sit for a number of the faculty children. Some of those friendships have lasted a lifetime. Rosie moved to Miami with the girls after Seth died, but I stayed in touch with Joan, and also Fred and Daphne Knight, and when I began teaching at Benson years later, they made me feel quite welcome. So yes, I'd say it was a close group.

"But even though the department was like a family in some ways, there was a certain amount of tension. When one person gets tenure, for instance, it usually means that someone else will be passed over. There was always competition for grant money, a better teaching schedule. And of course, there was the research, not only the usual need to publish or perish, but the extraordinary pressure of working for the government during wartime. One Saturday, a few weeks after Thanksgiving, I convinced André to come out of the laboratory long enough to have dinner with me. I cooked at his apartment, and I built a fire, because I thought it might relax him. I remember we sat drinking our coffee in front of the fire, and it was very cozy, with the first real snow of the season on the ground. But he couldn't unwind. He seemed terribly frustrated, and I broke my own rule and asked him if something was wrong at work.

"'He's just going too fast, Betty,' he told me. 'He wants to win so badly, he's playing with things none of us understand, and I'm afraid that something terrible could happen.' That's all he said, and I think he regretted saying it, though it was so very vague. I never asked again. A month later, he was dead. He'd never told me he was going away, but he'd taken other research trips at the last minute, so it didn't seem out of the ordinary.

"The plane crashed, and André was dead, and Bill Langston, and Seth Adelson. The pilot too, of course, but none of us knew him. He was young, though, that much we read in the papers, and his family was surprised, since they thought he was somewhere in Europe. But again, it wasn't the kind of thing you asked questions about. Patriotism demanded a certain lack of curiosity. Like the posters, said 'No careless talk.'

"It was Rosie Adelson who called me, absolutely hysterical. 'They're gone, Betty,' she told me. 'All three of them. They're gone.' I'll never forget her voice as long as I live. I dropped out of school and moved back to New York. That's where I met Alan, who was working on Wall Street. We were married within a few months, a time I barely remember. All I could think of was André, and I married Alan for no better reason than to have someone to fill up the emptiness. I'm not sure why he married me. With my Barnard education, I suppose I seemed a worthy wife to have on his arm at cocktail parties. I apologize if I sound bitter. I don't really blame him. He's no longer living, and it's no use to speak badly of the dead. The marriage dissolved in less than two years, quite a scandal in those days. My parents were mortified. The only positive thing to come out of that time was my doctorate, which I completed at Columbia. I couldn't bear to write about Alma-Tadema, so I threw away all the work I'd done and started over."

"I'm so sorry to upset you."

"It's not upset, exactly. It's just . . . deep feelings. Feelings I thought I'd laid to rest fifty years ago. Then, last month, it all came back. But let me back up a bit. A few months after the plane crash, something strange happened. I got a package in the mail, a book of Yeats poetry. It was marked to a certain page, a poem called 'The Lake Isle of Innisfree.' I'd never read it before, but I've known it from memory ever since. The beginning goes,

"I will arise and go now, and go to Innisfree,
And a small cabin build there, of clay and wattles
made:
Nine bean-rows will I have there, and a hive for
the honeybee,
And live alone in the bee-loud glade.

And I shall have some peace there, for peace
comes dropping slow,
Dropping from the veils of the morning to where
the cricket sings;
There midnight's all a glimmer, and noon a purple
glow,
And evening full of the linnet's wings."

"I never found out who sent it to me. That is, not until a few weeks ago."

"It was André Sebastien. He was still alive."

"So you know."

"I've suspected. But how did he contact you again after all those years?"

"I was sitting right here, in this chair. There was a knock at the door, and there he was. Older, much older, but I would have recognized him anywhere. His jet-black hair had turned entirely white, and he was terribly thin. He looked exhausted. In fiction, I suppose I would have fainted dead away. But I just stared at him, wondering if what I was looking at could possibly be real. You can't imagine what it was like, to have a ghost fifty years gone suddenly appear on your doorstep. I couldn't speak. The eyes were the same brilliant blue I remembered, and I suddenly realized how old I was, how I must look to him after all those years, and I was ashamed.

"He must have seen it on my face, because the first

thing he said was 'Betty, you're still so beautiful. My lovely, lovely Betty.' In retrospect, I think I must have been in shock. He took me inside and sat me down, and we talked for hours and hours. It all seemed like a dream, even as it was happening. The young man I'd lost fifty years ago had come back to me, and in so many ways he was exactly the same.

"Naturally, after the first shock had passed, I had so many questions. He didn't explain everything. He said he didn't have much time, that he knew he was dying. He might only have a few months left to live. 'I have to make things right, Betty,' he told me. 'After all these years, the truth has to come out. When I die, the truth will die with me.'

"I asked him to tell me about the plane crash, but he wouldn't say much. 'There wasn't any plane crash.' That's all he'd tell me. He said I'd learn everything soon, but he needed to make it right before he could tell me. He kept repeating that: 'make it right.' I asked him how he'd lived, what he had done all those years, and he was more willing to talk about that. He said that after he left Gabriel, he went up to Quebec, way up north, where his mother had been born. He changed his name, opened a grocery store, and just . . . lived. Once a few years had passed, he said, it was almost as though André Sebastien had never existed. The only contact he ever had with his old life was to send me the poem about Innisfree; it was his way of telling me not to worry. But when he found out he was dying, he knew he had to come back to Gabriel and tell the truth."

"But how did he find you?"

"I asked him the same question. He'd subscribed to the Barnard alumni magazine, so that he'd be able to follow my life from a distance. That was how he'd found out I was married, and of course he had no way of knowing about the divorce. All those years, he thought I was another man's wife. And just a few days after he came back to me, he was dead. I knew in my soul he hadn't committed suicide. He was going to live out whatever time he had left here, with me, in this house. I couldn't believe he would abandon me a second time.

"When his body was found, it was like losing him all over again, only this time there was no one I could turn to. You must understand, Miss Bernier. You of all people know what it's like to believe in your heart that a man did not take his own life. I knew someone had killed André. Whomever he'd told his secret hadn't wanted it to see the light of day. I didn't know where to turn. The news story about his death had been written by Adam Ellroy. All I had was the name. So one night, about a week after, I called him at home. I told him I knew it hadn't been a suicide. I gave him what little information I had, and begged him to look into it. He was polite, but I knew he might not take me seriously. He asked me if I had any proof, and I had to admit I hadn't.

"And then, a few weeks later, I saw the front-page story. Adam Ellroy had killed himself, jumped in the same gorge where they found André. I'm not a stupid woman, Miss Bernier, and I have never been a hysterical woman either. But not for one moment did I believe it was a coincidence. I began to get frightened. I thought about going to the police, but I doubted they'd put much credence in an old woman's fears. Then the notes started coming, and I knew whoever had killed them wouldn't hesitate to harm me as well. I've been paralyzed. I haven't left my house in days, not even out to the front stoop to get the mail."

"Please, think. Do you have any idea at all who might have killed them?"

"I've spent so many hours thinking about it. All I can tell you is that whatever André was hiding must have had something to do with his research. It must be connected to the physics department, or the army, or the government, since I believe he was working for them at the time."

"But there's something else I don't understand. When you called Adam, did you mention something to him about the *Monitor*—the newspaper from July eighth?"

"It was something else André said to me. He saw the paper sitting here on the table, and when he read something on the front page, it seemed to upset him. 'It's still going on, Betty,' he said. 'The lies are still going on.' I asked him what he meant, but he wouldn't say more. When I called your friend Adam, it was one of the few hints I could give him as to what might have been on André's mind."

"Do you remember a man who worked for the physics department—a janitor named Yitzhak Dershowitz?"

She started to shake her head. "Wait. Yes, I think I do. They had a large family, six or seven children. Yes, I remember them now. They were immigrants—Russian, or perhaps it was Polish. I always thought . . ."

"What?"

She held up a thin finger and didn't speak for another ten seconds. "I'm trying to consider how to put this without sounding like an elitist. Although I suppose that at my age, one is entitled to say anything one wants."

"Please, go ahead," I said, surprised at how much I wanted to jump out of my chair and shake her into answering. What would my mother say?

"What I'm trying to say is that the family kept to itself

a great deal. Whether or not the marriage was what you'd call happy, I couldn't say. But I would say there was always something . . . bitter about them."

"Bitter? How do you mean?"

"The few times I ever spoke to Mr. Dershowitz, I always got the impression that he was far more intelligent than he let on."

"I don't understand."

"Once . . . Goodness, it's so hard to remember after so many years. But I do recall that once I interrupted a conversation between him and André, and Mr. Dershowitz seemed very uncomfortable and walked away. André said they'd been talking about physics, and I gathered that André was quite impressed by how much he understood. And I recall that on one occasion, André told me that he'd caught Mr. Dershowitz in his laboratory, not cleaning it, but going through his things."

"He thought he was going to steal something?"

"Oh, no. I don't think that was the sense I got from André at the time."

"But what do you think it meant?"

"I can't imagine."

"Do you know Stewart Day? The vice president for university relations?"

"An administrator? Heavens, no. We in the art history department have always tried to stay as far away from Yaukey Hall as we could. Why do you ask?"

"I've seen a photograph of Yitzhak Dershowitz. Stewart Day looks enough like him to be his twin. Or his son."

I stayed as long as I could and tried to get her to eat a little, but I had to leave for work at three. She gave me a kiss on the cheek, and I said I'd come back later to see if she needed anything.

I never made it. The police found her at the bottom of

the stairs after an anonymous phone call brought them to her door. Her neck was broken.

The story ran in Saturday's newspaper, under the headline "Retired Benson Art Historian Dies." Gordon wrote it, and afterward he told me that for the first time in his life he noticed that the first part of "deadline" is just "dead."

29

ALL THE LIGHTS WERE TURNED OFF IN MAD'S APART-
ment, the streetlights casting jumpy patterns on the floor
as a bulb flickered somewhere. My eyeballs ached from
crying too much with my contact lenses in, but Mad's
body was warm and his arm was around me. He stroked
my head and told me everything was all right, but even he
didn't sound convinced. Neither did Gordon, who sat opposite us in Mad's old wicker chair drinking a Corona. It
was two o'clock in the morning, and I hadn't moved from
Mad's couch for hours.

It was Gordon who found me downstairs in the
morgue, hunched over in a corner and crying hysterically.
I don't remember much about it, but Gordon tells me I
was quite the basket case. He apologized before he
slapped me hard across the face, and to this day, though
he's still one of my best friends, I could swear he enjoyed
it a little too much.

Gordon told Bill I was sick, then parked me at Mad's

and went back to the paper. Mad offered me some tea, and that made me start crying all over again. He was just trying to make me feel better, but all it did was remind me of Betty Barrows.

"She was so scared, Mad. I should have known she was in danger. What if my going to visit her was what got her killed?"

"Is there any chance it was an accident? You said she was pretty old, and upset. Maybe she really did fall down the stairs."

"Oh, Mad, I can't believe that any more than I believe that Adam accidentally fell into North Creek Gorge."

"I don't believe it either. And I think it's time we finally went to the police."

"We're so close. I know we are."

"Alex, this is ridiculous. Someone killed André Sebastien to cover this thing up. Then he killed Adam, and now Betty Barrows. What else has to happen before you smarten up?"

"I promise I'll talk to Chief Hill on Monday, okay?"

"Monday? Christ, Alex, we both know his home number by heart. We can call him right now, tell him about Stewart Day, the whole damn thing. What the hell is wrong with you?"

"Forty-eight hours. That's all I'm asking. Every instinct I've ever had is telling me something is about to break. I keep thinking about what Betty Barrows said, that this all went back to what Sebastien was working on, whatever happened fifty years ago. We know there was never any plane crash. So why did someone say there was?"

"I can only think of one reason, and that's to cover up how they really died."

"But what if we're not just talking about the three sci-

entists? What if we add the other two deaths into the bar-
gain? Peter Murphy's car accident, Marion Hazel's house
fire. We've got five people dead, or at least disappeared.
You're the science guy, Mad. What could possibly have
happened?"

"Maybe the same thing that's happening now. Someone murdered them, and made it look like accidents."

"But *why* would someone want to murder them?"

"There was a war on, Alex, and we're fairly sure that
Sebastien was working on something related to the Manhattan Project. Maybe someone killed them to stop what
they were doing."

"Who would have done that?"

"How about the Germans? The Japanese? Somebody
who didn't feel like having an atomic bomb dropped on
their head? Oh, forget it. It's ridiculous, anyway. None of
the really important research for the Manhattan Project
was done at Benson. Some of the theoretical stuff, sure,
and several guys went to Los Alamos. But the facilities
didn't exist to let you get anywhere near building an actual bomb. You can't do that kind of research in a regular
lab, not if you want to stay in one piece."

"So where does that . . . Mad, wait a minute. What if
that's exactly what happened? What if there was some
sort of lab accident? That would account for the deaths,
and it would also give a damn good reason for covering
it up."

"No way. If somebody detonated an atomic bomb on
campus, you could have seen the mushroom cloud from
Syracuse. Unless . . . Wait a second. There was something
I was reading about . . ." He jumped off the couch and
pulled out one of his god-awful physics books. "Here it
is. Something called a 'nuclear fizzle.'"

"A nuclear whatzzle?"

"Fizzle. I won't bore you with the details. It's an explosion, a relatively small one. It wouldn't necessarily do much damage."

"Big enough to blow up a building?"

"I don't know for sure. Probably not. It depends."

"A laboratory?"

"I'm no expert. I think so. But that's the kind of research they did at Los Alamos, not Benson. It would have been way too dangerous. And besides, you'd need a good-sized chunk of plutonium."

"But what if somebody *was* doing that kind of research here at Benson?"

"In the middle of a campus full of kids? Everything's different when you're at war. But nowadays, you might call it criminal."

"Sebastien told Betty Barrows he was afraid something terrible was going to happen. What if it *did* happen? 'He's going too fast, he wants to win too badly.' That's what she told me he said. What if Sebastien saw it coming?"

"But there's no evidence that kind of research was ever done here."

"Think, Mad. Wouldn't the whole point of covering it up be so there *wouldn't* be any evidence?"

"Did Betty Barrows know who Sebastien was talking about?"

"She wasn't sure. But don't forget, we're not just talking about things that happened fifty years ago. Three people have died in the past few weeks. Someone's out there *now* who doesn't want the truth to come out. Betty Barrows said she thought it all went back to the government, the army, or the physics department."

"The feds? Holy shit. What are we talking, conspiracy theories?"

"It sounds crazy, I know."

"I'm not sure what's worse—the feds or the army. Jesus, I'll take a bunch of pissed-off physicists any day. Besides, maybe we're just going off the deep end."

There was a knock on the door, and we both froze until Gordon came in. "Jesus, you ever thought of locking the door?" He laid a six-pack of Corona on the coffee table. "Alex, you're going to kill me."

"For anything in particular? Or just because it feels good?"

"For scaring the shit out of you in California."

"What are you talking about?"

"Remember what I told you about Langston? That he was in town the weekend Adam died? Well, he wasn't. At least we don't have any evidence that he was. Listen, Alex, I'm really sorry. I should have stuck to the golden rule, confirmed it three times before I told you. But you were out there with him, and I just kind of lost it. But I went to check my facts afterward, and I tracked down the clerk who actually made the calls. Turned out to be some twit they hired for minimum wage."

"Christ, Band," Mad said. "We're *all* twits they hire for minimum wage."

"You're not wrong. But anyway, this chick can't have an IQ in the triple digits. She told me she thought she was supposed to record every single call she made, not just the ones where she actually talked to somebody. So the records mean nothing at all."

"You asshole," I said. "I took your word for it. And the one time in your life you screw up, you practically get me accusing Will of murder? How the hell am I supposed to explain this to him?"

"Did you actually tell him what I told you?"

"No, not exactly. But he'd have to be an idiot not to figure out there was something wrong. I *told* you it had to be a mistake. For fuck's sake, Gordon, how much else have you screwed up?"

"Calm down, Alex," Mad said. "I can't believe I'm sitting here defending the New York wonder boy, but it's more fact-checking than I ever would have done. Let's just get over it. Besides, we know a shitload more than we did then." While I fumed in the corner, he filled Gordon in on what we'd been talking about.

"A nuclear fizzle?" Gordon said. "I've never heard of it. So, you can have a nuclear explosion without really having a nuclear explosion? Is that it?"

"More or less," Mad said. "Basically, a fizzle is what happens when your reaction goes too slowly. Or else it can happen by accident if you mix the wrong stuff together. Something similar killed a guy at Los Alamos— Slotin, I think his name was."

"But what about the radioactivity?"

"There would be some. I couldn't tell you how much. I just cover this stuff, remember?"

Mad's phone rang then, the old black rotary-dial bleating like a dying sheep. "Could be for me," Gordon said. "I told Bill I'd be over here."

He was right. The call was for him, and as he listened, a pinkish tint started to connect the freckles on his forehead. "I'll be right over," he said finally.

"What the hell is up?" Mad prompted.

"One of my cop sources called looking for me."

"Yeah, and?"

"It's over," he said. "Stewart Day confessed."

30

HE'D BEEN HEADING DOWN THE HILL FROM CAMPUS, PAST the Tibetan monastery on Browning Street, when the cops stopped him. He wasn't speeding, or even driving that erratically. But apparently in his zeal to get wherever he was going, he forgot that Browning runs one-way *uphill*. This town is full of one-way streets, which is a convenient way for the police to catch drunk drivers. But as it turned out, Day wasn't even that far over the legal limit. What he was, though, was hysterical. From what Gordon's cop sources told him, Day just kept saying "it's not my fault" over and over until one of the patrolmen wanted to sock him so badly his partner had to hold him back.

I have no idea whether the confession will hold up in court, considering his whacked-out mental state and however much he'd had to drink. They gave him one of those walk-the-line, touch-your-nose sobriety tests, which he failed miserably, and they read him his rights and hauled him down to the police station. The whole way down he was singing like Maria Callas—about how it was an accident, that he didn't mean to hurt her, that it was positively, definitely, and most emphatically *not his fault*. If I'd been in the patrol car, I would have wanted to deck him too.

The university counsel is a guy named Sandy Timmerman, a man so uptight he makes Stewart Day look like a patchouli-wearing hippie, and for the past fifteen years has won the local press corps's poll for the most unpleasant person to deal with on the entire campus. Timmerman was the first one on the scene after Day got arrested; I don't know how he found out about it so fast, but he managed to get Day to shut his mouth before he completely ruined his life. My mom's a lawyer, and she tells me that if Day were her client she could get him off the hook faster than you can microwave a burrito.

At that point, of course, none of us were sure of how things had really gone down at Betty Barrows's house. All I knew is what Day had been ranting before Timmerman showed up. "It's not my fault. I didn't do anything wrong. I just wanted to talk. I never laid a hand on her. It's not my fault . . ." He kept mumbling something about his father, and how it was a crime that a PhD should have to work as a janitor just to make a living, and how important he was back in Poland. He'd been coherent enough to tell the cops who he was talking about—that it was Professor Spencer—and of course it turned out that he was the one who made the anonymous call. I suppose you have to give him some credit for that—for being enough of a human being to call someone and not leave her lying there for God knows how long.

But after Timmerman got to him, it was obvious that Day wasn't going to say anything more to the cops, much less the press. He'd been ticketed for going the wrong way down a one-way street, which isn't exactly a capital offense, even with Republicans in the statehouse. We had no idea if he'd be able to convince the cops that Betty's death had been an accident, and although the pieces were falling into place, we still didn't have enough evidence to tie him to Adam.

"What do we know about what Day was up to the day Adam died?" Gordon asked from a plastic chair in my backyard. The temperature had hit ninety-seven at noon, and we were drinking a pitcher of frozen margaritas. Salt clung to the rims of the red plastic glasses, Shakespeare chased the chipmunks, and it was hard not to feel just a little relaxed. We knew who had killed Adam, and proving it was just a matter of time.

"During the day, he was sailing with his family," I said. "It's that night that's the question. The university council was having its midsummer meeting at the Davidson—that's the Benson hotel—and Day was there until around midnight. We got that from one of Dirk's pals at Benson Catering."

"Okay," Gordon said. "You're probably sick of hearing this, but let's think about it logically. We don't know exactly how Day ended up over at the old lady's house, but . . ."

"Me," I said. "I have the worst feeling it was because of me. I told her we thought someone in the Benson administration was involved. Then I went and asked her about Stewart Day and whether she thought he could really be one of the Dershowitz kids. One of the last things she said to me was that she couldn't stand it anymore—waiting there all helpless by herself. What if she decided to take it all on herself? Maybe she thought she could get him to admit everything, and we'd both be out of danger. What if she called him up and . . ."

"That's just speculation," Gordon said. "You're beating yourself up for nothing. If we're going to prove anything, we need to go over the facts one by one. And let's not forget Trevor Hoffman. Do we think he didn't have anything to do with this after all?"

"I don't suppose we're going to get anything else out of the frat brothers, are we?" Mad asked.

"Doubtful," Gordon began, "but I could . . ."

"The *fraternity*," I shrieked. "I can't believe I didn't think of it before. Day was president of Gamma Sigma Rho at Dartmouth. What was it? The Beta chapter. And isn't Benson the Alpha chapter?"

"So you think Hoffman killed Adam to help out a frat brother?" Mad said. "You've gotta be kidding me."

"Hold on a minute," Gordon said. "Didn't you tell me Hoffman's whole family was career army? His grandfather was in World War II? Maybe he's connected up that way."

"What?" Mad asked. "Semper fi, let's go throw some old guy off a bridge?"

We went on like that for a couple of hours, each of us proposing theories with varying levels of absurdity, the other two shooting them down with varying levels of politeness. We finally ran out of energy around two, when I pried Mad's fingers off his drink and kicked the two of them out. I'd already made plans to go over to Will's place, ostensibly to go swimming. The truth was, I had big plans to apologize for suspecting he was a homicidal maniac.

"Do you have a tennis date?" I asked when he answered the door in goofy white shorts and a polo shirt.

"In a few hours," he said against my neck. "Would it

be impertinent if I asked you what you were wearing under this?"

"Bikini."

"Excellent answer." He kissed me again, very well in fact, and when he ran his hands under my sundress his shorts didn't hide much.

"Listen, have you seen this morning's paper?"

"Not yet. Why?"

"Let's go outside and talk, okay?" We settled on a deck chair, me lying back and him perched on the end.

"What's happened?"

"Stewart Day got arrested for drunk driving."

"The bloody fool's been nipping at the flask again, has he?"

"Apparently. Will, it's not funny."

"I'm sorry, Alex. I'm just not particularly fond of him. No one was hurt, I hope."

"No. Well, yes, but not how you think. I've got some bad news, Will. Professor Spencer's dead."

"Who?"

I'd been about to stretch out a hand to tousle his hair, but I dropped it. "Betty Barrows Spencer, the art history professor."

"She was in the car?"

"No. It looks like she fell down the stairs and broke her neck."

"That's . . . terrible."

They were just two words, but there was something wrong about the way he said it. To this day I can't put my finger on what it was that warned me—either the weird echo in his voice or the way his body seemed to tense up all of a sudden. It wasn't anything you'd notice unless you were as physically attuned to the man as I was. All I can say is that at that moment, Will didn't seem upset. He seemed *relieved.*

I'd been about to blurt out everything I knew about Betty Barrows, but whatever I was picking up from him stopped me. "You didn't hear?"

"No. What happened?"

"She fell down the stairs in her house."

"That's terrible," he said again, a little more convincing now.

"Won't you go to the funeral?"

"What department did you say she was in?"

"Art history. She was emeritus."

"Oh, yes, of course. I've heard of her."

"Heard of her?"

"Didn't she have something to do with the art museum?"

"Yes."

"But what does this have to do with Stewart Day?"

"I don't know," I said weakly. "They're both in the paper today."

"Was it an accident?"

"Day? No, he just went the wrong way down Browning."

"No, I mean . . . Professor Spencer. Was her death an accident?"

"Why wouldn't it be?"

"I don't know. You made it sound so melodramatic."

"Don't you want to go to the funeral?" I asked again, and he seemed to start to relax.

"Perhaps I will."

"Didn't you know her?"

"Only vaguely."

I stared out at the pool so I didn't have to look him in

the eye. "I thought she might have been a friend of yours."

"What department did you say she was in?"

"You already asked me that. Twice. Art history." I heard Betty Barrows's voice then, and since I don't really believe in ghosts it must have been in my head. *I got to be quite close to Rosie Adelson, and also Joan Langston. I used to baby-sit for a number of the faculty children. Some of those friendships have lasted a lifetime.*

"Are you all right? Alex?"

"I think I'd better get out of the sun." I jumped up from the chaise and bolted through the sliding-glass doors, too fast probably. "I should get going . . ."

"Are you sure you should drive? Why don't you lie down on the couch? Do you want some water?"

"No, really, Will. I'd better get going." He was holding on to my arm, and when I tried to pull away he wouldn't let me go.

"What's wrong with you?" he asked, and there was an edge in his voice I'd never heard before.

"Would you please let me go?"

"Please don't leave."

"Stop it. You're hurting me."

"I'd never hurt you."

"Odd thing to say when you're breaking my arm."

He let me go then, and from the way he dropped my arm it seemed he hadn't realized he was holding it in the first place. "Alex, what's gotten into you?"

I know I should have left then, convinced him everything was fine and gotten out of there as fast as I could. Yes, I was confused, with Stewart Day and Trevor Hoffman running around in my head. But as I look back on it, I can't believe I wasn't more frightened. If he'd wanted to kill me, he could have done it then and there—or long before that, come to think of it. But I was so angry, I felt like he was the one who ought to be scared of me. "That's the problem with liars," I said finally. "They never know when to just stick to the truth."

"What are you talking about?"

"Will, think. For God's sake, you spent thirty years in school. You should know better. You should at least have admitted you knew her. She used to baby-sit you, for Christ's sake. She was one of your mother's best friends."

"Who? Alex, sweetheart, what's wrong? What's gotten into you?"

"Christ, I am such a pathetic little idiot." My voice was starting to shake a little. "I don't know what's wrong with me. All the time . . ."

"Alex . . ."

"Betty Barrows. Betty Barrows Spencer. When I poured out my goddamn heart to you upstairs in your bedroom, when I told you about Adam, all about his murder, I told you I was looking for Betty Barrows. And you never once mentioned that you've known her all your life. Oh, *God*. You're in this up to your neck, aren't you? I don't know how you did it . . ."

"Alex, you're being completely irrational."

There was still something wrong about the way he was reacting, and I tried to put my finger on it. He was properly confused, with just the right amount of righteous indignation. But—there it was—he wasn't really *surprised*. Something about the way Will Langston was behaving was just too . . . prepared. Like he'd always been ready for this.

We'd been standing just inside the patio doors, and even though I probably could have gotten away then, I crossed farther into the room and sat down on the couch. You always hear about the survival instinct—fight or flight—but I can't say I was thinking in terms of either one. Mostly, I was just thinking, *Fuck you.*

"It's crazy, Will, but I believe you do care about me. And do you know why? Because I think if you didn't, I'd already be dead. I'd have fallen off a bridge somewhere, or down the stairs. Or maybe you would have gotten more creative with me—slit my throat on the way home from the movies, and left me at the dump."

"Alex, *stop it.*" There was real passion in his voice now, and pain.

"You know," I said, looking right into his eyes. "You're going to have to kill me too."

"Alex . . ."

"Because this is never going to go away. I'll leave it up to you, Will, you and your conscience. If I'm wrong, you can chalk it up to hysteria, and maybe someday you'll forgive me. But if I'm right, you'd better listen to this. I will never give up. I will never go away. I'm not sure how I'm going to prove it, but I will. And when I do, as God is my witness, I'll rip your heart out with my fucking fingernails."

He didn't say anything, just sat there staring at me. He'd begun to look genuinely upset, and it threw me off. Doubts nagged, and I pushed them down. "How about if I tell you what I think happened? I've thought about this for weeks, and I still don't understand it. The more information I got, the less sense it made. Maybe I would have thought about it before if I hadn't gotten involved with you. But I got sidetracked by goddamn Stewart Day, and those idiotic frat boys. And then there was that conference, and you had an alibi. Even when Gordon said you might be involved, I couldn't believe it. I thought there had to be some other explanation. I'd look at you, and I just couldn't believe it."

"Is this some kind of sick joke?"

"Good try, Will, but too late."

"What's too late? What are you talking about?"

"Just listen. Here's what I think happened. A long time ago, something terrible happened in your father's lab. It killed him, and several other people, but somehow it was covered up. Then a few weeks ago, André Sebastien came back to town, and he was determined to tell the truth to someone. I think that someone was you. Whatever he told you, you killed him to avoid having other people find out about it. Then Adam started asking questions, and you killed him too. Then I came along, and for whatever reason you let me live. But then I found Professor Spencer, and you must have been terrified she'd tell me everything. Maybe you didn't realize that she didn't know very much, but you killed her anyway. And Stewart Day said it wasn't his fault. He must have been telling the truth."

"I didn't kill her, Alex. I swear to God. I haven't seen her in weeks."

"*Stop it.*"

"I'm not lying, Alex," he said, and there was a different tone in his voice. Weariness, distance, as though he were talking through a tunnel at four A.M. "No more. I'm not lying anymore."

"What are you saying?"

"I didn't kill her." He laid his elbows on his knees and leaned forward over the glass tabletop, talking to his own reflection. "Please believe me. I didn't kill her. I'm guilty of a great many things, but I had nothing to do with that. I could never hurt Betty any more than I could hurt you. She was like family. I'd known her all my life. What kind of monster do you think I am?"

"I don't know, Will. What kind of monster are you?"

The words seemed to fly over the coffee table and strike him. His head snapped back, and when I saw his eyes there was genuine grief in them. "Alex, you know me. My whole life I've tried to help people. I'm a doctor, for God's sake. All I ever wanted to do was make something good out of one of the most evil things ever conceived of. Don't you know that?"

"Will, for Christ's sake, just tell me the truth."

He stood up, and for a minute I thought he was leaving the room. But he went to a cabinet, pulled out a bottle, and poured himself a water glass full of something. "I don't suppose you'd care for one?" I shook my head. "I can't believe I'm drinking at two o'clock in the afternoon. It's not a habit of mine. But I'm badly in need of a drink right now." He gave a laugh, strangled and unconvincing. "There goes my tennis game." He drained the glass in three gulps, and I could smell the liquor now. Scotch.

"What was it all about, Will? Money? Isn't it always about money?"

He shook his head, staring into the empty glass. "Alex, would you believe me if I told you I never wanted any of this to happen, that I'd give anything in the world to be able to go back to the beginning and take it all back?"

"No, Will. I don't think I would fucking well believe a goddamn word you say."

"Please, Alex. This is hard enough. Please don't be so . . . so cold."

"Goodness, Will, I'm sorry if I'm being rude. But I have a sneaking suspicion that I'm about to hear you confess to killing the man I loved. Now, I'm sorry if that sounds too melodramatic, or I'm not behaving in a sufficiently civilized way. I'll have to remember my manners the next time I screw a serial killer."

It was out of my mouth before I could stop myself. If you want to be generous, you could call it a tactical error; if not, you could call it pretty goddamn stupid. But I was upset, and he was acting all whipped and guilty, and I went too far. I hadn't been paying enough attention to his mood, or realized how close to flipping out he actually was. Maybe it was the scotch. But suffice it to say, he flipped.

"The man you *loved*?" He stalked across the room and dragged me up from the couch, practically lifting me off the ground with one hand. He was stronger than he looked, but I already knew that. "Don't be so bloody naive. You think you loved him, but how could you love a man who treated you like a whore? Who crawled into your bed whenever it suited him?"

"Stop it. *Stop it.*"

If he heard me, he didn't show it. He let go of my wrist and grabbed my head in both hands, holding on so hard there were big purple spots where his face used to be. "I had to do it. Don't you understand that? Don't you understand that I didn't do anything I didn't have to do?" He kissed me then, pressing his lips against mine in a way that even Sade couldn't confuse with passion. Was I scared of him then? You bet your ass. I tried to push him away but he only pressed harder.

"Will, please stop it. Let me go," I said when he finally came up for air. I tried to make myself look him in the eye but the best I could do was stare at his Tretorns. "I'm . . . I'm sure you had your reasons." He held me at arm's length for a moment, then threw me down onto the couch so hard I sank into the crack between the cushions.

"Don't move," he said when I started to scramble back up. "And for Christ's sake, don't even try to humor me."

"I'm not."

"Of course you are. You should see yourself. You're terrified. All you want is to get away from me. But, Alex, you don't understand. You don't see that I would never hurt you."

"You keep saying that, but you keep hurting me."

"I never meant for this to happen."

"Then please, Will. Please let me go. I won't tell anyone."

He laughed, the same strangled little bark as before. "Frailty, thy name is woman. Five minutes ago you said I'd have to kill you to keep you quiet."

"I didn't mean it. I was only being macho." He wandered back toward the liquor cabinet, and I started to judge the distance between the couch and the patio doors. I either had to go around the glass coffee table or over it. I wondered which was faster.

"Can I trust you, Alex? Can I really trust you to leave this alone?"

"You can trust me." *Sure, you can trust me. You can trust that as soon as I get out of here, I'm calling the cops.*

"Do you promise?"

"I promise." I snuck a look at him over my shoulder. He had his back to me, fumbling with something on the bar. I was about to leap up and make a run for it when I sensed him behind me, felt the hand around the neck and the jab in my arm. I had enough momentum going to get to my feet, but my knees buckled and I toppled to the carpet. The last thing I remember is Will Langston standing over me through a bug-eye lens, holding a hypodermic needle, and looking like he was about to cry.

31

As I write this all down, I have fantasies about making it way more interesting than it was, infusing it with metaphor and onomatopoeia and some touches from a Sharon Stone film. I think about writing that I woke up handcuffed to Will Langston's bed, me wearing his dead wife's nightgown and him threatening to eat me alive. In my dreams, Will is just about to fillet me with a butcher knife when Adam rushes in—not dead, just a victim of mistaken identity and a little amnesia. As Will is dragged off to jail Adam asks me to marry him, and we live happily ever after, and our children all go to good colleges.

This is not what happened. Actually, I woke up tied to a chair in the living room with the same nylon cord Will used to lash the covers on his sailboat. Humiliating. He didn't have a gun, or a knife, or even a baseball bat. He was just sitting on the couch, sucking down scotch so fast the bottle might as well have had a nipple on it. He looked awful. "Ah, she's coming to." I tried to see who he was talking to, but no one else was there. Uh-oh. Having him speak to me in the third person did not seem like a good sign. "Is she ready to listen to me now?"

"What . . ." My mouth felt like the inside of a lint trap. "Can I please have some water?" He had a glass on the table, and I wondered if he knew I'd need it after whatever he shot me up with. He held the glass up so I could drink, and though I had a momentary instinct to spit it in his face, I was too thirsty for bravado. "What did you give me?"

"Just a mild sedative." He sat back down.

"Just a mild sedative you happened to have in your living room?"

"I thought I might have to use it someday."

"On me?"

"I had to make you listen to me, and I knew you just wanted to get away. But you've got to listen to me, Alex. If you listen, you'll understand why I did what I did. Maybe you can even forgive me."

You whacked out son of a bitch. "Would you please untie me?"

"No.

"This is ridiculous. Will, this is *me* you're talking to. *Alex.* My hands are falling asleep. If I promise not to leave, will you please untie me?"

"I'm sorry."

"How long do you plan to keep me like this?"

"Until you've heard the whole story."

"And then what?"

"That will be up to you."

I didn't even want to think about what he meant by that. "Then I guess you'd better get it over with."

"Do you promise you'll believe me?"

Was he kidding? What was I going to say to a guy who had me trussed up like a hog? "Yes, Will," I said with as much sincerity as I could fake on such short notice. "I'll believe you."

"Alex, before I say anything, there's something I need you to understand. What happened between you and me was the truth. When I told you I loved you out in California, I meant it. I know that may be hard for you to understand right now, but it's absolutely true. Do you believe me?"

He was out of his mind, but I decided it was best not to mention it. "I believe that you believe it."

"This is no time for word games."

"Then I don't know how to answer."

"Fair enough. Are you comfortable? Do you want another drink of water?"

"Comfortable? Will, you tied me to a chair. Now why don't you just say what you've got to say and get it over with?"

He got up to get another drink. "I suppose I always knew the truth would come out. No matter what I did to hide it, it just made it worse, like the monster in Greek myth that grows back two heads for every one you chop off." He turned to face me, breathed in deep, exhaled. "It's a very complicated story, but I'll try to be succinct. I'm supposed to meet my tennis date"—he looked at his Rolex—"in forty-five minutes. But I'll tell you everything. The truth, the whole truth, and nothing but the truth." I thought he might get too drunk to talk, but when he sat back down, the glass was only half-full this time. Or considering the context, maybe I should say it was half-empty.

"It all began . . . No, that's not right. I should say it all ended. Everything ended for me the day André Sebastien came into my life. It was in July. July 8 to be exact, at nine-thirty at night. I was sitting right here, on this couch, reading, and the doorbell rang. I opened it to find an old man standing there, and I only had to take one look at him to know he was dying. He had that wasted look you see in patients whose time is numbered in months or even weeks. He said he was an old friend of my father's, and desperately needed to talk to me, and of course I asked him in.

"He sat down across from me, right where you're sitting now, and the first thing he said was, 'You're so like your father. It's as if I'm looking at an older version of Bill Langston.' At first I thought he was confused, maybe a bit senile. Then I realized what he was saying was perfectly accurate. I'm almost fifteen years older than my father was when he died, and the fact that I'd already outlived him by that many years had never struck me before. 'The last time I saw you, you couldn't have been more than two years old,' he said. 'Sometimes I can't believe all the time that has passed, all the years I've kept the secrets.'

"Then he told me he was dying, pancreatic cancer, and he only had a few months left. 'I'm afraid all of this will come as a shock to you, and I'm sorry,' he said. 'A son has a right to be proud of his father. But the lies have gone on too long.'

"I didn't take him seriously at first. I thought he was just a confused old man. But I thought there'd be no harm in hearing him out, offering him a drink, and sending him on his way with a clean conscience. Then he told me that for the past fifty years, he'd gone by the name René Lecuyer. But he said his real name was André Sebastien.

"Of course, I recognized the name immediately. For as long as I could remember, my mother had made sure I knew what happened to my father, how he'd died a hero, he and Sebastien and Adelson. So when Sebastien introduced himself, it only made me more certain I was dealing with some sort of crackpot. My thoughts must have been obvious, because he said he knew he must sound insane. But he begged me to hear him out. He said he thought I had a right to hear it first, before he went to the press and the international scientific community.

"Then he told me what I suppose you've already figured out, Alex. He said my father didn't die in a plane crash. In fact, there never was any plane crash. And what's more, my sainted father hadn't even been a war hero. Oh, I suppose he was a hero in his own mind. But from the story André Sebastien told me, I'd describe him more as a megalomaniac than anything else, and a dangerous one, at that.

"He said it all began when the war department started recruiting scientists to work on what would eventually become the Manhattan Project. The best minds from all over the country were brought together, men from a variety of fields—chemistry, physics, engineering. Even back then, Benson was one of the premier research universities in the country, and my father fully expected to be asked to participate, and of course, he was. But when it came time to choose someone to head the project, he was passed over. My father was a very ambitious man, and he didn't take it well. He'd always despised Oppenheimer, and the idea of working under him galled him. According to Sebastien, my father was obsessed. He was determined to be the one who invented the bomb, and to hell with everyone else. So the race was on—not only between us and the Germans, but between my father and the rest of the Manhattan Project. He wasn't a traitor; Sebastien told me that as though it were some sort of consolation. He genuinely believed he could design the bomb on his own, just him and his handpicked research team, more quickly than a massive research project could. Unfortunately, he had friends in the war department, and in the Benson administration, who agreed with him.

"He was given the wherewithal to build a small research facility. Secret, underground, like something out of a spy novel. Apparently the only way to get in was through a tunnel connected to the basement of the physics building. Who needs to go to the movies, right? My father was told to assemble a team of three men. He'd worked with Adelson for years, and he wasn't hard to convince. He was Jewish, after all, and he had family in Europe. Sebastien was harder to recruit, but he was brilliant and my father wanted him—and my father always got what he wanted. His military benefactors arranged to have two people from the army assigned as support staff. Their names were Peter Murphy and Marion Hazel. The woman had been an army nurse, but Sebastien gathered she had some sort of high-level security clearance. The man was career army, but he'd been wounded somewhere and discharged. He'd lost two brothers in the war, and there was no question about his loyalty.

"Sebastien said he was concerned from the beginning that something terrible might happen. With a staff of just five people, they were juggling two research projects— the genuine work they were doing for the government as part of the Manhattan Project, and the secret part, that only they and a few others knew about. The latter took place underground, in facilities that were superior to anything else on the Benson campus—but still, Sebastien thought, not sufficient for what they were dealing with. He tried to talk to my father, but he wouldn't listen. Sebastien said he didn't realize until almost the very end that my father actually intended to build a prototype in the underground lab. For that, you need plutonium, and Sebastien never thought my father would be able to get any. It was more strictly controlled than you can possibly imagine. Hanford—that was the reactor in Washington State that produced plutonium from uranium—was able to make less than a kilogram of it a week. But my father had immensely powerful friends, and someone in the war department was able to smuggle him a relatively large quantity of it. Sebastien had no idea how, but whoever did it must have been very high up, because my father got his hands on some plutonium even before Los Alamos did.

"At that point, there was a terrible argument between the two of them. Sebastien told my father he was putting thousands of students at risk, maybe the whole population of Gabriel. You have to remember, in those days not even the people who ran the Manhattan Project knew just how much destructive power they were dealing with. Even when they did the first test detonation at Alamogordo in July of 1945, they weren't sure the sky wouldn't be set on fire. Sebastien knew my father was playing God with things he didn't understand.

"By January of 1945, things had really started to degenerate. The tension between Sebastien and my father was almost unbearable, and Adelson was stuck in the middle. The other two, Hazel and Murphy, were military people and did what they were ordered, which in this case was whatever my father wanted. My father knew he couldn't avoid being sent to Los Alamos much longer—scientists had already been there for two years. His private little research project was going to be over and he'd have to kowtow to Oppenheimer. Time was running out.

"Now, this next bit may seem irrelevant at first, but

you'll see in a moment why it's important. As his work became more stressful, Sebastien was seeing very little of his fiancée, Betty Barrows. He told me he felt terribly guilty about that. He loved her, and he desperately wanted to marry her, but he was afraid all the pressure he was under was destroying their relationship. On the day of the accident, he was supposed to be in the lab. But he'd been late for a dinner date with Betty, and by the time he got there, she'd left. He looked around campus for her for the better part of two hours. By the time he went back to the lab, it was too late. There had been an explosion, and the tunnel connecting the lab to the physics building had collapsed.

"Sebastien was a little vague on what happened next. He said he just walked off campus and hitched a ride from the first person who'd pick him up. The driver was on his way to the Adirondacks, and he camped out there for a few days with nothing but the clothes on his back and whatever he had in his pocket; some money, a few photographs. He didn't know what to do. He felt responsible for what had happened, felt he could have prevented it somehow.

"By the time he came out of the woods, it was too late. He was already dead, or at least everyone thought he was. Sebastien wasn't sure how it all played out, but he assumed that when my father failed to make his daily report to his friends in the military, they sent someone to investigate. He said they must have found what was left of the laboratory and realized they had one hell of a problem. They could hardly admit that these kinds of experiments were going on at a college campus, in the middle of a town full of civilians. They couldn't risk what an accident like this could do to public support for the eventual use of the bomb, that it might be perceived as something too dangerous to build.

"When Sebastien got to a town and saw a newspaper, he realized what must have happened. He certainly knew there hadn't been any plane crash. The military had concocted the story to cover up their deaths, and Sebastien later found out they'd gone so far as to crash a plane in the Rockies. He wasn't sure how they came up with the pilot, but he guessed they probably used the name of someone who'd been killed in action elsewhere. They burned down Marion Hazel's house, and crashed Peter Murphy's truck. She didn't have any family to be concerned with, but Murphy had a wife and son. To ensure they didn't ask too many questions, they were well provided for. Apparently, all his widow wanted was some money to live on and Benson educations for her son and any grandchildren she might have. When the time came, my father's friends in the university administration made sure they got it.

"Once the so-called accidents had been made public, Sebastien couldn't do anything but disappear. If he resurfaced, the plane crash would have been exposed for the hoax it was. And he felt terribly guilty for not stopping my father, reporting him somehow. In some ways, he believed he should have died in the laboratory with the others. He went up to Canada, where his mother had grown up, and his fluent French allowed him to blend in. But he never stopped thinking about Betty Barrows—and he never stopped wondering what went wrong. Over the years, he kept up with the research in his field, and eventually decided that it must have been a fizzle. He got the cancer diagnosis early this year, and the desire to tell the truth about what had happened began to gnaw at him. Of course, he also wondered whether the research he'd done had caused the disease, especially whatever radiation he was exposed to when he tried to go back to the lab that night. He finally worked up the courage to come down here and tell the truth: first to me, then to Betty, then to the world.

"He told me all this sitting across from me on the couch, right where you are now. And when he was finished, I didn't know what to say. I no longer had any thought that he was insane, or that he was making it up. It was all just too strange to be fiction. Anyone trying to invent a story wouldn't need to concoct one as outlandish as that—secret laboratories, government conspiracies. It was so crazy, it had to be true.

"The story had taken a long time to tell, and it was past midnight. He seemed exhausted, and it turned out he'd walked all the way here from Betty's house. Naturally, I offered him a ride. But all I could think about was the fact that the Langston Foundation was built on a lie. It was founded in the name of my father—that sounds like some sort of prayer, doesn't it? He was supposed to be this great war hero, great and gallant and brave, a man who'd given his life in the name of science. But he wasn't. He was just a megalomaniac who'd gotten three people killed in the rush to preserve his own ego. The *bastard*. Oppenheimer was twice the man he was, and Hans Bethe, and all the others too. Even if you believe that what they created was wrong, they didn't knowingly risk innocent people's lives to do it. Ironic, isn't it? The sole purpose of the Manhattan Project was to wipe out whole cities. And I've committed murder to hide the fact that my father was responsible for the deaths of three people, just three."

"Christ, Will, how could you do it?"

"They always say you don't remember your own wedding. There are so many people, and everything is just a whirlwind. I remember my wedding very well, every detail. But I have almost no memory of the first time I took a human life.

"As I was saying, when we were in the car all I could think about was that the entire Langston Foundation was based on a lie. My father, the man I'd spent my whole life either hating or trying to outdo, was nothing but an egomaniac. You have no idea—no, you're too young. You've no idea what it's like to look back on your life and feel like it's all been wasted, chasing a ghost. And I knew I was about to lose everything. You came to that fundraising dinner with me; you should know how the foundation depends on the whims of the men who write the checks. There's always someone else out there who needs the money as badly as you do, another cause that's equally worthy. When my father's reputation was destroyed, the foundation was going to go with it. And the foundation was all I had left of Laura. It was founded for my father, yes, but she made it what it was. She spent twenty years of her life building it up, charming the money men, traveling to every godforsaken corner of the world. She sacrificed everything for it, even gave up having children. In the end it even cost her her life. I couldn't . . . I just couldn't let it all be for nothing.

"You know how sometimes you're driving and you can't remember how you got from point A to point B? It was as though I were on autopilot. When we got to North Creek Bridge, Sebastien asked me to stop. It was jarring when he spoke; I was so far into myself, I'd nearly forgotten he was in the car with me. He told me the overlook had been one of his and Betty's favorite spots, and he hadn't seen it for fifty years. You know how beautiful the view is at night—all the lights of Gabriel are laid out in the valley, and you can see the Bessler towers across the way. He didn't say anything, just stood at the rail looking out. No one else was around—it was late, and most of the students were gone for the summer. All I could hear was the sound of the water below us, rushing over Gabriel Falls.

"And then it struck me that if he were gone, my life could be worth something again. It's not that I had any sort of vision. But as I was standing there on the bridge, I could picture a scale. On one side was everything the Langston Foundation had accomplished, all the lives it had saved with the research it had funded, all the good it could do if it was allowed to survive. And on the other was one frail old man, with only a few months left to live. It was only a matter of weeks until he died, and an agonizing death at that. I realized killing him was a kind of euthanasia. So I walked up behind him, and pushed him over the rail. He didn't cry out. He just gasped, and that was the end of it. I never even heard him hit the ground. Then I got back into my car and drove home."

"You actually convinced yourself you were doing him a favor?"

"He was dying, Alex. Don't you see? I'm trying to show you I'm not some kind of monster."

"If you want to prove it, why don't you untie me?"

He looked at me sideways. "Can I trust you not to try to leave?"

"I swear I won't. I want to hear the rest of the story." I wasn't lying. He must have been able to tell, because he got up and disappeared into the kitchen. The sight of him coming at me with a steak knife was less than comforting, but all he did was cut the rope from my arms and legs. "I need to stand up."

"Go ahead." I got up and stretched, realizing absurdly that I was still wearing my bikini under my sundress. A couple of hours before, I'd been on my way to apologize to Will for suspecting him. And now here I was, getting the whole confession from him in first person singular. "What I wouldn't give for a cigarette."

"Would you like one?"

"You've got some?" He tossed me a pack of Dunhills from a drawer in the bar. "I'm shocked. I never imagined you smoked."

"I don't do it very often."

"Then again, I never imagined you kill people. Got a light?"

32

"When André Sebastien was dead, I thought it was over. I thought I could just put it behind me, go on with my work. At first, I thought about it all the time. Then after a while, it only struck me once or twice a day. And one morning, I woke up and realized that I hadn't thought about it the entire day before. Then your friend Adam called for an interview, and I agreed without even asking him what it was about.

"When you commented on the Hopper painting in my office, it was on the tip of my tongue to say that your friend Adam had also admired it. You see, Alex? I'm not very good at this sort of thing, am I? I might have exposed everything with one careless sentence. But that was the first thing he said when he came into my office—that he liked the painting. He said the woman in it reminded him of someone he knew, and later on I wondered if he'd been talking about you.

"When I realized what he'd come to talk to me about,

my gut reaction was that I'd been found out, but he had no idea. He said he was working on a story, and in connection with it he wondered if I knew anyone named René Lecuyer or André Sebastien. He said he knew Sebastien had worked with my father in the forties, and wanted to know if I could help him dig up any information on him. I put him off, told him I couldn't help him but I'd call if anything occurred to me.

"I didn't even think about killing him at first. But your friend Adam struck me as extremely persistent, and I realized it was only a matter of time until he put everything together. I knew that if I could only get rid of this one man, everything would be all right—I could have my life back, and do my work, do some good.

"But Adam Ellroy was no helpless old man. I was going to have to have a plan, perhaps even an alibi, and it had to happen before he figured out too much. I'd tried to ask him, subtly, if anyone else knew he was working on the story, and I gathered that no one else did. He said it was some kind of special project of his. I could only hope he hadn't told anyone else—or if he had, the investigation would die with him. The weekend of the conference in Chicago seemed like the perfect opportunity. I had to make some complicated travel arrangements—I'll get to that later—and on Friday I called him at home and told him I'd found some important information. I said it was highly confidential, and I could only meet him at night, someplace private. We settled on three o'clock in the morning, late Saturday night. I suggested the bridge, hinting that the location would help me explain how René Lecuyer had died. He agreed to it quite eagerly, and I got the feeling the whole business appealed to his sense of adventure."

"It would have."

"First, on the previous Thursday, I left one of my cars at the Syracuse airport and flew back to Gabriel under another name. Then I left for Chicago with the rest of the Benson group, and attended the conference Friday and Saturday. Saturday night, after all the speeches and drinks were over, I put the "DO NOT DISTURB" sign on my door and got a taxi to the airport. I flew back to Syracuse, again under another name, then drove down to Gabriel in time to meet Adam. You see, there are no flights into Gabriel that late at night, and in any event I couldn't risk being recognized.

"I got to the bridge first, and waited until your friend arrived. He was right on time, and he seemed excited, friendly. I'm certain he never suspected a thing. I didn't have any clear idea of how I was going to do it—after all, your Adam was no weak old man. He was a great deal younger and stronger than I was. Then the opportunity presented itself. We were both standing next to the rail, and I had him absorbed in whatever fiction I'd decided to spin for him—I couldn't remember now if I tried. He was writing in his notebook, and it gave me the chance to take him by surprise. I grabbed his legs and knocked him off balance over the rail."

"You son of a bitch."

"He . . . he managed to grab the bottom part of the railing when he fell over it. He hung there, and I never thought he could hold on. But he must have been even stronger than he looked, because he started to pull himself up. There's nothing there for your feet to grab on to, so he had to do it all with his arms. But he was strong enough to do it. He was confused, of course, and he kept saying, 'What the hell is going on?' asking me to help him. I just stood there. I didn't know what I was going to do if he managed to pull himself back up onto the bridge.

I went to my car and took the tire iron out of the trunk. When I came back, he thought I was going to help him, throw him a rope, but instead I raised up the tire iron to strike him. You can't imagine the look on his face. I've never seen anything like it. Pure horror.

"At the last minute, I couldn't do it. I lost my nerve. I leaned over the side and grabbed his hand, tried to pull him up, but his weight was dragging me down. I couldn't get a good hold on him. Somehow I lost my grip, just as he was reaching up to grab the next rail. I could hear him cry out the whole way down, fainter and fainter, until he finally hit the ground, and everything was quiet. It was the loudest silence I've ever heard.

"I just stood there, at the rail, for what seemed like hours. I was about to drive away when it suddenly occurred to me that even though he was dead, there might be a paper trail. I had no idea what to do about it if there was. He hadn't locked his truck, so I looked through it. There were notebooks in it, at least ten of them, and I took them all. The one he'd been holding when he . . . went over the bridge had fallen with him, and I just had to hope it wouldn't be found. When I looked through the glove compartment, I found what I hoped were an extra set of keys, and that's when it occurred to me that I might be able to search his apartment. I knew I was taking a risk, but I didn't have any choice. I went through his desk, but there was too much for me to deal with, and time was running out. I had to leave for Syracuse to catch my flight back to Chicago. So I just took everything—all the notebooks, all the files. I hoped I could look through them and bring everything back before they were missed. I thought about trying to look through his desk at the *Monitor,* but I never quite had the nerve. The lights are never turned off there, and I couldn't take the chance.

How could I possibly explain myself, riffling through a reporter's desk? I just had to hope there was nothing incriminating there—or if there was, it wouldn't make sense to anyone else.

"I dropped all the files off here, drove back to the airport, and flew to Chicago. By the time I got back to the hotel it was ten o'clock in the morning. No one had missed me. I sat there, listening to the speeches, thinking, Can anyone see it in my face? Was it possible to tell, just by looking at me, that I'd just committed murder? No one could, of course, and there was something fascinating about the thought. I should have been exhausted, but I was wide awake—adrenaline, I suppose. I finished out the conference and went back to Gabriel with everyone else from Benson. Once I looked through all the paperwork I'd taken from Adam's apartment, I realized there was nothing incriminating.

"Finally, I thought it was over. My father's secret was safe, my wife's memory was safe, I was safe. I didn't think there was much risk that Betty Barrows would interfere—Sebastien had made a point of saying that he hadn't told her anything yet. Then you appeared. I knew what you were after from the moment you walked into my office with that ridiculous story about French-Canadians."

"But if you knew, why did you offer to help me?"

"I could hardly refuse. All I could do was try and make sure you didn't get anywhere."

God, I'd been such an idiot. "The head of the physics department said he was surprised their records didn't go back that far. But they did, didn't they?"

"You're a very smart girl, Alex. I found them the same day you first came to my office, and I burned them. No one had looked at them in years, and I knew they'd never be missed. Most departments really don't keep things around that long, so there wasn't much danger. And as for helping you find some old professors, I knew the only one left was Henry Singer, and he's senile and couldn't tell you anything anyway." He was wrong, of course. Professor Singer's photograph had been the key to the whole thing.

"I tried to keep an eye on you, take every chance to steer you in the wrong direction. I . . . followed you, hoping I could figure out how much you knew. It wasn't easy. I was terrified you'd track down Betty Barrows, and between the two of you you'd put all the pieces together. I started sending her the notes then, hoping I could scare her into leaving town. And then I sent them to you."

"You didn't just send them to me. You broke into my house, you son of a bitch. You weren't really in Houston until yesterday, were you?"

"I came back Wednesday. Alex, I was desperate. I had to scare you off. But I never would have hurt you. You have to believe that."

"What a shame your charity didn't extend to Betty Barrows."

"No, Alex, it's not true. I swear to you, I didn't kill her. I had no idea she was dead until you told me. I have no idea what happened to her. If Stewart Day says she fell down the stairs by accident, then that must be what really happened."

"I thought you hadn't heard anything about that."

"I read the paper while you were . . . While you were sleeping."

"Wait a minute. There's one thing I don't get. What in God's name does all of this have to do with B-GLAD?"

"B-GLAD?"

"The gay and lesbian living center. Somehow, it's connected to all this. André Sebastien was interested in the story, and I never understood why." I took a good look at Will for the first time since he started talking. His slumping shoulders made his polo shirt look too big, and he'd begun to slur his words from all the scotch.

"The clearing, where those two boys were attacked," he said. "I'm surprised you haven't figured that out. The explosion had to have left a huge mess of concrete and God knows what else—fifty years is nothing when you're talking about radioactivity. It was obvious nothing else could be built on the land above it. Remember, my father had friends in the Benson administration. They made sure that nothing would be built on that land, not ever. You have to understand that a college of this size has a great deal of institutional memory. Things are passed down from one president to the next, one administration to the next. Unwritten rules. There will never be anything but red tulips planted outside the faculty club. No part of the university art collection will ever be sold. And there will never be anything built on the land that covers my father's laboratory. The gay and lesbian group can protest all it wants. It may happen somewhere, but it will not be there."

"You mean there are people in the administration who know about all this?"

"Not the murders. No one knows about that but me and you. But about the laboratory and my father's experiments, yes. There would have to be others who are aware of what happened."

"Who?"

"Even I don't know that. Possibly the university president, but not necessarily. Presidents come and presidents go, after all. But the head of the board of trustees has more power over Benson's fate than anyone else. I'd be willing to wager that he's the keeper of the flame. Perhaps there are others as well, though no one could prove it. If it were ever to come out, the administration would express the deepest shock, I'm sure. But, Alex, we still haven't talked about the most important part. Us."

"Us?"

"You and me, together."

The tone in his voice gave me a sweaty feeling at the back of my neck. Even when he was talking about pushing Adam off a goddamn bridge, he hadn't creeped me out like this. "What do you mean?"

"Alex, listen. This is very important. When you walked into my office, I knew it was a sign. It was like a blessing."

"Excuse me?"

"It was a sign that I had done the right thing, that the good of the many really did outweigh the good of the few. I'd been so alone since Laura died, so empty and weak. And when I finally found the strength to do what had to be done, it brought you to me. Don't you see? If I hadn't killed Adam, you and I might never have met. But from the first time I saw you, I knew it was possible for me to live again. You reminded me so much of Laura—not physically, of course. But you had her spirit, her intellect. Even your laugh is very much the same. And my God, you'd even gone to the same college. I told you once before. It was like you were a gift, one I was afraid I had no right to unwrap. But even while I was trying to hide what I'd done, part of me was hoping you'd find out, that you'd learn the truth and eventually you'd understand. I knew that if we could just get through all the ugliness, we could have a future together. We could have children. I could have the life I'd never had time for before. But I'd make time, Alex. For you, this time, I would."

He wasn't joking. There wasn't even a trace of sarcasm

in his voice. The word "sociopath" tripped across my brain, and not for the first time. "You're sick."

"You're upset, I know. Sweetheart, I completely understand. I've just told you a very long and complicated story. You need time to come to terms with it."

Get a handle on yourself, Bernier. What you say right now will make a difference for the rest of your life—specifically, whether or not you have one. "Will, I'm . . . I'm so confused."

"Of course you are. But I'm here to help you." He held out his arms.

You are the most disgusting human being I have ever met, and I would love nothing more in the whole world than to kill you with my bare hands. This was my id talking, but for once in my life I didn't listen. Instead, I forced myself to walk toward him. I may even have smiled. "You mean, you did all this for me?"

"For us. Alex, I did it for us."

"Nobody's ever done anything like that for me before."

"No one has ever loved you as much as I do. Alex, please say you believe me."

"Of course I believe you."

"Do you love me?"

"I love you." I stepped into his embrace and kissed him. His tongue went into my mouth, and I tried very hard not to throw up.

"Thank God." He hugged me like an anaconda. I could barely breathe, and whatever hope I had that he'd gotten drunk and weak went out the window. He swept me off the floor like a groom on his wedding night, and before I knew what he had in mind he was carrying me up the stairs. *Holy shit.* He careened a bit from side to side as he want up the staircase, but he set me down on his bed very gently, and knelt on the floor. "Alex, my love, this is the moment of truth." I was too scared to say anything. "This is when we pledge ourselves to each other forever. But I have to know it's what you really want."

He was talking like something out of a bad romance novel, and I nearly laughed out loud. Come to think of it, it was probably just hysteria. I tried to make myself answer him, but I couldn't. I just kissed him again, and hoped it would pass for whatever he was looking for. It must have worked, because he pushed me over backwards onto the bed, running his hands under my sundress. I felt him tug at my bikini bottom, pull it down my thighs and around my knees. I've heard about women who've survived being raped, or who've been paid to have sex with men they loathe. They all talk about being disconnected from their bodies, feeling it happen to someone else even though it's happening to them. I wish that had been the case with Will that day, but the truth is I felt the whole thing, felt his weight on top of me and his doctor's hands like sandpaper on my skin. One word kept going through my head, and it wasn't "no" or "stop" or even "help." It was just *Adam.*

I could almost see him then, the way he was that last night we were together. Just for a second, maybe because I was so desperate to think about anything except what was really happening, I closed my eyes and pictured Adam alive as I hadn't been able to since I saw his body on the bridge. It's strange now to think how vivid the image was, and at such an awful moment, but I'll always believe it's what saved me. *I won't let you do this to me,* I thought. *I'm not sure, but I think I'd rather die.* A second later, I got a chance to prove it. Just as Will Langston pulled away to reach down and shove himself into me, I pushed against him, rolled over toward the end table, and grabbed the first thing I touched.

It was a sculpture his wife had given him, I found out

later. The irony is not lost on me. I swung it as high and as hard as I could against his face just as the surprise was starting to register. He fell down against the bed and was struggling to get up when I hit him again, on the side of his temple this time. I wanted to keep hitting him, smash again and again until the brains leaked out of his skull, but I didn't. I just bound him with the scraps of nylon he'd used to tie me to the chair and picked up the phone. Then I dialed 911, and watched the blood drip out of his ear while I waited for the police to come.

EPILOGUE

~

THAT WAS IT. NO DRAMATIC FINISH, NO HAND-TO-HAND fight to the death. Just a numbness, as I lingered in the vestibule until two uniformed officers came to the door. I'm sure it helped that I knew them both from covering cops, and although I guess they could have cuffed me right then and there, they didn't. I told them Will Langston was upstairs, and that he'd killed at least two people, and that they'd damn well better get Chief Hill.

I'm not sure who called Sandy Timmerman, but he showed up right after the cops. At noon, Dr. William J. Langston Jr. was driven from his house in the back of a squad car, and that's the last I ever saw of him. He pleaded not guilty, and the trial will happen sooner or later, unless he cuts some sort of a deal. I probably could have been in a world of trouble—I suppose Will could even have charged me with assault if he'd wanted to. He's calling it a lover's quarrel. But with all the evidence we've got, nobody believes him.

Still, a guy with his money and connections never gets the death penalty. I'm willing to bet he'll plead insanity eventually, and live out his days in the presidential suite at some fancy mental hospital. He's a doctor; maybe he can do research on himself.

The buzz on the Langston Foundation is that it's finished. Ironically enough, the pundits are saying that it wasn't Langston Senior's guilty secret that caused its downfall—it's the fact that its president turned out to be a homicidal maniac.

As for Stewart Day, I like to think he's occupying what the TV preachers call "a hell of his own making." Unfortunately, that particular purgatory is nothing worse than a minimum-security work camp, the sort of Club Fed you see on *60 Minutes*. He pleaded no contest to the drunk driving charges, and his lawyer convinced the cops that Betty Barrows's death was really an accident. And although I'd be more than happy to hand him the blame, the more I think about it, the more I believe he's telling the truth.

Day never said a word about it in public, of course, but Gordon got an earful from his cop sources. My first instinct about what happened had been right. Betty really had called Day after I left, and I still can't figure out what she thought she was doing. Maybe she was trying to finish something that had started fifty years ago, get some answers to the questions she should have asked when she was my age. Maybe she just got sick of sitting there cloistered in her house, scared and helpless. But the truth is, I think she was trying to intervene on my behalf, to settle things herself and keep me out of it, and for that I'll always feel guilty, even if I live as long as she did.

When she'd called accusing him of murdering André Sebastien, Day had no idea what she was talking about.

All he'd understood was that she knew the truth about his past, and his secret was in danger of being exposed. He'd gone to her house in a frenzy—begging her to keep her mouth shut, even offering her money—and he must have scared her half to death. She tried to get away from him, and she'd almost made it to the top of the stairs when she lost her balance and came tumbling down, nearly taking him with her. He didn't even stop to see if she was dead before he took off.

The rest of the day, what happened after I left Will's house, is mostly a blur. We called Bill, and he got the publisher off the golf course. Eventually, just about every member of the *Monitor* newsroom was called in, and the overtime budget for the rest of the year was blown to hell. We broke the story in Monday's paper, with joint bylines for me, Mad, and Gordon, and a special note from the publisher essentially saying that it was highly unusual for reporters to write about issues they're closely involved with, but the nature of the story made it unavoidable. In other words: We're breaking this story, so screw you.

The wires and the TV and radio guys picked it up the next day, and things have been unbearable ever since. They're calling it the story of the century, and every news organization you've ever heard of wants an interview. You wouldn't believe how persistent these people are, trying to convince me that Barbara Walters or Diane Sawyer or Maria Shriver or Bryant Gumbel or Mike Wallace is the only journalist alive who can do my story justice. Would you believe one of the producers of *Larry King Live* showed up on my doorstep with a fruit basket? How am I supposed to handle this?

The *Times* came nosing around seconds after the paper hit the streets—and for the one time in history, the *Gabriel Monitor* kicked its ass. Not that there was ever a level playing field—we lived through the story, after all—but I know Gordon got some pleasure out of it. After this, I doubt he's going to have to put in a full year in purgatory before he gets his ticket back to paradise. It might be nice if I could report that he's developed so much affection for small-town America he's decided to tell the *Times* to go to hell, but . . . fat chance. If they make him an offer, he'll crawl back to New York over broken glass.

A few days after Will's arrest, some guy from the university courier service delivered a package to my house, a wooden box big enough to fit a kiddie swimming pool. After everything that had happened, Dirk was afraid it might explode, but when I pried it open with the backside of a hammer it turned out to be the Hopper painting. No note, no explanation; just a million-dollar work of art dropped off on my doorstep like it was an order from J. Crew.

Maybe it was Will's way of trying to make up for what he did, or some weirdo declaration of love. I guess I'll never know for sure. You're probably thinking that I should have donated the thing to a museum, but I just couldn't; now that I'm writing it down, I'll probably have to declare it on my income tax. The painting takes up one entire wall of my bedroom, and the fact that I wake up and go to bed with it is probably a little psychotic. I know I'll never look at it without thinking about Will Langston. But painting or no painting, I would have thought about him every day for the rest of my life.

Do I hate him? I've thought about that a lot lately, cooped up in my house with the goddamned Gulf War press pool on the front lawn. And my conclusion is: Yes, I hate the son of a bitch. Maybe if I was a good Christian—or any kind of Christian, for that matter—I'd find it in my heart to forgive him.

Forget it. The man practically destroyed my faith in human nature. Okay, maybe that's too melodramatic. Let's just say he did a stealth job on my psyche. But the worst thing of all is that he took Adam, erased him from the face of the earth. And for the rest of my life I'll wonder: Was he the one? Was Adam the man I was supposed to marry? Was he supposed to be the father of my children? Is whoever I end up with—if I end up with anybody—just going to be some second-class substitute? I don't know, and frankly it's all too much to handle right now. I just want everyone to go away, and I want to put on my headphones and run around the block with my dog like I used to.

When I got home from the paper that Sunday night, it was something like three o'clock in the morning. Of course I couldn't sleep, and I turned on the radio to the Benson student station. It must have been Seventies hour, because they played this old song by the Five Stairsteps. It's called "Ooh Child," and it's always gotten to me because it's so doggedly, idiotically optimistic. It speaks of things getting easier, about clearing your head and walking in the sunshine, and living in a world that's a whole lot brighter than the one we've got.

Even though I'm no more religious than Adam was, I like to think the lyrics were some sort of sign that I'm going to get over this eventually. People can handle a lot more than you'd think they can; the human capacity for healing is something amazing.

But sometimes, when I lie in the dark with the dog at my feet and try to get to sleep, I can't help but think that the world would be much brighter if Adam were still in it. All I can do now is remember him. And if feeling better means forgetting, I'd rather hold on to the pain.

—Gabriel, New York
August 18

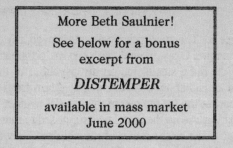

More Beth Saulnier!

See below for a bonus
excerpt from

DISTEMPER

available in mass market
June 2000

They found the first body in April, which is when things tend to turn up around here. The sun came out for the first time in six months, the top crust started to melt, and some poor bastard cross-country skiing in his shirt-sleeves saw her foot sticking out of the snow. He'd practically skied right over her, he told the newspaper later, and that seemed to upset him most of all—the thought that if he'd looked away for a second, he might have run her down and desecrated her more than she'd been already.

But he didn't. He caught sight of her two yards in front of him, and he said that he never thought it was anything other than a corpse. He didn't think it was a doll or an animal—whatever it is people usually say. He was just skiing along, thinking that it was a great day to be alive, and the next thing he knew he had to make himself fall over sideways to avoid running over a dead girl.

The man was a scientist, an associate professor of chemistry with a cool head and a woolly beard, and he had the presence of mind not to touch anything. He just hustled back to his Volvo and called the cops. By the time the police got through interviewing him six hours later, he was wishing to holy hell he'd gone rock climbing instead.

The first thing they noticed about the body was that the knees were scraped and bloody, as though she'd been praying on cement. Then they saw that the palms of her hands were the same, bruised and raw, and they wondered

1

if she'd tried to crawl for her life. There was no purse, no identification at all. She was a girl in her early twenties, with straight teeth and good skin. She was apparently healthy, until someone intervened. She was naked, and she was dead, and she was found outside a town where there are fifteen thousand others just like her.

It's hard to describe what happens to a place when a dead girl is found. You know somebody had to put her there, and to do it, that somebody must have been among us, and for that space of time no one was safe. If you're a woman, which I am, you realize that but for a bit of blind luck it could have been you. It could have been your mother, or the lady who does your manicure, or the girl in your class you can't stand but wouldn't want that to happen to; you realize you really *wouldn't* wish it on your worst enemy.

If we'd been in a different sort of place, one that didn't have social consciousness hemorrhaging from every crack in the pavement, everyone might have been satisfied with gossip and low-grade fear. But folks around here believe in action, because it's the only thing that keeps us warm in the winter, and sure enough someone up on campus organized a meeting. As is the tradition here, they advertised it by chalking RALLY FOR WOMEN'S LIVES on various spots on the sidewalk, and before you could blink someone else went around and turned all the Es in WOMEN into Ys.

"Do you think they'll ever catch the chap?" my roommate Emma asked in her *Masterpiece Theatre* accent. "Or will it remain, as the French say, '*un crime insoluble*'?"

We were stretched out in the living room of our house on the outskirts of downtown, a Victorian of the dubious structural quality that landlords are willing to rent to three veterinary students, one ornithologist, and an underpaid reporter. There were twelve of us altogether, if you count the three dogs and four cats. Marci is from San Diego and all of four-foot-eleven in her Keds; C.A. is an Army brat who has, on more than one occasion, made good on her threat to bench-press Marci. They're both third-year vet students and the workload means they're hardly ever home. Emma, who comes from London and never lets anyone forget it, did vet school in the U.K. and is here for a fellowship in radiology. Steve, our token guy, is an ornithologist who studies night migration. I'm still not clear on what this is, but it seems to involve lots of time in the woods, freezing his butt off and wearing headphones.

I'd only lived with them since January, when their fifth roommate took off for a research job down South. I'd been looking for a place since my housemate Dirk and his boyfriend Helmut had their commitment ceremony and moved in together. They found me my new spot through Steve, who's Helmut's ex, so it's all very symmetrical.

"Of course they'll catch him," C.A. said. "What else have the cops got to do all day? They'll solve it, they'll convict him, and ten years from now they'll finally fry the son of a bitch."

"Do you kiss your mother with that mouth?" Marci said. "And you know they don't fry them anymore. They give them the needle, like a schnauzer. It's veterinary science's contribution to the justice system."

"You Yanks do cherish your capital punishment," Emma said from my BarcaLounger, where she was letting her dog Tipsy lick gin and tonic off her fingers. He's a standard poodle she got from the animal shelter when she moved here, and named him in honor of her lush of an ex-husband.

"You know, Ems, I recall that at the end of those Agatha Christie mysteries, they took the killer out and hanged him, so there's no need to go all civilized," Steve said.

Emma tossed back the rest of her drink. The dog looked depressed.

"So has anybody heard anything else about the murder?" C.A. asked, sounding like she was enjoying it more than decency allowed. "How about you, Alex? You read the newspaper. Come on, you *are* the newspaper. What's the scoop?"

"Nothing new," I said. "Just a rehash. City editor's going nuts. They still haven't ID'd her. They're checking missing persons for the whole Northeast. Ontario, too."

"I can't believe they don't even know who she is," C.A. said. "Wouldn't you think they'd at least have figured out that much by now?"

Emma plucked the newspaper from the coffee table. "She was rather pretty, too. Pity." After the body was found, a police artist did a color sketch of the girl. She stared out from beneath the *Gabriel Monitor*'s masthead like something not quite dead but not really alive, either. The description said she was five feet tall and 105 pounds. When she was alive, people probably called her "perky."

"She remind you guys of anybody?" C.A. asked.

"You think you know her?" I asked. "For real?"

"Look at those eyes. The totally vacant expression. Dye the hair blond, add a couple of pounds, and who've you got?" C.A. jumped off the couch with her brassy brown curls waving around like garter snakes and snatched the paper from Emma. "Hello. *Hell-o* guys. Are you guys out to lunch or what? Take a look at her. It's our very own girlie girl. It's Marci all over again."

Marci opened her mouth, let it stay like that for a minute, then shut it again.

"Really, Cathy Ann," Emma said. "That was quite uncalled for. Particularly the crack about the weight."

"But just look at the—"

"Okay, kids," I said. "Can we calm down? She didn't mean it. She's just being a smartass. Come on, let's have another drink and—"

"She's right." The four of us stopped and stared at Marci, who was nose to nose with the newspaper.

4

"Who's right?" Steve said. "Not C.A. C.A.'s *never* right. Trust me on this. I've done studies."

Marci shook her head hard. "No, she's right. Look at the drawing. *Look* at it . . ."

"Nonsense," Emma said, taking back the paper. "It doesn't look a thing like . . . Oh, dear."

"Well, so what?" I said, plopping down on the couch next to Marci. "So you look like her. So what? I mean, clearly it's creepy and all . . ."

"Don't you get it?" Marci said with a little croaking sound. "These people, they have types. What if whoever killed her is still around? What if he likes girls who look like . . . like us?"

"You know what? Pretty soon they're going to catch the guy and send him someplace where he's dating guys named Spike. You'll see. It'll all be over in a couple of days."

I was trying—and let's face it, failing—to sound tough. But the truth was that the whole situation got to me, like it got to all of us. I'd seen death before, up close and personal, but it didn't make it any less frightening. The dead girl in the snow was about our age, could have fit right there in our living room. The thought of her made us feel both stronger and more fragile. More than anything, she made us think how lucky we were just not to be her.

We stayed up absurdly late that night talking about it, maybe a little bit scared to go to sleep because of what we might dream. And we might have stayed just a little bit scared if there hadn't been another dead girl, then another and another. And we might have had more midnight talks, thinking of the whole business in the third person, if I hadn't found the second body myself.